Time of the Stonechosen

Time of the Stonechosen

Book Two of the Soulstone Prophecy

Thomas Quinn Miller

Published 2016 by Creativia
Paperback design by Creativia (www.creativia.org)
ISBN: 978-1530414710
Cartography and illustrations by Thomas Quinn Miller
Cover art by http://www.thecovercollection.com/
Edited by D.S. Williams

http://thomasquinnmiller.com

A Request from the Author

First of all, thank you for purchasing this book. After finishing, please consider giving it an honest review on Amazon and/or Goodreads. Reviews are incredibly valuable for me in promoting my work and is the best way to say thank you.

Learn more about the world of Allwyn and the author at http://thomasquinnmiller.com.

Dedications

In memory of Kurt Heath Maddox.

This one is for you. I miss ya, Buddy.

As in all things, I thank my wife and

children for their love and support.

Acknowledgments

I would never have been able to bring Ghile's story out into the light of day without the help of my beta readers. They were there to pick it up and dust it off whenever I dropped it. So a big "Thank you" to Clane Kaluna, Noel Mock, James Calder, Robert Sobon, and June Balmforth. I appreciate your help, scrutiny, editing, grammar checking and all around general thoughtfulness.

Stonechosen

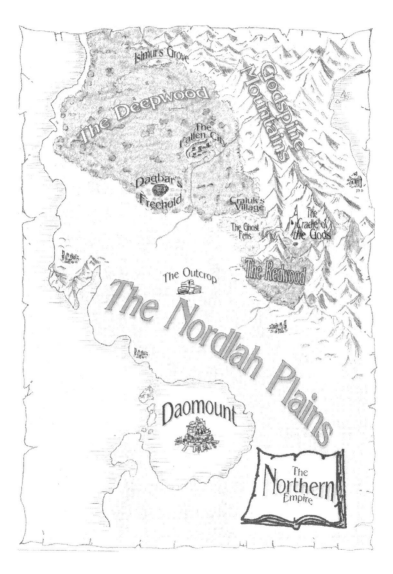

Contents

Part III   **292**

Prologue

 HE golden rays of the morning sun glinted across the water as the griffon broke through the low-lying puffs of clouds, its white-tipped wings trailing faint lines of vapor. The warm southern winds played through Safu's leonine fur. A deep-throated screech burst from the griffon's beak and she craned her feathered neck to look back at her rider.

The armored dwarf leaned forward in his saddle to pat the griffon's muscled side. "We are home." Even though the words were lost in the wind, Safu seemed comforted.

Finngyr took in a deep breath and let it out slowly. The taste of the salty air only deepened the feeling of home. Far in the distance, across the blue waters of the Innersea, the capital city of Daomount gleamed.

The white washed walls of the uniform buildings reflected the sun and made the mountain city glimmer. The many docks stretched out like fingers into the surrounding waters. The trade barges and fishing vessels spread about like pebbles being scattered before them.

Finngyr banked Safu into a low arcing dive, affording him a better view of his home. The Histories taught that the city of Daomount had been built atop the mountain which the god Daomur cast down upon the god Haurtu, trapping him beneath. The surrounding waters rushed in to fill his tomb, forming the Innersea.

Finngyr looked out over the island city jutting from the water.

He knew most thought this nothing more than a legend. But not him, he knew it to be real. Real as the god he communed with in his prayers. Real as the danger which now threatened both those who thought it legend and those who still held faith in their hearts.

Finngyr relaxed his grip, feeling the reins slide through his leather gloves. Safu knew their destination near the city's summit as well as he did. It only took her a moment to notice. With a screech, the griffon dove, broad powerful wings beating as she adjusted her course.

As one of the three holy orders of Daomur, the Temple of Justice was near the summit of Daomount. It shared the summit with the Temple of Art, where the Artificers praised Daomur through creation, building and enchantments, and the largest of the three, the Temple of Law, where the Ritualists – custodians of the holy book of Hjurl and marshals of government – interpreted dwarven law.

Finngyr's heart swelled with pride as he approached. There was a time when the Temple of Justice was the largest of the sects. During the Great Purge, when the progeny of the Hungering God, Haurtu, had to be eradicated from the face of Allwyn; The Knights of the Temple of Justice numbered in the tens of thousands. Now, only a thousand years later, they numbered in the hundreds. Where once they were armies, now they led the armies of the empire, under the Ritualists' scrutiny and the benign neglect of the Artificers. The Knight Justices were now a relic of a bygone age.

The muscles in his neck and jaw ached from clenching. He could feel his anger rising and worked to fight it down. Like all dwarves, he had been taught to keep his emotions in check from a young age. The Lawgiver's justice was best reflected on with a clear mind, free of emotion. Something Finngyr was finding more and more difficult. Even this view would only calm him for a short time.

Finngyr had found a true vessel of Haurtu the Hungerer. Not just some human whelp who showed the dimmest spark of potential, but one already possessed by a soulstone. He'd found one, then let it escape!

Frustrated, he tightened his knees and felt Safu bank in response. Finngyr forced himself to relax and looked out over the water. Taking deep breathes, he recited one of the many prayers to Daomur.

"Your word is law
I am your vessel.
I deliver your law.

Your word is justice.
I am your vessel.
I deliver your justice.

Your word is truth.
I am your vessel
I deliver your truth.

In Daomur's judgment, we are preserved."

He rested his hand upon the metal shaft of his hammer, tracing the intricate engravings through rough leather gloves. He wanted nothing more than to feel the comforting weight of the ancient relic in his grip as he intoned the holy prayer. It was through these most sacred and holy weapons of his sect, said to be blessed by Daomur himself, that a knight justice could identify those chosen by the Hungering God. When he felt divine presence emanating from it, he knew, with surety, his god anointed him to enact his divine mandate and Finngyr would sing Daomur's praises as he culled the tainted human from the herd. Never was he more fulfilled than those brief moments when he was the blessed hand of his god on Allwyn.

The hammer's touch and the prayer took him back to the memory of his encounter with the Stonechosen and Finngyr flinched yet again for not being better prepared.

He'd travelled with Safu to the Cradle of the Gods, a backwater human containment on the fringe of the empire. It was his first appointment outside the ever hostile Nordlah Plains. When he received his orders, he thought he was being banished for some unknown transgression. He thought it would be easy.

Finngyr had been more interested in showing the Cradle's Overseer, Magister Obudar, how a loyal citizen of the empire should treat humans than in performing the Rite of Attrition. Even though the rite had been the reason he was sent there.

If he had only placed more focus on his duties: performing the rite, seeking out those abominations whom were potential vessels of the Hungering God's return, and culling them from the human herd; he could have captured the Stonechosen. And once more, the scene played out in his mind, perhaps for the thousandth time.

Just beyond the edge of the town of Lakeside, he'd walked into the clearing. His armor was resplendent, engraved with the sigils of his sect. He stood looking out over the herds of humans, their faces flickering with the light from the immense bonfires, holy hammer resting in his hands.

Finngyr was born to deliver Daomur's judgment on these savages, yet even as he exulted in serving his god, he felt the familiar itch which always preceded battle. To him, the search for potential vessels of the Hungering God was a war. Since taking his oaths, he had served in the Nordlah Plains where barbarian warriors fought to a man against Daomur's judgement. Every inch taken was a struggle.

Here, in this so called Cradle of the Gods, the foul humans lined up like lambs for the slaughter, their cow-eyed loved ones clung to each other, helpless and waiting nearby.

Bile rose to Finngyr's mouth as he marched past the line of dwarf guards sent to oversee the rites. He'd made sure their armor gleamed and their weapons held a keen edge. For all the good it had done. Normally, he would have waded into the thick of battle, his brethren knights at his side, ancient hammers meting out Daomur's justice. It was an insult, this line of docile humans, these borderland guards.

Finngyr strode down the line, pausing only to hold his hammer before each human in turn. Most stared at their feet, some watched with bewildered faces and just for a moment, one looked as if it would reach out and touch the hammer.

Make that mistake.

And as he suspected, the hammer remained dormant in his grasp. Humans lacked the capacity to understand what they beheld and while Finngyr held no love for them, he would follow Daomur's law. He would only cull those whom the hammer marked as a vessel, in self-defense or against those who would stop him from performing his holy duty. In Daomur's name he wished one of these humans would try to stop him.

The sensation caught Finngyr off guard at first. He stood before a tall, lanky whelp. The human's shoulders sagged and its thick dark curls partially hid its vacant eyes.

His god's presence flowed into him.

What was happening?

The most Finngyr ever felt was a slight sensation, the tiniest presence of the divine. Some Knight Justices confided they were not always sure when they did feel it and would cull the human just to be safe. But this! Daomur's presence flowed out of the hammer in waves; a hum like a thousand trapped hornets about to burst forth.

The other humans in the line gazed open-mouthed when the hammer trembled in his hands. Finngyr could only stare as white light burst from it, the glare blinding. The human whelp stood staring now, confusion and then dawning horror on his face.

This was no potential vessel of the Hungering God. This was a stonechosen, one already possessed. Finngyr knew what must be done.

"I cull thee!" Finngyr roared, as he brought the hammer around his back and over in a crushing blow, with all of his faith behind it.

He felt the impact, waited for the give of soft flesh and the familiar crunch of bone, but it never came. Instead, it felt as if he struck stone. A blinding flash of light and what felt like hot wind buffeted him, hurling him back, the hammer flying from his grasp.

Finngyr landed hard and tightened his muscles to keep the air from being knocked from him. Curling up as much as his armor would allow, he rolled with the momentum and rose in a crouch, his side axe already in hand.

The sounds of screaming filled his ears and he could just make out indistinct shapes running past him. He couldn't focus his eyes. The residual image of the flash still filled his vision. He had lost his hammer. What had he hit? Surely the blow killed the whelp?

"Dwarves! To me!" Finngyr roared. He made his way forward. Shadows danced before him. Something pushed into him, he removed it with a swipe of his axe and was rewarded with a satisfying scream.

"Do not stand before me! I walk in Daomur's grace and all who oppose me die in his name!"

Apprentice and journeymen priests from the Temple of Artificers labored away on the statues and wall carvings which were so plentiful in Daomount. Most of his race paid homage to the Lawgiver through stonecraft or commerce. Finngyr's was a different calling.

He passed one of the open markets, surrounding a Bastion, gatehouse to the Underways. Other than by ship, they were the only other way to leave the city. Unless, you could fly.

Safu's shadow glided over the Bastion and the caravan assembling at its entrance; the caravan's laden wagons preparing for the underground journey to some far off place in the empire.

Finngyr thought of the caravan as blood, the Underways veins and Daomount, the empire's beating heart.

Finally, he reached the summit, home to the judicial and temple districts. Safu descended in slow circles, setting down on a long precipice of stone, jutting out from the side of the Temple of Justice like a waiting hand. She cantered along the expanse and into the griffon paddock proper, her still-beating wings kicking up dust and straw.

Challenging screeches came from a scattering of stalls on the stable's many levels. Safu raised her head and straightened her feathers, answering in turn with her own challenge. If it were not for the powerful enchantments placed on the griffon tack and harness by the Artificers, the griffons' natural territorial instincts would have them shredding each other with beak and claw.

From a third floor stable door, two pages scrambled out and descended a series of wooden ladders with practiced ease. Finngyr didn't recognize either of them. But, as pages, they were the lowest members of the temple, so it was not surprising.

Reaching down from his saddle Finngyr patted Safu behind the wing, where her golden tinged feathers gave way to sleek hair. The muscles controlling her wings went taut beneath his riding glove as she stretched.

"His word is law," Finngyr called to the pages. He disengaged the riding harness with a practiced slam of his fist. Safu lowered her head at the sound and in one movement Finngyr swung his leg over the saddle and slid down.

He was already removing his pack and hammer when the two pages, both barely old enough to be called beardlings, raced up behind him and bowed deeply at the waist.

"His word his law, Knight Justice," they intoned in unison.

"See to Safu. Her nest is at the top." Finngyr pointed to the fourth level. He heard a groan at his announcement. The exercise pages received from climbing up and down the numerous ladders in the stable was just as much a part of their training as learning to handle the order's steeds. That sort of dissension would never have been tolerated when he was a page.

Finngyr turned and stared at them, but could not determine which one had made his disappointment known.

"She will need to have her talons cut as well," he added, eyeing each of them for any further signs of discontent.

The pages bowed in unison.

Satisfied, he walked past them. One of the most difficult and dangerous jobs involving the griffons was cutting back the talons on their front claws. Behind him, Finngyr heard a satisfying thump as the innocent page repaid his partner, who stifled the resulting moan.

It was good to be home. Finngyr needed to pray, to give thanks for his safe arrival. Then, he would report to Lord Captain Danuk and consult the Book of Hjurl, particularly the Prophecies of the Vessels. They needed to know he encountered a true stonechosen and not just a potential vessel. He needed to discover which forbidden city the stonechosen now journeyed towards. Then he would know where to hunt.

He would find Ghile of Last Hamlet. And this time, he would not escape.

Part I

1

The Ghost Fens

HIS *time I'm going to win.*

Ghile summoned his force shield just in time to parry the overhead strike of the huge stone axe. The weight behind Two Elks' swing jarred Ghile's arm, sending white-hot pain racing up and into his shoulder. Ghile doubted he could lift the axe, let alone swing it with such force.

"Good. Use your magic," Two Elks said.

Two Elks followed the deflected strike with another and another. Each driving Ghile further down, buckling his knees. He felt like a stake being driven into the ground by a mallet.

Ghile tightened his grip on Uncle Toren's fang blade. *No, my fang blade,* he thought. He waited for the next blow to land and then followed it with a quick lunge, ducking around the side of his force shield.

Two Elks must have anticipated the move. He released his two handed grip on the axe and struck the back of Ghile's blade wielding hand with a sharp slap of his own. The blade broke free of his grip and spun across the clearing to stick next to where Riff was lounging.

"Hey!" Riff shouted. He gave them both a withering stare.

Ghile shrugged and offered a weak smile.

Something slammed into his calves. The sodden ground rushed up to greet him in a wet embrace of reeds and moss. Even though the spot they chose to rest for the day was on high ground, the damp of the Ghost Fens still leached up into the soil. Ghile thanked the All Mother for the soft landing as he lay flat on his back and stared into the bluish mists above him.

"Hand too strong on blade," Two Elks said.

He was still in a crouch from the move he'd used to sweep Ghile's legs. He finished his sentence by bringing his axe over his head in a killing blow and stopped it just short of separating Ghile's head from his shoulders.

"Look at enemy, watch eyes." Two Elks gestured towards his own eyes and then proffered a hand to Ghile.

Of his companions, Two Elks was the oldest, having seen maybe thirty years. He was also difficult for Ghile to understand. Ghile didn't know if this was due to Two Elks' weak grasp of their language and he just couldn't find the words to express himself, or if he was naturally just a quiet person.

He was the first Nordlah Plains barbarian Ghile had ever met. They might all be as stoic, for all he knew. The vast plains Two Elks called home lay to the west of the Cradle of the Gods, beyond the Redwood. If all the barbarians were like Two Elks, they were a tall and hardy people indeed.

"You think too much before you do," Two Elks said.

Ghile nodded and exhaled a deep breath, hoping the pain in his back and shoulders would exit with the air. This was the seventh fighting lesson in as many days. They trained with both blade and spear, with Two Elks taking his promise to train Ghile to use the fang blade to heart.

He still found it hard to believe Uncle Toren had given up the knife. Only Fangs, guardians of the Cradle, were presented these enchanted dwarf-forged blades. No human was allowed to craft metal, by dwarven law. A human, other than a Fang, found in possession of an enchanted blade risked death at the hands of the dwarves.

Ghile looked to where the fang blade landed. The deer antler handle struck a sharp contrast to the surrounding moss, only a portion of the blade's shining steel above the ground.

Two Elks shook his offered hand over Ghile. "Up. We go again."

The blade pulled Ghile's thoughts to his uncle and his family. How he missed them!

But, there was nothing for it now. He was Stonechosen and he was going to have to learn to fight. Even if it killed him. Well, even if Two Elks killed him.

Ghile cleared his thoughts and reached into himself. It was almost second nature to find the inner force and focus it with his will. He was aware of every sound around him. The Ghost Fens were alive with croaking frogs and chirping crickets. The hum of hovering midges, hunting for exposed skin, fought for his attention. He let their droning fall away and looked inward.

He pushed out with his force shield, forcing it against the ground beneath him, using it to propel his body. He flew forward towards the fang blade, and using the momentum, he curled into a roll and came up into the defensive fighting stance Two Elks taught him only days before; his body turned slightly, presenting a smaller target to his opponent, the blade held in his hands before him.

Two Elks nodded. "Good."

"That's enough, Two Elks," Gaidel said. There was a tone of command in her voice, young though she was, which left little doubt Ghile's lesson was now done.

She leaned against a nearby tree from where she'd been watching. Tree might have been too generous a word. Her slight weight was enough to cause it to lean, threatening to pull free and fall into the glowing water a short distance below.

The Ghost Fens were named from the cold bluish glow found in any water which pooled and stagnated long enough. That and the heat robbing mist, which hung low over it like a damp woolen blanket left out overnight.

"He needs to rest. It will be dark in another couple of hours," Gaidel said.

"Explain to me again, Revered Daughter, why we are traveling by night?" Riff asked.

Ghile frowned at the way Riff drew out 'Revered Daughter'. Riff had questioned every decision the druid made since leaving the Cradle, determined to chip away at any authority she tried to instill over the group.

Gaidel was only a couple of years older than Ghile, but even so, she had a way of carrying herself, a way of standing and speaking which made Ghile naturally defer to her.

Her long red hair was pulled back in a tight braid, further accentuating her bare scalp, the entire front half shaved, from ear to ear. The strange blue curving tattoos, which marked her as a Redwood Druid, flowed across her scalp in place of hair.

Above all others, druids were respected by people of the Cradle. It was the druids who saved the human race from extinction back during the Great Purge. Ghile now knew they had once been priestesses of the Hungering God, or Haurtu, the God of Learning and Wisdom as he was known back then.

But, it was their prayers to the All Mother which awoke her and resulted in her stopping the decimation of his race over a thousand years before. No small wonder they were known as the Daughters of the All Mother and treated with such reverence. Ghile eyed Riff. *Well, by most anyway.*

"It will be easier for the cullers to spot us if we move by day," Gaidel said.

Riff nodded at her answer before she even finished speaking. It was the same answer she gave each time he asked the question. Riff plucked another pinkish mushroom from a clump near where he was lounging and squeezed it between his fingers.

Riff discovered that particular variety of mushroom on their second day in the fens. When squeezed, they emitted a wet flatulent sound which still made Ghile snicker, despite the disapproving stares it drew from Gaidel.

She closed her eyes and took a deep, steadying breath, waiting for Riff's deliberate long pause to end. Riff watched her like a cat pawing at a mouse.

"I understand that," Riff finally said. "But I don't see how anything could see us through this thrice damned mist, day or night."

Ghile watched Two Elks, who had already found his fur blankets and began laying them out across a patch of somewhat dry reeds and thick spongy grass, having grown accustomed to this type of banter between Gaidel and Riff. His guardianship of Gaidel did not seem to extend to protecting her from being teased. Not that Ghile felt she needed it. She more than held her own against Riff's taunts.

"It is not up for debate, sorcerer's apprentice," Gaidel said. She didn't draw out Riff's title, not willing to be baited this time.

Riff leaned back, shaking his head. He fished for another mushroom.

Ghile cleaned the fang blade on his leggings and took care sliding it into its sheath. He sat down near Riff. They had both gathered reeds and piled them into bedding when they made camp earlier that morning. Ghile had plenty of sleep already and didn't understand why Gaidel felt he needed more. Over the past days, she often asked him how he felt or if he was in need of a rest. Ghile didn't think she gifted the other two with the same attention. He'd pondered over this more than once.

Ghile watched Daughter Gaidel as she spoke to Two Elks in hushed tones, idly scratching Ast, one of his two Valehounds, who lay near her. The two Valehounds, Ast and Cuz, were his father's hounds, but they were his now. Where they never listened to any of his commands before, the power of the soulstones embedded in his chest allowed him to feel their thoughts and touch their minds. He focused and the two hounds raised their heads, eyes watching him.

"She can't get enough of me," Riff said, punctuating his statement with another squashed mushroom.

Ghile rolled his eyes and laughed. "Obviously."

"You are getting better, Sheepherder. You almost had him that time," Riff said.

"Really?" Ghile asked. He thought he was getting better. The fang blade didn't feel as awkward in his hand anymore.

Riff laughed and rolled his eyes in imitation of Ghile. "No."

Ghile picked up a clump of moss and threw it at him.

"Be careful, do you not see my feet are bare?" Riff said.

Ghile leaned back and rested the back of his head on his hands. He wasn't tired, but if he didn't make an effort of at least appearing to rest, he knew he would draw Gaidel's ire. He shook his head at Riff's comment. "Do you threaten me with your stench, Sorcerer?"

Riff smirked and rolled over to lean toward Ghile. "A sorcerer does not only hold a source in his hands. He but needs it to touch some part of him to use it to cast. So be warned."

Ghile smiled at the mock seriousness in Riff's tone. He knew Riff could hurl fire and control water, but knew he could control earth and metal, too. Riff even said a strong sorcerer could control air. Though, Ghile had never seen Master Almoriz, Riff's mentor, do that. "I will take your words to heart, great sorcerer," Ghile said with the same mock seriousness. He bowed his head and held his palms out and turned upwards toward the sky in a show of respect.

"See that you do," Riff said. He leaned back and crossed his arms behind his head and closed his eyes with a sigh of contentment.

The way Riff relaxed there in the middle of the Ghost Fens, Ghile would have thought he rested upon a warm fur laid before a hearth. He was happy Riff came with them. The two of them joked often and neither the wet of the fen or its annoying insects could dampen their spirits. This was the first time Ghile had left the Cradle. True, he'd not seen much yet, they still had not reached the bottom of the many tiered levels of the Ghost Fens, but Ghile was out of the Cradle and gone was the bleak future he feared as a sheepherder in Upper Vale.

The Ghost Fens were not the way any sane human would choose to leave their valley home. Normally, they would have traveled down out of the Vales and past Lakeside on the shores of Crystal Lake, then into the Redwood that covered the lowlands of the mountain valley. Onwards they would have gone, past Redwood Village, where Riff and Gaidel were from and then descend the cliffs near South Falls. Then they would arrive in the portion of the Redwoods his people called the Drops.

Not that many would make the journey. He never had. He had heard tales of those places around the hearth fire, having never ventured further than Lakeside himself. Even fewer would dare risk traveling further than the Drops.

It was against Dwarven law for humans to travel unaccompanied between settlements. Only druids, their shieldwardens and sorcerers were permitted outside the settlements.

Their dwarven overseers left little doubt how dangerous the wilds were. The dwarven human catchers were the least of one's worries in the wilds. Nordlah barbarians roamed the plains, along with blood-thirsty orcs and vargan that prowled the forests.

Not even the dwarves took that route. They used the Underways, tunnels of their own making which reached throughout the empire. Ghile had never seen them, but knew one opened up under the stone Bastion in Lakeside. The Underways were the domain of the dwarves.

Ghile's path led in a different direction. The Ghost Fens were a more direct route, which gave them the added bonus of secrecy. No one traveled through the Ghost Fens to leave the Cradle, and for good reason. There were no real trails to speak of and the Fens were broken into tiers, much like giant steps, with treacherous cliffs separating each level. The waters from Crystal Lake flowed down onto each level, where it gathered before spilling over to the lower level.

They had been wading through thick swamp grass and reeds pushed up against pools of water for over a week now. During the day, they sheltered in the many copses of willow and alder that found purchase on the infrequent levels of higher ground. Each time they came to another one of the waterfall covered cliffs which divided the tiers, they had to use rope to lower themselves down.

Ghile feared the Ghost Fens got their name from the ghosts of all the souls who became lost and drowned. But the answer was revealed to them on the first night when the sun set and the waters began to glow with the same soft blue as the waters of Crystal

Lake. This, combined with the perpetual mist clinging stubbornly to the fens both day and night. Ghile could see how legends of ghosts began.

∧

The group broke their fast in the evening with hard bread and cheese. Riff moved between them and with a touch and softly whispered incantation, removed all the damp from their clothes. It never lasted long, but it was like having a dry change of clothes each day. Between Riff's ability and Gaidel's healing touch, for the others at least, Ghile felt confident the natural dangers of the fens would not stop them.

They had only been trudging through the blue mists a short time before they reached the edge of their current tier.

"Don't drop me!" Riff called from below.

Ghile leaned out over the edge to get a better view. Riff hung from the end of the rope about half way between Ghile and Two Elks above, and a waiting Gaidel below. Ast and Cuz sniffed the ground near her, still wearing the patchwork leather harnesses Two Elks had hastily fashioned to help lower them down. "Stop complaining, Riff. Two Elks isn't even straining," Ghile said.

It was true, the barbarian slowly lowered out sections of the thick rope hand over hand. His large corded muscles were taut, but his expression was relaxed. "The sorcerer is light. Daughter Gaidel was heavier," Two Elks said.

Ghile laughed, even though he wasn't sure Two Elks meant it as a joke.

"I'm down," Riff called from below. Two Elks took the now-slack rope and tied it to a nearby jut of rock.

"I lower you, Stonechosen, then climb down. I no need rope," Two Elks said. He gave the rope a few tugs to test his handiwork.

Ghile shook his head. "We have been over this, Two Elks. We need the rope and there is no need for you to risk yourself."

Two Elks shrugged and shouldered his large kite shield. He backed over the edge, looking behind him as he descended.

It took Two Elks half the time to make the climb than it took to lower Riff. Ghile heard the call from below and began untying the rope.

At first, Riff accused Ghile of just showing off, but Ghile knew it was more for practice. The more he used the new powers gifted to him by the soulstones, the more control he had over them. Ghile called and then dropped the rope over the edge, knowing Two Elks was already gathering it on the other end.

Ghile retrieved his spear leaning on the rock face next to him and stepped out over the edge.

The wind swept past him as he gained momentum. He plummeted towards the upturned faces of his companions. Before his new powers, he would have been terrified, flailing his arms and screaming all the way down, but now he just watched the ground approach, using his arms to keep himself upright.

With only moments to spare, Ghile pushed with his mind and felt the invisible force extend from the bottom of his feet. In his mind, it was like a billowing cloud spreading out thick below him. He felt the force as it reached the ground. He allowed it to slowly give way under the pressure. He quickly slowed and bent his knees into a crouch, to absorb some of the fall. He concentrated on the force until the strain was too great and he was only a couple of feet above the reeds before releasing it. He dropped the remainder of the distance and landed on the soft ground with a muffled squish.

"Even though you are stonechosen, Ghile, you still feel pain and can be hurt. Broken legs are going to leave you in agony. I cannot heal you and it will slow us down while we wait for your powers to mend you," Gaidel said.

The two Valehounds bounded up to greet Ghile. "I'm fine," Ghile said. He reached down and gave both Ast and Cuz a good scratch in turn.

"That is not the point," Gaidel said, crossing her arms for emphasis, "there is no point in protecting you, if you take every opportunity to risk yourself."

Ghile was about to respond, a lopsided smile on his face. He looked to Riff and Two Elks for support. Both were staring at him in silence. He could feel the weight, like dwarven stone, behind those stares. He would not get reinforcements from either of them. His smile dissolved, along with his rebuttal. "Alright, I'll be more careful. But try to understand, Adon said I have to use my powers if they are to improve."

Ghile saw the uncomfortable look come over Riff's visage at the mention of Ghile's older brother. Adon was culled by the dwarves many years ago back in the Cradle. Adon was also Riff's good friend. Adon now appeared in Ghile's dreams and taught him how to use the powers the soulstones granted him. It all sounded ridiculous to Ghile, if he truly thought about it.

"Well, try to practice your powers when you have both feet planted on the ground," Gaidel said. Gaidel motioned for Two Elks to lead the way. "We should continue."

She didn't wait to see if the others followed, as she struck out behind the barbarian, her eyes scanning the sky.

"Well, we'd better go, her greatness has spoken," Riff said with a wink.

Normally, he would have smiled and winked back, but he only nodded. The idea they were protecting him didn't sit too well with Ghile. He was the youngest of them. He wouldn't hesitate to admit they were all more capable of defending themselves. But Ghile thought of them more as his companions and guides on this journey, not his protectors. Apparently, he was the only one who saw things that way. "Come on, boys." Ghile motioned and Ast and Cuz splashed through the reeds in great bounds, with little care for the amount of mud they sent flying with each leap.

Riff gave a half-hearted kick after them as they passed, before following. The two Valehounds paid him little heed. Their once-white coats were covered in mud, their shaggy fur hanging limp from their thick frames. Ghile trudged into the fens after them, his mood now as damp as the rest of him.

2

The Knight Captain

"THOUGHT I would find you here."

Finngyr did not look up from his prayers at the words of the visitor. He wasn't surprised when he heard the sound of metal on stone and the grunt of accepted pain as the visitor knelt down beside him. Finngyr also made that sound when kneeling to pray. The heavy thud of a hammer was followed by the clink of its handle. He waited; when the visitor didn't speak further, Finngyr returned to his prayers.

A short time later Finngyr opened his eyes. He had chosen one of the smaller chapels which lined the outer walls of the Temple of Truth. They were more conducive to private prayer. A single shaft of light, let in from a high-placed window, lit the simple altar and the room's only other two occupants.

Finngyr looked at his uninvited guest, who knelt next to him, eyes still closed. Finngyr bowed at the waist, without rising.

"His word is law, Knight Captain Danuk," Finngyr said.

The older knight justice did not respond, but continued with his prayers. Finngyr waited, watching the knight captain's lips moving beneath his tightly braided beard. There was almost as much gray as red in the beard and receding hair. Dust motes floated around him and settled onto the polished steel of his shoulder plates.

The Knight Captain's hammer rested before him, identical to Finngyr's except for the wear and unique scratches, marks it earned through centuries of use. He wondered at how many other Knights in service to Daomur wielded these two relics, resting before them. How many more would, after they were bones and dust?

Finngyr looked up and found Knight Captain Danuk studying him with a calm expression.

"It is good to be back, is it not, Finngyr?"

"Yes, Knight Captain, it is."

The two of them knelt there in silence, both staring at the carved altar. The hammer and scales, the symbol of their god, coaxed from the stone long ago.

"Come. We will go to my quarters and I will have some food brought up from the kitchens. You can give me your reports," the Knight Captain said.

"Sir, there is something I must tell you. I—"

"There is much you must tell me, Knight Justice. We received a message from the Cradle shortly after you left. But by Daomur's beard, I will hear it over full plates and fuller tankards." Knight Captain Danuk grasped his hammer and worked his way up slowly, accompanied by more than a few grunts.

He took four respectful steps backwards before turning and leaving the chapel. Finngyr rose, repeated the four backward steps and followed.

"Then, I have some news for *you*, Finngyr. There are interesting happenings on the Nordlah Plains."

⋀

"Stonechosen, you say? You are sure?" Knight Captain Danuk said. He leaned into his high-backed oak chair and shook his head.

The Knight Captain had changed into a simple white tunic, thick with embroidery around the neck and sleeves, and a wide, woven leather belt. His armor lay on its stand near the hearth. The two pages – adolescent dwarves who saw to the armor's polishing and starting the small hearth fire, sprinkling it with incense – now stood to either side of the table, waiting to fill a tankard or collect an empty plate.

"I am sure," Finngyr said.

He too, had changed into a tunic like the Knight Captain's. They were favored in the mountain city. Even here, at the summit, the ocean breeze carried a touch of warmth.

The Knight Captain's quarters, like most officers' quarters in the temple, had an open, easterly facing balcony to take advantage of the trade winds.

"It was a tall and gangly whelp. Seemed as surprised as I was. The hammer put off a bright light and almost vibrated out of my hand." Finngyr shook a leg of ham to demonstrate. A rogue piece of meat escaped to the floor, only to be scooped up by one of the attentive pages. Finngyr never noticed.

"And you smote him, you say?" Danuk asked.

"I do say! The force of the blow threw me back. The flash was blinding. Felt like I struck stone." Finngyr brought the leg of meat down with both hands in front of him. "I rolled with the force of the blow and came up with my side axe in hand. I was still blinded when I called for support from the poor excuses for what that backwater settlement calls guards."

Danuk nodded at this statement, as if it was well known.

"But, then all the bonfires from the human's festivities exploded with flames that soared into the sky and then back into themselves, throwing fire and ash everywhere," Finngyr finished.

"That has the sounds of ancient human magic, like in the stories of the Great Purge, that does," Danuk said. He held out his tankard over the arm of his chair to be refilled.

"Exactly! The local magister kept a pet sorcerer, so I naturally had him arrested and took control of the settlement's guard."

"Naturally," Danuk said.

"But, I could not find the boy. I even razed its village, in hopes of drawing it out." Finngyr leaned back in his chair, moving to take a drink from his tankard and then stopping. He stared off into the late afternoon sky and the gathered shadows on this side of Daomount. Off in the distance, he could see the sun almost resting on the waters. The shadows of the mountain city reached out for the retreating light like a drowning dwarf.

"Ahem," Danuk said.

Finngyr continued. "It was then the Magister quoted the Book of Hjurl to me. A passage concerning the trial of the vessels. "Now marked, his chosen must gather, where once his progeny thrived—"

"His hunger compels them to journey," Danuk intoned.

"In his cities they survive," the two finished in unison.

Finngyr set his tankard down and leaned forward over the table. "I need to consult the Prophecies, Knight Captain. I need to see if there is any clue as to which of the forbidden cities Ghile Stonechosen might go to. I let him escape once. I seek redemption. I must find him and bring him here."

The Knight Captain held up a finger to stop Finngyr, his face lost in thought.

Finngyr felt his temper bubbling below the surface. He swallowed it back down like bile. It would serve no purpose to show the

Knight Captain how much his emotions held sway over him. Daomur taught control over one's emotions, to ponder his laws with a clear mind.

"Finngyr, you might have just helped answer something which has been puzzling us. You recall I mentioned news concerning the Nordlah Plains?" The Knight Captain was also leaning forward now. "If you encountered a stonechosen in the Cradle, that means there are others." He paused for a moment, letting those words sink in. "To think the Time of the Stonechosen has come during our lifetimes. It makes sense. The plains barbarians do not follow their normal migrations. Where we expect to find the various tribes, there are none. Where they would normally gather in force to fight against their culling, the pathetic few we do find throw themselves into combat. The few who survive, tell us nothing of the location of the others."

Finngyr could not push down the feelings of jealousy at the thought of his brother knights diving into battle. He should be there, performing the Rite of Attrition on their chosen, culling those who stood in his way. This was the first time in all his years of service to the Temple he'd been sent anywhere but the plains. "Sir, if I may ask. Why did you send me to the Cradle?" Finngyr said.

The Knight Captain shook his head. "I was not the one to make that decision, Finngyr."

Finngyr stared across the table. That didn't make sense. As his superior, the decision of who to send should have been Knight Captain Danuk's. He would have been ordered to dispatch a knight justice, but which particular one was left to him. "You are my captain," Finngyr said.

"True. But the order to send you to the Cradle of the Gods came from the Lord Knight Justice Gyldoon himself." Danuk raised an eyebrow and watched Finngyr.

Finngyr stared at his superior officer. The Lord Knight Justice was the head of their order and sat on the Judges' Council of Daomount. He was the oldest member of the order and one of the only dwarves still alive who recalled the last Time of the Stonechosen.

"It appears our Lord Gyldoon has the gift of prophecy, Knight Justice," Danuk said.

Finngyr couldn't explain why the Lord Knight Justice himself would give such an order. Different thoughts were spinning through his mind, each fighting to move forward and to be given attention before being pushed aside by others. The gift of prophecy was not among them. "No. It doesn't make sense. If he knew or even suspected that the Time of the Stonechosen has come, then why would he not tell us? Tell the Judges Council?" Finngyr said.

"I do not know. Nor is it my place, or yours, to question that decision," Danuk said.

Finngyr thought to respond and caught himself. "Of course, Knight Captain."

The Knight Captain appeared mollified by the response. "But if it is the Time of the Stonechosen, then maybe others have arisen among the barbarians and they travel to the cities as well? We hunt in the wrong places."

The two sat there, the gentle wind and the crackling of the small fire the only sound. Occasionally one of the pages would scuff a sandal on the floor.

"I will seek an audience with the Lord Knight Justice," Danuk finally said.

"Might I accompany you, sir?"

Danuk shook his head, even before Finngyr finished his request.

"That would not bode well for you, I should think. That brings me to the other news I meant to share with you this day. The Magister from the Cradle sent word via a runesmith a few days ago. Most likely right after your departure. It seems they have a rebellion on their hands there. They are placing the responsibility for that rebellion firmly on your shoulders, Knight Justice."

Damn you, Obudar!

"They are requesting troops be dispatched to their aid and had the forethought to mention the annual tithes have not left their Bastion."

Twice damn you, Obudar!

"The Judges Council has been hearing your name on the lips of more than a few high merchants, who will feel a personal loss in their purses from this rebellion in the Cradle."

Finngyr closed his eyes and leaned back. He could see his chance of catching Ghile the Stonechosen slipping through his fingers like so much sand.

3

Predator and Prey

T was all Ghile could do to concentrate on his next step. The muscles in his legs screamed in protest as he waded through the chest deep water. He pulled his boot free from the sucking mud, only to stagger forward and force it back down into its clutching grasp once more.

On it went. He had no idea how he kept going – pull, step, pull, step. Behind him, he could hear Riff's heavy breathing and occasional curses as he cleared the air around him of swarming insects. In front of him, Daughter Gaidel held her staff over a downturned head, plodding along. Even Ast and Cuz panted nearby, tongues lolling as they paddled to keep up.

Only Two Elks seemed unaffected by the exertion. The barbarian had cut a winding route through the night, trying to keep to higher ground whenever possible. That too was tiring, since what little ground rose out of the fens was bordered by reeds and every bit above water choked with plants.

At least Ghile's new powers allowed him to see where he was stepping when they were not in the glowing water. Riff had fallen on more than one occasion when they moved across land at night.

Two Elks almost had to separate Riff and Gaidel, when Riff once again pulled his everflame from one of his many pouches. Everflame was the symbol of a sorcerer. Only they could transform a regular flame, causing it to lose all heat but give light for months, though nothing fueled it. It could even act as a source for the sorcerer's magic. Ghile had seen Riff use it to deadly effect against the worgs in the battle on the Horn.

Gaidel would not suffer anything that increased their risk of being seen and confronted Riff each time he drew it out. It was only when Two Elks added the light could attract the Ghost Fen's nocturnal predators that Riff finally put it away.

They had descended the last tier of the Ghost Fens the previous morning and camped along its base that day. It was much warmer here, out of the mountains. Ghile's hopes that the perpetual mist would clear was short lived; it clung stubbornly, even here at the fen's lowest level.

With the heat came the insects. Though, they didn't seem to appreciate the way he tasted, they apparently considered sorcerer a delicacy, having swarmed Riff incessantly.

After a morning of more weapons training with Two Elks, Ghile slept like the dead. They set out with dusk and had been trudging along ever since.

The ghostly mist painted everything in its bluish glow, overpowering the dull yellow of the rising sun. Ghile almost wept with relief when Two Elks called for a rest on a wide hillock. With the coming dawn, Daughter Gaidel had permitted a small banked fire. It licked the stuffy morning air. Ghile and Riff huddled nearby, enjoying the reminiscent comfort of its crackling flames more than the resulting heat.

Riff moved among them, mumbling the incantation to draw the moisture from their clothes. It was only a little time later when the four travelers and two mud-covered hounds rested on the dark hillock, surrounded by the mist and ghostly blue waters, the tiny yellow flames of the banked fire flickering between them.

Ghile's boots hung upside down on sticks, as close to the fire as he dared. Though they were dry, he liked the warmth when he pulled them on in the evening. He was still picking at the bones from the last of the fish Gaidel had caught earlier, as he eyed Two Elks.

Two Elks was already asleep, his chest moving in a slow easy rhythm. His arms cradled the stone axe. His kite shield, the sign of a shieldwarden, was laid over him like a turtle's shell. The night's march must have tired him more than Ghile first thought. Normally, they would have worked on weapons training right after eating. Ghile gave thanks for small blessings and quietly made himself comfortable.

Gaidel sat across from him, her legs folded beneath her, eyes closed. She spent most mornings in this state, humming softly to herself as she communed with the All Mother. He listened and noticed, not for the first time, how her humming followed along with the sounds of the fens.

He closed his eyes and felt a dull throbbing in his chest, like a muscle strained by a long day's toil. But it was no muscle, the throb came from the two soulstones embedded deep in the bone, just beneath his skin.

Ever since the other stonechosen, the young girl made of smoke, had appeared in his dreaming, he could sense her direction. He knew he could follow the throb and it would lead him to her. The problem was, it would lead him over any mountain or across any canyon in his path. He could use this strange attraction between the stones to find her, but he couldn't follow it blindly.

He wondered if she could feel the strange 'stonecalling' as well. If so, was she trying to find him? If she was, what would happen when she did? The only other time he'd encountered another stonechosen, the goblin Muk, they'd fought to the death and now the goblin's soulstone resided in Ghile's chest.

"What do you know of our destination?" Ghile asked Riff.

Riff leaned on one elbow, a hand absently held toward the fire. He smirked before answering. "To which do you refer: The Fallen City, the Deepwood, or this Dagbar character?"

Ghile hadn't realized his question was so open ended. Riff had a tendency to make light of most situations and rarely was straightforward in his answers. He would drag his responses out and try to leach every ounce of humor he could from each one. Ghile found it enjoyable in times like these. It was good to have someone to remind him things were only as bad as he wanted to see them.

Riff's mentor, Master Almoriz, the Sorcerer of Whispering Rock, told them they should seek out a tradesman named Dagbar, who lived in a human settlement like the Cradle. Of course, this settlement was on the edge of the Deepwood, forest of the Elves. Ghile knew as much about the Deepwood and the elves as he did Dagbar or the Fallen City.

"One is as good as the other," Ghile said.

Riff considered for a long time. The sound of Gaidel's soft humming filled the silence.

"Master Almoriz spoke of the Fallen City. It was one of the largest human cities before the Great Purge. I do not know what it was called before then. But, as one of the largest cities, it drew the attention of Daomur himself.

"Master Almoriz said Daomur split the ground asunder with his great hammer, causing the city to collapse inwards. I do not know if it is named for the hubris of the humans who lived there, or for the punishment Daomur inflicted on it for Haurtu's actions," Riff said.

Ghile wondered what the stonechosen girl was doing in such a place. He discovered his first soulstone in the ancient ruins at the base of the Horn, the large mountain which cut the upper part of the Cradle into Upper and Lower Vale. He later came to understand it had once been a temple. He had not thought to ask Muk, who was now in his dreaming, where the goblin had found his soulstone. It was something he would have to do.

"Now the elves, let's see…" Riff wrinkled his forehead as he searched his memories. "Other than humans, the elves were the only other race who suffered as many losses during the God Wars and it is said they are not a prolific race to start with," he said. "I have never met one, but they are said to be beautiful to look upon. It is also said their goddess, Islmur, dotes on them. They do not call themselves elves, either. But, I cannot remember what Master Almoriz called them." Riff shrugged. "What I do remember is they fought alongside the dwarves during the Great Purge and took from us the language of the gods, taught to them by Islmur herself. Master Almoriz said it was the language the sorcerers of old used to command great magics. The powers some of us are blessed with today, are mere shadows of the power they held." There was no mirth in Riff's voice when he spoke of the elves or their goddess. "Anyway, after Haurtu was exiled from Allwyn, Daomur forbid Islmur or the elves to share the god's tongue with anyone," Riff finished.

Ghile could not imagine what powers they must possess. The few sorcerers born to the human race were thought of as mere tinkerers. They made everflame torches, put edges on tools and weapons which hardly showed wear from use, and mended pots.

Since becoming Stonechosen, Ghile had come to understand they had more power than they shared with others. A sorcerer could force his will on the environment, making it change to his desires. But, they needed to touch a small token of whatever they affected. Riff called it the source. His belt held various 'sources' in numerous pouches and bags.

Ghile had seen Riff hurl forth a gout of flame from his hands, using his everflame as a source to fuel the magic. He'd also seen the sorcerer Almoriz control a field full of bonfires, causing their flames to take to the skies and then come back down and crash into themselves, sending burning ash everywhere. Master Almoriz had done this to cover Ghile's escape from the dwarven culler.

"As for Dagbar, I know no more than you. He is a merchant in a settlement somewhere on the edge of the Deepwood," Riff said.

Ghile looked around him and shook his head. "I can't believe this is all really happening, Riff."

"What do you mean?" Riff said.

"It seems like yesterday I was tending the flocks, leaning on this spear, and wishing something exciting would happen. Now look at me."

"It sounds like you should be more careful what you wish for," Riff suggested.

Ghile nodded, tossing small weeds into the flames as he considered.

"Do you think my family is alright?" Ghile asked.

"I'm sure they are, Ghile. Your uncle is a Fang and your father a chieftain. They will see to your people."

"I can't believe Last Hamlet is gone. I can't help—"

"Oh no, don't start that again," Riff interrupted. "How many times do I have to tell you; what those thrice-damned dwarves did to your village was not your fault?"

Ghile raised his hands in surrender. "Alright, alright."

The two sat there in silence, listening to Gaidel's soft humming. Ghile had just noticed Gaidel was no longer accompanied by the sounds of the fen, when she opened her eyes and stared right through him.

"To arms, we are not alone," she called.

⋏

Gaidel sat in the relaxed position she had been trained to from her earliest days as a druid.

Most people would find sitting with their legs bent under them, their back rigid, unbearable after a few minutes, but Gaidel could maintain the position for hours.

She was not fully lost in the song. In that state she was completely enveloped and lost in its sounds, having no awareness of what went on around her. She could only remain fully in the song for a short time, for fear of being swallowed and carried away by it.

It was for that reason Gaidel practiced this technique every day. She followed the same process she used to enter the song, but stopped just before leaving her body and immersing herself.

In the beginning, she could hear nothing, the pain of the position and her mind constantly distracting her. Over time, the pain subsided and her mind calmed until she was able to detect the faintest whisper of the All Mother's dream.

Gaidel was humming along with the song, listening to its ebbs and flows. Everything that was the All Mother contributed its voice to the cacophony. The wind, with its bright full timbre, quickly danced over the slow drumming boom of the ground; the small copse of trees' warm graceful voice moved in methodical rhythm.

She could also hear Riff and Ghile talking softly across the small fire from her, while also hearing Riff's own song flow by.

Gaidel felt every living creature on Allwyn had its part in the endless song of the All Mother. That was, until she met Ghile. Ghile no longer had a song.

It had not been long since they fought the goblin and his worgs on the Horn. She was still upset at Ghile, for recklessly running off ahead of them in pursuit of the goblin, while the rest of them battled the frost wyrm. They were meant to protect the Stonechosen. Luckily, Riff was able to break free of battle and follow. By the time she and Two Elks defeated the beast and tracked Ghile and Riff to the cave, the battle with the goblin and his worgs was over.

Ghile succeeded in rescuing his uncle from the goblin, but suffered serious wounds. Gaidel feared she had already failed in the task Mother Brambles had given her in protecting Ghile when she entered the cave and saw Riff huddled over Ghile's slumped form. She immediately entered the song and tried to speed his healing.

It was one of the first lessons taught to young druids and she had done it many times before. Once in the song, she sought Ghile's song, yet found nothing. Even the worst of creatures, who were living against the path Allwyn set for them, had a discordant song.

But Ghile's song was gone.

Gaidel could only come to one conclusion. Ghile was no longer a part of the All Mother. Gaidel was honor bound to protect him, but she wished she knew what it was she was now protecting. What other changes were the soulstones causing in him?

The change in the whispers of the All Mother's song jarred Gaidel back to the present. She could hear new rhythms.

Five creatures were stealthily approaching. They were large beasts, hunters. All were female and Gaidel could hear the hunger and need to feed their young in their song. The song was strong and in tune with the All Mother. She was not deep enough into the Dream Song to reach out to them, to try and dissuade them from attacking. Even if she had time to swim deeper into the song and try to get them to hear her voice, she doubted they would listen. They were attuned to the All Mother and following their true path. It pained her to think they would have to harm these creatures, But she had to warn the others.

"To arms! We are not alone," she called.

∧

Two Elks sensed trouble even before the little daughter called out her warning. The ceremony which bound them as druid and shieldwarden had entwined their two songs as one.

He was upright, with the comforting weight of his shield along one arm and the balanced weight of his stone axe in the other.

He did not yet know what he faced, but he was ready to defend the little daughter if she needed to fully enter the song. He banged his weapon against his shield and roared a challenge into the dawn-tinged mist.

Two Elks slid his bare feet through the damp foliage, there was no time to don his boots. He wanted to be sure there was nothing to trip him or make him stumble.

The little daughter stood next to him, her back instinctively to his, her staff held parallel before her in a defensive position.

So, whatever the threat, she had chosen not to call upon the All Mother to help defeat it. *Good*, he thought to himself. Whatever they were about to face, she felt them capable of handling it.

The young Stonechosen and sorcerer were on their feet and staring into the mist. Neither of them were covering the other.

Two Elks noted Ghile still held the dwarf-made blade too tightly in one hand. He was readying the spear the people of the Cradle favored in the other. Ghile stared into the nearby waters. Unlike the sorcerer, who tossed his head left and right, the young Stonechosen seemed to know where the threat came from.

His two Valehounds crouched protectively to either side of him, their hackles raised and throaty growls filling the otherwise silent morning.

The water in front of Ghile and the hounds exploded with two sleek, black shapes. Well-muscled and still glistening with the water's bluish glow, the two predators flew towards the Stonechosen and his hounds.

A third shape broke the surface to the left of the sorcerer, using the distraction of the other two as cover. It slipped quickly from the water and belly-crawled toward Riff's blind side, the black skin of its muzzle pulling back to display thick, bony ridges. Two long black tails swished close to the ground as it lunged. Two Elks barely had time to cry a warning when two more of the creatures exploded from the water beside him.

$$\Lambda$$

Ghile, his exhaustion gone, flung his spear just as the two feline creatures exploded from the water. He was rewarded with a satisfying thud as the spear sank deep into one of the creature's protruding shoulders, just beyond its head. The creature twisted in midflight, its four limbs slashing the air in unison with its two-pronged tail. It crashed into the ground in front of Ghile and then disappeared under the white fur and raking claws of Ast and Cuz.

The second of the two landed between Ghile and Riff, snapping at Ghile's legs, forcing him to fall back. The thick bony ridges these creatures had in place of teeth made a sharp crack with each bite, leaving little doubt they could break bone. Ghile fell further back from the assault, swiping his blade in defensive strokes to guard his retreat.

Behind the advancing creature, Ghile saw Riff raising his hands, everflame playing through the sorcerer's fingertips, causing the flames' reflection to dance across his grinning face. The creature had exposed its back to Riff and he wasn't going to pass up the opportunity.

Ghile heard Two Elks' warning just as Riff screamed and fell to the ground. Another of the creatures had snuck up behind him and locked its jaws onto Riff's leg. It immediately began dragging Riff back towards the water with powerful jerking motions. Riff clawed at the muddy ground and grasping at nearby plants and shrubs, anything to stop from being pulled away from the others, his everflame falling to the ground forgotten.

The creature before Ghile stopped its assault and began backing away, keeping between Ghile and the struggling Riff. Its yellow eyes were locked with Ghile's and somehow, he knew it was a she and hungry. He could sense they only wanted one of them and would take Riff and leave the others in peace. He could feel his consciousness slip deeper into those yellow eyes. He could see small black cubs in a deep warren, rolling and snarling as they played over the sole male, who lounged and waited for the females to return.

Ghile shook himself out of it and his surroundings snapped back into place. He realized it was the powers of his newly acquired soulstone.

He had to save Riff.

He risked a look at Gaidel and Two Elks. They were both engaged with one creature each, their backs together. The swamp cats lunged forward, snapping their jaws, but seemed more interested in keeping Two Elks and Gaidel busy than actually attacking. Ghile knew there would be no help coming. It was going to have to be him. He had to do something now.

He focused his mind on the sounds of Ast and Cuz. He could feel them behind him. The swamp cat he had wounded with the spear was no match against the two Valehounds. These creatures were quick, but not as big as one of the wolves which prowled the mountains around the Cradle. Ghile kept his fang blade before him, and focused on Cuz.

Help me.

Ghile felt the wet fur brush past his waist as Cuz barreled into the swamp cat who was blocking Ghile from Riff. The two animals fell into a rolling ball of hisses and barks. There was no way Ghile was going to get past the two in time.

Even though he'd had the second soulstone for weeks, he had not entered the dreaming to learn its powers. He realized now he'd spent too much time practicing combat with Two Elks. Well, there was nothing for it now; he concentrated and reached out to the mind of the swamp cat who held onto Riff.

Ghile tasted sweet warm blood in his mouth. He felt the soft give of flesh and the resistance of bone. His two tails were lashed securely around his prey's other leg and even now, he felt the cool comfort of his watery home as he slid into its protection. He thought of his litter back in the warren and how pleased his mate would be with this kill.

Ghile had the sensation of leaning into an open hole and then falling in. His consciousness was somehow now inside the swamp cat. He screamed and a feline squall filled his ears. This was wrong. He had to get out. He had to get out.

Λ

By Daomur's short hairs, his leg hurt! Riff tried to focus, but the pain cut through everything. He'd dropped his everflame when the thrice-damned swamp cat had snuck up and bit into him. He should have seen it coming. It would have been nice if someone had actually said they were about to be attacked by a pack of swamp cats, instead of just yelling "To arms!"

What could he do without his everflame? It was hard to concentrate through the pain. Maybe if he waited until the cat had him in the water to use it as a source? He could force the water down its throat and choke the thing before it ate him. He could feel the strong grip the creature had on his other leg. Its tails were almost as strong as its damnable bite.

Without reason, the swamp cat's eyes went large and it let go of him. It began squalling like the Hungerer himself had a hold of it. Riff stared for a moment in shock, before grabbing his wounded leg. The cat thrashed, half in and half out of the water.

Well, you don't have to tell me twice, he thought.

Riff rolled over and crawled the short distance to his everflame. He almost cried when he felt its gentle reaffirming warmth. Everflame gave off little heat, but as a source, Riff could channel it into real fire. He tried to squeeze the pain from his mind and take in the battle. Ghile's two hounds were more than holding their own against two other swamp cats. Both Gaidel and Two Elks seemed no worse for wear, but had not been able to land any telling blows against the two cats which danced about them. Of everyone, he seemed to be the only one who had been half eaten.

"Figures. Fine, you want to pick on the little guy, huh?" Riff glanced at Ghile, who stood near him with a blank expression on his face. "What are you doing, Sheepherder?" Riff said. Well, at least he was nearby. Now to show these swamp cats what happens, when you try to eat a sorcerer who has his own stonechosen.

Ghile couldn't free his mind from the creature. He could feel it near him, it was as confused and panicked as he was. It wanted to flee, Ghile could feel it trying to control its limbs in vain. He was trying to stand, but his paws didn't bend right and he kept falling on his side. His tails were slapping his sides and face, further confusing him. He just wanted out.

Riff came into view. He called for help, but it only came out as another high pitched whine. Ghile watched in horror as Riff hopped to maintain his balance on his good leg and raised the everflame before him.

As the flames washed over him, Ghile felt his fur curl and melt. His flesh bubbled under the heat. The pain was like nothing he'd ever experienced. His screams were torn from his throat by burning air and then he felt nothing as he was hurled into darkness.

4

Return to the Dreaming

HILE listened to the gentle lapping of nearby waves. He could hear birdsong in the distance. There was a warmth on his skin. Sunlight.

He exhaled. He was in the dreaming again. The forested island in the center of the great lake, surrounded by mountains. He was safe.

Something hit his head. "Stupid boy!" The something croaked at him. It slapped him on the head again. "Muk not teach you how stone work yet," it said.

Ghile opened his eyes and shielded his head. Another blow slapped into his arms. The goblin was bouncing from one long, floppy foot to the other. His wrinkled green skin and overabundance of warts, combined with long floppy ears, would have been comical, if not for the rows of sharp jagged teeth in its downturned mouth and current attitude.

Muk struck at him again.

"Stop hitting me!" Ghile said. Ghile reached into his mind and grabbed raw thought. He formed the thought into a tangible force and pushed it out before him like a wad of wool. He didn't want to hurt the little pest, but he also didn't want to be hit on the head again.

Muk screamed as he was thrown back, landing hard on the beach among scattered pebbles. He sat up and shot Ghile a withering glare.

"That no way to treat dream teacher! I not teach stupid boy nothing." Muk got up and adjusted the rags he was wearing, as if they were the finest festival clothes.

Ghile couldn't help but chuckle, which only set the goblin cursing in his own tongue and bouncing from one foot to the other again.

Another gift of the soulstones, was Ghile could understand every word of the goblin tongue. He blushed.

"He is right, Brother. That is no way to treat your teachers," Adon said.

Ghile wasn't sure when Adon had arrived, or if he'd been there the whole time. His face reddened and he immediately felt foolish. Ghile rose off the beach and ran his hand through his tangled curls. "I'm sorry, Adon. I wasn't trying to hurt him. He was hitting me on the head."

"I can't really blame him, what you did was foolish," Adon said.

Ghile's brother was tall, just like him. He looked the same as he had on the day he failed the Rite of Attrition in Lakeside, all those years before. The same dark hair as Ghile's, same high cheekbones. Even with everything that happened, it was still a mix of joy and confusion whenever Ghile saw Adon, joy at being reunited with his brother and confusion because Adon had been culled by the dwarves. Yet here he was.

Muk walked up beside Adon and stood next to him, barely taller than Adon's knee. The obstinate goblin purposefully crossed his arms over his chest and added a 'harrumph' for good measure.

"You look well, considering," Adon said.

With a start, Ghile remembered the flames as they leaped from Riff's hands. He felt his flesh scream with the kiss of fire. The fight in the Ghost Fens! Ghile thrust his hands before his face and examined them, followed by his arms. There were no burns. With relief, he remembered the wounds he suffered in Allwyn did not follow him into the dreaming.

"Wait, how do you two know what happened? Can you see into Allwyn?" Ghile said. He'd never really thought on it before. Adon never said he could see what was happening when Ghile was awake. Ghile couldn't decide if the idea of them being able to see things he did was something he liked or not.

Adon walked over and put a hand on Ghile's shoulder. "Be at ease, Brother. We can only sense when you call upon the powers of the soulstones. And then, it is only the briefest of images. Much like seeing the dreamings of the other sleepers," Adon said.

"What sleepers you mean?" Muk asked. He looked between the two humans in confusion.

Ghile recalled Adon sharing his experience after he was culled, after he'd died. At first, Adon was reluctant to talk about it, but over time, he finally shared his time spent floating in a dream-like sleep. He had compared it to lying in a pitch black field surrounded by others. He could sense their presence, but not see them. They were all speaking at once, sharing stories of their lives, their experiences. Over time, Adon was able to single out individual stories from the others. Then, he could start to see what the others had seen, experience what they experienced. It was how he'd learned the old ways from the ancestors. How he had learned to use the powers forgotten by humans since the Great Purge.

"Who sleeping?" Muk said. He appeared to be getting agitated again.

Adon made a calming gesture with his hands. "I will explain it to you later, Muk. For now, we need to focus on Ghile and his training."

Ghile shook his head and sat back down, crossing his legs.

"Adon, I cannot stay. There is a battle in the Ghost Fens, we were attacked by these black cat-like creatures. They came from the water. I must return."

Ghile tried to relax. He focused on returning to Allwyn. The last time he was in the dreaming, Muk taught him how to wake up. He had to relax and focus his mind. He had eventually felt his feet sink into the earth and spread out like roots, his head and hands rising up to become limbs of the Great Oak that occupied the center of the island.

Nothing was happening. Ghile opened his eyes to find Adon watching him with a concerned look, while Muk stared at him as if he was an idiot.

"Ghile, you have been hurt. I'm afraid you cannot leave until you've healed," Adon said.

"But it was the swamp creature who was burned, not me." Even as Ghile spoke, he could vividly remember his fur and flesh melting under the heat. He shuddered and tried to shake the feeling off, like it was a wasp which had landed on him.

Muk poked himself in the head. "You hurt here. You go too deep in swamp cat. Become cat. Dangerous. Only control one that way. No have control of your body. You stupid boy. Why you no come here to learn new powers sooner? You stupid boy."

"All right, Muk. That's enough," Adon said. He stepped forward and extended his hand to Ghile.

"Come with us, Brother. You're here for the time being and you need to learn how to use your new powers."

Λ

The three of them made their way through the island forest. Ghile tried to take everything in at once. He had not been in the dreaming since he defeated Muk and the worgs on the Horn.

The forest seemed to be in a perpetual state of summer. The green leaves hung thick above them. The sky was cloudless. Only once had Ghile seen the sky anything but clear. On one of his visits, he arrived to a brewing storm. He'd searched through these very woods looking for Adon. He'd been angry then and wanted to confront his brother. He'd accused Adon of being the god, the Hungering God. Even now, walking behind Adon and Muk, he was not really sure who they were. This dream Adon looked like the brother he remembered. He spoke like Adon and acted like him. He stared at the back of Adon's head, as if the answer could be found there.

Muk scampered along, taking two to three steps for every one of theirs. Ghile had not known the creature before he died, so didn't know if this Muk was the same one who captured his Uncle Toren and used him as bait to lure Ghile to that cave.

Regardless, this goblin had been stonechosen, like him. But, now, Muk's soulstone was in Ghile's chest, next to the one Ghile had found in the ruins at the base of the horn. He absently ran his hands along the two soulstones, embedded in his chest, just beneath his skin.

Ghile ducked under a low hanging branch and recognized this part of the forest as where the shadow creature had once tried to lure him away. He looked around, expecting to see the skulking creature peering out around one of the trees, wringing its hands, watching him.

Adon said the creature was here when he first arrived. For what purpose, if any, Ghile didn't know. All he did know was the creature tried to attack Adon on numerous occasions and tried to lure Ghile away from Adon, deeper into the forest. Adon said the shadow was trying to isolate Ghile, so it could attack him.

If Ghile was being honest with himself, he wasn't entirely sure that was true. He wouldn't admit that to Adon. Adon had seemed quite sure that was the reason and told him on a number of occasions to be wary of the creature. But, it never openly attacked Ghile.

He felt more than confident enough to protect himself from the shadow now. He decided the next time the shadow showed itself, he would follow it and see where it lead. Maybe he would finally start to get some answers about this place.

The trio entered the large clearing which surrounded the huge oak tree growing from the center of the island. The tree made the surrounding trees look like shrubs. It reminded Ghile of the way the Horn towered over his valley home. But where the Horn was dark and ugly, the great oak was majestic and full of life. Ghile found he missed the big tree, as much as the rest of the place. This place, this dreaming brought him comfort, relaxed him. He could think of no better place to learn.

Adon turned around before one of the great roots of the oak. The roots easily rose twenty feet in the air. Ghile and Adon had spent many evenings sitting on them, looking up into the boughs of the oak, talking.

"So, let us begin with what you already know," Adon said. He pulled a handful of stones from a pouch on his belt and tossed them towards Ghile. As soon as they left his hands, they raced towards Ghile.

Ghile focused his mind and brought the image of the force wall from his mind and into reality. The shimmering wall stretched out from his hand. As he had done in the past, he did not make the wall solid to just reflect the stones. As soon as he felt the pressure of them impacting his shield, he allowed the shield to give under the force. The three stones slowed and hovered momentarily before being shot back towards Adon.

Adon smiled and redirected the stones with a wave of his hands.

"Good. Now follow me." With that, Adon turned, took two steps and then soared into the air to land lightly on top of one of the oak's enormous roots.

Ghile nodded and ran forward. He focused and pushed his force shield out from the bottoms of his feet with as much power as he could and found himself vaulted into the air. He easily cleared the height of the root and as he felt his speed slowing, he waved his arms to keep his feet beneath him. He continued to hold the image of the force extending out from his feet and allowed the force shield to absorb the impact of his landing. When the pressure was too much, he released it and landed lightly on the top of the root, next to Adon.

"Well done," Adon said.

Adon stepped off the root, but instead of plummeting down, he raised one hand and floated forward through the air. He glided down to land gently next to a clapping Muk.

Ghile jumped off the root and followed. He extended his force shield out from his extended hand. He stretched it wide and thin until he felt it catch the air. He used this trick to clear the chasm during his manhood tests. He thought of Gar then and could see his cousins accusing eyes as Gar fell to his death. Ghile felt himself falling too. He had lost his concentration and with it, his force shield. He brought up a shield beneath him and only just broke his fall, tumbling to the ground.

"Ghile, you must maintain focus. The shield is an extension of your mind," Adon said.

Muk was clapping even harder and making a sinister wheezing sound Ghile took to be laughter. In all the other training sessions with Adon, he'd never had an audience. The addition of Muk was not going to make these sessions any easier.

"I'm sorry, I pictured… I will maintain focus," Ghile said.

Adon nodded. "Now, I know you used the force power to fill that worg's mouth and break its jaws. You need to continue to think of different ways to use it. There are no limits, except for those you impose on yourself."

"There is the limit to how far I can extend it. That, and I can only extend it from my own body," Ghile said.

"Your own mind," Adon corrected. "You extend it from your own mind. But now you can touch other minds."

Muk stepped from behind Adon. The little goblin's demeanor had completely changed. He had his hands behind his back and wore a somber expression.

Ghile couldn't help but grin when Muk stated, "Now Muk teach."

Adon cleared his throat and shook his head when Ghile looked up. But, Ghile could see Adon holding back a smile of his own.

Ghile cleared his throat and listened attentively to the little goblin.

Muk walked around him slowly. "When animals near, you feel it. In here." Muk poked his head again. It was apparently a gesture he was fond of. He did it with more force than was necessary and Ghile couldn't help but wince each time he did it. "The closer the animal, the easier it be to sense and control," Muk said.

Ghile looked around the clearing and for the first time, realized he'd never actually seen another animal in the dreaming, other than those in the clearing and the shadow creature. *Of course there were other animals,* he thought. He'd heard the birds singing from the nearby trees many times.

Muk was still speaking, but Ghile had already closed his eyes and focused his mind. He reached out, mentally searching. From the experience he had with the swamp cats, he was a little more cautious. It reminded him of when he woke in the middle of the night back in Last Hamlet and had to find his way out of his father's roundhouse without stepping on someone or knocking something over.

He sensed a number of small, for lack of a better word, bubbles... there. The bubbles were small and if he had eyes in his mind, he would say they glowed slightly. They were a short distance away from him. He tried to focus on one of them and was disoriented when he felt his conscious rush towards it, closing the mental distance in less than a heartbeat. He fought the forward momentum and stopped abruptly.

The small bubble of light floated there. He could sense it was a bird, one of the house swallows which made their nests among the rafters of his people's roundhouses. He loved watching them swoop in through the windows and doorways in the spring, back from wherever they had been through the long winters.

He felt another presence beside him and felt, more than heard, Muk's chastising voice.

"You too hasty. I not finished. Why you focus on one? Try sense others, all at once," Muk said.

Ghile nodded and then thought how useless such an action was, given the circumstances. He relaxed and was jolted back away from the single swallow and could again sense the others.

"Good. Now reach out and see yourself grasping each ball of light and crushing it like egg."

Ghile didn't know if he was more disturbed by the image of crushing the minds of these small birds, or by the sound of glee in the goblin's voice.

"Are you crazy?" Ghile said. He opened his eyes and glared down at Muk.

The little goblin opened his eyes, a genuinely confused look on his face. "No. Why ask?"

"Why would I want to shred their minds? They're harmless swallows," Ghile said. A wind rustled through the trees and the clearing. Ghile brushed a loose lock of hair from in front of his eyes. "This is what you want to teach me? How to crush creatures' minds?" Ghile looked to Adon, who stood a short distance away watching. "Adon, I won't do it."

Adon looked at the trees and nodded to Ghile. "He is right, Muk. There is no need to kill these birds. I think Ghile has enough control to try something a little more complex than attacking their minds. But Ghile," Adon added, "there may come a time where you are in danger and understanding you have the ability to perform such an attack may be the difference between life and death."

Ghile sighed. He ran his hands through his hair and nodded to Muk. "Teach me how you controlled the worgs."

Muk stared at him for a moment before answering. It was obvious he didn't appreciate being told what he was to teach. It was also obvious he was a little disappointed in not seeing the swallows having their minds shredded. "Reach out to birds' minds. Feel they should listen to you, feel they need to do as you say. My dream teacher explain it to me by describing how we speak to young," Muk said.

"Your dream teacher?" Ghile had not considered it, but it made sense that Muk, as stonechosen, would have had a teacher. "What do you think happened to him once you, um, you know, died?"

Ghile didn't want to upset Muk, but he was curious as to how this all worked. Adon had been here when he first came to this forested island. Muk appeared after Ghile joined with the second soulstone. If he was killed by another stonechosen as Muk was, would he appear in their dreaming to teach them what he knew? He wasn't so sure he would be inclined to teach someone who'd just killed him.

"I not know," Muk said. If it bothered Muk, he didn't show it.

Adon cleared his throat. "Ghile, focus on your training for now. We can discuss this later."

Ghile again wondered if this was indeed Adon. There were so many unanswered questions about all this.

"Alright, the swallows," Ghile said. He reached out with his mind. This time, he did not close his eyes. The small bubbles appeared there in his mind as little floating lights. He did as Muk said and thought of how they should listen to them, how they were supposed to listen to him.

Nothing happened. The swallows were still in the trees and didn't seem to be any different.

"Now call them," Muk said.

No sooner had Ghile thought they should come to him, than one of the little blue colored birds swooped down and landed on his shoulder. It tilted its small delicate head and stared at him expectantly. It was soon joined by the others. They swooped in, chittering away. They were hungry, Ghile realized. They had not told him; he'd just felt it. The first one to land on him hopped closer to his face. Ghile could sense its mind, that little bubble of energy, floating there in his mind's eye. He had the urge to push his consciousness against the bubble.

Ghile was instantly staring at his own enormous face. He was hungry and he could feel his tiny heart fluttering incredibly fast in his chest.

His human face had gone slack and emotionless. His eyes were open, but blank, empty. It reminded him of the way some people looked when they were daydreaming.

The urge to fly filled him and he took to the sky. His sharp angled blue wings cut through the air as he swooped across the clearing. He began beating his wings furiously and rose with each downward thrust. It was an incredible feeling and he couldn't hold it all in. He shouted. The sound that came out of him was more of a cheerful warble followed by a 'slee-plink'.

He banked sharply to his left and circled around. Some of the other swallows had also taken to the air. He must have lost control of them when he entered this one. He could see Adon and Muk were talking to his human form, but he couldn't hear them. He thought about the swallow he was 'riding'. Where was it? Was it in here with him? He tried to sense it, but couldn't. It must still be here with him, he didn't know how to fly, yet he somehow knew what to do. He hadn't thought about what he needed to do, just what he wanted to do and he'd done it.

He circled around again and rose higher. He had a clear view of the clearing. What an incredible feeling it was to fly! He would definitely be doing this again.

Far below, it looked like Muk was starting to get angry. He was hopping again. Ghile thought about being back in his own body and he was instantly there.

He was disoriented, tired and extremely hungry. The sound of Muk's croaking flooded into his ears. Ghile shook his head, trying to clear it.

"You hear me?" Muk said.

"Yes, Muk. I hear you now. I entered one of the swallows. I was flying," Ghile said.

"I didn't say do that. You need listen, not go jumping in animals. That what hurt you before," Muk said. His voice had risen even higher.

At least he'd stopped hopping up and down, Ghile thought.

Luckily, Adon stepped up and took control of the conversation. "Ghile. You now have the power of two of the soulstones. You need to work on combining their powers, as well as mastering each one individually."

Adon reached into his pouch and pulled out a stone. Ghile recognized it as one of the stones from the shore. Adon searched the trees and then pointed at one. "There, Ghile. See that swallow there on that lower branch?"

Ghile had to squint, but could make out the small blue swallow. He nodded.

"I'm going to hurl this stone at it. Use your force shield and protect it," Adon said.

With that, Adon tossed the stone forward and it streaked off towards the unsuspecting sparrow.

Ghile started to say he wasn't ready when Adon released the stone. But, there was nothing for it. Ghile reached out with his mind. He felt his consciousness streak towards the swallow. He focused on the image of the shield, spreading out before him as his mind entered the swallow. He felt the impact of the stone as the shield deflected it. The force of the blow threw him off the branch, but he spread his wings and turned the plummet into a swooping dive. Ghile willed himself back into his own body and opened his eyes. "What is with you two and trying to kill those poor birds?" said he demanded.

"That was well done, Ghile" Adon said, apparently choosing to ignore Ghile's question.

Muk turned and began walking towards one of the many trails that led from the clearing surrounding the oak. "Come, we find something bigger to work with," Muk said.

5

The Book of Hjurl

 INNGYR squeezed the bridge of his broad nose to try and ease his headache. He'd spent too many hours staring at these tablets. There were just enough glowstones spread out among the ancient stone tablets to keep him from tripping over one, but not enough to allow for reading. No outside light made it this far into the Ritualist's temple and he had to make do with their feeble light and the resulting headache.

Were the Ritualist's bats? If Daomur gifted them with the ability to enchant the heavy, head-sized circular glowstones to produce light, why couldn't the priests make the effort to have them give off a little more illumination? He wished, not for the first time, open flames were not forbidden near the tablets. What he wouldn't give for a lantern, or some reading candles.

He straightened and knuckled his lower back. His muscles ached in protest, but he ignored them until he felt a satisfying crack. The stone wall behind him was joined with an outer wall. The room was tall enough to allow for a few arched windows, evenly placed to let in more light. Surely the Ritualists could contract one of the journeymen from the Temple of Art to perform such work? The Artisans were always looking for something to chisel on.

If it wasn't for the headache, he would be fine with the dim light. It fit his mood. He had spent too much time in the Temple of Law over the last few weeks poring over these tablets. Finngyr was a dwarf of action and all this time waiting and studying went against his base nature.

After his meeting with Captain Danuk, Finngyr thought he would have a short wait before being disciplined for his decisions in the Cradle of the Gods. He hurried here, to the Temple of Law, as soon as his duties allowed, to study this portion of the Book of Hjurl concerning the Prophecies, thinking he had little time before he would be summoned to receive his fate.

All twenty-seven tablets filling this small antechamber were etched with the Prophecies of Hjurl. He had read over them to find any clue as to where the human vessel would go. As the days wore on and no summons came, he continued to return here and study.

After the first few days, he sought another meeting with Captain Danuk to no avail. It seemed the captain was too busy with the goings-on in the plains to grant him another audience. Finngyr was tempted to storm into his office after the first week, but knew protocol dictated he follow proper channels to request an audience with a superior in the order.

Damn their bones. Didn't they understand there was a vessel of the Hungering God roaming loose out there? Why was he still here?

His earlier wanderings further out into the Temple District had not gone well. The district was always filled with priests and politicians, debating this law or that edict. He had no patience for their constant blathering or their impertinent stares. It seemed the tales of his deeds had spread quickly. More than once he heard his name spoken while passing a cluster of his brethren.

He confronted one group of adepts from the Temple of Law when he overheard one of them questioning, in a whisper meant to be heard, why the Knight Justice was not already supervising human prisoners in the Underways, an insult of the highest order.

As if he would perform a job for the lowest of commoners, who were not even true citizens of the empire. He was a member of the church and a full citizen.

Finngyr's jaw tightened, only agitating his headache. If only he could have set those Adepts straight. The silent smirks they gave him when he demanded they repeat what they'd said still set his blood boiling. Of course, he could do nothing and had not ventured forth into the district since. He was already in enough trouble without adding a public display of emotion on top of things, like some beardling who had forgotten his teachings.

All dwarves learned from an early age that emotions only clouded thoughts. Daomur's laws called for a clear mind. The open expression of emotion was considered rude behavior, at best. When was the last time his thoughts were clear of anger? Even now it seeped into his thoughts, wearing away at his resolve. Finngyr crossed his arms, as if he could crush the unwanted emotion from inside him with sheer strength.

"His word is meant to be considered with a clear mind, Knight Justice," a voice said.

Finngyr relaxed his grip, releasing a breath he hadn't realized he'd been holding. "I did not hear you enter, Priest Eriver," Finngyr said without opening his eyes.

The old priest harrumphed.

Other than himself, the wizened priest was the only other visitor to this part of the temple Finngyr had seen. He wondered why the priest even came down here. He never consulted the tablets concerning the Prophecies. Was he merely checking up on him?

"Still with us, I see?"

Finngyr grunted and pretended to return to his inspection of the tablet in front of him. Brother Eriver began all of their conversations with that statement. If they could be considered conversations. They consisted of the old dwarf talking at Finngyr and Finngyr trying to ignore him until the priest grew bored and wandered off.

"Always you Knight Justices and the Prophecies!" Priest Eriver said. "As if they were the only tablets ever chiseled."

Finngyr continued to stare at the etchings. This portion of the Prophecies was a series of fragmented thoughts, concerning Daomur and dreams. At least they were complete sentences. Most of the prophecies were cryptic chants.

"You know, Hjurl, bless his name, didn't even carve these tablets?" Priest Eriver went on. The priest hobbled over to stand next to Finngyr and waited to see if the Knight Justice would answer this time.

Finngyr knew it wouldn't matter whether he did or didn't. He looked at the older dwarf and waited.

The priest's bald pate was wrinkled with age and mostly occupied by a large brown birthmark. It made Finngyr think of spilled gravy and that reminded him he'd not eaten since early morning. What gray streaked hair remained, was wrapped around his head like an old ferret, trained to hold up his wispy beard. "It was his sons who took up the hammer and chisel when he was too feeble to continue the work on his own."

Finngyr had heard all this before. To hear it again was bad enough, but with his headache, each word felt like an artificer's hammer chipping away on the inside of his skull. "It is too dark in here," Finngyr said, trying to change the subject.

"You need spectacles. I have told you this before. You're as stubborn as stone."

Brother Eriver had told him this before and the old dwarf's gall still annoyed him. The Lawgivers were a blunt sect. There were few things as direct as a Lawgiver's tongue. Normally, Finngyr would have appreciated such directness. But, not when it was at his expense.

"There is plenty of light in the chambers holding the other tablets of the Book, priest. You Lawgivers only care for your dry laws."

It was the headache. He wouldn't have taken the bait and referred to the sect with the derogatory name if not for the headache. The Temple of the Ritualists were responsible for overseeing ceremonies and law. It was true they worked closely with the civil government.

Largest of the three temples, they were also the keepers of the Book of Hjurl. Their secondary role was to interpret the laws of society derived from the Book. To refer to them as Lawgivers was to imply they did not interpret Daomur's words, but dictate them.

Finngyr could see the veins in the old priest's head swell and one of his eyes squeezed tight from the pressure building beneath the surface. Finngyr could see the priest regaining his composure after a few seconds and knew the energy was going to be directed into a reproof that, when it came, burst forth like a river over its damn

"Lawgivers? Dry laws? Hjurl, bless his name, was the first dwarf. Daomur chiseled him from stone and took a small piece of himself and placed it into the Hjurl's chest to give him life and you consider the discussions those two had, the discussions etched into those tablets out there 'dry laws'? Those first days spent discussing life and existence? What it means to be a dwarf? How our creator meant us to live a life which would honor him? Dry laws indeed!" The priest waved his hand to take in the whole chamber. "These tablets you have spent so much time studying, were carved near the end of his life. When Hjurl was decrepit and too old to even hold the hammer and chisel. Ramblings near the end of his life, ramblings of many things."

"Prophecies," Finngyr corrected when Eriver stopped to draw breath. Finngyr was not one to back down. He had spent weeks poring over these particular tablets. The Temple of Justice was largely founded on the Prophecies. He could not conceal the exasperation from his voice. "This portion of the Book of Hjurl is known as The Prophecies, Priest."

"So, the student instructs the teacher, then?" Eriver began tapping his sandaled foot against the stone. The sound echoed in Finngyr's ears and played on his headache. "This portion of The Prophecies speak of the mad god, his imprisonment, escape and retribution. The Prophecy of the Vessels," Priest Eriver recited.

"Exactly," Finngyr said.

The priest stopped tapping and held a gnarled finger up like a sprung trap. "Did you know it is written in those dry old laws, as you call them, that Hjurl, bless his name, spent the last years of his long life lost in a half conscious state? It was his ramblings during that time which fill these tablets."

Finngyr's head throbbed with each pulse of his heart. His headache had grabbed the priest's words and slammed them down onto Finngyr's head, mocked all the time he had spent here these past weeks, searching for answers. "The Time of the Stonechosen has come, priest." Finngyr pronounced each word slowly, letting them seethe out of him. He stared hard at the old dwarf.

Brother Eriver stared back, one eye still wrinkled in consternation. "Oh, you Justices would like that wouldn't you? The Time of the Stonechosen. The Soulstone Prophecies fulfilled. Where are these stonechosen, these vessels occupied by the Hungerer himself to facilitate his second coming?"

Finngyr tightened his hand on the empty air where he wished his hammer to be. The Knight Captain Danuk took Finngyr's report, which Finngyr later dictated to an acolyte of the Temple of Law to be transcribed to the Knights Council. The Knight Captain said he hoped this would shed some light on the strange occurrences in the Nordlah Plains and help determine if the Time of the Stonechosen had arrived. Then nothing.

"Always you Justices with your warnings and predictions. Is that how you justify your actions in the Cradle of the Gods, Knight Justice Finngyr? Hmm? Caused an uprising. All those lost profits. Why hasn't the Lord Knight Justice brought this news before the High Council? All I have heard discussed in the High Council was what was to be done about *you*." The old priest blinked at him and waited.

I had him and I lost him. Finngyr's headache and anger were gone, drowned in thick heavy remorse.

Eriver must have seen Finngyr's thoughts reflected on his face, because the old priest's features softened. "I am an old dwarf and rise too quickly to a lively debate. Do not let my words affect you, so. Our sects have always quarreled so, Knight Justice." He waved his hands as if they would clear away everything that had just transpired.

Ghile Stonechosen had been before him and Finngyr had let him escape. The sole reason for his existence was to protect his people, prevent the return of the Hungerer by culling those humans who could be his vessel and he had failed. A Stonechosen was out there somewhere on Allwyn, growing in power because of him and his inadequacies. He had let himself be duped into giving up the hunt by coin mongers and now it was coin mongers who were going to decide his fate. Not realizing they were condemning themselves, all of Allwyn, by condemning him. And now, on top of everything, this old priest pitied him.

"His word is law, Priest Eriver," Finngyr finally said. He walked from the chamber, his thoughts weighing heavily on him. He left the priest there alone, staring after him in the meager light of the glowstones.

6

Plans within Plans

 INNGYR tucked his shoulder and rolled with the blow. It was a good strike, he had to give the beardling that. Had he stood his ground, it would have broken bone. As it was, the quick reaction resulted in some pain and maybe a healthy bruise come the evening.

The sand covering the ground of the temple's training arena cushioned the roll and Finngyr was back on his feet, a good defensive distance from both of his adversaries.

The two young dwarves were in the training rings when he arrived. He came early in hopes of having the place to himself. Finngyr did not care for the Master of Arms and knew he didn't usually arrive until well after breaking fast. He needed to work out his frustrations and the laziness which had crept into his bones since his return to Daomount. But these two were already here, going through their fighting forms.

They were young, barely more than squires. But the one with the thick red hair – Horth was his name – more than made up for his youth with sheer girth. He was the one who almost landed the bone-crushing blow that sent Finngyr diving.

The other – Kjar – was dark haired and lean. He had the perpetual squint of the dwarves from Orehome, the southernmost mountain city of the empire. The biggest thing about him was his nose. Its deformed shape suggested it had been broken more than once. Not even the thick mustache he grew diminished its size. Finngyr intended to add an additional break to that number this morning.

The two circled to either side of him, trying to flank him and divide his attention. He shuffled back and to the side, keeping them in view. He shifted his grip on the practice hammer. It was lighter than his own, even with the stone weight placed in its center. But the balance and size were right enough for training.

Sweat streaked Horth's face. He wasn't used to long, drawn out battles. Finngyr could tell he liked to use his size and strength to end fights quickly. Kjar, on the other hand, seemed perfectly content to shift from one defensive stance to the other, squinting all the while over that melon of a nose, biding his time. He was a planner. But, would he hesitate when the time came to strike?

Finngyr brought his handle up and forward, turning the weapon's head down past his body in a reverse, upward swing. He couldn't put much strength behind the move, but it was meant more as a distraction. He shifted forward towards Kjar, who reacted quickly enough to avoid the blow, sliding to the side.

Finngyr carried the swing up and over; turning his body as he went, he brought the swing all the way around and behind him, continuing the momentum. He turned his body, redirecting the swing into a horizontal arc, right into the incoming Horth. The large dwarf had seized the opportunity to launch a strike at Finngyr's exposed back when he thought the attack was focused on his companion. Just as Finngyr knew he would. Finngyr's hammer caught him solidly in the thigh, sending Horth's strike wide. The large dwarf tumbled to the sand.

Finngyr had just enough time to recover before Kjar struck like a viper, combining blows from both the business end and the tip of the hammer's handle. Finngyr was caught off guard at first. He expected the attack, but was not accustomed to this fighting style. It must be yet another thing the young dwarf brought north, along with that squint. It was all Finngyr could do to keep his hammer before him, using both hands to block the flurry of blows. The clack of wood echoed off the circular stone walls.

Unfortunately for Kjar, his blows fell into a rhythm Finngyr detected and when the next strike came, Finngyr let it slide along the shaft of his hammer instead of taking the hit squarely. Finngyr lunged forward, sending the end of his hammer's shaft square into Kjar's nose with a satisfying crack.

The young dwarf's forward momentum halted as he stumbled to the side, blinking. Blood already flowed down into his thick mustache, followed by a string of curses that would have made a dock hand proud.

Finngyr slid left and turned into a defensive crouch, in case Horth was on the attack again. The flame-haired dwarf was down on one knee, nursing his thigh and shaking his head at Kjar's misfortune. "How is it your nose always finds a way to get hit?" Horth said.

"Phaw," was Kjar's only response as he pinched off the bridge of his nose in an attempt to control the bleeding.

"Your attack was adequate, Knight, but you fell into a rhythm," Finngyr said.

"Well, fought, Knight Justice," Horth said.

Finngyr grunted and walked to the raised stone edge of the fighting ring. It was one of three such rings that made up the training arena. He leaned his sparring hammer against a bench and grabbed a towel. Even this early in the morning, the sun's warmth had Finngyr's wool trousers and broad waist sash damp with sweat. Black curly hair lay flat against his bare chest and back.

He poured a mug of water from a nearby jug and drank deeply. The water was cool. He didn't notice the page who had filled it. The newest members of the Temple of Justice saw to all the mundane needs and were beneath notice. He wasn't sure if it was the exercise or teaching a couple of beardlings some humility, but Finngyr felt a little better.

He sat down and watched the two as Horth examined Kjar's nose. A few squires came in and occupied one of the other rings, going through morning ritual stretches.

Finngyr remembered a time when all the rings would have been full with knights and squires. There were two other practice areas which were converted to other uses long before he was born.

His sect was in decline and seen as less of a necessity by the empire. The Knights of the Temple of Justice were only needed to cull the human settlements and keep the forbidden cities' goblin populations under control, which the empire was seeing more as a religious tradition than the essential need that it was. Only in the Nordlah Plains were humans still in any form of open rebellion. But, there were no tradable commodities in the plains, thus as long as the few Bastions guarding the underways and the forbidden cities were protected, the empire did not truly care what the nomadic plainsmen did.

The humans in the outlying settlements produced desired goods and performed the menial work noone else wished to do. Even in the cities, human servants were used to run errands and wait on their dwarven overseers. Finngyr thanked Daomur their human stink was not allowed in the judicial and temple districts.

As long as it did not impact trade, the Knights would be allowed to perform their sacred duties. Finngyr spat into the sand as if the bad taste those coin mongering simpletons left in his mouth was something physical, like soured ale.

"That is a foul face indeed," Knight Captain Danuk said.

Finngyr had been so deep in thought, he had not heard the captain approach. He rose smartly and bowed. "Knight Captain," Finngyr said. He tried to keep the hope from his voice. Had the time finally come?

Danuk nodded in reply and then motioned for Finngyr to take his seat before joining him. Finngyr's earlier opponents were back in the nearby ring, sparring. The two veteran knights sat together and watched.

"Those two have yet to be blooded," the Knight Captain eventually said.

"Aye and it shows," Finngyr replied. "But, they fight well enough for a couple of beardlings."

Knight Danuk grunted and continued to watch them in silence. "That is good to hear. They will be joining you."

Finngyr wasn't sure he'd heard correctly. "They will what, Knight Captain?"

"Be joining you. You have an assignment. Though, I'm not sure what the Knights Council was thinking. I requested you and every other knight able to hoist his hammer assigned to the plains."

"I'm not being assigned to the plains?" Finngyr said. He was not sure if that was good or bad. A part of him wanted to be back there, the other wanted to find the stonechosen he had let escape and drag its mangled body back to Daomount.

"All I know is you will not be reporting to me. You are to report to the Lord Knight Justice Gyldoon himself. That is all I was told." Danuk's tone said he would be interested in any information

Finngyr cared to add. The Knight Captain continued to stare out over the training area as he spoke, but Finngyr could see how the last statement pained him to admit. It meant whatever Finngyr's fate was to be, it was decided.

At least whatever his punishment was, he would still be performing Daomur's holy will. He was being assigned somewhere. But where would he go with two untested Knights, who had not even performed their first rites yet? He could understand the Knight Captain's unease. The assignment should have been passed down through him. This breach in protocol could not bode well for Finngyr. If Lord Knight Justice Gyldoon needed to be seen taking a personal hand in this, it could only mean the High Council had instructed him to see to Finngyr's fate himself. The Lord Knight Justice would not be pleased, to be ordered to discipline one of his own by the High Council.

"You might want to clean up first. The Lord Knight Justice awaits you at the central shrine." The Knight Captain's words shook Finngyr from his musings.

Finngyr was up and moving, remembering at the last second to turn and bow. "His word is Law, Knight Captain."

"I'll let these two know to get ready and meet you at the stables," was all the Knight Captain said in lieu of a response.

Finngyr straightened his robes for the fifth time. He wished he had been given enough time to don his armor. But, he was worried he had kept the Lord Knight Justice waiting too long by just washing and throwing on his ceremonial robes. His neck and collar were still damp from his hastily-rinsed hair. He rarely wore these robes and was used to the feel of his armor. The freedom of movement the robes granted felt wrong. "Damnable cloth." He felt naked.

He made his way up the stairs leading to the central shrine. The Temple of Justice was located near the summit of Daomount and the main chamber at the top of the temple. It was only accessible by a long flight of white Orehome marble stairs, each broad step worth a small fortune.

Finngyr had been in full armor the last time he was here during the Blessings. He recalled the plates of his armor reflecting the early morning light, shining through the temple's high arches.

The shrine was built to hold thousands of worshipers. Finngyr had only ever been to the main chamber during the Blessings. Nothing filled him with more pride and honor for his sect than the Blessings. The ceremony that heralded the Knights setting forth to deliver Daomur's judgement on the humans throughout the empire.

Where before Finngyr had been surrounded by fellow knights, lost in their numbers, his footsteps now echoed off the pillars, lining the stairs like sentinels, judging each of his unworthy steps.

At the summit of the stairs, the warm, salt-touched winds gusted through the chamber, sending the numerous banners, bearing Daomur's hammer and scales, snapping. He took in the majestic view of the shrine and the Innersea, beyond the shrine's thick columns.

In the distance, the Lord Knight Gyldoon knelt before the final set of steps that led to the main altar. Two knights, fully armed and armored, knelt a short distance behind him. They both rose at Finngyr's approach. By their demeanor and the way they held their weapons, Finngyr knew they were veterans and more than ready to sacrifice themselves to protect the Lord Knight Justice.

Finngyr stopped a safe distance away and took a knee before bowing low and placing a fist on the smooth floor. He stared at his stone-faced reflection in the marble floor. The time had come to know his fate. "Daomur is the truth and his word justice!"

The two bodyguards inclined their heads and responded in unison, "Let our hammers deliver his truth!" Their words were all but lost in the vast chamber.

"And so they shall, so they shall," Lord Knight Gyldoon said as he rose. His voice had the gravelly sound of the old, but with an undeniable strength still beneath it.

When one of his knight protectors stepped forward to help him to his feet, he swatted the proffered arm away. "Go! Guard the stair. Knight Justice Finngyr and I will speak alone," the Lord Knight said.

Both protectors dropped to a knee and bowed deeply. They rose, backed away and turned to walk past Finngyr. He could feel their eyes on the top of his helmetless head, almost make out their dour expressions in their reflections on the floor. They must be as confused by this summons as he.

"Rise, Knight Justice Finngyr. I would have a look at you."

He rose to his full height and stood there, silent, but proud. He would not play the part of the chastised child.

"You were to deliver his judgement. Find the Fallen One's chosen and destroy them else their powers grow." The Lord Knight's blunt statement, a quote from the Blessing Ceremony, would have had less impact had it been a gauntleted fist to the jaw. There was no accusation there, no blame. Just a matter-of-fact pronouncement that left Finngyr broken in its wake.

He had failed.

Finngyr swallowed and took a deep breath, staring forward. He did not want the doubt that was inside to be read on his face.

The Lord Knight stared at Finngyr for what felt like hours. Finngyr squared his shoulders and resolved to stand strong under that gaze. He was a knight justice. He would suffer the fate of his failure.

"Walk with me," Gyldoon said.

Finngyr blinked.

Gyldoon clasped his thin hands behind his back and began a circuitous route through the shrine. Finngyr moved to take a place his right and slightly behind, giving him the position of honor, and followed in silence. Finngyr had never been this close to the old dwarf. He studied him as they walked. The Lord Knight Justice must have been large in his youth. Time had pulled on his frame, but Gyldoon's shoulders were still square and his back straight.

"Did you wonder why you were assigned to the Cradle of the Gods?" He didn't look back as he spoke. He simply stopped near one of the many marble columns and looked down over the city and surrounding sea.

"Yes, Lord Knight Justice." Finngyr said.

"A simple 'sir', is sufficient, Finngyr. We will be here all morning if you insist on complete titles."

"Yes, Lord Kn— sir."

"Good. At least you can follow some orders. Well? Why do you think you were sent there, of all places? "

Finngyr swallowed. "I thought I had done something wrong, sir." That was the truth of it. Finngyr could see no other reason to pull him from the Nordlah Plains and send him to that backwater settlement.

"Did you know; legend has it that settlement was named the Cradle of the Gods because it was the birthplace of the Primordials?" Gyldoon said.

"No, sir."

"The ruins that lay scattered at the base of the large mountain called the Horn were once one of the largest cathedrals dedicated to Haurtu the Hungerer. A place of study and learning. A place of the mind."

Finngyr remembered flying over the ruins when he accompanied the guards on their way up the valley to the Stonechosen's village. It had seemed an unremarkable pile of stone. Nothing compared to some of the ruined human cities Finngyr had seen.

"I believe those are the places where the soulstones of Haurtu appear in Allwyn. Those places where once his power was focused. It is why I personally selected strong loyal knights to perform the Right of Attrition in the settlements at or near those locations."

Did Finngyr hear correctly? So he was not punished but hand-picked, personally selected? Loyal? Wait, weren't all knights loyal? Finngyr fought down the urge to rebuke that statement. He grabbed the nearest thought and focused on it instead.

"Why now, sir? Why this year's rite?"

Gyldoon did not answer right way. Finngyr could tell the Lord Knight was weighing his next words carefully.

"If one studies the Book of Hjurl and is devout, the clues are there," Gyldoon finally said.

Studied? Devout? Finngyr drew a deep, calming breath. He had pored over the Prophecies until his eyes burned. There were none more devout than he. Was he being baited? It was obvious the Lord Knight was holding something back and it maddened Finngyr that he could not question the Lord Knight's answer.

The only portion that even mentioned the soulstones was the Prophecies of Hjurl, wasn't it? He had seen nothing to say when the Time of the Stonechosen would come, let alone where the soul-stones would appear.

Finngyr swallowed before replying. "Lord Knight Justice, forgive my impertinence, but why not tell the Judges Council this? If you suspected the Time of the Stonechosen had come, and you thought you knew where the soulstones would appear, why not report this to the Council and send the might of the empire to those places?"

Gyldoon again did not answer right away.

Finngyr recognized the Lord Knight's fight for self-control. He fought the same battle so often in himself. Gyldoon raised an eyebrow and looked ready to chastise him, but then swallowed it down instead. "Because the Judges Council would ask the very question you have asked and believe my answer as much as you do now."

The old knight rubbed his hands together and continued walking. They did not speak again for several minutes. Finngyr turned over the implications as he followed. The Lord Knight's next words were spoken with a note of tiredness in his voice.

"A knight justice should not get as old as I am, Finngyr. The battles I have seen, have been through. Any one of them should have brought my end upon me. The wounds that should have claimed me, only to heal so that I could fight on. I used to think Daomur had some special purpose for me." Gyldoon held his hands before him, studied them in the dawn light.

Finngyr saw the thickness and odd curves in the Lord Knight's joints.

"The pain brought on by age seeps into me, Finngyr. It far outweighs the pains of old battle wounds. Did you witness the light when you struck the stonechosen?" Gyldoon said.

The question caught Finngyr off guard. "Sir? The light? Yes, yes, sir, I did. I was blinded by it."

"What did it feel like when you struck the creature?" Gyldoon said.

Finngyr had barely finished saying "stone", before Gyldoon was nodding, a distant look on his face.

"So the time is upon us."

Gyldoon reached out and placed his gnarled hands on Finngyr's shoulders. His yellow-tinged eyes grabbed and held Finngyr's own with sheer intensity.

"You have failed me and the order, Finngyr. But, if given the chance, to redeem yourself, would you seize it?"

Finngyr didn't understand. Was he to be given another chance? Knight Captain Danuk said he was not being assigned to the plains. That the Lord Knight Justice had a special assignment for him. When Finngyr responded, each word hung heavy with conviction. "With all my being, Lord Knight Justice."

Gyldoon continued to stare into the younger knight's eyes, weighing him. "Every year, during the Rites of Attrition, the merchants complain about trade and business. How important the settlements are to the empire. Then the Judges council consults with the three Temples of Daomur. The Artificers' coffers, like most of the governors who sit on the Judges Council, are lined by the merchants and guildhalls. The Ritualists spew their rhetoric of carefully weighed choices and restraint. They pay lip service to the importance of the Temple of Justice, but speak of it in dribble about the importance of traditions.

"Your actions in the Cradle of the Gods have drawn much attention, Finngyr. You are exactly what the merchant's feared. As a result, the Judges Council was more upset about that burned village and the riots than any rumors of stonechosen." Gyldoon smirked. "Did they seek my counsel? No, they asked in what way you would be disciplined to set an example for the others of our sect."

By what right did those coin mongers and wordsmiths have to question the Knights Council?

It was by divine right that all knights of the Temple of Justice were assigned their duties by the Knights Council, of which Lord Knight Gyldoon presided over.

But, as the smallest sect in the Church of Daomur, the Knights held little sway over the Judges Council, unlike the other two major sects, the Ritualists and the Artificers.

"As long as the Temple of Law and the Temple of Art are in power, the merchants have control of the Judges Council. If we are going to protect the empire from this threat and itself, I need to seize control. To do that, I must prove the Time of the Stonechosen has indeed arrived and to do that I need proof. I need to show them a stone-chosen," Gyldoon said.

"If it could be proven that the time of the stonechosen has come, then the laws are clear and the Judges Council would have to listen to the Knights Council of the Temple of Justice, above all others. It would mean supreme control over all the military of the five mountain cities and the entire empire," Gyldoon said.

Again the weight of Finngyr's failure to capture Ghile Stonechosen rose unbidden like bile. Had he succeeded, the Lord Knight Justice would have what he needed and even now, a righteous purge would be sweeping across the empire.

But, the Lord Knight Justice said he sent knights. There were others chosen and sent to these special places he somehow knew about. "Sir, what of the others? Did none succeed?"

"All that returned failed me."

"That returned?"

"Of all the Knights I sent out, only one is unaccounted for."

Then, there was still hope. Finngyr was torn. A part of him hoped this remaining knight would succeed, a part of him wished for his failure. He swiftly chastised himself. He would not let his own hubris cloud his thoughts. "Sir, how many did you send out?" Finngyr said.

"Three to the lost cities in the Nordlah plains. Of those three, all returned with talk of large tribal gatherings, but due to the number of humans, were unable to get close and had to return. The ones I sent to the ruined city on the forgotten coast returned with no sightings. Only Knight Justice Griff, who I sent to Dagbar's settlement near the Fallen City, has not returned."

The Fallen City, as it was named in the texts, was one of the cities Finngyr had marked as a potential destination for Ghile Stonechosen. "Why would that city be a potential source of a soulstone?" Finngyr said.

"I chose it because the city was destroyed by Daomur himself. It is written, he caused the ground beneath it to open and swallow the city whole. No other city drew his direct attention during the Great Purge."

Finngyr nodded. If there was another stonechosen there, then it would make sense that would be the city the boy would go to.

'Now marked, his chosen must gather, where once his progeny thrived' The old human cities.

"As punishment for your poor decisions in the Cradle, you are not going to be assigned to the Nordlah Plains. But, as Captain Danuk has called all able Knights to join him in the plains to confront those gathered tribes and deliver the Rites of Attrition on the barbarians, I still need someone to see what happened to Knight Justice Griff. You and two newly-appointed knights are to travel to Dagbar's Freehold to discover what happened to your fellow knight."

"There were no messages sent by the runesmiths, sir?" Finngyr said. Something as important as a Knight Justice not returning would warrant using the runesmiths to communicate with the settlement.

"Of course. A message was sent and a reply received. It said the Knight Justice arrived, performed the Rite and left. Nothing more."

"I assume no troops have been dispatched to the settlement?" Finngyr said.

"Even if you were not in trouble with the council and I could convince them troops should accompany you, they would not be sent. Dagbar has powerful friends within the trade houses and on the Judges Council itself. He does not like government troops in his settlement. He is an Allwynian and uses his own guards to protect the Freehold," Gyldoon said.

"An Allwynian? How can an Allwynian hold a position of Magister?" Finngyr said. Allwynians were dwarves who worshiped Allwyn the All Mother. There was no law that said a dwarf must worship Daomur, but as the creator of the dwarven race and creator of their laws and basic tenets of life, almost all did. So much so, those very few who didn't were thought to be mad at a minimum. But they were never given positions of leadership or power.

"As I said, he has powerful friends and his reach is long. Dagbar is not only a Magister, but an Ambassador to the Elves of the Deepwood. All exotic wares, medicines, logging, mining, sweet leaf and most importantly, silverwood, pass through the Freehold." Gyldoon said. "Oh, how the wealthy would tremble if their supplies of silverwood ran low. How else would they determine their status?" Gyldoon motioned dramatically, then looked ready to spit in disgust.

He didn't, of course. Not even he would do such a thing in this sacred place.

"At first, you must not upset Magister Dagbar. Do not presume to assume control of his guards, either. You are there on a diplomatic mission for the temple. Find out what happened to Knight Justice Griff and that is all," Gyldoon said.

"Then why the two additional knights, sir?"

The Lord Knight Justice didn't appear bothered by his impertinence. "Don't be thick. Because you cannot be trusted on your own, of course. So says the Judges Council. Though, I have little doubt why some on the council so readily agreed to this as a satisfactory form of punishment for your transgressions."

Finngyr's confusion must have shown on his face because Gyldoon sighed and continued. "They think you will upset Magister Dagbar and give them all the reason they need, to point to yet another decision I have failed in, and remove the last vestiges of power I have in the say of running of this city! We are of like minds and I am putting much trust in you. I would have liked to send others I trust with you, but all able Knight Justices are needed in the Nordlah Plains and I dare not risk drawing attention to your true purpose. So, two freshly-raised squires have been chosen to accompany you, at the behest of the council. Pay heed, they are freshly-raised and must not be allowed to hinder your true quest."

Finngyr could feel the weight behind those last words. He nodded.

The Lord Knight's tone grew icy. "If there is even a hint of a stonechosen there, you must do whatever it takes to bring it to me. Nothing is more important than that. *Nothing.* Do you understand?"

"I will see it done," Finngyr said, hurriedly taking a knee and bowing deeply.

Gyldoon lifted Finngyr's head with his fingers, until their eyes met.

"The Temple of Justice will once again take its rightful place at the head of the empire. We will lead our people back onto Daomur's righteous path and remove the threat of the Fallen's progeny once and for all," Gyldoon said.

"His word is law," Finngyr intoned.

$\wedge$

The griffon folded her wings tight against her body, pinning Kjar against the strap he was trying to tighten. "By the sun and stars, this one detests me," Kjar said. He braced his gloved hands against the griffon's side and pushed, forcing the wing back.

Finngyr sat impatiently on Safu, watching. He had shown up at the stables before first light and had Safu in the paddock, saddled and ready for flight, when Horth and Kjar arrived with the first rays of light barely touching the freshly-raked sand.

"Put your riding gloves on after you have her saddled, Kjar, son of Kath," Finngyr said. He enjoyed using the young knight's patron names. All dwarves used patron names until they had established themselves and their places in society. As newly-dubbed knights, both Horth and Kjar no longer used their patron names, but Finngyr had learned what he could in the short time he had about his new companions, including their lineage.

"She is only testing you, Kjar. Give her a good knee, that will teach her," Horth said.

Finngyr eyed the big lout. Horth had little trouble saddling his own griffon, using his immense strength to keep the creature in line. Finngyr had learned much about this one. Horth's father was a captain of the caravan guard, for one of the wealthiest merchant families in Daomount. Horth's belt and riding gloves looked new and were bordered in elegant gilded designs. Finngyr had little doubt where Horth procured the additional funds for such extravagance.

"I pray your male loses his bridle, Horth, son of Hornuk. I would wager he would have a lesson to teach *you*," Finngyr said.

It was the enchanted bridles, specifically the griffon's head harness, that kept the aggressive creatures affectionate towards their riders. Over time, if the knight treated the griffon with respect, the creature would form a natural bond to its rider. A knight never knew how long he might be in the field and there were not always artificers available to repair and enchant damaged gear. There was more than one tale of a knight being turned on by an unbridled, mistreated griffon.

Horth visibly seethed, but said nothing.

At least he could hold his tongue when he should.

Kjar removed his gloves and started in on the strap again. Safu screeched and scratched the sand with her front talons. She too, was impatient to take to the air.

Horth's male griffon ruffled its neck feathers and lifted its head in a show of dominance. Horth quickly tightened his grip on the rein and yanked back sharply. "There'll be none of that," he said. The young male's long, leonine tail lashed violently from side to side, but it obeyed its rider.

"There, that sees it done," Kjar said. He climbed into the saddle and locked his riding buckle with a sharp click. He then donned his gloves and took up the reins.

Finngyr knew he had much to answer for. But he wasn't sure the burden of these two was fair punishment.

"Safu! Fly!" With that, Finngyr took to the air over Daomount, the other two knights following.

7

Aftermath

AIDEL was tired of walking but knew she had to push on. Her legs ached with the effort of pulling them through the thigh deep water. They should have been resting by now, but she needed to put as much distance as possible between them and where they fought the swamp cats. What other troubles had the noise of battle attracted?

She looked back at Riff. He was trudging along stoically. He must have felt he was being watched because he looked up from his efforts and gave her a quick smile and a wink, even though the strain of keeping pace was plain on his face.

She turned before he could see her face redden. How the man infuriated her! He had turned that fire of his on three of the swamp cats before the others finally broke off their attack. The smell of burnt hair still clung to her.

She had entered the 'Dream Song' and healed Riff's leg. There was no way he would have been able to continue on with such a wound, though under different circumstances, she would have left him with a nice limp to teach him some humility.

Unfortunately, there was nothing she could do for Ghile.

She was a druid and not being able to heal the Stonechosen troubled her more than she cared to admit. His limp form hung over Two Elks' shoulder. If the additional weight bothered her shieldwarden, he didn't show it. He cut a steady swath through the waters before her, sending out V-shaped ripples in his wake.

Ghile's two Valehounds waded along slightly ahead of Two Elks. They'd stayed close to Ghile since he fell unconscious. She'd searched him for any obvious injuries, but there were none. It must have something to do with the soulstones. Whatever the reason, he had not woken up, no matter what she tried. She only hoped he would snap out of it soon. If there was any more trouble in the Ghost Fens, they would need him.

Far ahead in the distance, she could just make out the line of trees marking the end of the fens and the border of the Deepwood. The mist of the Ghost Fens was not as thick here, but unfortunately, there was not much land either.

They had left behind the small patches of reed-covered ground a few hours ago and been wading through the black waters ever since. The muddy bottom pulled at her boots. At least hers rose up to her thighs and were tied tightly. Riff had to remove his ankle high boots and complained bitterly whenever he stepped on something or felt something slither across his exposed feet.

She didn't want to think about what might be in the water. She just needed to get them into the Deepwood.

She looked to the skies yet again, the action almost second nature since fleeing the Cradle. The mists were not as thick here as she would have liked. If a culler passed overhead now, they would be easily spotted. Fortunately, the skies were clear of anything larger than birds.

The only good side of moving into the open water was Riff's constant complaining about the insects had tapered off. It seemed the biting insects that flourished in the fens kept near the pockets of land. Only dragonflies and water striders noted the group's passing.

Gaidel looked over her arms and noted she had not been bitten once. If not for Riff's constant belly aching, she wouldn't have even noticed the insect's presence.

Yet another blessing from the All Mother. One of the benefits of entering the Song. Patron Sister Bosand would have been quite perturbed with her novice, forgetting something so fundamental.

She had not seen the Patron Sister since she and Two Elks were bonded.

The great fire that burned that night not so long ago, had warmed the front side of her body while the winds of the Nordlah Plains cooled her back. She'd stood next to Patron Sister Bosand.

Sister Bosand wore that cynical expression she always wore when she observed something she didn't quite approve of. The graying strands that were normally visible in her otherwise dark hair were hidden by the bonfire's glow, giving her the appearance of someone much younger than her forty-something years.

As a patron sister, Bosand had taken Gaidel under her wing since the day Gaidel's foster father Orson approved of her joining the sisterhood at the summer festival almost two years before.

Gaidel learned from Sister Bosand what it meant to be a druid. She instructed her in the ways of wood lore and healing. Most importantly, she taught Gaidel how to join the All Mother's Song, the true gift of the Druids. By slipping into a trancelike state, Gaidel could join the essence of herself with everything around her. In this state, she could, look back in time, and given enough practice, to the future.

In those two years since being inducted, this was the first time Patron Sister Bosand had left the Redwood. They traveled deep into its confines, only rarely coming close to the Cradle. But, they always stayed under its protective boughs.

Even though the Patron Sister never said anything, it was obvious she was as uncomfortable as Gaidel to be among the barbarians who called the plains, with its rolling tundras and vast steppes, home. Every denizen of the Cradle was raised to fear the barbarians of the Nordlah Plains. The residents of the Redwood, which covered the Cradle's southern boundaries, more than most since the barbarians raided into the Redwood every spring thaw.

Besides herself, Patron Sister Bosand, and her shieldwarden, there was only one other at the bonfire who was not a native of the Nordlah Plains and was the very person who requested their presence at this gathering, Mother Brambles.

Mother Brambles sat alongside three other Mother Druids, all Nordlah barbarians, in the center of the gathering. The four sat in a line, legs crossed, with eyes closed and hands joined, lost in Allwyn's Song.

Even though Mother Brambles stood out as much as the rest of them, she seemed completely at ease. Even her giant bear, Babe, was nowhere to be seen. Gaidel noted that the other three Mothers were also not protected by their totem animals. This was the first time Gaidel had seen Mother Brambles without her large protector.

Here in the middle of a gathering of hundreds of barbarians, Gaidel could think of no better time for a protector. At least Rachard, Patron Sister Bosand's shieldwarden, was nearby. He glanced at Gaidel and gave her one of his reassuring winks. As old as the Patron Sister, Gaidel had come to look at him as a doting uncle. Where the Patron Sister was no nonsense, Shieldwarden Rachard was quick to find the humor in any situation.

So here she stood, surrounded by tribes from throughout the Nordlah Plains. Hundreds of men and women, every one of them a warrior. She marveled at their great height and builds. Even the women looked formidable. The gathering reminded Gaidel of their summer festival in Lakeside. But where her people spent their days trading and celebrating, the barbarians spent them drinking and fighting. Gaidel was aware of no fewer than five deaths in the two days she had been here. The warrior's wounds too great even for Druidic healing.

She turned away from the light and heat of the bonfire. She could no longer see the ruins of the city, but the outlines of its tallest buildings jutted out above the horizon, resembling jagged teeth.

This was the closest Gaidel had ever been to one of the ancient cities of her kind. They were forbidden places. Dwarven law called for death to any humans found within their confines. But here, in the plains, the barbarians held them sacred. And though they did not live in them, needing to follow the great tusker herds for survival, they gathered near them for festivals and ceremonies.

Some of the barbarians stood on what looked like the remains of giant dwarven statues. Three plainsmen had climbed on top of a nearby bearded stone head, its vacant eyes seeming to watch the ceremony with them. The ground around them was churned up. The stone dwarves looked different from the human ruins, newer. Gaidel wondered if they were placed to ward off the plainsmen. If so, it seemed to have little effect.

"Daughter Gaidel, pay attention. The ceremony begins," Sister Bosand said. She tapped Gaidel on the arm, the way she always did when explaining something she felt important. "Took them long enough. My legs are starting to cramp," she added, shifting her weight.

Rachard laid a comforting hand on her side.

Sister Bosand quickly swatted it away and whispered something harsh to her shieldwarden, words that Gaidel couldn't hear.

Rachard simply smiled and said nothing, staring ahead at the three plainsmen and one plainswoman entering the central clearing.

They were even taller and more muscular than most of the barbarians, even the woman. Each of them had the long black hair and deeply-tanned skin of their kind. The way they carried themselves made Gaidel think they must be leaders or hold other positions of importance.

Gaidel recognized a couple of them from the combats that occurred throughout the day. She was brought up in the Three Arrows tavern in Redwood Village, considered by many to be one of the toughest villages in the Cradle, but she had been horrified at the violence she witnessed today.

The manhood test of her people might result in a few bruises and the occasional broken bone, but rarely was there a death. The feats of strength and combat she had been made to endure today could easily end in the death of one of the participants. Gaidel was at a loss to understand what they were fighting for, but the culmination led to this ceremony.

Patron Sister Bosand scolded her for asking too many questions, but Shieldwarden Rachard at least tried to explain things to her.

"Now understand my grasp of their tongue is poor, Daughter Gaidel. Not much better than my understanding of their ways. But don't let 'um fool ya. They may seem barbaric, but the Nordlah tribes have rules for everything. These contests are just their way of determining who from the gathered tribes will have the honor to take on some sacred test," Rachard said, scratching his beard. "Near as I can tell, all the tribes have come together. I tried to find out more, but I nearly insulted the one I was talking to by asking. The way I understand it, the ones who win all these tests will be allowed to enter the ruined city. I don't know what for. Apparently to hunt for something or other that is sacred to them,"

So at the end of a day of bloodshed, the four victors now stood before the line of Mother Druids. The song of the four mothers grew louder now that the victors arrived. The surrounding plainsmen began a low chant, accompanied by the smack of fists into open palms. Gaidel wished she spoke their language so she could understand what they were chanting. Whatever it was, it was the same series of words over and over.

One of the mother druids opened her eyes and rose from her seated position. Even from this distance, Gaidel could see the flow of the Song in them. Tiny dots of light, like shooting stars, flashed across her eyes.

She pointed at the largest of the four who had come forward. He was easily the largest man Gaidel had ever seen. He was also completely bald, his face and scalp heavily scarred. The Mother Druid called out some chant and the crowd erupted in cheers. The massive barbarian raised his fists into the air and roared to the sky.

Rachard leaned in to Gaidel. "A face only a mother could love, eh?"

Patron Sister Bosand shushed him.

The next mother stood, this one used a walking stick to steady herself. Her skin hung from her bones like a sack. If she was not moving and singing, Gaidel would have thought her a corpse.

She pointed at the female among the four and called out a different chant. The crowd erupted into cheers again.

Gaidel noted that the portion of the crowd which cheered was different than the first. She realized it must be the members of the tribe of the one selected, who were cheering for their champion.

Gaidel wondered how many different Nordlah tribes gathered to compete in these violent games, and to what end?

The next mother stood and went through the same ritual as the two before. The tribe members of the third champion cheered. Only Mother Brambles remained. She finally rose and stepped forward.

The remaining barbarian lifted his chin in anticipation, but otherwise remained still, waiting for her words. Mother Brambles pointed at him and spoke the language of the plains with the same sharp dialect. But instead of cheers, there was a moment of silence followed by a mixture of gasps and roars of outrage.

Shieldwarden Rachard stepped protectively in front of her and Patron Sister Bosand. Luckily, no one had brought weapons to the ceremony, but Gaidel held little doubt that the gathered crowd would have no trouble beating them to death with their bare hands.

Gaidel moved instinctively closer to Shieldwarden Rachard, but then noticed the nearby tribesmen were moving away from her, not moving in to attack. She looked from one dark face to another. Some eyes held confusion, but more than one looked resentful and angry. Many looked from her to Mother Brambles. She wondered what Mother Brambles had said and why they were all looking at her now?

She looked back to the center of the gathering and found Mother Brambles focus was now on her, along with her outstretched finger. She repeated whatever she had said before.

Gaidel looked over at the one remaining barbarian, who also now stared at her. Where others looked upon her with confusion or anger, this one seemed to have set his jaw and was weighing her worth.

Something in Gaidel snapped. Who did he think he was? She set her fists on her hips and stared back at him in full measure.

"It cannot be," the Patron Sister said.

Bosand moved closer to Gaidel and put a protective hand on her shoulder. "Mother Allwyn protect you child. You are to be bonded."

The sounds of the crowd mixed with the crackling of the bonfire to form a cacophony of noise that faded to the background as Gaidel took in the word her Patron Sister had spoken.

Bonded.

It was not until a druid was ready to be separated from her patron sister that she was bonded to a shieldwarden. It was then his job to protect her with his life. The bonding process joined them forever, linking their individual songs together as one.

Never had Gaidel heard of a plainsman being bonded to a druid from the Redwood. By the looks on the faces around her, she was not the only one.

Many members of the crowd were still shouting and shaking their fists. Whatever honor that was meant to be bestowed on this barbarian, Mother Brambles had taken it from him by declaring him a shieldwarden. Had this been her reason for summoning them here all along?

Gaidel looked at the other Mothers who stood near Mother Brambles. Mother Brambles had moved up to the barbarian and repeated herself. She pointed once again at Gaidel. The other mothers looked to the crowds and then each other. It was obvious from their expressions; they were weighing their next actions carefully.

It was the Mother who looked like a corpse who finally made a decision and moved up beside Mother Brambles and repeated her words. Once she spoke some of the crowd stopped shaking their fists and quieted. Others just spat on the ground and stormed off.

When the other two Mothers moved up beside Mother Brambles and repeated her words to the lone barbarian, the remainder of the crowd quieted.

All eyes were on the lone barbarian now.

Waiting.

He straightened his shoulders and nodded his head with one sharp bob.

All eyes then seemed to settle on Gaidel.

Mother Brambles motioned her forward.

The only sounds that accompanied her steps were the sound of the flames. She could feel the heat of the bonfire build as she neared Mother Brambles and her soon to be shieldwarden, it reflected the burning in the pit of her stomach.

"Little Daughter."

Two Elk's voice brought her back to the present.

He stood in the black fetid water, staring at her, Ghile hanging limp over his shoulder. "Movement in trees. We not alone."

8

Living on the Edge

 "HAT are we waiting for?" Riff said.

His gait now included a pronounced limp and he winced with each step. He struggled to keep pace with the group as they made their way around the broad-boughed trees and moss covered rocks that bordered the Ghost Fens.

They had reached the shore without any further incident. Between them, they had spotted at least five different humanoid creatures moving through the trees during their approach. Since they reached land and turned south, the number had doubled.

Whoever or whatever they were, they were keeping their distance. Both of Ghile's Valehounds had their hackles raised and took turns barking their warnings into the forest.

Gaidel heard birdsong following them. The amount of whipper and redbeak calls she heard were too many for such a small area. Their watchers were using the calls to communicate. The only thing she was sure of was they were not vargan or dwarves. Neither would use birdsong to communicate.

"I said we are not attacking and I meant it. We do not know their numbers or their intentions," Gaidel said.

The sorcerer's aching feet were apparently adding to his temper and he seemed ready to pick a fight. *This one is too quick to battle for my tastes,* Gaidel thought.

Riff ducked under another moss-laden limb and continued his tirade. "So, we're just going to keep traipsing along until we walk into an ambush? Is that your plan, oh wise one?"

Gaidel tightened her grip on her staff and bit back the insult that jumped to her lips. At that moment, she wanted nothing more than to beat Riff senseless. Instead of giving in to her anger, she settled for glaring at him.

"Enough!" Two Elks said. He placed Ghile's limp form on the ground. Ast and Cuz began sniffing and licking Ghile.

Two Elks slung his large kite shield from his shoulder and settled it in place on his forearm.

"They come," he said.

Gaidel heard it then. Two Elks had kept the fens to their left, but in all other directions she heard the sounds of movement. She gave one final glare at Riff and moved to Two Elks' side. She took a deep steadying breath to clear her mind, the Song ready on her lips.

"Finally!" Riff said. He pulled out his everflame and grimaced as he set his bare feet in the soil.

The Valehounds growled deep in the back of their throats, hackles raised.

A human's voice, deep and resonant, called out from somewhere in front of them, the accent strange to Gaidel's ears. "Hold dem hounds. We no wanna fight. We wanna talk."

"Riff, grab them," Gaidel said.

"You grab them, Druid. I'm not dropping my guard." His gaze darted back and forth, looking for a target.

Two Elks turned a baleful glare on Riff. "Riff, take hounds." He lowered his shield and relaxed his stance. "I not ask twice."

Riff let out an exasperated sigh and limped over to grab the two Valehounds by their collars. Neither Ast or Cuz seemed ready to charge forward, though if they did, it was unlikely Riff would have been able to stop them. He whispered some reassurances to them. Ast gave a couple warning barks and then was still.

Two quick calls of a blue jay came from up ahead and the forest exploded with motion as shapes appeared all around them. Over a dozen different humans, melted out of the surroundings, their skin covered in dry mud. Foliage hung from them. Most had bows, drawn and ready.

A short stocky one stepped forward. The blue and white of his eyes stood out in sharp contrast to his mud covered skin and slicked back, short-cropped hair. He didn't have a bow in his hands, but an axe. "We no wanna hurt you or da hounds. But we will defend aw selves." He was the one who'd called out before.

Gaidel was surprised to see his axe was made of some yellowish-brown metal. A human with a metal weapon. She wondered if he was a Fang of his people.

Gaidel stepped forward and leaned her staff against a nearby limb. She held both her hands before her, palms upward and inclined her head.

"I am Daughter Gaidel of the Redwood Druids. This is Two Elks, my shieldwarden. The man holding the hounds is Riff, a sorcerer of the Cradle. Why do you hinder us?"

The surrounding humans broke out in excited whispers. Gaidel noted they were of various ages. The ones nearest them were all adult warriors, but more than a few further back were boys, others older, wrinkled with age beneath their camouflage. They were mostly unclothed. All were clad in various furs and what looked like hairless skins from some green animal.

The stocky man who had spoken, whistled again, silencing the others. He slid his axe into his fur belt and proffered his hands in a gesture like Gaidel's.

"Ma name is Craluk. We be look'n ta trade."

A short distance behind Craluk, one of the younger ones let out a series of short chirps. It reminded Gaidel of a squirrel. A few of the other humans chirped back.

Craluk whistled sharply and the others fell silent. He walked forward.

Two Elks stepped up to stand just to the side of Gaidel. Craluk barely reached Two Elk's chest. He was shorter than Riff, though almost twice as wide.

Gaidel heard the sounds of tightening bow strings around them. She placed a hand on Two Elk's arm.

"Please, Craluk. We have little, if anything to trade. We only wish to be on our way," she said.

"What wrong with 'um?" Craluk motioned to Ghile.

"Why do you want to know?" Riff said.

"It be said a druid be a right powerful healer. Why you not heal this'n hea?"

His accent was thick, but understandable. His question was a fair one. Gaidel felt the weight of eyes on her. She looked to Two Elks and even Riff. Both simply stared back, waiting to see how she answered. If she told the truth, that Ghile was stonechosen and was no longer a part of the All Mother's Song, how would Craluk and the others react? If she told them they were fleeing a culler and were in search of another soulstone to help Ghile fulfill a prophecy, would their quest end here, before it even started?

From the beginning Gaidel had fought for leadership of their group. She thought it her responsibility from the start. Now, with everything riding on her next words, for the first time, she doubted herself. Was she a leader? "I can heal a person here." Gaidel motioned to her whole body. "He is hurt inside here." She pointed to her head.

The same one that had chirped excitedly before lowered his bow and whispered, "Craluk, sure'n she help—"

Craluk made a sharp slicing gesture at the boy. "Enough, Lotte. Shut it."

"Do you have someone who is injured?" Gaidel asked. She looked from Craluk to the one he called Lotte. Lotte quickly smiled and nodded, but stopped when Craluk looked his way.

Gaidel could tell Craluk was experiencing the same inner battle regarding leadership that she was. He was weighing his next decision and all the ramifications it would have on him and his group.

He issued a short, three chirp whistle. Bows were lowered and a few of the men even smiled to one another, nodding.

"Come. Follow. It'll be dark and ain't safe in da wood afta dark," Craluk said. He turned to go.

Gaidel watched as Craluk made silent gestures to his men and began walking back the way Gaidel and the others had just come.

"Craluk, wait. I thought you wished to trade? Where are you going?" Gaidel said.

He stopped and motioned for them to follow. "Trade in da village. It be this way, hea."

Gaidel motioned back in the direction her group had been going. "But the place we seek is that way."

Craluk looked out into the trees, as if he could follow her gesture and see where they were headed. "If ya be head'n to da Freehold, it be too fa ta reach a'fore night. Ain't safe afta dark, for certain. You be a druid and a sorcerer, but not even you be safe afta dark, for certain. Betta come with us. You rest, eat some. Then, we trade."

Gaidel didn't like being told what to do by anyone. Especially not by someone who just assumed she should listen. "And if we refuse?"

Craluk shrugged. "Then we go to da village and be safe. In da tomorrow we track yuns. Then, we take whatever the dead ones leave of ya."

Riff cleared his throat. "I think following them sounds like an excellent idea."

⋀

Riff was in a foul mood. The swamp cats had tried to eat him. The insects were in the process of finishing the job. His feet were killing him. The over-sensitive Gaidel refused to heal him. The parts of him that were not sore, were wet. He was in a foul mood indeed.

He needed a warm bed and a warmer meal. A little village girl to keep him company wouldn't be turned away either.

The only reason he was out here was to protect Ghile, who had passed out the first time they encountered trouble and not woken since.

Riff followed a short distance behind Two Elks, along the sorriest excuse for a trail he ever had the pleasure to limp along. These mudmen really needed to get out more. Half of them walked ahead of them and the other half behind. Convenient.

The talkative one, Lotte was his name, was right behind him. Every time Riff had turned around, the kid gave him another annoying smile. What was he smiling about, when he was covered in mud and twigs? Riff shook his head and gave his underarm a sniff. He needed a bath, too. What was the likelihood there was a nice inn at the end of this trail? Riff glance around at Lotte's mud-covered face and was rewarded with another annoying smile. *Not likely,* he thought.

"By the gods, what do you keep smiling about?" Riff called over his shoulder.

"Do ya joke on me? We ain't had no visitors fer a long while. Now, when we need da most help, da muther answers our prayers right certain. Sends us one druid and one sorcerer. How can I not be a smile'n?" Lotte said.

There he went again, about needing help. Riff had tried getting more details about this help they needed along with more information about what the leader of the mudmen had said about dead ones from Craluk, to no avail. *'It'll be dark and ain't safe in da wood afta dark.'* That hadn't been ominous at all. Riff leaned out around Two Elks and caught of glimpse of their leader, Craluk, all the way in the front. Unlikely he could hear all the way back here. Time for some answers. "Yes, you are lucky indeed. So, tell me, how do these dead ones make the Deepwood unsafe after dark?" Riff said.

"Because da dead ones take ya and turn ya into dead ones, fur certain," Lotte said.

Riff stopped walking and turned around to stare at the boy, who offered yet another stupid grin. "Come again?"

"Da dead ones. They come git ya at night and take da liv'n. It is why we finally approached ya. If ya gone any further, we no make it back to da village afore dark."

Riff wasn't sure which concerned him more. What the mud boy was saying or how he was saying it. Like he was talking about the weather, or what he had for breakfast. Riff looked around and noted the sun sat low on the horizon, painting the sky orange and red. If the last few days were any example of things to come, Riff didn't like his odds if the dead decided to take someone. He was sure he would be first on the menu. He slapped at something climbing along his neck.

"Walk faster," Riff said. He focused on walking without such a pronounced limp. "How much further to your village?"

"Not much. So, ya Cradle-born then?"

"Yes."

"What it be like up thar?"

"Fascinating place. Listen, why did you wait until the last minute to approach us? We backtracked all the way back to where we left the fen. We could have been to your village by now," Riff said.

"Craluk be right fussed over if'n it be worth jumping you. It was when da big one named ya sorcerer and you named the other druid that Craluk fixed on talk'n with ya," Lotte said.

Again as if he was talking about the weather, Riff thought. What was wrong with this kid? "Wait, if the dead walk the Deepwood, what about the elves? I thought the Deepwood was their domain?"

Lotte was walking faster and trying to keep up with Riff. He took a deep breath before answering. "Elves don't come this far out on da edge. It be safe from the treefolk out hea. Too far for them ta come and too far for da dwarves to come. We be safe hea. Well, that be afore da dead ones."

"What do these, dead ones, look like?" Riff said.

It was obvious to Riff that the young Lotte liked to talk ... a lot. He was hitting his stride now and fell into a matter-of-fact pattern as he filled Riff in on all the details of the dead ones.

They looked like whatever they were before they became dead ones. They had seen dead ones who were human, goblin, even vargan. They were all ghostly pale with deep red veins running all through their flesh, except the vargan, of course. But Lotte assumed they were covered in veins beneath their fur. Their eyes were big and pale white. They could see really well at night and traveled in packs, but most of all, they were vicious. The only thing that seemed to scare them was fire.

It was then Riff noticed how dark it was and decided to bring out some light to see by. He took out his everflame, which fascinated Lotte.

They arrived at what the mudmen considered a village shortly after nightfall. Thick black trees rose out of the fetid waters of the fens. The people of Craluk's village had built wooden platforms around the base of them, a good distance above the water. Where no trees offered support, the industrious villagers had chopped down smaller ones from within the forest and driven them down deep into the wet soil beneath the dark water. Bowed bridges of wood and rope swayed between platforms, creating a swinging maze of pathways.

Small reed huts, their pointed thatched roofs overrun with moss, squatted atop the platforms like toads, barely leaving space to walk. Most huts were hidden under the curtains of moss drooping down from every exposed limb.

Signs of daily life in the swamp were everywhere; scraped hides stretched on drying frames, freshly mended fishing nets hung over railings, clutches of defeathered birds and gutted frogs hung from the hut's eaves. Numerous rope ladders stretched down to the water's surface, where wooden canoes rested, their paths still discernable by the trails of cleared water through the duckweed.

Hard-shell gourds hung everywhere, hundreds of them. All hollowed out and cut to release the light from whatever was burning within them. The ones nearest to them and the edge of the village were cut with wide circles, to produce as much light as possible.

Riff doubted if the moss and trees could conceal this place from view with this much light. Cullers and man catchers were known to patrol between the settlements looking for runaways. The place was awash in the light, obviously to protect them from the dead ones.

If the dead ones did not get them, the cullers eventually would. Hopefully, he would be safe here for just one night. If Craluk had not stopped them, they might have run into the dead ones unaware and with Ghile unconscious and pretty much useless for anything other than a meal.

Riff thought on that for a moment. He concentrated on the everflame in his hand and spoke the words he had been taught by Master Almoriz. He could feel the power flow into him, ready to be channeled out through the flames. He could feel the pure open connection he had to the magic whenever Ghile was near. Even unconscious, Ghile seemed to augment his channeling. Not completely useless, then. He would have to keep the sheepherder close, conscious or otherwise.

The village's residents, equally covered in mud, came out of the huts and along the bridges to greet them. Wives, their hair filled with numerous, brightly-colored feathers, hugged husbands as children squirmed between them, vying for attention. Others openly stared and pointed at the newcomers. The excitement in the air was palpable. Lotte wasn't the only one thrilled by the strangers; dogs of all sizes hurried forward to sniff at Ast and Cuz, who seemed equally intent on saying hello. Riff knew they were about to become the center of attention and he still had an important question for Lotte.

"You said you needed our help. What did you mean?"

Lotte continued to wave excitedly to the others and point at Riff and his companions. "Oh, be Craluk's yungin, Ollin. He was taken by da dead ones. But, we took 'um back," Lotte said, with more than a bit of pride in his voice.

"So help me understand where we come in?" Riff said, over the gathering din.

"He be a dead one now. Da Druid will fix him back fur certain."

∧

Riff slapped at another insect that was circling his face, looking for a place to land.

One of the village women brought a gourd of thinned mud to the hut Craluk had them escorted to. She explained it would ward off the many insects that seemed to be a constant nuisance here.

Two Elks put it on immediately. Gaidel didn't recall him complaining about the small biting pests, but she saw several red welts on his thick arms as he was applying the mud.

Riff had flat out refused and no amount of talking could sway him. She had finally given up. If he was going to let pride get in the way of common sense, so be it. He could suffer the bites along with his sore feet.

She was going to apply the mud to Ghile, but he seemed to be as unaffected by the insects as she was. Another effect of being stone-chosen, she guessed.

The villagers also brought fresh water and food, mostly heavily salted fish and some sort of small crustaceans, flavored with a lightly bitter sauce made from nuts.

Gaidel asked where they obtained the salt and one of the village women showed her roots from a tree, which also produced the bitter nuts.

Gaidel hadn't realized how hungry she was until the smell of the food reached her. She ate heartily as the women shared their method of boiling down the roots to extract the salt.

Riff waited until the women left to tell the others about the conversation he'd had with Lotte. "So you see, you're going to have to heal a dead boy or I'm pretty sure we're going to be next."

"Are you sure you heard him correctly?" Gaidel asked. Other than stories to scare small children, she had never heard of the dead returning to Allwyn.

"I would see this… dead one," Two Elks said.

It annoyed Gaidel that Two Elks was so quick to take Riff at his word.

"Aren't you two listening? You can't heal someone who is already dead. When you can't help this boy, we're going to be of no more use to them," Riff said. "Lotte said they were thinking of robbing us originally. These people don't live in the settlements, they're outlaws. You saw their metal weapons."

All humans were required to live in settlements by dwarven law. Any humans found outside of the settlements were outlaws and were treated as such. It was not unheard of to find small bands of humans who survived on their own. The Nordlah barbarians were perfect examples of this. They seemed to thrive on the plains. But, they were also constantly being attacked by the dwarves and forever on the move. Craluk's people seemed to have found somewhere safe to exist and Gaidel knew they would do what they must to keep themselves safe, even make or steal metal weapons.

Two Elks worked the last bits of tender white meat off a slender fish bone before tossing it back into the bowl. "Enough. We are guests here. We have taken their…" He looked to Gaidel.

"Hospitality," she said.

"Yes, hospitality. If they ask for this, we must help," Two Elks finished.

Riff stared at the two of them and finally shook his head and sat down. "Great, one calls me a liar and the other is more interested in being a good guest."

Riff looked at Ast and Cuz, who had nuzzled up on either side of Ghile and were currently watching the proceedings, tails thumping against the mat-covered floor. "What do you two think we should do?"

Ast cocked his head to one side and raised his ears. Cuz barked.

"Calm yourself, Riff. Once we have eaten and rested we will ask about this boy. Until then we will be on our guard. If what this Lotte said is true, then there is something in the Deepwood which could keep us from reaching Dagbar's Freehold. For tonight, with Ghile still unconscious, this place is safe enough. If these people meant us harm, they have had a number of chances to act," Gaidel said.

"Calm myself? What about the lights? You know that culler is searching for Ghile. How can he miss these lights? This place is a beacon."

Two Elks leaned back and belched. "I grow tired of talk that means nothing. It is not our time to die. We have full bellies, shelter and a fire. This I know. Riff talks only of what he doesn't know. No more talk about nothing or I will throw you outside." With that, Two Elks pulled his axe next to him and rolled onto his side.

Gaidel watched as Riff opened and closed his mouth a few times. When he looked at her, she quirked an eyebrow and gave him a questioning smirk. She could see how badly he wanted to say something. She would enjoy watching her shieldwarden toss Riff out like her father used to do to the rowdier patrons at the Three Arrows.

It seemed a lifetime ago when she left her home in Redwood Village. Growing up in a tavern made her accustomed to people and noise. Always someone to talk to, always something going on. Her new life as a Redwood Druid was such a sharp contrast, her previous life seemed like it belonged to another person. She watched Riff finally give up and drag his furs off to the side, away from them, and lay down.

Why Mother Brambles decided Riff needed to join them, she still didn't know. For all the good it did Ghile. They hadn't even left the boundaries of the swamp before he came to harm. If anything, the sorcerer was slowing them down. He was no traveler, that was for certain. If he didn't toughen up, he would never make it to Dagbar's Freehold. A small voice in the back of her head reminded her she could heal his wounds. Fine, in the morning she would see to him. She sighed and went to check on Ghile one more time before bed.

Both Ast and Cuz watched her expectantly as she checked Ghile's temperature and breathing. He had not eaten or drank anything since the battle, but he seemed fine – too healthy, in fact. The combat training Two Elks had been giving him seemed to have caused a growth spurt in the young uplander. His clothing was stretched taut over his frame. *What other changes were those soulstones working on him,* she wondered.

At least they were out of the Cradle and through the fens. Patron Sister Bosand always said when you were faced with a large problem, break it down into small, manageable pieces. Tomorrow, she would see about this dead one and trading for supplies for the journey to Dagbar's Freehold. She unfurled her sleeping furs near Two Elks and laid down. She continued to mull over the things they still needed to do until sleep took her.

Gaidel sat motionless as Two Elks scraped the sharp blade of his flint knife along her scalp. The skin not covered in the blue swirling patterns that marked her as a druid was bright pink. He shook the blade in the small bowl of water and continued to shave the front part of her scalp. It was a routine they went through most mornings, Two Elks shaving Gaidel's head and then his face. His people refused to grow facial hair as an insult to dwarves, who prized their beards.

The inside of the little hut had warmed considerably from the sun's morning rays, which struggled to find small gaps to push through and share little beams with the hut's inhabitants. It was still early and Riff, Ghile, and the two Valehounds still slept.

There was motion outside the tent followed by someone clearing their voice. "Morn'n in da hut. It's Craluk. Reckon I could come in?"

Two Elks wiped his knife on his trousers and moved over to shake Riff awake. Riff was still wiping the sleep from his eyes when Gaidel bade Craluk enter.

Craluk passed through the doorway followed by Lotte and two other men Gaidel recognized from the day before. They all proffered the upturned hands and bowed deeply.

Craluk gave Lotte a harsh stare before speaking. "Been told what Lotte shared with Master Riff. I apologize for what he done said. Our problems be our own and we ought not burden you with um."

Lotte stared down at his feet and said nothing.

Even if these people chose to live as outlaws, they still followed the strict laws of hospitality Gaidel had learned in her short time with the Nordlah barbarians. Craluk's people were all short of stature and square shouldered. They did not look at all like Two Elk's people, except for the same colored hair. Gaidel found herself wondering how long they had lived out here and where they originally came from. As hosts, they could not ask for their guests help and Gaidel knew Craluk felt Lotte had shamed them.

"Craluk, you and your people are honorable hosts. We are indebted to you for sharing your food and providing us shelter," Gaidel said. She glanced at Two Elks, who gave her an almost imperceptible nod. "I would gladly do what I can if you would allow me to see your son." Behind her, Gaidel heard Riff groan.

She found Two Elks already beat her to glare at Riff, who quickly put up his hands in a gesture of surrender.

"Fine, fine," Riff said.

Craluk nodded and motioned for them to follow, the relief obvious on his face. He must have been afraid that Lotte hurt his chances to get help.

Gaidel, Two Elks, and Riff followed the others out of the hut and over the swaying walkways. The two Valehounds remained at Ghile's side. The young stonechosen couldn't have asked for a better pair of guardians.

There were a few villagers already up and going about their morning activities. Canoes were already out in the water, the villagers in them stopping at various poles protruding from the water and pulling long vines attached to woven cages. Others were packing nets and three pronged spears into the remaining canoes.

Craluk stopped before a curtain of green hanging moss. Gaidel could just make out a single hut a short distance beyond. It sat alone under the protective boughs, separate from the others.

"It be dark up in there, as the light hurts Ollin's eyes. Move slow like and don't git near'n his head or he'll take a chunk out of ya," Craluk said. He pulled the mossy curtain aside and gestured for them to enter.

Gaidel stepped under the canopy, followed by Two Elks and Riff. As soon as they came near the hut, they could hear something thrashing around inside. A deep throated growl, like that of a caged animal, drifted out from the darkness. Gaidel found the hair on the back of her neck standing up and her fists clenched.

She took a breath and knelt down to look into the opening. Something small and pale lurched forward out of the shadows. Its pupilless eyes were as pale as sheep's milk, as was its skin. Thick red veins bulged against the pallid flesh which seemed barely able to contain them. The creature that at one time had been Craluk's son,

Ollin, now gnashed its teeth like some savage beast, straining to reach Gaidel.

It was bound around the ankles and wrists with thick leather straps, which were tied to each other in turn and also to a single wooden pole back in the center of the hut. Gaidel had started forward when she felt Two Elk's hand on her shoulder.

"Careful, Daughter Gaidel. It is not at the end of its bonds. It stops at the edge of the light."

He was right. It stopped at the edge of the little light that filtered through the canopy above them. Even this small amount of light kept it at bay.

"Two Elks, you will have to hold him, so I may enter the song," Gaidel said.

Two Elks grunted and placed his shield and axe down before he stepped forward. He moved carefully, bending down and holding his hands out in front of him.

The creature stopped its struggling and hissed, tracking Two Elks movements.

"Ollin, we are not here to hurt you," Gaidel said.

Ollin's head snapped towards Gaidel and he hissed again. Two Elks slowly extended one hand towards Ollin as he moved closer.

Ollin sprang forward at Two Elk's outstretched hand. His teeth snapped down where Two Elk's hand had been a mere second before.

Two Elks lunged forward then and wrapped his arms around Ollin, pinning Ollin's much smaller arms to his sides. Ollin thrashed his head, trying to lock his teeth into something, but could not and finally settled for banging the back of his head against Two Elk's chest.

If it bothered the barbarian, he didn't show it. Two Elks nodded to Gaidel. "Little one is strong."

Gaidel stepped forward and took a closer look at Ollin. The boy was young, probably only seven or eight years old. He had stopped his struggles to stare at Gaidel and issue another low menacing hiss. Gaidel grimaced. Ollin's tongue was as black as pitch.

Gaidel began to sing. She let the sound of her voice resonate deep within her. Closing her eyes, she breathed in deeply, clearing her mind of thought. She opened her senses. She willed herself to become one with the song and felt the essence of herself spread out and meld with everything around her.

At once, the song of the All Mother poured in, filling her like an empty vessel. A song only a druid could hear, feel, and taste. She sensed more than saw the others around her as she swayed with the rhythm. She could feel the song flowing through her, trying to pull her along. Somewhere in the distance, she could hear herself singing.

The waters of the fen beneath her danced around her slower song, ignoring it. Water, air, fire, these things were beyond her reach, their song being too quick and confusing, hard to become one with.

Gaidel listened and heard the song of the others around her, Two Elk's was the easiest to sense because it was already in perfect tune with hers. It was this bond that joined them. She sensed Riff's song. He was scared, his song undulated with his fear.

She focused and tried to hear Ollin's song. Where was it? It should have been as easy to hear as Riff's. Gaidel changed her pitch, searching. As her song reached higher, she became aware of Ollin's song. But it was wrong, so utterly wrong.

Whatever had happened to Ollin had changed his song. It was as if there were holes in it now, like part of him was missing from Allwyn. There was still enough of Ollin there to recognize as Ollin, but it was intertwined with an emptiness, something not of Allwyn.

Gaidel had felt that emptiness before. When she had tried to heal Ghile. But unlike Ghile, this nothingness had a song, a faster song, like that of water. The tune of whatever had Ollin in its grasp was some corrupted form of water. It dominated Ollin's song and Gaidel knew she could not possibly coerce it to release its grip on the boy.

Gaidel stopped singing and opened her eyes.

Ollin was thrashing again, but Two Elks held him firm. She shook her head at Two Elks. "There is something in him, some kind of corrupt water, a poison of some kind. It will not heed my song."

Riff moved up closer. "Can you not just heal him? If he drank something that did this to him, can't you just heal him of it?"

"No, it isn't something that is in him," Gaidel said. She wasn't sure how to explain it.

"Whatever it is, it is him now, it is part of his song, part of him. But, it is some kind of corrupt water, I recognize that much of its song."

Riff looked behind him at Craluk and the others. It was obvious to Gaidel that he still didn't trust their hosts. When he turned back to her, she could see he had set himself to some decision.

"Right, if it is water, then it will have to listen to me," Riff said.

"What are you talking about," she asked.

He knelt down and hopped off the walkway and into the black waters below, sending the duckweed spreading out in a growing circle. "Just trust me," Riff said.

He motioned for Two Elks. "Bring him to me, in the water."

Two Elks didn't move. "He is bound to pole," he said.

"Craluk, cut him free of the pole," Riff said. He didn't wait to see if his orders were being followed, but began running his hands through the water and taking deep breaths.

Gaidel moved to the side as Craluk drew a jagged knife and stepped past her. She could see the concern in the chieftain's face.

She knew Riff was afraid of what would happen if they couldn't help the boy, but she would not endanger the child further.

"Riff, what are you planning to do? I don't understand," Gaidel said.

Riff motioned for Two Elks to join him once he saw Crulak had cut the leather straps that secured Ollin to the pole.

Two Elks looked to Gaidel and waited. She didn't know what Riff had in mind. Sorcerers could not affect the living.

"Gaidel, listen to me. I'm pretty sure what I'm about to try is going to hurt Ollin. A lot. I need your help. I want you to start healing him once I begin," Riff said.

Gaidel didn't know what to do. She looked at Riff and then at Two Elks. A part of her resented Riff telling her what to do. He had been against this entire idea before. What if he hurt the boy?

"Gaidel! We can do this." He glanced at Craluk and the others. "We have to."

She cursed, but nodded and jumped down into the water next to him.

As soon as Two Elks moved out from the protection of the hut, Ollin began to scream and doubled his efforts to break free. His skin immediately began to discolor and become blotchy. It was as if the sun was bruising him.

Two Elks jumped down next to Gaidel and Riff. As he sunk into the soft soil, he almost lost his balance and his grip on Ollin.

Riff had already began chanting under his breath, both hands beneath the surface of the water.

Other villagers gathered behind Craluk and along the various walkways, their curiosity overriding their fear.

As soon as Riff touched Ollin's flesh, it began to hiss and bubble. His skin split, spraying black blood. An equally black smoke poured forth from the wound, snaking down towards the water.

Gaidel entered the song. Having found Ollin once, it was easier this time. She sang higher until she found him. Riff was right. Whatever he was doing, it was killing the boy. In the song, it sounded like Riff was ripping Ollin's song apart.

Then she realized the parts of the song that remained were dropping in pitch, sounding more human. Gaidel concentrated on those parts of the song. She began to sing with it, filling in what was missing, healing it, and with it, Ollin.

She concentrated on the high pitched tearing. With each section that Riff freed, she waited for it to fall in pitch and right before it drifted away, she would wrap it in her song, fill the holes left by the magic Riff worked. Little by little, she was coercing Ollin's song whole again.

Gaidel lost track of time, focusing on the song, the next missing piece. She had to keep singing.

She didn't think about how much healing she was doing or how much still needed to be done. She focused all her attention on the next piece and then the next.

When Gaidel finally opened her eyes, Two Elks was holding her.

She was disoriented, like she always was when she left the Dream Song. Two Elks was the only thing that kept her from slipping into the murky water. She was cold from the waist down, her body numb.

But if Two Elks was holding her?

She saw Ollin in Craluk's arms. Craluk must have jumped in while she was healing the boy. Ollin's skin was a healthy shade of pink and he was asleep, breathing deeply. Beside him Riff was nodding to her.

"We did it," he said. "Together."

The one named Lotte had also jumped into the water next to Riff. Riff had a hand on Lotte's chest, holding his attempts at hugging the sorcerer at bay.

Lotte was grinning from ear to ear.

Part II

9

Akira Dreamwalker

HILE reclined on one of the lower branches of the Great Oak, the thick bark rough beneath his hands. He was still well above most other trees on the island, but the Great Oak was an adult among children. Above him, its massive trunk and numerous limbs disappeared in shadow. He had been higher since his return to the dreaming, his powers were growing. There was a time when even its roots seemed out of his reach. The new soulstone had not only introduced new abilities, it strengthened the old ones.

A full moon hung low in the sky tonight. From his vantage point, Ghile could see out over all of the forest and the surrounding lake beyond. The moon's gentle light reflected in the still dark water, coloring the surrounding mountains in varying shades of grey. It was a calm night with nary a breeze. The air hung heavy with the smells of damp soil and that comforting smell Ghile found in all growing things. The perfect time to relax and think.

Upon first returning to the dreaming, he had been too tired to do anything but collapse at the end of a day's training. As his skill increased, Ghile spent his early evenings thinking of home and the family he'd left behind. He missed the warmth of his bed, his mother's cooking, Tia's laughter and even his father's stern gaze. He wondered where his clan was, now that Last Hamlet was gone, razed to the ground by the dwarves.

But as his time in the dreaming went on, more and more often these quiet times were spent contemplating more what lay before him than what he had left behind.

Ghile knew he would have to return to Allwyn soon. If he was honest with himself, he had been putting it off. At first he convinced himself it was because he needed to train here with Adon and Muk. He definitely had honed his skills. His ability to leap from the tall roots of the great oak up to its lower branches, where he was now, was proof of that.

Under Muk's tutelage, Ghile gained better control over his ability to mind-link with animals. Besides the numerous birds, there were also hare and deer on the island. He even used his new gifts to summon fish to eat.

At first this bothered him. It felt unfair somehow. Adon asked him if he would prefer spearing them or piercing their mouth with hooks. How was using his now-natural gifts any different? If anything, it was kinder.

The idea of shredding a creature's mind still made him queasy, but he had discovered a way to cause the animal to lapse into unconsciousness beforehand. He discovered it first with the fish and had since used it to call and collect all his meals.

No, the training was why he was here, after all, but not why he had delayed his inevitable return to Allwyn. More and more recently, his thoughts always seemed to return to her. He had secretly hoped she would return. The girl made of mist, the other stonechosen.

He wished he had asked her name before she vanished. She was like him. Chosen to fulfill a prophecy, she probably knew as little about as he did. He couldn't help wondering if she was afraid like he was. Did she question her every decision? Ask why it happened to her? But his questions would have to go unanswered. He had not seen her since.

Ghile knew he was imposing on his new companions back in All-wyn. Either they were still waiting for him in the swamp, in which case Riff would by now be completely devoured by the bugs, or they had moved on and were carrying his body. He felt a surge of guilt at the thought of Two Elks being burdened by his sleeping form. What of the others? If they were on the move and encountered trouble...

No, he had waited long enough. He was being selfish. It was time to return. He would find Adon and Muk to say goodbye and go.

Having made up his mind, he stepped off the branch and fell rapidly. The moonlight would have made it possible for most anyone to see well enough, but Ghile could see perfectly well in almost complete darkness. Yet another gift of the soulstones.

His descent was leading him towards another limb. He focused and used his force energy to push off and go around the branch as he fell past. He did this with a casual flick of his head. It came so easily to him now. He did this once more before the final drop to the ground.

He landed softly, his force energy dissipating at the last second. To anyone watching, it would have appeared Ghile had stepped off the limb a couple of hundred feet above him and continued walking when he reached the ground. Ghile couldn't help but smile at something Adon had said earlier that day, "You are coming along, nicely."

It was strange how much Adon's praise meant to him. Even the approving nods from Muk brought with them a sense of pride. From his earliest memories, he had never been good enough at anything.

He grew too quickly when he was young and as a result was awkward and self-conscious. As the second born son of Last Hamlet's chieftain, it had originally been easy to stay in the background. That all changed when Adon was culled. All eyes turned to him after that and he had struggled under the weight of the collective gaze. He suspected that was why Gar and Bralf had singled him out for their bullying. His thoughts lingered on Gar and turned dark before he pushed them down.

He had changed so much since finding the soulstones. Here was something he was good at. No, he corrected himself, something he excelled at. As his control of his new found powers grew, other tasks came easier to him as well. He didn't feel so awkward when he moved. Training with the fang blade and spear felt more natural. He had confidence in himself and his abilities.

In his short stay in the dreaming he could easily sense the presence of nearby animals and reach out and touch their thoughts. He could temporarily touch minds and see through their eyes, control their movements. It was almost second nature to extend his force shield through another creature he was in contact with. It wasn't difficult to control two, three or even four different force shields at a time now.

If the animal was large enough, he could leech some of its life force to share some of its abilities for a short time. He was careful with this power, though. If the animal was small, it would kill it. Ghile refused to hurt an animal if it wasn't necessary, regardless of what Muk said.

Of all the animals on the island, the raven and the stag appealed most to him. There was such a primal feeling of strength when he mind-touched a stag. He most enjoyed leeching life force from them and then running alongside them through the forest.

Ravens were such intelligent animals. It had surprised him how observant and curious they were. He found they were the easiest to mind touch of all the birds on the island.

Ghile reached out with his mind there at the base of the Great Oak. He sensed the life force of the islands tiniest forest denizens, but there was nothing larger than a dozing rabbit nearby.

Ghile looked down the various trails that lead from the clearing around the Great Oak. He wasn't sure which one to take. Without any nearby animals to allow him to scout the area, he was on his own. This was the first time he had decided to leave the limbs of the great oak in the evening after settling down. He wasn't sure where to look for Adon and Muk.

Movement on the edge of the clearing caught his attention. Crouched down beside a lone beech tree, the shadow creature watched him. If not for his enhanced vision, the creature would have been impossible to see. It was wringing its hands, an action Ghile now associated with it. Whatever the creature was, it was no animal. Ghile had not sensed its presence.

Ghile had been wondering when the shadow creature would make its next appearance. He didn't reach for his pouch of stones or make any other quick movements, he didn't want to scare it off this time. He had made up his mind to see what it wanted.

He walked slowly towards the creature with his hands up and open in front of him. When he was halfway into the clearing, the creature cautiously slid out away from the safety of the trees and motioned for Ghile to follow.

Every time before this, Ghile either ignored the creature or attacked it. Adon had warned him from the beginning, the shadow creature meant them all harm and was not to be trusted. Even after he learned enough about his situation to question whether it was really Adon he was learning from, Ghile blindly followed Adon's lead. Until now. No, now was the time to find out if this skulking creature of shadow really meant him harm.

"Lead on," Ghile said.

The shadow creature looked ready to leap into the air, but settled on nodding its head enthusiastically. It motioned again for Ghile to follow before turning and heading deeper into the forest. It had an odd, shuffling gait and Ghile had no trouble keeping up with it. It stopped every so often to look back over its shoulder and make sure he was still following.

Ghile studied it as they made their way through the moon dappled undergrowth. It was easily as tall as he was, though because of its timid posture, it only came up to just above his waist. Like him, it was lanky, ungainly looking. Ghile couldn't help but feel a bit sorry for the thing, the way it skulked about. Even now, it constantly tried to watch everywhere at once, seeming to be afraid of everything.

The creature reached a small outcropping of rock, scurried up on one of the lower stones and turned to wait for Ghile, arms wrapped around its knees, hugging them close to its chest.

Ghile stopped and waited for it to do something. But, it seemed content to wait as well. Ghile supposed he was going to have to start this off, whatever this was.

"Well, you finally have me here..."

The shadow creature took one last look around, and seeming satisfied they were alone. It slowly rose to its full height.

Ghile couldn't breathe. All those times before he knew the shadow creature seemed familiar and now he knew why. The shadow was his own. Ghile stood alone in the middle of the forest, moonlight shining down through the canopy, staring at his own shadow.

The realization seemed to set his shadow self into motion. It took two steps back and dissolved into a black swirling smoke. The smoke settled into a large open space under two of the stones that made up the outcropping. Within their confines, a swirling black doorway formed.

Ghile somehow knew he was supposed to step into it, that this was the reason, the purpose the shadow was here in his dreaming. Was this the trap Adon had warned him about? Was this some trick to lure him into this black doorway? Where did it lead? Well, only one way to find out. There was nothing for it now.

"I hope you don't mean me harm," Ghile said, stepping forward.

"I do not," a young female voice said from behind him.

Ghile stumbled and spun around.

The fear of being surprised was instantly replaced by a fire-like heat that washed over his skin, a warmth he only felt when he was in the presence of another soulstone. The slight irresistible pull he had been following since leaving the Cradle felt like the tug of a fast flowing river rushing around him, dragging him along.

She was just as he remembered her. She was human, not much older than he was. She wore the same simple gown, the same swirling grey color as the rest of her. She looked like she was made of smoke from her long, loose flowing hair to her tiny perfect bare feet.

"What is your name?" The words tumbled out of Ghile before he knew he had said them. The question had been with him since they had last met.

"Akira," she said, in a soft melodious voice.

Ghile didn't know what to say. He just kept repeating her name over and over in his head, as if he was afraid he might forget it.

"You are?" Akira said.

"Huh? Oh, uh, Ghile."

"You are closer, Ghile." She looked from his face to his chest. "I can feel your presence now." Akira tilted her head and closed her eyes as if listening for something. "You have entered the Deepwood," she said. Her accent was still difficult to understand, but there was something so intriguing about it.

Ghile wasn't really sure where his physical body was. But if what she said was true, then Gaidel and the others had continued on and left the Ghost Fens.

Ghile remembered his shadow.

He turned. The shadow door was gone, along with any sign of the shadow creature, his shadow self.

Ghile quickly turned back to Akira, for fear she too would disappear. She still stood before him, watching him curiously. She leaned her head to the side to look past him.

"Before you had said something was wrong. That you couldn't wake up?" Ghile asked.

Akira nodded. "Yes. I do not understand why. But I cannot."

She must be in her dreaming, as he was now in his. But somehow she had the ability to project herself into his dreaming. Was this the power granted to her by her soulstone?

"You mentioned your brother?" Ghile said.

"Yes. His name is Ashar." Akira looked away then.

Ghile was afraid he had somehow upset her. "Is he alright? I didn't mean to upset you."

"No, it is not that. Ashar is well. He protects me, my body, while I am asleep. We do not know why I cannot wake up."

"How long have you been trapped in your dreaming?" Ghile said.

Akira reached up and touched her soulstone. "Since I found this."

"In the Fallen City?"

"Yes."

"How do you know your brother is with you?" Ghile asked. There was a part of him that feared her brother had fled and left her lying alone, abandoned, in the middle of some ancient human city.

"I visit him in his dreams. He is trying to discover a way to wake me. He protects me. But we are alone and there are things in the mists."

"We journey to Dagbar and from there—"

"No, you must not," Akira said. She had stepped forward and tried to place one of her small hands on his arm. The smoke that made up her hand dissipated as it reached him. When she drew her hand back, the smoke drift together and reformed.

"Dagbar is a dwarf, he is dangerous. He will turn you over to the cullers," Akira said. "Do not go to him. Please there is no time. You can feel the pull of the soulstone. Follow it. Please I need your help."

Ghile found himself nodding. He wanted to help Akira. She seemed so afraid and he just wanted to make her feel safe. He found himself agreeing before he had even decided to. "I will, please do not be afraid. I'm coming," Ghile said. A part of him was yelling at him, for agreeing so quickly. What had come over him? Don't be afraid? What was he saying? Didn't she understand what was going to happen when they met for real? The pull of the soulstones was muted here in the dreaming, but Ghile could still feel it, knew by Akira's actions she could as well. He recalled the intensity of the feeling when he first encountered Muk. The need to have the other stone.

The swirling smoke that was Akira slowly began to drift apart. Any other doubts about going to her drifted away with it.

"No, don't go!"

"Goodbye, Ghile Stonechosen."

Ghile stood there, helpless, as she disappeared from site.

"Please, don't leave, I—"

As the last remnants of her vanished from sight, Ghile thought he saw a smile touch her lips. He could feel his heart drumming in his throat, his face flush. He stood there, long after she was gone.

⋀

Akira floated silently in the dream mists. The guilt of what she was doing tore at her insides. She felt the familiar itch in her eyes as the tears began to gather along her eyelashes. She breathed in deeply, swallowing, trying to hold them back. One lone teardrop fell and instantly transformed into the same grey mist that surrounded her, then drifted apart, returning to the mists.

The powerful attraction of Ghile's soulstones only made her feel worse. She concentrated on her brother, Ashar. She pictured his thin angular face, his high cheekbones, and thick brows, which were always furrowed in concentration. She pictured him working over his mortar and pestles, flasks, and funnels; fussing over his draughts and elixirs.

She felt the pull deep in her chest at first, like a rope tied just behind her navel that was suddenly pulled taught. She began floating through the mists. She kept the image of her brother in her head as she gained speed.

Images formed around her – two lovers embracing; a small child running in fear, only to trip over nothing; a goblin standing on a mound of junk, cheering. When she first entered the dream mists, she had been thrown from one dream to the next, with no control of her movements. Every glimpse of a dream, no matter how small, sucked her inside.

She knew the images for what they were now, others' dreams, formed from the dream mists. She had spent much time wondering if that were true or if it was the other way around, if the dream mists were birthed from the dreams.

But now, they were but minor distractions to pass by, share a glimpse of themselves and then fade away behind her. Before, she might have stopped and entered one that caught her attention, spent time in another's dream just to see something other than the mists. But her heart was heavy, so she just drifted past.

The only memory strong enough to push its way through her melancholy was the same one she always had when traveling through the dream mists. The image of her and Ashar, running through the enchanted mists of the Fallen City. The dream mists and the enchanted mists that perpetually hid the city in its bowels like some thick soup, were somehow connected. How long had it been since that day? The last day she had spent awake...

"Akira, hurry! There is no time, they are almost upon us," Ashar said. He had stopped running to turn and urge her on. He reached out and took her hand, pulling her along.

The whoops and cries of the goblins echoed through the mists all around them. The unpredictable creatures infested the Fallen City, somehow unaffected by the effects of the dream mists.

They ran.

Jagged stone pillars and broken walls of greenish-black stone, covered by slime, streaked past.

Ashar had spent hours gathering, categorizing, and studying the slime on their many previous trips here. But now, he didn't even give it a glance as they fled from their pursuers.

A knot had formed in Akira's side and she tried gulping in air to slow the pain. She had to run through it. It was her fault they had attracted the attention of so many of the goblins that scavenged throughout the ruins. They were usually easy enough to avoid, the city was huge and the mists made it difficult to see more than a few feet in any direction, especially this deep.

They passed more jagged columns, all in neat rows. They were somewhere in the temple district, near the center of the bowl. They had been chased deeper than they had ever been before.

The Fallen City sat in a deep chasm, a literal bowl formed in the land and filled with this impenetrable enchanted mist, allowing only the tallest of the ancient buildings to breach the upper surface, like the fingers of some drowning god.

Ashar dragged her down a set of lopsided stairs, more a slide now. They tumbled together at the bottom, but Ashar was up quickly, reaching for one of his flasks.

His eyes darted left and right, looking for where to go next. They seemed to have slid into a dead end. One of the many sinkholes that pockmarked the bottom of the chasm.

"Get behind me, Akira," Ashar said. He ripped the small flask from one of his many belts. He began the soft low chant that Akira knew he used as a sorcerer, to channel his power. The liquid in the flask took on a bright red hue.

Akira knelt down and began backing away from Ashar. Using her hands to feel her way, she pressed her back against a large, slime-covered stone along the steep side of the sinkhole.

Was this it? Was this how their lives would end? It pained her to realize she was going to be proven right.

She had warned Ashar that no amount of Magister Dagbar's promised rewards was worth the danger of the Fallen City. How many arguments had they had? How many times had she refused to risk another journey here, only to join him in the last minute?

Every time they returned to the Emporium, Ashar assured her they had ventured into the mists for the last time. Only to come back days or weeks later, with another urging from Magister Dagbar and Master Dowynn.

Magister Dagbar knew he broke the very laws he was supposed to enforce. He knew the dangers of the Deepwood and the Fallen City. But each time Ashar returned, Master Dowynn would give him a different task, something else to research, at Magister Dagbar's urging.

The first goblins appeared at the edges of the sinkhole. Akira could make out their squat shapes and long, protruding ears, hear their sniffing as they searched the two humans out. The two mist shrouded forms turned to four, then eight.

Ashar hurled his first flask and reached to tear two more from his belts. His aim was good and the small sound of breaking glass was deceptively unassuming compared to the loud boom of flame that followed. Blood red fire billowed out from the broken flask and ignited the mist.

The screams of the nearest goblins were lost in a roar of flames.

Akira turned her face away from the flames and used her arms to shield herself from the wave of heat and debris she knew was about to follow.

The flash revealed a dark hole a short distance away from Akira. The flames died away and with them, the revealing light.

The sound of Ashar's chanting and the breaking of glass gave Akira the forewarning she needed to focus on the spot where she had seen the hole.

The flames that followed revealed the hole and a short distance into it as well. It was deep. Maybe this was not the end of them, after all.

Akira called for Ashar as she scrambled for the opening. He was reaching for another pair of flasks.

Above them, the goblins closest to where the flash impacted were simply gone, consumed by the magical flame. Others were screaming and flailing their arms in a hopeless attempt to put themselves out.

Other shapes were appearing out of the mists, but luckily, they seemed more interested in watching the suffering of their brethren than pursuing her and Ashar.

Ashar hurried past her and pulled an everflame from one of his many pouches. He waved it inside the opening, and seeming content, ushered Akira inside before him.

Luckily, the hole was not the home of one of the city's denizens. Due to the strange dream-like effect the mists caused, most creatures from the Deepwood avoided the place. But spiders as large as dogs or larger were not uncommon, nor was finding the carcass of a goblin bound in webbing and stuffed away under an outcropping, or hanging from a building.

Akira half climbed, half slid down a short tunnel formed by a collapsed wall. At the end, she dropped a few feet to a slightly slanted floor. The ceiling had been forced down under the weight of debris, but she could almost stand here.

It was a small space, the walls had been pushed inward and the ground was covered with fallen stone. Akira watched as Ashar hurled another of his flasks. He was outlined in the flash, a black shape surrounded by red. He began his descent towards her and Akira moved farther into the space to make room. She almost screamed when she saw a slender hand jutting out of the stones next to her. It only took her a moment to realize it was part of a broken statue, more than likely crushed by the compacted ceiling.

With Ashar's arrival, his everflame illuminated the rest of the room. There were broken pieces of statues scattered everywhere. The collapsed ceiling must have crushed them.

"Ashar, look at this," Akira said.

Ashar had always shown great interest in the art of the ancient city, particularly the statues.

He did not turn around, but said, "Not now. It has been a while, Akira. Drink another mist antidote."

Ashar concentrated on the tunnel they had entered by. He grabbed a small flask from his belt and consumed the contents.

She didn't feel the dream-like effects of the mist yet, but she hastily did as she was told, swallowing down the acrid liquid, but continuing to study what she had found.

The bust lay nearby and the expression on the face drew Akira's attention. The head tilted slightly up, giving the face a conceited air.

"This should keep them out," Ashar said.

He threw a flask into the tunnel entrance which, like the others, exploded once its contents were exposed to air. But instead of fire, this one shot forth white webbing, filling the entrance.

Akira looked back to the bust and knelt down next to it. She made to brush the small bits of debris from the lips of the face when her other hand adhered to the stone. "Ashar," she said.

"That will keep our pesky pursuers from searching too far into the tunnel. They are not fond of the hunting spiders," Ashar said, catching his breath as he admired his handiwork.

Akira tried to use her other hand as leverage to free herself, but it too, held fast to the strange bust. "Ashar!"

He was at her side in an instant. His eyes went wide with shock and his first action was to drop the everflame and grab her by the shoulders, trying to pull her back. Her hands were fixed and he only succeeded in dragging the bust clear of the other debris.

"No, no, no," Ashar said as he stared at the bust's chest.

Akira was still trying to free her hands. They were growing warmer. The chest of the bust had a series of mounds on it, which formed a spiral pattern.

Ashar placed his hands over the small mounds and pushed down. Akira didn't know what he expected to happen, maybe this was some ancient trap he had learned about from Master Dowynn. Ashar and Master Dowynn were the only humans Akira knew who could pull words off of objects. "Come on, come on," Ashar said, pushing down harder.

"Ashar, my hands are burning." Akira heard a low hum, it sounded like bees. The humming was coming from the statue.

"No, this is not supposed to happen. Akira, I will fix this. I promise," Ashar said.

The statue began to glow from within.

"Akira, I'm sorry. I will fix this. I promise," Ashar said.

The statue was glowing too brightly to look at and the hum now filled the room.

The heat transformed into intense pain. Akira felt a slicing pain along her palm. She screamed. Akira could see a circular mound moving just under her skin, dragging searing pain along behind it.

Ashar took her face in his hands and turned her towards him. It was hard to hear him through the loud hum, or see him through the tears. The last thing she remembered was Ashar's tear-streaked face as he repeated "I'm sorry", over and over.

Akira floated silently in the mist. The tears fell freely now, joining the dream mist as soon as they fell away from her. She looked at her hand where the soulstone had entered so long ago and then touched her chest where her single stone now resided.

Of course, this was not her hand or her soulstone. Not really. Here, she was made of the stuff of dreams, like everything else. Her true body was in Allwyn, with Ashar.

Akira focused on her brother again and continued forward. The image of Ashar looking out over the sea appeared before her.

She stepped through and was behind Ashar then. He was looking out over the sea, his hands clasped behind his back. She recognized the place. He dreamed of it often. He had described it to her when they were little, but she didn't remember it.

The small wattle and daub hut that was their home in this settlement sat a short distance away. The winds that blew in from the ocean and raced across the beach brought small flecks of sand, that had long ago scoured this side of the hut smooth.

Ashar stood before the squat driftwood fence. Its chaotic shapes, bound together by rope, only enhanced the beauty of the place. Akira wished she remembered the place of her childhood. Ashar assured her she shouldn't.

The human settlement of Oceanwood was no more. Its residents now either dead, like their parents, or moved to other human containments. The entire settlement, fell victim to the 'Justice' of the dwarves, as Ashar put it.

"You spoke with him?" Ashar said. He had not turned around, but continued to stare out over the ocean.

"Yes," Akira said, stepping up next to him. The sand, carried on the wind, blew through her. She wished she could feel the sting of it on her skin. She would welcome the pain.

"Where is he now?"

"He has entered the Deepwood," Akira said.

"Good. Good. It will not be much longer, sister."

"Ashar, are you sure this is the only way?"

Ashar turned to stare at her. His deep set eyes locked on her. He didn't blink. Recently, the intensity she saw in Ashar's gaze discomforted her. He had given so much to try and help her since she had found the soulstone. He had done everything he could to wake her. To free her of the stone's control. "Akira, did I not promise you I would do everything to set this right?"

She nodded. They had conducted this same discourse so many times before. She knew better than to argue, she only wished there was some other way.

Ashar sat down and closed his eyes.

"Ashar, please don't go. I... I would like to stay here for a while. The ocean is so beautiful."

"You know I must prepare, Akira."

She nodded. She tried to lock the colors in her mind. The blues of the sky and dull green of the ocean. The multiple shades of brown in the driftwood fence.

Suddenly, Ashar was gone and with him, his dream.

Akira floated in the mists once again.

Alone.

At first, after finding the soulstone, she found herself in her own dreaming. It was a beautiful place. A forested glade, a river cutting a gentle path along its edge. Her mother had been there to greet her. It was her mother who had taught her the ways of the dreaming. Had tried to teach her how to return to Allwyn. It had not worked. Over time, her mother faded, then the river and finally the glade. All faded into the grey mist of the dreaming.

Now, she was truly alone.

10

The Fallen City

SHAR opened his eyes. His vision filled with the total darkness only found deep in the bowels of Allwyn. Or in this case, the lowest reaches of the Fallen City. He sat up slowly. He was shivering. No matter how many blankets or furs he added to this stone slab he used as a bed, its hard surface still sucked heat from him.

Much like this accursed place sucked at his soul, he mused. "It will be over soon, sister."

He half expected to hear Akira answer. She was still so beautiful in his dreams. It was such a double-edged sword each time he saw her there.

Enough of this. There was still much to prepare before the next stonechosen arrived.

Ashar reached out, feeling for the dusty edge of the side table. The stone was cold beneath his fingers. The clink of empty bottles mocked his fumbling until he found the stone cup that concealed the everflame. He tossed the cup aside. The glow of the everflame's heatless light skittered across the walls of the cramped chamber.

He continued to fumble among the half-emptied flasks covering the night stand, holding each up in turn and scrutinizing its contents, until he found one which still held a small amount of his tonic. He swished it around and studied it through the glass until it was the right consistency. He drank down the sickly yellow solution, grimacing at its acrid taste and then discarded the empty flask among the others. He would need to make another batch soon.

Grabbing his useless leg, he swung it out and over the side. He pushed himself up and retrieved his staff from where he had left it. Ashar had to put most of his weight on the staff. It would take time for the tonic to work and the pain to subside before his leg could properly support him. Even then, he still needed the staff. Luckily, this chamber was near to his work.

He made his way out of the little chamber. The sound of his staff and dragging leg echoed dully off the damp, glistening walls.

The stone corridor was draped in shadow, but, even from a distance, the flickering light of the laboratory provided enough to see by. He continued down the hallway, the thousand stabbing needles in his leg slowly replaced by a throbbing numbness as the tonic did its work.

His leg was yet another reminder of the debt he owed Dagbar. A debt he would pay upon the dwarf tenfold. True, Dagbar had not inflicted the wound that maimed him, but it all led back to the dwarf. Ashar caught himself absently running his hand along the part of his black robes that covered his mauled thigh. A habit he had begun whenever he was lost in thought. He clenched his hand into a tight fist.

No, Dagbar was responsible for him being here, for what had happened to Akira, his leg and the reason he had to waste his talents in this forsaken place.

The humiliation maddened Ashar. In his youth, his mentor Master Dowynn had taught him to look up to Dagbar. Master Dowynn respected, even revered, the dwarf magister. Master Dowynn had honestly believed every word the dwarf spoke about restoring the balance and equality of the races. He had lapped it all up like a dog.

Ashar knew that was all humans were to the dwarfs. They were nothing more than dogs. Pets to entertain them and do their bidding. To be tossed aside when no longer needed or killed if they were disobedient.

The dwarves called the human's homes settlements. They were internment camps. Dwarven law even allowed them to slay humans found outside the camps, those not under the dwarven yoke. He remembered one instance when Dagbar praised the writings of Hjurl and pointed to the laws against slavery as an example that the dwarves had lost their way from the beginning times. That their God of Law had instructed them to watch over the human race, Daomur never meant for things to devolve to where they were now.

Ashar now knew Dagbar only told Master Dowynn and the others what they wanted to hear, told them what Dagbar needed them to hear, to trick them, to convince them to do his bidding. The Emporium, his Freehold was no different than any other human containment.

It took Ashar losing Akira to open his eyes. How long had he searched for a soulstone in the Fallen City? How many times had he and Master Dowynn secretly scoured through the ancient texts and forbidden writings of their human ancestors? The only reason Dagbar had taught them the forbidden knowledge of reading was to make it easier for the dwarf to reach his goals.

Ashar had been tricked to believe he was chosen. He was the one destined to find a soulstone and bring about the return of Haurtu and with his return, free the human race and return balance to Allwyn.

Ashar kissed his fingers and touched his head then his heart, a gesture that paid reverence to the great Haurtu. A gesture reminding Ashar that the mind comes before the heart. Knowledge before emotion. A practice lost in time. Like so much other knowledge lost during the Great Purge, when the dwarves and elves tried to erase humans from existence.

Ashar had been ready to help restore balance. To become stonechosen and then prepare for the challenge of the vessel, the final joining with Haurtu. Such lies Dagbar had told him. It was in taking Akira's sleeping form back to Dagbar, in asking him to reverse the process and free her from the burden of becoming a vessel that Ashar discovered the truth.

Dagbar had looked him and Master Dowynn in the face and said once chosen, it was irreversible. A fact Ashar now knew to be false.

Dagbar could never have realized the gift of reading he gave to Ashar would reveal the dwarf's falsehoods. For Ashar discovered in the ancient writings a way to do just that. A way to free his sister.

How Dagbar had tried to play him for the fool! So convincing when he placed his hand on Ashar's shoulder and wept for the loss he was to suffer.

She was too weak, he said. We must not let her wake until the true stonechosen arrives to claim her stone.

To kill her, he meant! The true stonechosen? Wasn't Ashar supposed to be the true stonechosen? The lies poured from Dagbar like water from a flask.

Oh, why had Master Dowynn done as Dagbar had commanded and administered the elixir of sleeping death to his beloved Akira? She was like his own daughter. Why hadn't he stopped him?

Where was the determination Ashar had now? At least he had enough courage to steal away with her in the night and bring her to the only place he could think of that would keep them both safe. Safe until he was able to punish Master Dowynn for his weakness and Dagbar for his lies.

Ashar entered his laboratory. He passed between two of the many tables he had found throughout the city and had brought here. Across their various surfaces, elixirs frothed and boiled in their beakers. The lights of the many tiny flames reflected through them to cast a myriad of colors about the large circular chamber. Ashar felt the calming effect work always had on him. It centered him, focused him to task.

He stopped and checked the viscosity of one of his unguents. Too gummy, he mused. He dug through nearby baskets, looking for the ingredient he needed. He only found a small amount of what he sought.

Damn, out again.

He stopped and listened for the telltale click of claws on stone that gave away the location of one of his goblin thralls. Nothing. He usually could hear them, even over all the bubbling and hissing.

His thoughts returned to his sister. They better not be trying to exhume her again. He made his way to the center of the room. The two small circular mounds of stone lay untouched. He awkwardly knelt down beside one and rested his hand on the unyielding cold slab. He could sense her under there, asleep, wasting away.

He knew she could not die, but after a time, he could no longer watch her skin tighten and grey, her hair, once thick and vibrant, become mere threads.

It pained him to lie to Akira, but he had to keep her complacent if he had any chance of freeing her from her soulstone. If she knew the truth of what he had planned, she might try to stop him – she was still blind to the ugly truth that was life. He had to protect her. He could not stand the thought of what the dwarves would do to her or the thought of another stonechosen consuming her.

No, this was the only chance she had. He'd promised her he would make it right and he would. Ashar had no intention of fulfilling the soulstone prophecy. Not once he discovered how the soulstones fueled his magic. No, he would use the power promised him to free his sister and then repay Dagbar tenfold. Repay them all for their lies.

He looked at the other nearby mound. The vargan stonechosen was the first to feel the pull of his sister's soulstone. He absently rubbed his mauled thigh. What strength the beast had. But now its soulstone fueled Ashar's powers, as well. Soon, he would add the boy stonechosen and then have enough soulstones to punish Dagbar and then perform the ritual to free Akira.

He heard the tell-tale click of claws on stone. "Come!"

Two pallid goblins skulked out from behind nearby tables. Blue veins pulsed just below white flesh. Their rapidly rising chests reminded him of small birds. Drool fell freely from their open mouths. One brushed against the other as they approached, causing the other to bare its fangs and hiss. The two tensed and squared off on each other.

"Attend me," Ashar said. Were there only two left? He could only afford to send one to gather ingredients. He needed the other to tend the fires.

"You. Go beyond the city. I need more wormwood bark." Ashar held forth the last bit he had found. The goblin thrall he had indicated skittered forward and sniffed hungrily at the bark.

Of all the mist thralls, the goblins were the most resourceful and cunning. It was a pity there were only so many of them left. They were the first he began experimenting on. It had taken time and cost many.

Humans from the outlying farms of the Emporium were next. He began to turn them into mist thralls, more to punish Dagbar than anything else. They were not as cunning as the goblins nor as fierce as the vargan. They were also not equipped with sharp claws and teeth like the others. All attempts to enhance their physical form had failed. The noise those particular test subjects made had grated on his nerves to the point of almost not making it worth doing the experiments in the first place.

Almost.

Yes, the goblins were his favorites. They were also the only ones who seemed to retain some of their base nature. Being natural sneaks, they could avoid the accursed elves and their fae in the surrounding Deepwood with regularity.

The elves were a drain on his other thralls, but an acceptable nuisance. They were a natural defense, keeping everyone else away from the city. They were solitary creatures, never gathering in great enough numbers to pose any serious threat. Best of all, they, along with their fae minions, seemed to fear the dream mists.

"Go!"

The goblin thrall snarled its pleasure and hurried from the lab on all fours. Ashar dismissed the other with a wave.

"Now to see to the boy, dear sister."

Ashar breathed in deeply, taking the mists deep into him. He then began to chant the words of power, the words even Master Dowynn did not know, forbidden words thought lost in time. He drew upon the mists that cursed the Fallen City and used them as the source of his castings.

He sent out his summons.

He needed the mists, they were integral in not only creating the mist thralls, but also in summoning and controlling them. The dream mist was a gift from Haurtu. Much easier to use than air, it connected all it touched. An abundant and never-ending source for his magic. As long as he did not succumb to its hallucinogenic effects.

He had been lucky to find this tower. Not only was it mostly intact, but its jagged summit just pierced the top of the mists and allowed access to much needed fresh air.

Ashar had long ago learned the ingredients needed to mix the antidote, which shielded him from the effects of the dream mists, but he sometimes forgot to retake them and the mists' effects took longer to take hold here.

He refocused on his summons. Before Akira became stonechosen, he would never have had the strength to reach out of the city. But now, with her and the vargan stonechosen lying by her side, there was no place within the mists he could not reach.

Based on what Akira said, the boy was young and already had two soulstones. He also only had a small group of followers to protect him. This was Ashar's chance to acquire what he needed.

The longer he waited, the more precarious his position became. It was only a matter of time before the elves considered him a great enough threat and attempted to brave the city's mists. Or worse, Dagbar finally decide that Ashar was beyond redemption and report his and Akira's existence to the empire.

The culler who had stumbled upon him after visiting Dagbar's camp had cost Ashar dozens of thralls. That reminded him, he would need to check on Knight Justice Griff and see how his transformation was coming. Every situation, no matter how dire, could still produce something positive. Ashar smiled contemptuously. "Dagbar taught me that," Ashar said.

Across the many tables, the goblin thrall stopped feeding one of the many flames and hissed as it lowered its head in supplication.

Ashar cackled and returned to his musings.

He knew he could not survive an organized assault by the dwarves or the elves. Not yet. He still needed time to prepare, grow stronger. But, with two more soulstones, he would have what he needed. The young approaching stonechosen was his best chance to fix everything. And once he had the power of all four soulstones fueling his magic, then he would be unstoppable.

He heard screams, followed by the rattling of cages drifting down from the upper levels. Those who had not yet turned. Good, the mist thralls were responding to his summons. He would need to work on turning as many captives as possible once he had the other soulstones.

A pack of thralls appeared at the top of the stairs. They were mostly vargan, with a smattering of humans among them.

Ashar had only ever climbed those winding stairs to the top once. At any other time, he would have marveled at the view over the Fallen City, but until Akira was free and Dagbar paid for his lies, Ashar did not have the luxury of enjoying such frivolities.

The thralls descended the stairs that clung to the outer walls. The humans, like all mist thralls, ran on all fours. Ashar noted they almost kept pace with the vargan, which was impressive. Yet another gift his potion bestowed upon them.

The creatures finally reached the bottom level, some of them leaping the last section of stairs in their haste to reach him. They all stopped a short distance away, their chests rising and falling at that abnormally fast rate he had come to associate with them.

"Good. You must go to the south, to the edges of the Deepwood. A small group of humans' travel through the woods there. They will be somewhere between the Ghost Fens and the human settlement I sent you to raid. Find them. Kill them all and then bring the male bodies back to me," Ashar said.

He knew they would be unable to truly kill the stonechosen, but the wounds caused would force his body to shut down while the soulstones healed him.

Of course, he would never be allowed to wake. Ashar looked at the two stone tombs in the center of the room. The crushing weight of the boy's tomb would see to that.

Ashar needed to see to his studies of the ancient texts. There were a few, as yet unanswered questions regarding the soulstone ritual.

Soon, he would have everything he needed.

11

The Outcrop

INNGYR disengaged the intricate steel harness with a practiced slam of his fist and swung his leg over Safu's feathered back to slide down from the griffon with practiced ease.

"Thank you, Safu." He undid the straps that held his hammer and pack, all the while taking time to stroke her muscled side and whisper encouragement.

Safu eyed him approvingly, the thin transparent membrane of her eye flicking rapidly.

"You have carried me this day in safety and comfort, and I thank you." It was the same thing he always said to her while dismounting. He had learned early on the importance of the bond between knight and mount. He breathed in her comforting scent, a combination of down and musk. A lesson not enough knights appreciated by far, present company included.

Finngyr undid the buckles of his riding saddle and heaved it off Safu, propping it on a nearby stone spur. The stone was part of the large outcropping where he had chosen to stop and make camp for the evening. The outcropping jutted up out of the Nordlah Plains like a giant clawed hand grasping towards the sky, breaking the monotony of the smooth rolling hills. The red stone stood out in stark contrast to the sun-baked yellow grass and cloudless sky stretching on forever over this hostile land.

Finngyr had camped at this landmark before, on this very plateau, and knew it meant they were halfway through their journey. They were a week north of Daomount and three days into the plains. Their destination lay to the north, but Finngyr couldn't help but look west. If he flew in that direction for ten days he would be able to join his fellow knights. Them and whatever smattering of the empire's military the High Council deigned to send with them, to deal with the gathering barbarians.

With the information he now had from the Lord Knight Justice, it didn't take a beardling to figure out why the humans were gathering. They knew the Time of the Stonechosen was upon them. They knew and were gathering to protect those abominations. He should be there to stop them. He breathed in, as if the call of righteous battle was a scent he could inhale and savor.

It was not the first time he wished he was there with his brother veteran knights, instead of here with these two youngling ingrates. Neither had even earned the title of Knight Justice, having never officiated over a culling ceremony, or Rite of Attrition, as others of weaker dispositions named it. They were freshly raised knights with no respect for anyone or anything.

It was obvious they felt this assignment was beneath them. They never came out and said it to Finngyr's face, even they were not that stupid. But, through hushed conversations and shared looks, Finngyr knew the truth of it.

Finngyr turned and ran his gloved hand over Safu's beak and enchanted bridle. He drew in a calming breath. "Go now and hunt.

Return at my call," Finngyr said, completing the ritual. Safu took to the darkening sky, the powerful strokes of her wings kicking up a cloud of dust.

Horth, having just slid down from his griffon, covered his face, coughing. "A little warning next time, Finngyr?"

Horth turned his back to Finngyr and started in on the straps holding down his riding saddle. Where Finngyr had a simple backpack, Horth's gear filled a pack and two swollen saddle bags. Like his belt and gloves, the saddlebags were not simple, but made of fine leather with detailed etchings. Horth was a dwarf who appreciated the finer things and had the coin to pay for it. His father's association with the coin mongers appeared to be a lucrative one.

Kjar's griffon pranced impatiently nearby as the lean dwarf still fought with his riding buckle. He had been trying to imitate Finngyr's quick release since first seeing it a week before, to no avail. Even after a week, Kjar was still awkward in the saddle. He spent as little time with his mount as was necessary and never spoke to it save muttered curses. His griffon fought against the bridle as soon as Kjar gave the reins some slack as he tried to work the buckle free.

Horth smirked. "Having trouble, Kjar?" He slapped his own griffon hard on the hind quarters, near its leonine tail. "Go hunt!"

Enough was enough.

He would not suffer the impertinence and ineptitude of these two any longer. They would know their place before they reached the Freehold. Too much rode on his quest. They would know their place before they left this outcrop, or they wouldn't leave it at all.

Horth turned from the billow of dust, not bothering to watch his griffon's departure, and right into an explosion of rock shards and debris.

"What in the name–" Horth fell back, stumbled over the uneven ground, and dropped heavily onto his back.

Kjar's griffon bolted to the air with an indignant screech. Startled and still half in the saddle, Kjar and his curses rose back into the sky with it.

Finngyr stepped over what remained of the stone he had just crushed and let his ornate hammer fall to rest on his shoulder, its immense head framing his own like a dark halo. He didn't need to look at his hammer to know the smooth metal surface was unblemished. He leaned forward to tower over the now-prone Horth. "Your lack of propriety is at an end. You will address me by title and name, Knight Horth," Finngyr said.

"What are you on about?" Horth actually had the audacity to look incredulous. Finngyr didn't know if the reddening of the bigger dwarf's face was from embarrassment, or rising anger. Horth slapped some of the dirt off his hands and started to rise.

Finngyr's boot caught him soundly in the breastplate and down he went again. "Think of this as the pebble that broke the human's back. I am going to let you up in a moment, Knight Horth. When I do, you have a choice to make. Either you will rise, address me as Knight Justice Finngyr and then bow and ask forgiveness for your arrogance and lack of discipline…"

Horth sputtered and started up again. Another boot returned him just as quickly to the ground.

"…or you will rise, collect your hammer, and try to kill me. I say try, for I will surely kill you." With that, Finngyr stepped back and hefted his hammer off his shoulder and let the haft fall into his other hand with a slap of finality. He limbered his shoulders and waited, his face a stone mask.

Horth didn't rise immediately. He took it in turn to glower at Finngyr and glance into the sky at Kjar, who still hadn't gotten his griffon under control. Finngyr could see Horth weighing his options. It was obvious he wanted nothing more than to attack Finngyr, but without the aid of his thin southern companion, he didn't have a chance of besting the more seasoned knight and he knew it. Some other thought played behind the beardling's eyes.

Finngyr glanced in Kjar's direction and couldn't suppress a satisfied smirk. "Well, Knight Horth?"

"The Judges Council will hear of this!" The words all but tore themselves past Horth's lips.

"The Judges Council? Surely you mean the Knights Council, Knight Horth? For wouldn't a young knight, freshly raised from squire, complain to the Council of his sect instead of going directly to the great Judges Council?" Finngyr said. He raised an eyebrow to emphasize his question. He could see the dawning realization on Horth's face. The young knight had made a mistake in his anger and let slip what Finngyr expected all along.

"My father—"

"Will mourn the loss of his over-indulged and treacherous son. Decide, Knight Horth, or I will crush you where you lay and be better off for it." Each word was measured and said with a cold certainty that would have had no more effect had Finngyr roared them like an enraged human.

"Orcs!"

"Orcs!" Kjar shouted again. He had his griffon in check, though he turned in the saddle trying to look in every direction at once. His griffon hovered a short distance above them. "What are you two doing down there?"

Finngyr only spared him a glance. "I grow weary Knight Horth, and your time grows short."

Horth held up a shaking hand. "No, Finngyr, please wait! Orcs. Kjar has spotted orcs. Now is not the time. We need—"

"What did you call me?" Finngyr said.

"In his holy name! Knight Justice Finngyr! You are Knight Justice Finngyr."

Finngyr never took his stare off Horth as he called to Kjar. "How many and from what direction?"

Other than the sounds of the griffon's beating wings, the outcrop was silent. After what seemed minutes, but was no more than seconds, Kjar answered. "Thirty or more. I'm not sure. They are coming around from both sides and from below. What are we going to do?"

Finngyr nodded at Kjar's words, but continued to stare at Horth. "Well?"

Horth swallowed and spoke the words hastily, glancing left and right as they tumbled out. "I most humbly, em, ask, that you... um... forgive me, er, my disrespect, Knight Justice Finngyr."

Finngyr could hear them now and so could Horth. They were close. The sounds of bare hands and feet slapping stone, grunts coming from deep-barreled chests, even the rattling of bones.

Finngyr had faced orcs before. They were not uncommon in the Nordlah Plains. They shared a common enemy in the humans and like them, were primitive and no match for an armed and armored dwarf. Most of the time they stayed clear of them. The Bastions were too well fortified and heavily guarded to have anything to fear from orcs.

Though they were powerful warriors, there were only a handful of tribes in the plains. Their constant blood feud with the humans, and the orc's ridiculous beliefs, kept their numbers at a minimum.

So why were they attacking now? If they spotted the griffons' land, they were well hidden enough to have slipped away without detection. What would make them seek out three obviously superior dwarves? An idea struck him. "Is there a watcher among them?" Finngyr called to Kjar.

"What?" Kjar shouted back

"A watcher?"

"What in great Daomur's name, is a watcher?" Kjar called.

The orcs were the creations of Hideon, God of Hate. His subsequent fall to Haurtu the Devourer during the God Wars was not something the proud orcs ever seemed to accept. It seemed their history taught Hideon turned his back on the orcs and left Allwyn out of disgust for some apparent weakness in his progeny. The shamans of the orcs believed only an act of great courage in battle would draw Hideon's attention and allow the shamans to implore his return.

Thus, normally not a danger, an orc warband with a watcher with them, meant they would only attack a foe worthy of their god's attention. It was always easy to pick out a watcher. Orc shamans practiced ritual scarring.

"A shaman, Knight Kjar! Is one of their number clothed different and covered in scars?"

"Yes! I see him." Kjar called almost immediately, pointing further down the rocky slope.

"Good. Take to the sky and once the battle begins, it is your sole purpose to kill him," Finngyr said.

Kjar nodded and with a sharp jerk on the reins, turned his griffon. Wooden javelins flew through the air where the young knight had been only moments before.

The roars rose in a unison around them as the orcs made the plateau. The ones below appeared first, grey hands gripping red stone. The hands were followed by large, elongated faces, all tusks and snarls. To both sides of the ledge, others leaped from rock to rock, racing to be first to close with the enemy. The smallest of them towered over Finngyr and was almost as wide as tall. Thick pelts and hide stretched over muscled bodies, grey skin left bare in places to display prominent battle scars. The jawbones and skulls of animals, surfaces orange with the reflection of the setting sun, were haphazardly tied in place to act as shoulder guards or tooth-rimmed gauntlets. Tiny deep set eyes, burning with hatred stared out of each grey face.

"Don't just sit there in the dirt, Knight Horth. Time to work out those saddle sores."

Finngyr paid no more heed to Horth and took in the surrounding landscape to find the best place to make his stand. There was no need to charge into this fight, it would come to him. Had he trusted Horth more, he would have gone back to back with him; as it was, he liked his odds on his own.

He found a relatively flat space near the outer edge of the plateau, with little to no rocks to trip him up, but close enough to the edge to have a height advantage over those who came at him from below. As if to prove he had chosen well, a clawed hand slapped against stone, not a pace away from him, the ugly brute attached to it rising into view a moment later. Finngyr's steel-capped boot caught it below the jaw, sending the orc back to the rocks below.

There was no time to watch the orc fall as a battle cry erupted to his left. The first of the orcs who made the plateau from the side reached him. This one was big, even for an orc. It roared a challenge into the sky, foam and spittle flying past the tusks of its pronounced jaw.

"Your god can't hear you, oaf!" Finngyr spat and stepped in with a wide swing of his hammer. The arcing blow was more to judge distance and see how quick his opponent was. It was a common tactic when fighting against a warrior with a two-handed weapon, to follow in after a wide swing. The orc obliged, coming in with a downward swing of its stone spiked wooden club.

But Finngyr was ready and rushed in to close the distance. He still caught a portion of the blow, but this close in, there was little strength behind it, even though it still would have splintered the skull of a human. But dwarves were made of sterner stuff and Finngyr shrugged off the blow. Not so for the steel vambrace Finngyr planted into the orcs midsection, or the follow-up downward thrust with the end of his hammer's handle.

The first pushed the air from the creature's lungs and the second landed on the top of the creature's knee with a satisfying crunch. Against most opponents, Finngyr liked to keep distance, but this orc was twice his size and had the advantage of reach.

Already close, Finngyr spun full circle and crouched even lower, letting his hammer gain momentum as he did. It would have been easy enough to jump over this blow, but the strike to the knee had done its job, as Finngyr knew it would. The spinning hammer smashed into the already-wounded leg, causing it to bend at a quite unnatural angle. The orc toppled over.

Normally, Finngyr would have finished his opponent, but more orcs already closed on him from behind the downed orc, their faces a mix of eagerness and bloodlust. This was not a fight to protect land or food. This was a display. A display of strength and raw savagery to appease a dead god who would never be sated.

Finngyr slid back and to the side, keeping the downed orc between him and the others. It caused the two closing orcs to spread out and go around their fallen companion.

Finngyr feinted to the right and then lunged left to bring his hammer head up and block the downward strike from the first incoming orc. It's stone headed axe shattered against the enchanted metal of the hammer. Finngyr didn't hesitate, but lunged back to his right and swung hard in an upward strike that smashed the spearhead of the other orc, who rushed in to skewer him in the back while he focused on the other. It too, exploded into dust from the enchanted hammer blow.

Finngyr firmed his grip on the hammer and intoned a prayer to Daomur, a deep throated rumble which reverberated deep within him. He could feel the presence of Daomur in the hammer. Daomur's magic passed through the objects his progeny created in his name. From the bridle that helped control the griffons, to the armor Finngyr wore, his god's magic infused them. But none compared to the ancient hammers his sect wielded in Daomur's name. The vibrations in his throat were mirrored by those from the hammer. The weight of the hammer disappeared and it felt like he was holding little more than a stick.

Finngyr swung the hammer back around his head and across in front of him; the head thrummed with holy might as it passed through the first orc and then the other. It then connected with the first orc Finngyr wounded, who had chosen a bad time to stand and rejoin the fight.

Blood and bits of bone were all that was left in the hammer's wake as all three orcs, or what remained of them, flew away from Finngyr like leaves on the wind.

Even as he brought the hammer around, he could feel the vibrations fade and the full weight of the hammer return. But the communion with Daomur, that intimate joining, revealed all of Finngyr's suppressed emotions and brought them bubbling to the surface.

Not just the emotions his race was taught to keep buried deep within and out of the public eye, but the deeper personal emotions of discovering a stonechosen and then letting him escape. Being outsmarted by Magister Obudar back in the Cradle of the Gods. The humiliation of returning to Daomount empty-handed. The looks from the other denizens of the summit at his failure. And finally, the disrespect these two mockeries of his order had shown him. He felt the emotions wash over him in waves. He let them all go, let them pour forth and be purged in Daomur's light.

Finngyr rushed into the oncoming orcs with abandon.

/\

Kjar circled high above the battle. The coppery smell of blood wafted up with the cries of the dying orcs. His original intentions were to stay here and see how this fight played out. The number of orcs was well past ten, fifty more like. All he had to do was wait it out and watch Finngyr fall and he could return to Daomount to give his report, having barely escaped, of course.

But, no sooner had Finngyr dispatched three orcs with one blow than he charged into another group, even larger, and begin laying waste to them. Every swing of his hammer brought death. No more javelins came Kjar's way and even the orcs who'd just made purchase on the ledge ignored Horth and moved to engage Finngyr. It made no sense. Why attack the obviously more dangerous opponent? Were the orcs in such a hurry to die? At first, Kjar could not believe his luck, but orcs kept falling and Finngyr showed no signs of tiring.

If the orcs would have just rushed him en masse, they could have brought him down by sheer numbers, but they seemed to want to fight in either single combat or in numbers no greater than two or three.

Horth was holding his own against the two orcs he now fought, he had slain two others, but he was nothing compared to Finngyr. Kjar knew Finngyr was good in battle, but this was beyond anything he had seen. Was this the battle prowess of all veteran knights of the Temple of Justice in Daomount? Kjar wondered how there were any Nordlah Barbarians left on the plains.

In the southern lands of the empire, a Knight of Daomur needed to be quick and strike fast. They spent their time moving through the forbidden cities, dealing with the multitudes of goblins that infested them. The handful of human settlements near his southern city of Orehome where all docile. Were the barbarians as fierce as this knight? What had he gotten himself into? Kjar had traveled north through the underways as a merchant's guard, after a poor decision involving a wealthy noble and the noble's only daughter. He joined the Temple of Justice in Daomount only because it was the least selective of the orders and in need of initiates. He thought himself a cunning opponent and even sometimes felt the power of Daomur emanating from his hammer. But even from this distance, he could feel his god in Finngyr, lending his might to the knight.

In that moment, Kjar's outlook on Finngyr changed. Horth had let him in on his secret and promised to give him a cut of the take if he helped Horth make sure Finngyr failed in this mission to find the lost knight and most importantly, suffered the wrath of Magister Dagbar. Horth had not shared who their benefactor was, but it didn't take a scholar to know the coin came from a merchant house who employed a certain knight's father.

Kjar was not as devoted as most, but he considered himself a pragmatic dwarf and knew which way the wind blew. He could now see his best chance of survival involved staying on the good side of the knight below him, who was cutting his way through orcs like the hand of Daomur himself. To do that, he needed to follow orders.

He scanned the battle.

The red-hued sun sat fat on the horizon, splashing the last of its light across the outcropping and the small plateau where the battle still waged. It took him a moment, but he spotted the orc shaman standing on a spur jutting out a little above the battle. Gesturing wildly, it shook its spear to the sky and pointed down at the battle.

Were all the creatures mad?
Kjar banked his mount and dove towards the shaman.

/\

Finngyr didn't know if it had been minutes or hours. Each grey skin he slew was replaced by another. He fought to hold onto his hammer, blood from the numerous wounds he had taken ran down his arms and threatened to loosen his grip. He could not afford to lose the weapon, having thrown both his axes already. They were somewhere on the plateau, lodged in orc skulls. If he survived much longer, he would lose the light and then the battle. He could already see the white reflection of eyeshine, as the orcs adjusted to the darkening sky.

It was only when the ecstasy of Daomur began to wane that he remembered Knight Kjar and the shaman. What was the dwarf waiting for? As if in answer, a large shadow swooped down and past him. Finngyr took a glancing blow to the back and shoulder, rolling forward with the momentum.

He came up, bringing his hammer over and into a downward stroke that crushed both an orc and the pitiful attempt it made at blocking with its axe. Finngyr stumbled forward with the remaining momentum and caught his balance just in time to block a spear thrust from a new opponent.

He roared his defiance back at the screaming orcs, but still they came. Finngyr spit blood into the face of the spear-wielding orc as he spun past him and clipped the back of its head with the butt of his hammer. He sensed, more than saw, movement on his left and spun to strike.

Horth raised a bloodied hand. "Knight Justice, stay your hand!"

Finngyr looked left and right for the next attack, but none came. The orcs were fleeing. Their howls and yells still filled the darkening sky, but they were cries of anguish instead of rage. Above them, Finngyr could just make out Kjar's griffon holding the remains of the orc shaman, its rear leonine paws relentlessly rending what remained of the shaman.

Finngyr felt the last of his strength leave with the fleeing orcs and he fell to one knee, the haft of his hammer all that kept him from falling completely. He looked to Horth, who was as bloodied and stood bent, hammer resting across his knees as he fought for breath and watched the retreating orcs. "I do not understand; we were almost beaten."

Finngyr pointed towards Kjar, who had already landed a short distance away. "The shaman," was all he managed to say before blackness began closing in on the edges of his vision. He tried to shake it off. He tried to rise and slipped in blood and something else, stumbling to the side and landing hard.

From the edges of his failing vision he could see Horth walking towards him, hammer in hand. Then there were two of him. Finngyr fought to clear his vision.

A wing buffeted Finngyr as Kjar's griffon appeared between the two knights. Blackness wash over Finngyr, threatening to pull him under and then Kjar was at his side.

"I am here, Knight Justice Finngyr. Here, your hammer. Take it. Say the words with me. Knight Justice, focus. Say the words. Daomur is my strength..."

"His might passes through me."

"His light shines from me."

"I am but his vessel."

"He fills me so I may continue to serve."

As Finngyr repeated the chant with Kjar, he felt the thrum in his hands as Daomur's healing flowed into him, strengthening him. His skin itched and grew tight as his flesh knitted back together.

Finngyr's vision cleared. Kjar knelt next to him praying. A short distance away, Horth lay on the ground rubbing his head and glaring at Kjar.

Kjar opened his eyes and glanced between the two knights. He shrugged. "My apologies, Knight Horth. I still have not yet learned to handle my griffon, eh? I was almost too late. Forgive me, Knight Justice Finngyr."

Finngyr nodded at Kjar's words and with the help of the younger knight, stood up. He shouldered his hammer and approached Horth, who had not healed himself yet. Finngyr extended a hand to him.

"Well?"

Horth stared hard at Finngyr. He swallowed. "Well what, Knight Justice Finngyr?"

"You still owe me a bow," Finngyr said.

12

Awake in Craluk's Village

HILE awoke and tried to sit up. At first, his body didn't respond. His eyes watered and he blinked to clear them. A light blanket covered him, tucked in at the sides. The restrictive blanket and lack of movement made it difficult, but with effort, he freed a hand and reached up to clear the grit that crusted his lids.

Cuz licked his face. Both Valehounds were resting on either side of him. They nudged his hand as he made to wipe away the drool, each fighting over who would receive the first scratch.

"Hello, you two." Without realizing it, his thoughts touched theirs. Their feelings of concern washed over him. He could sense they were relaxed and not on guard. Cuz was a little hungry. Wherever he was, he was safe for the moment.

Even though it was dark, his enhanced vision took in what little light there was and allowed him to see clearly. He was inside a small, thatched hut. He could hear voices coming from outside, many of them. There was also music. It sounded like some kind of celebration. Even though he didn't recognize the song and the high twangs of the musical instruments were foreign to him, images of Last Hamlet and his clansmen filled his mind and it took a moment to shake the feeling he was home. Where the memory had been, a hollow feeling of loss remained.

He tried to get up. His legs resisted the unfamiliar movement. He must have been asleep for quite a while this time. The amount of time that passed in the dreaming was not always the same as in Allwyn. He was discovering that sometimes what felt like weeks in the dreaming, had only been a day on Allwyn or vice versa.

The thatching of the hut was covered in patches of moss and swarmed with all kinds of flying insects. So, they obviously hadn't traveled too far from the Ghost Fens.

His companion's possessions were located next to nearby bedrolls. Gaidel's things were lined up neatly to one side near Two Elks'. Riff's were scattered off to the other side of the hut and taking up more room than was necessary.

Ghile tried to swallow, but his mouth was so dry. He finally forced one that pained his throat. If there was some sort of celebration, then there would also be food and drink. Both appealed to him right now. Not to mention, his companions were probably there. Though he had mixed feelings on sharing what he had learned and what he was going to have to tell them, he was of a single mind when it came to filling his belly.

He took the time to gather his belongings, finding them stacked neatly along one wall. He left his spear, but hung the fang blade from his belt.

Ast and Cuz made to come with him, but he mentally commanded them to stay. After scratching and petting each of them, they happily obliged, laying back down and resting their heads on their paws. He pushed back the heavy blanket covering the entryway and stepped out of the hut.

The small village was not so much on the edge of the Ghost Fens, as hanging over it. He made his way along the well-lit walkway, tentative at first, as he tested some of the more questionable looking boards.

He followed the music and voices. The talk was interspersed with laughter. He found himself smiling as he moved towards the revelers, the merriment infectious.

When the villagers on the edges of the celebration saw him, some stopped to point, others smiled and clapped. Why were they all covered in mud? They were all human, but they were definitely shorter than the people of the Cradle, if not wider. They seemed comfortable enough with his presence and though most were armed, they did not appear threatening.

Ghile found Riff seated between two mud-covered girls. They seemed enraptured with his every word as he waved his hands, in the middle of one of his tales. He stopped when he noticed Ghile.

"Well, look who is back among the living," Riff said.

From across the fire, Gaidel rose.

Ghile smiled and waved to her. He could see Two Elks sat cross-legged next to where she had been, accepting a bowl of food from a nearby villager. Ghile could see a number of bowls and gourds scattered amongst them.

"Hi, Gaidel. Might I have some—"

Ghile didn't know if it was the sound of the slap, or his exclamation at the blinding pain on the side of his face that caused everyone around them to go silent. Even the musicians stopped playing.

"What was that for?" Ghile demanded, rubbing his cheek. He jerked his arms up defensively, when it looked like she might strike him again.

Gaidel pushed past him and stormed off in the direction he had come from.

What in the name of the Devourer was going on? Ghile thought.

Ghile looked to Two Elks and Riff for some sort of explanation. Two Elks watched with an amused expression as he continued to sip from his bowl.

Riff guffawed. "Welcome back, Sheepherder."

Λ

"I said I was sorry, Gaidel. How many more times must I say it?"

They were all back in the hut. Two Elks had been thoughtful enough to bring food and drink with him and offer it to Ghile, but Ghile hadn't had an opportunity to try any of it.

"What you did was foolish and reckless," Gaidel shouted at him. "How are we to protect you, if you throw yourself into danger at the slightest provocation, using powers you don't even know how to control?"

Ghile blinked. "I've already explained I was trying to help fight off the swamp cats. Did you really expect me to stand idly by, while the rest of you risked your lives? How was I supposed to know Riff was going to strike the one cat I tried to mind control?" he said.

"Sorry about that," Riff said.

Gaidel glared down at Riff, who shrugged innocently.

At least Riff was kind enough to apologize, Ghile thought. Gaidel was just being unreasonable. Her anger was like a spring storm in the Cradle, whipping him relentlessly.

"Listen, I'm sorry alright? I shouldn't have tried to use the powers before being taught how," Ghile said. "I'll be more careful next time."

"Sorry? Careful? Next time?" Ghile could see Gaidel wanted to say more, but was too angry to find words. He had never seen her this angry. He would rather face the swamp cats again, than endure this tongue lashing. She reminded him of his Aunt Jilla when she had a go at his uncle.

"So this is funny to you, is it?" Gaidel said.

Uh-oh. Ghile raised his hands, shaking them furiously. "No, no, no, I was just—"

"That enough, Daughter Gaidel," Two Elks said.

"I don't know," Riff said. "I thought she was just starting to get warmed up."

Both Ghile and Gaidel stared daggers at the sorcerer.

Two Elks continued. "He learn from mistake. He say this many times. He stonechosen. Must fight."

"It is our responsibility to—" Gaidel began.

Two Elks raised a hand. "It shieldwarden res-pon-sibility protect druid. This mean I protect you from all? Even protect you from you?"

This blunt statement brought Gaidel up short. Even the way Two Elks had stumbled over the word 'responsibility' didn't seem to have lessened the word's impact.

Gaidel looked ready to start again when Riff cleared his throat. "Look, Gaidel, I was scared we might have lost him, too."

She blinked and looked between them all. Whatever anger was still left in her visibly dissipated. She sighed and sat down next to Two Elks. "I wasn't scared," she all but whispered.

Ghile watched her tentatively. He wasn't sure it was safe to start eating yet. The sound of his stomach growling echoed in the uncomfortable silence.

Two Elks motioned toward the food. "Eat."

Ghile dove in with vigor. It was spicier than he was used to and he drained his drinking cup quickly.

"So, you have been training to use your new powers?" Riff said.

Ghile nodded and answered between mouthfuls. Ast and Cuz followed his hands, watching every bite as if the next handful was sure to be for them. "Yes. The goblin, the one from the Horn. It, well I think it's the same one, anyway – it's in the dreaming now, teaching me."

"Awkward," Riff said. "Not at all put out that you killed it, then?"

Ghile smirked, but both Two Elks' and Gaidel's faces remained impassive. They seemed more intent on Ghile's words.

"No, Muk, its name is Muk, doesn't seem to mind. That's why I wonder if it's really the same goblin, or just the soulstone's version of him. It's hard to explain. Muk speaks about a dream teacher when he was alive. The one that taught him. It reminded me of how Adon was there to teach me. Adon is my dream teacher. Well, my first one, at least. Now I have two."

Ghile filled his cup with more water and continued.

"I've been training to sense animals. I can look through their eyes now, inhabit their thoughts, control them even. I can use my force shield through them. Muk also taught me how to… well, I guess you would best describe it as 'borrow' their abilities for a short time. Though, it's dangerous for them if they are small creatures." Ghile's eyes brightened. "We found this stag in the forest. It was so strong looking." Ghile held his hands before him. "Its chest was so thick. Anyway, it began to run and I reached out and could feel its strength filling me. The next thing I knew, I was running along with it and I was keeping up, leaping over the fallen trees, running as fast as it was. It was incredible."

The others were staring, Riff smiling at him. Gaidel's expression more thoughtful. He realized he had probably just shared more about the dreaming with them than he ever had before.

He suddenly felt self-conscious. "Anyway…"

"Well, while you were in dreamland, learning to be one with the animals, Gaidel and I were here in the real world, saving the day," Riff said.

Ghile finished eating, as Riff recounted how he and Gaidel had saved the young boy, Ollin from whatever had infected him. The celebration Ghile had awoken to was for them.

"Craluk thankful for saving his son," Two Elks said. "He offered a guide. What is wrong?"

Ghile was shaking his head. "No, we must go straight to the Fallen City," Ghile said.

"What?" Gaidel and Riff said in unison.

"No, Ghile. We're supposed to find this Dagbar, Master Almoriz said—" Riff began.

"I know what Master Almoriz said, but this Dagbar is not to be trusted."

"Says who?" Riff asked, his voice rising.

"I… it's…" Ghile hadn't told them about Akira's appearance in the dreaming. He'd confided in Master Almoriz back in the ruins about her and her calling him to the Fallen City, but he never told them it was Akira who told him about the others and that she was stonechosen like him. Now was as good a time as any, he supposed.

He told them of Akira's visits to the dreaming and what she had shared with him about Dagbar. He left out how much his heart raced each time he saw her, as he recounted his story.

"Ghile, she is stonechosen," Gaidel stated simply when he finished.

"So?" Ghile said.

"So, you know what must happen when we find her," Gaidel said carefully.

Ghile did know. He had been pushing the thought back to the farthest corners of his mind. Yes, he knew. One of them would have to die. Different thoughts rushed about inside his head, each fighting with the other for attention.

"I know," Ghile said finally. "But, she said she was asleep and couldn't wake up. She said her brother was with her. They were in the mists. There were other things in the mists, too, things she was afraid of."

"I don't see how she or her brother are going to be happy to see you, Ghile. It might be a trap," Riff said.

"She said Dagbar was a dwarf and he was going to turn me over to the cullers. I don't believe it's a trap, Riff. I think she is telling the truth."

"Somehow I don't think she has your best interests at heart, Ghile."

"And you do?" Ghile all but shouted.

When he saw the pained look on Riff's face, he immediately wished he could take it back. Instead, he just stared.

"Ghile, she is stonechosen," Gaidel said again, as if everything that needed to be said was summed up in that one point.

Ghile knew both Riff and Gaidel were right. Akira was stonechosen. When they did finally meet, Ghile would feel the pull of her soulstone. Not the muted pull in the dreaming, but the same feeling he had when he first encountered Muk in the cave on the Horn.

How strong that desire had been. Ghile had never wanted anything more in his entire life. The thought had been all encompassing. Even though he knew the pain that would follow, had experienced it already, he knew he would feel the same when he found Akira.

Ghile stared down at his hands, saying nothing. He could feel the others watching him. He didn't know what to say. How had his life gotten so complicated?

He thought of his family back in the Cradle. Where were his parents now? They would know what to do. Was Tia all right? He wondered if his kin from Last Hamlet was still hiding in the ruins at the base of the Horn, or if they had returned to what was left of their homes and began to rebuild? Were Uncle Toren and his father even now making plans to avenge Last Hamlet? If so, isn't that where he should be? Ghile felt a hand on his. Gaidel was beside him.

"I'm sorry I struck you," she said.

Ghile nodded. "It's alright."

"Much to think on," Two Elks said. "I take watch." With that, Two Elks left the hut.

Riff patted Ghile on the shoulder before he started halfheartedly rolling out his bedroll. He wasn't even halfway down before he declared he must have forgotten something at the celebration and wondered out loud if one of the girls at the celebration might have seen it. He excused himself to find out.

Gaidel said nothing else and went to lie on her bedroll, her back to Ghile. He sat there, absently petting Ast and Cuz, lost in his thoughts.

Two Elks sat in the shadows of one of the trees whose limbs hung limp, as if it was weeping into the black water. He had put out the fires in the gourds near their hut. He didn't like them. They affected his night vision while making him too easy to be seen. He had found a place which allowed him to watch the hut, without being spotted by anyone who approached.

He understood why the villagers needed the lights, but they were caught between a wolf and a charging tusker. The very fires which protected them from the dead ones, would eventually attract the eyes of the dwarves. Maybe even the ones Two Elks was sure now hunted Ghile.

Two Elks looked up through the branches. There were too many nearby lights to see the stars clearly, let alone something flying through the night sky.

If the dwarf had not found them yet, then he had gone for reinforcements. Their descent from the Cradle had been too slow for them to be far ahead now. Two Elks had fought enough dwarves in his life to know the culler would not give up the hunt. Once on the trail, dwarves were tenacious.

They had made it this far, they would make it to this Dagbar's settlement. Probably to find the culler waiting. If not there, then he would be waiting at the ancient city. Two Elks brought his hand to his heart and then his lips at the thought of the ancient city. A gesture his people used, to remind themselves they followed the way of their ancestors in word and deed.

Two Elks knew about the ancient cities of their ancestors. They were sacred places to his people. The dwarves fought to keep his people out of the three cities within the plains, but his people always fought through. It was outside one of those cities that Two Elks was bonded to the little daughter.

He missed his chance to become a seeker and enter the city during that ceremony, a great honor. It looked like he would have another chance to enter a sacred city soon. They were dangerous places, even without the golem guardians the dwarves placed around them. He prayed to the ancestors that he met and dealt with the culler before they reached this Fallen City.

But when they did encounter the culler again, which Two Elks felt certain they would, they would need to be ready. He would continue to work with Ghile. The boy was doing well in their training sessions. Two Elks would never use as small a weapon as Ghile's blade, let alone a weapon that was dwarf made. But, Ghile was not large enough to use a man's weapon, like the great axe, with any skill.

The real issue for Two Elks was Riff. His magic was useful, but dangerous. He did not know how to fight as a member of a warband. Two Elks' people took many seasons to hone the skills needed, time this group did not have.

He thought again about putting the sorcerer in his place, but there was no time for Riff's wounded pride to heal. Besides, if Daughter Gaidel was to learn to be a leader, she would have to learn to handle people like the sorcerer. Two Elks would not admit it, but he found more than a little amusement from watching the two argue. He suspected there was more there than either the little daughter or the sorcerer knew. He would give Daughter Gaidel more time to establish her position before stepping in.

Two Elks sat silently in the darkness, considering many things, when he saw young Ghile emerge from the hut. Ghile stood there looking about for only a moment before spotting Two Elks and heading his way.

Two Elks looked around him to see if some stray light had given away his position.

Ghile moved some limbs aside. "My turn to take watch, I think?" He opened his palms and bowed his head.

Two Elks nodded, still a little bothered he had been spotted so easily.

He was not tired, so he motioned for Ghile to sit. The celebration had ended, villagers drifted off to their huts. Two Elks could see a few guards on other platforms, staring off into the darkness.

With the celebrations over, the sounds of the night slipped in to fill the void. Frogs and crickets competed with their calls. Something small splashed in the waters beneath them. Two Elks watched the slow moving ripples through the gaps in the wood.

He knew the boy wanted to talk. Ghile would open his mouth to say something and then stop, unsure of himself. Two Elks couldn't blame him, though he wondered why Ghile didn't speak with Riff. The two seemed close, like oath brothers, always laughing together like children. The boy's people were so protected from things in their valley home, under the watchful eyes of their dwarven masters. They were in no hurry to grow up, they didn't have to. Even their manhood tests, which was where Two Elks had first seen Ghile, happened late in life. Two Elks people blooded their boys after their tenth winter. It did not surprise him Mother Brambles sent them along to see to this 'Gwa A'Chook' Stonechosen.

"Dwarf's pet?" Ghile said.

His words shook Two Elks from his thoughts.

"What?"

"Dwarf's pet. You said dwarf's pet."

Two Elks had spoken aloud, but unconsciously and in his native tongue. Could it be?

"Ghile Stonechosen, can you speak the true language?"

"What language do you mean?" Ghile answered him in perfect Nordinian.

"Do not mock me, Ghile Stonechosen. The language you are speaking right now. The language of my people, the True Language. Where did you learn it?"

Ghile stared at Two Elks for a moment before raising his palms and bowing his head again. He weighed each of his words carefully before responding. "I think it's another gift of the soulstones, Two Elks. I hear your language, beneath words that I understand. When I answer you, I am speaking my language, but I can hear the words coming out as your language."

Two Elks nodded and made a warding gesture over his heart. "Truly, the Battle God has gifted you."

"Haurtu, you mean?"

Two Elks made the same warding gesture over his heart. "You are new to the True Language, Ghile Stonechosen, so I forgive your ignorance and take no insult from it. Your honor is clean. But, do not speak the Battle God's name in the true language. It is only ever said in ceremony or as a war cry for battle. Words hold power and names most of all."

Ghile swallowed and nodded. "I did not mean to offend, Two Elks. Why do you refer to Har…him as the Battle God? I have heard him called the Hungerer and even the God of Learning and Wisdom, but this is the first time as the Battle God."

Two Elks sat there and nodded as Ghile spoke. He had heard Ghile's people speak of the Battle God by other names and knew they feared him. He had to admit it felt good to be able to speak in his own tongue. There was much the boy needed to know and now Two Elks would be able to tell him.

"The tongue you are hearing is called Nordinian by outsiders, and the True Language by my people because it is the language of our ancestors. The tongue your people speak is Dwarvish."

Ghile stared at him. "It is? I didn't know that. I'm not sure how I feel about that."

It was difficult for Two Elks to read the boy's features there in the dark beneath the weeping tree, but it appeared Ghile was tasting his words for the first time.

"The past is in the past, Ghile Stonechosen. Do not dwell on such things. The Battle God called our ancestors to war against the other races. We are still at war. My people do not forget and fight on to this day."

Two Elks found himself using his hands to add emphasis to his words, in the way of his people. He didn't know if the boy would understand the additional meaning, but he slipped into the gestures naturally.

"Your people have forgotten, Ghile Stonechosen. You are like pets, staying where you are put and making gifts for your new masters."

Even in the darkness, Two Elks could see his words offended the boy. Good, he should be offended. In his culture, one might seek blood debt for such an insult. Two Elks knew enough about the Cradler's now to know no such challenge was coming, so he continued.

"You are Stonechosen now, you walk a different path." Two Elks reached out and patted him on the shoulder to show his approval. "The wise women of my people, those who have entered the age of the crone, like your Mother Brambles, know when the time of the seeking has come and bring our people together outside the sacred cities. There we compete for the right to be seekers and enter and search for the soulstones."

Ghile recalled Master Almoriz telling him of the Nordlah Barbarians and how it was a great honor to seek the soulstones. "Wait, the druids know when the soulstones will appear?"

"It is known only the oldest druids, those who sing long, know when the time of the seeking has come. Only they can call the tribes together and keep the peace between them during the gatherings."

"What happens when one of your people finds a soulstone?"

The boy was leaning forward now, hanging on his words. Two Elks liked this boy. It saddened him what he was about to tell him, but the boy needed to know what his fate could be.

"According to our chanters, few ever return. The time of seeking is rare. This was the only one in my, or my father's, or his father's, lifetime. It is known if more than one seeker emerges, they must battle until only one remains. Then that one will be Battle Lord and lead all the tribes against the dwarves."

"There was a seeking this past season?" Ghile said. "Did one of your people find a soulstone?"

"I do not know, Ghile Stonechosen. I was called to be a Shieldwarden and left my people. But…"

"But?" Ghile said.

"But, if there is a Battle Lord, they will seek you out and kill you," Two Elks said matter of factly.

The boy looked down. "Thanks for the vote of confidence, Two Elks."

"It is not the way of my people to twist words. Only the best of my people are chosen to be seekers. It is done so that if they become Stonechosen, they will be worthy to be Battle Lord and lead the tribes. You are a young warrior. Maybe with time, I could teach you. But I do not think we will have that time. We may be able to protect you long enough to reach the sacred city. You may find another soulstone and grow in power. But, if a Battle Lord has emerged from the plains, they will find you and you will die."

"Then why are you even here?" The boy's voice was strained. Two Elks could hear the fear and anger mixed behind the words.

"I am here, Ghile Stonechosen, because it is my duty. I was chosen to be a Shieldwarden to a Redwood Druid. The first of my people to ever be bonded to one of your druids. I was to be a seeker, but I was chosen by Mother Brambles and so I went. It was my duty."

"Mother Brambles? She was in the Nordlah plains? Why would—"

"The past is in the past, Ghile Stonechosen. For whatever reason, you are now stonechosen. It is your duty to seek other soulstones, to grow and learn. To find other stonechosen and defeat them," Two Elks said.

"What if I choose not to? What if I don't want to seek out other stonechosen or fulfill this stupid prophecy? I left the Cradle because my family was in danger if I stayed. There is nothing stopping me from leaving right now and going wherever I want to. Who would stop me? Would you stop me, Two Elks? You and Gaidel? Would Riff?"

The question hung there between them. Ghile strained with the effort of getting the words out and not allowing all the emotion he seemed to barely have in check from pouring out with them.

Two Elks took no insult from his words. The boy was afraid. It was understandable for a Cradler. "It is during our tenth winter that we take our manhood tests. The All Mother tests my people most heavily in winter. She sends winds and snows to cull the old and weak."

"Answer me!" Ghile said.

Two Elks held up a hand and when he spoke, it was with an inner calm his people held when they spoke of important things. "I am answering you, Stonechosen. Will you listen to my words?"

Ghile began to answer and then stopped. He finally nodded.

"Our tests not only require us to evade those who hunt us, we must also hunt. We must bring food back to our people to show we are not only strong warriors, but also able to provide for the tribe. During my test, I was blessed by the All Mother and found fresh tracks. Elk are prized by my people, second only to the great tuskers. I had found two, two young bucks, I discovered later. It was near a stream that I finally caught up with them."

"I chose the one I would take and closed the distance as they drank from a break in the ice. Again, the All Mother blessed me with favorable winds and none of my tribe nearby. It was a clean kill and a feat which normally takes many hunters. I would bring honor to my family with the kill.

"But, the other elk did something most unexpected. It did not flee when I struck the first one down. It did at first, startled by my attack, but then it turned and stood its ground. It refused to leave. It is not my people's way to take more from the All Mother than we need. I tried scaring it away, but it refused to go. Others of my tribe found me then, standing over my kill and screaming at an elk to leave."

"What... what did you do?" There was no more anger in Ghile's words.

Two Elks pulled his furs to the side, showing a long, deep scar running from his chest down along his side. He couldn't help but smile. "I was honor bound to only take what I needed and that elk was honor bound to stay by its friend and deny me my prize. I have no better words for it. I would not kill it even though it did its best to kill me. The other hunters intervened on my behalf once I fell and did not get back up. They killed the other elk to protect me and returned me to the tribe."

"But they caught you. Did that mean you didn't pass your test?" Ghile said.

"No, Ghile Stonechosen. I passed the tests. You see, none of the hunters would claim having taken me." Two Elks could still see the pride on the faces of those men as they stood over him. "The druids will tell you balance above all things, but I think they are wrong. I think honor, doing what is right because it is right, is most important. You will do what you must, because it is the right thing to do. It is what you must do, as will I. I protect Daughter Gaidel and will do as she asks of me if it is within my ability and will not bring her to harm."

Ghile didn't seem to be listening to those last words. "Is that how you got your name... Two Elks?"

Two Elks nodded. "Yes, my man's name."

Ghile leaned back and the two of them stared into the night. After a time, Two Elks felt sleep calling and left Ghile beneath the weeping tree.

He wasn't sure, but as he left he thought he heard the boy whisper, "Duty above all things."

13

Gone

"THEY'RE gone!" Riff said.

He pushed his way past the villagers who crowded around Gaidel. The news traveled quickly that morning and there had been a steady stream of villagers, both curious and concerned. At Riff's arrival, Gaidel broke off her conversation with Craluk, the village leader.

"What do you mean they're gone?" she said.

"Which word confuses you?" Riff answered in an irritated tone.

His chest was rising and falling, hair damp against his head. He must have run through the entire village. The sun was barely above the green boughs of the Deepwood, but the morning mists had long burned away and the day promised to be warm.

Riff slapped at one of the many insects trying to land on his face. He still refused to use the protective mud. The man was so stubborn.

She didn't answer him right away, fighting down the first response that sprang to her lips. It would have been too easy to direct her frustrations at Riff. After his idea of combining his powers to free the boy, Ollin, from whatever strange magic had possessed him and simultaneously adding her powers to heal him, Gaidel thought Riff was finally taking his role in their group seriously. But, he went right back to carousing with any girl who raised an eyebrow his way, even if she was swathed in mud. Now he seemed back to his old self and was taking any opportunity to annoy her.

The thought of how she had gone from a simple tavern girl in Redwood Village to a druid guarding one of the stonechosen still staggered her. A stonechosen who had now disappeared.

She contented herself with staring daggers at Riff. It would have to do. It would not do to let him get under her skin at this moment. She turned her attention back to Craluk. More of the villagers appeared, the throng growing around them.

"Craluk are you sure no one saw Ghile or the hounds this morning?" Gaidel asked again. "It is still early. Maybe someone who stayed awake late into the evening who is not yet awake?"

Gaidel tried to get an idea of how many villagers gathered around them. It was difficult to do, since she could barely see over their heads. Though the numbers had increased, she was sure there were still more at the celebrations last night than were here now. Someone had to have seen him.

How could Ghile leave in the middle of the night with those hounds and not be seen? The three had been in the hut when she fell asleep. Two Elks said Ghile came out to take watch and that was the last anyone had seen of him. It was not until Riff returned to the hut in the early dawn that Ghile's absence was discovered. She spared a sidelong glance at the sorcerer. She didn't want to show the discord in their group to the entire village, but she would box his ears if he complained of being tired.

"Ain't none seen the boy fer certain, Daughter Gaidel," Craluk said. He made a few intricate motions with his hands and a couple of the nearby men pushed their way out through the crowd. "But we look again since you is ask'n."

"There is no point, I've already looked. aThey're gone," Riff said.

She had been so angry with Ghile when he finally woke from the dreaming. Now, not even a day later, he was missing. She was doing a fine job of protecting him. What had happened to him? It couldn't be the dwarves. They were never subtle in their actions. If cullers had found them, they would have attacked the village in force. The Dead Ones?

"Craluk, when the Dead Ones come, do they take some and leave others? Could they have taken Ghile?" she asked.

Craluk was shaking his head before she finished. "Ain't like um, Daughter Gaidel. They go about in packs. Don't be misunderstand'n, they can be right sneaky, but only until they attack. They be right fearful of fire and we ain't ever had any come into the village proper. If'n it was them, they would have tried taken the lot of ya and killed dem hounds. Ain't never heard of dem taken no critters."

"Gaidel, his bedroll and pack are missing. Ghile left, he wasn't taken," Riff said.

"Are you sure?" Their hut had slowly filled with gifts left in the doorway by villagers, thankful for what they had done for young Ollin. It started with food, but had progressed to bowls, blankets and carved wooden figurines, as if each gift was trying to outdo the one before. There had even been some metal items, but those quickly disappeared into one of Riff's many pouches. There was more than they could ever carry. The hut was so cluttered, she hadn't even noticed.

A space cleared next to them as Two Elks, head and shoulders taller than the rest, stalked in with a purposeful gait. "Found tracks, Little Daughter."

Two Elks led them over the final bridge, the vines complaining loudly against the weight as everyone followed behind him. No sooner had they cleared the bridge's securing posts, Two Elks veered off the trail and through waist-high reeds. The barbarian began pointing at various broken or bent stalks and then stopped to kneel down.

Gaidel knelt down next to him, the others crowding around and looking to where he pointed. She could see the depression he was pointing at, but how he knew it was Ghile, she had no idea.

"This one, Ghile," Two Elks said, pointing to a nearby track. He motioned a short distance away, "There, one of his hounds."

"Him be a'sneak'n." Lotte's grinning face appeared next to Two Elks; he too, was studying the track intently.

"Lookee, hea. He not wearing boots and he was all up on his ball n' toes," Lotte said.

Two Elks nodded and gave the young villager an appraising stare.

"That doesn't make any sense," Gaidel said.

Lotte jumped up and moved deeper into the reeds, following the trail.

"He da best tracker in da village," Craluk said, with more than a little pride in his deep voice.

"It doesn't make any sense," Gaidel repeated.

"Sure it does," Riff said. "He's set off on his own."

Gaidel shook her head. Why would Ghile sneak off in the middle of the night? He didn't have any supplies other than the meager contents of his pack. Was he even able to hunt or forage for his own food? Where was he headed?

A short distance away, Lotte called, "He put on his boots over hea and started a runnin'."

Craluk shook his head. "One of da men woulda seen a torch a bobbin' through dem trees."

Two Elks grunted. Gaidel looked to Two Elks and knew what he was thinking. Ghile didn't need a torch to see at night.

The truth settled into Gaidel's gut and lay there like a stone. Ghile had left them. After everything they had been through to get this far. Gaidel could see Mother Bramble's disapproving face if she returned, having lost the young stonechosen.

"Can we catch him?" she asked Two Elks.

"Why should we, Gaidel? He obviously doesn't want our help," Riff said.

He stood a short distance away from her, Craluk and Two Elks. The villagers who had followed them waited on the bridge and trail, watching.

Riff motioned towards them. "He wants to run off and get himself killed, fine by me. Craluk has offered us a place here."

At that, the leader quickly smiled and nodded his agreement. "Y'all would be most welcome."

"They need help with these dead ones. They have lost others from their village. We could help turn them human again. At least we could be helping someone who *wanted* our help," Riff said.

The last sentence was spoken with more than a little venom. Gaidel realized she wasn't the only one hurt by Ghile's actions. She knew Riff had no real interest in this village or its problems. He preferred soft beds and a giggling girl on his knee, one not covered in mud. For some reason, the image that brought to mind bothered her. The sorcerer truly was insufferable. She stood up and wiped nonexistent wrinkles from the folds of her robes. "Thank you, Craluk. Your offer is most kind. But, we must find Ghile," she said.

"You know where he's headed, don't you?" Riff said.

"Riff, that is enough." She gave him a dangerous look. They had not been overly forthcoming with Craluk and the others for fear of their reaction. It would be difficult to explain why Ghile journeyed towards the Fallen City and why a sorcerer, a druid and her shieldwarden chased after him.

Riff looked ready to say more, but Two Elks chose that time to stand up and give him a look that left little doubt what would happen if he did.

Riff threw his hands in the air. "Fine! I figured as much. I'll go get my stuff. I at least owe it to Master Ecrec to recover the idiot's body." He stomped off through the reeds, waving away the villagers as they approached to ask him questions.

Craluk scratched his head. "Maybe the boy still a little sick in da head, no? He head'n straight inta the Deepwood. Elves shoa to get im, ifn the dead ones don't."

"We need to find him, Craluk. He is... important," Gaidel said.

"Shoa, Daughter Gaidel. I promised ya a guide. Lotte will go with ya. I reckon you can catch up with him a'fore too long."

"No, I couldn't ask you to risk yourselves—"

"I owe ya, fer whatcha done did fer me boy. It is done." With that, Craluk whistled for Lotte and waved him back.

Gaidel relented with a sigh. "We would be honored to have him. Thank you, Craluk."

He nodded and headed back into the village. Lotte ran past them, his smile taking up most of his face.

Gaidel turned to follow, when she felt a hand on her shoulder.

"There something I must tell you, Little Daughter," Two Elks said.

14

Into the Deepwood

HILE leaped the wide forested ravine, his necklace of worg fangs rising from his chest to hang suspended before his eyes. He cleared the other side with room to spare. He would make Two Elks proud. He would make them all proud.

He landed, using his force shield to slow his descent. The widening field flattened a large area around him. He dismissed the mental image with hardly a thought and resumed running before the first plant rose behind him.

He wondered how far the ravine stretched through the wood? He had been running nonstop since leaving the village. The Valehounds were having a hard enough time keeping up with him, without an obstacle like a ravine adding to it. He sent his mind probing out in search of Ast and Cuz. He kept his focus on the forest falling away before him, on the steady rise and fall of his chest. It wouldn't do to concentrate fully on finding them and run headlong into a tree. Not at this pace.

His thoughts were like tendrils, reaching, searching for life. He sensed the birds and other forest denizens. The wood was filled with them.

A furry carcass hung from his belt and slapped against his thigh in rhythm with his long strides. An animal he had never seen before, it resembled a ferret, but thicker, with red and grey stripes and a long muzzle.

He had barely slowed to scoop it up after using the power to kill it. He'd spotted it as it made a dash from cover at his approach. He reached out and mind touched it, consuming it as quickly and painlessly as possible. For a short time afterwards, his sense of smell was heightened, a gift from the creature. It would provide him with dinner tonight. A part of him felt guilty, but he had to eat.

He finally touched the minds of the two Valehounds. Ast was off to his left, Cuz to the right, guarding his flank. They were a good distance away and neither were struggling through the ravine. He could feel their exhilaration as they ran along, trying to keep up with him. He could smell the scents of the forest through their minds. He still marveled at the myriad of smells that existed in their world. The mind touch reminded him he was not alone. He would need to collect something for dinner tonight for them as well. Maybe a couple of fat rabbits, or another one of these striped creatures.

Rays of sunlight pushed through the thick canopy, like glowing columns holding up the green ceiling of some huge cavern, breaking up the perpetual twilight of the Deepwood. He tried to dodge them as he ran, as if their light would hurt him if it touched his skin, expose him for leaving the others. No, he had done the right thing.

He focused on how incredible he felt. He had been running since before the first blush of dawn transformed the blacks and greys of the wood into shades of green. He didn't need the light to see, what little light there was in this place. The soulstones granted sight even in the deepest cave. He learned that when he first faced the worgs and Muk back on the Horn. But he could see farther with the light and he preferred the varying colors to the different shades of grey his night vision brought.

He breathed in the cool moist air, heavy with the smells of the wood, letting it fill his chest until he couldn't hold anymore. He let it out slowly and evenly, just to test if he could keep his current pace and still control his breathing. Had he tried to run like this before becoming stonechosen, he would have been gasping for air, a stitch in his side doubling him over with pain. This truly was incredible.

He ducked under one of the numerous roots spreading out from the gigantic trees. Any one of the roots here in the Deepwood, was as big as the trunks of the redwoods of home. The roots he couldn't run under, he leaped over, long leaps helped along by the power of the soulstones. How could these new found gifts be the very thing that would lead him to his death? Or the death of Akira?

There, he had said it. He knew deep down, the decision to leave the others in the village, the need to run and jump, push himself to his physical limits, all came from the desire to not think about what *they* said he had to do, when he finally reached Akira. Last night's talk with Two Elks had settled things for him.

He didn't need them to tell him, he knew what the soulstones would make him feel. Even now, he followed the pull he felt deep in his chest, the pull that would lead him to her. He remembered the yearning to have Muk's soulstone when he first saw the goblin. He had never wanted anything so much before in his life. Now, as he drew closer to Akira, he could feel the tingling, the urge slowly building. It was his desire that showed him the direction. Or was it?

Were these feelings even his, or were they the desires of the soulstones? He wondered more than once if it was the two soulstones now burned into his chest, into his very bone, that made him feel this way. Was this their desire coming through him? It made sense.

Ghile remembered the intense pain he'd felt both times he found soulstones. No one in their right minds would want to feel such pain, to experience them crawling under the skin like slugs until they reached the chest and burned themselves into the bone next to the others, forming that strange, spiral pattern. And if it was the soulstones causing this desire, then it was something he could fight.

He did want to find Akira. But, he wanted to find her so he could help her. He wanted to help her brother, Ashar, to free them and then flee the Fallen City. Then what? Where would they go?

Ghile slowed his run to a walk and ran his hands through his hair. Even if he wasn't tired, his body was showing the signs of exertion; sweaty brown curls clung to his forehead. He took another deep breath and sent out a mental summons to Ast and Cuz. There was no need to keep up this pace any longer. It was hard to tell how late in the day it was in the gloom of the forest, but they had covered much ground and he was hungry. There was no way the others would be able to catch him, even if they were able to find his trail. He hoped they wouldn't. He hoped they would return home and forget him. He could hear the two Valehounds rushing through the undergrowth.

The others. He felt the guilt for leaving them like something rotten, at the bottom of his gut. They had given up everything to come with him. Two Elks carried his unconscious form out of the Ghost Fens. They faced swamp cats and the frost wyrm, all because of him. But he had to do this. Had to leave them. It wasn't only about Akira or what Two Elks said.

What if one of them died? He remembered how bad Riff's leg had been savaged by that cat. Daughter Gaidel healed him, but what if next time she was too late? Could Ghile live with himself if one of them died because they were trying to protect him? No, it was better this way. This way he would not be responsible for their deaths and they would not be able to make him take Akira's soulstone.

Ast and Cuz reached his side. Ast nuzzled against his waist, hoping for a scratch. Cuz sniffed at the dead animal hanging from Ghile's belt. He moved Cuz's snout away with a laugh and brush of his hand. "This one isn't for you, boy. I'll find you another one later. Okay?" Ghile formed a mental image and pushed it towards Cuz. "How would you like a fat tasty rabbit?"

Cuz barked his appreciation. Ghile could sense the pleasure coming off the Valehound in waves.

When he'd first started communicating with the two hounds, he'd tried speaking to them like he would another human. But he learned his ability to communicate with animals didn't change the way they thought or how they thought. It seemed to be mostly emotions and images. When they were hungry, images of hunting for prey or eating would replace the words of humans. With the Valehounds, it was as much about smells as any other senses. He still had a hard time absorbing all the different smells they could sense. They could almost communicate through shared smells alone.

He also found it interesting that the smells were the same. A tree or a tuft of grass smelled exactly the same to Cuz, as it did to Ast. He remembered a time long past when Adon pondered that very question. They lay awake one summer's night in Upper Vale. They had chosen to sleep outside the roundhouse that night, and even made a small fire to chase off the always-present chill in Upper Vale. Adon went on and on about how what he thought green looked like, might not be the same as what Ghile thought green looked like. Ghile remembered laughing at how frustrated Adon became each time Ghile acted like he didn't understand. Now he knew it was the same for everyone and everything. At least for animals and himself, that was. He would have to tell Adon, the next time he saw him in the dreaming.

"Ouch!" Something small and sharp struck Ghile in the head, followed by several other small, painful stings in his neck and shoulders. Almost without thinking he crouched, extending his spear to the side for balance and raised his other hand to form a mental shield. The protective dome snapped into existence above him.

Other small spear-like missiles bounced off the shield. Above him, scores of small flying creatures, trailing dust of multicolored hues, dove towards him on tiny, translucent wings. Each banked before reaching him and hurled something.

Ghile dropped his spear and touched his neck. He felt something stuck in his skin. He winced as he pulled it out and examined it. A long thin thorn-like spear, covered in a purplish syrup and his own blood.

Small shouts proceeded pain shooting up from his feet and legs. He tried to dance back and tripped, something clinging to his leggings in several places. Small brown creatures, each no bigger than a potato, swarmed over him. Their faces were covered with grizzly green beards beneath enormous warty noses. Each waved a jagged stone or a small, sharpened stick.

Ghile could hear their shouts. Beneath the strange unintelligible croaks and whoops, he could sense more than hear the words, translated by the soulstones.

"Stop the human!"

"Trespasser!"

"It is not marked, get it!"

Marked? Ghile thought. *Stop the human?* Above him, he could hear the same sentiments, but in high, flitty voices.

Ghile focused and pulled in the shield above him and then pushed it out from all around him. It happened even before he could think about the fact he had never made one so large before. All about him the sounds of his attackers became muffled. The small potato-like creatures tumbled away in all directions.

Ghile gasped for air and realized he hadn't thought about that requirement inside the sealed shield. He quickly pictured a small space opening before his nose and mouth.

He breathed in the welcomed air and looked for Ast and Cuz. The two Valehounds lay nearby, panting and watching. Simply watching. A mixture of relief that they were unharmed, fought with Ghile's irritation that they were not doing anything to help him. Seriously?

He reached for their minds and sensed something wrong. A sort of haze permeated their thoughts. He wanted to push through it, to clear it, but had no idea how to begin. A few of the creatures not participating in the attack on him were stroking the Valehounds long white hair, further relaxing them. He could see small spear-like thorns, like the ones that had struck him, hanging from their pelts.

Ghile stood up and imagined more of the area around his face clear from the mental shield. Sound rushed in as it became reality. The attack continued, small projectiles hailing down from above and the potatoes, having regrouped, slamming sticks and stones against the shield around his shins and feet.

Realizing neither he nor his Valehounds were in any real immediate danger, Ghile spent a moment to take it all in. What were these things? He had never seen them in the Redwood. He could see other types mixed in among the colored, butterfly-looking ones and the big-nosed, bearded potatoes. There were living mushrooms, and others that resembled large insects. The one thing they all had in common was they didn't like him being here. "Why are you attacking us?" Ghile asked.

The change was almost instant. The chaos of noise and motion becoming silent and still. Even the flying ones stopped and hovered, staring at him in confusion.

"I said, why are you attacking us? We have done you no harm," Ghile repeated.

Some of them clapped and pointed at him, as if he had done some great trick. Others huddled together and whispered to themselves, all the while shooting him furtive glances. One of the potato men, for it seemed they were all bearded, ignored him completely and was curiously probing the mind shield near his feet with a stumpy brown hand.

When the silence broke, it broke like a sudden spring rain.

"Why are you not asleep?"

"Your own fault for not bearing the mark!"

"Who are you?"

"Can I ride your hounds?"

"How come I cannot hit you?"

"Where did you learn our language?"

"Why are you here?"

Ghile blinked and tried to shake away the barrage. "Wait, wait. One at a time." The change from violence to childlike innocence was so sudden in the creatures, Ghile couldn't help but laugh. There was something about them that he couldn't explain, but he found himself taking an immediate liking to them.

He thought of his little sister, Tia. How she would have clapped to see this multitude of woodland creatures and their rumpus!

The potato man who had been testing Ghile's mind shield called for the others to quiet down. Two of the butterfly ones began to mimic him and chitter between themselves.

When the creature seemed to think it had gotten as much silence as it was likely to manage, it motioned for Ghile to come closer.

"You're a human and don't belong here. So we attacked you. That is your answer. Now answer ours." The voice was deep and scratchy. When it spoke, its mouth opened wide and the whisker-covered cheeks bloomed out. It crossed its arms with those final words and glared up at him, waiting.

Ghile knelt before the blunt creature. "What are you?"

It continued to glare at him, waiting. A couple of the others had moved up to stand next to the first one and upon seeing its pose, copied the gesture and glared at Ghile as well.

"Oh, right. Of course, your questions." Ghile tried to sort through the earlier barrage. As much as he found himself liking these diminutive creatures, he wasn't sure he was comfortable sharing who he really was, or more importantly, his destination. But in answering anything other than his name, he didn't see how he could avoid it. He didn't know how they would react if they learned he was stonechosen. It seemed bad enough he was human. He could just walk away from them, they couldn't harm him after all, but there was Ast and Cuz to consider. It seemed he hadn't taken them into account when he decided to separate himself from the others, in hopes of protecting them.

Well, there was nothing for it. The truth, then.

"I am Ghile Stonechosen. That is Ast and the other Cuz. The answer to your other questions: why I am not affected by your poison, can speak with you, and your weapons cannot hit me, is in my name. I am stonechosen."

Ghile expected them to attack, or turn and flee in terror. He didn't expect them to simply stand there and nod, as if he'd just told them the sky was blue.

"Name's Gutroot. I'm a Hob," was the reply. Some of the surrounding hobs began repeating the word hob and nodding. They made Ghile think of a group of toads. The other creatures began calling out their names, as well as what they were. The ones that looked like butterflies were pixies. The bug-like ones, sprites. Their names were things of the wood, Thistlestem, Dewdrop, Blossom and so on. It became a game for them to vie for his attention and call out their names.

He didn't remember when he lowered his shield, but it was when he noted a number of the hobs working their way under Ast and Cuz and beginning to carry them away, that Ghile thought about his protection.

"Hey, what are you doing with them?" he demanded.

"They are coming with us," Gutroot said.

"With you? No, they're not. They are staying with me," Ghile said.

"Same," Gutroot replied. "You are coming with us, too."

"With you? Where?"

"To see the Alvar, of course," Gutroot called over his wide shoulder, having already turned and started to hobble away.

"Alvar?" Ghile said. "What are Alvar?"

15

Arrival at Dagbar's Freehold

 HE three griffons soared above the treetops, the leaves below a blur. The Deepwood was a sea of green beneath them.

They made good time and the knights could see the Bastion of Dagbar's Freehold, where it jutted above the forest's canopy. The sun sat high in the cloudless sky, the warmth of its rays making the tower appear to float on a shimmering haze.

Finngyr tightened his grip on Safu's reins and banked left. The other knights trailed close behind and followed his lead. He wanted to get a look at this place before landing. He was sure they would have been forewarned of his arrival. Something as important as a visit from three Knights from the Temple of Justice would have warranted the use of a runesmith. Magister Dagbar would be expecting them. *He would have prepared for them more like,* Finngyr mused.

Some type of pale wooden structure on the top of the Bastion caught his attention. It was square, similar to the tower it squatted on, but rose an additional two stories before angling up into a pitched roof. Why in Daomur's name, would a dwarf build something on top of a Bastion? Worse still, why build it of wood? Where were they to land?

The forest fell away beneath them to reveal rolling hills covered with cultivated fields of wheat, corn and barley, their square patterns pushing all the way up to the forest's edge. Finngyr expected to see the humans of the settlement scattered through them, working the land, but he saw no one. He guided Safu lower and noted high weeds amongst the crops. He had only taken this in when they passed over the first abandoned farmstead.

The door to the one story farm house lay forgotten in the weeds, a short distance from the porch. Even from this height, Finngyr could tell it had been torn off and thrown there. The animal paddock was empty, the water trough covered with a green film. It was the same with the other farms they took in, as they scouted the borderlands of the settlement. What happened here? Finngyr didn't see the telltale signs of the passage of a large force, the fields were not burned, just abandoned. They were too far into the Deep Wood for this to be barbarian raiders from the plains. If something happened here, why had Knight Justice Griff not reported it?

They flew low and followed one of the many roads that cut a straight line through the fields towards the Bastion. Dagbar's Freehold was built to the same design as the many Bastion's Finngyr had seen in the plains. The Bastion, the entry to the Underways, sat at the center of the settlement. From there, paved streets led away from its surrounding courtyard in the four cardinal directions to four fortified gates. The gates were connected by a protective stone wall, built in the shape of a square. Simple and efficient.

The majority of the buildings behind the protective walls were stone. There was a smattering of wooden structures peppered throughout, but most were of stone. This surprised Finngyr. There couldn't possibly be that many dwarves in this outpost. He was not aware of any sizable troops being assigned to the Freehold, either.

Where the outlying fields were devoid of life, the streets and buildings behind the protective walls was teeming with it. Humans and dwarves moved throughout the streets, shuffling their way around tents of every different design and color. Hastily erected paddocks held livestock of all sorts. Even the flat roofs of the buildings were crowded with makeshift shelters, chicken coops, and laundry lines. Human women squatted on the roofs, tending cooking pots, while their screaming offspring ran among them, pointing up at the griffons.

It wasn't until they made a second pass that Finngyr saw a small group of perhaps a half dozen dwarves and humans gathered outside one of the gatehouses. They held aloft triangular banners of blue and white, a white tree decorating the center – Magister Dagbar's trade guild emblem. It reminded Finngyr he was not just dealing with some unknown magister of a human containment, but a grandmaster of a trade guild.

Finngyr disengaged his harness as soon as Safu touched ground. "Thank you, Safu." He spoke the words of the riding ritual and then cleared his hammer and gear. He noted with satisfaction that both Horth and Kjar also thanked their mounts.

Finngyr took his time and watched the three griffons take to the skies, and only then turned to find a human male bowing before him, its palms turned upward. "May I take your belongings, Knight Justice?" The human was thin, its head clean shaven, with half its face stained blue. It made to reach for his pack.

Finngyr glared at it until it lowered its hand and stepped back hurriedly. Two other humans who had stepped forward to make the same offer to Horth and Kjar, followed suit.

A dwarf in deep blue robes stepped forward and inclined his head. "Greetings and well met, Knight Justices. Welcome to the Emporium. I am Magister Dagbar," he said in a thick northern accent.

Finngyr unfastened the clasp on his helmet and removed it. He had not missed that Magister Dagbar had only inclined his head, instead of bowing. He had also said 'Magister' instead of his higher rank of 'Grandmaster'. Was he insulting them by using his lesser title and paying respect as an equal, or saying they ranked no higher than a magister? Either way, Finngyr disliked him already.

Dagbar was wide, even for a dwarf, Finngyr would not have said he was fat, but he didn't appear to miss too many meals. He wore magister's robes of a deep blue with shoulder plates of polished silver with gold filigree. The robe was made of velvet from the south, a precious import unless Finngyr missed his guess. His flame red hair and beard were intricately twisted in long braids and heavily oiled. Not one finger was wont for a band of gold or precious stone. Most striking were the colors of his eyes. One was a deep blue, which matched his robe, the other pure white.

Both Horth and Kjar stepped up next to Finngyr and bowed at the waist. Finngyr frowned and inclined his head at the Magister.

"His word is law, Magister," Finngyr said. He let the traditional greeting hang there a moment. "I am Knight Justice Finngyr. This is Knight Kjar and Knight Horth."

"Yes, well, we have been expecting you. Though I must say, I do not understand the reason for your visit. One of your brethren, a Knight Justice Griff, I believe, was here not too long ago to perform the Rite of Attrition," Dagbar said.

"We will discuss that in due time, Magister, I can assure you." Finngyr motioned towards the gatehouse. "What has happened here?"

198

"Ah, well, that. Yes, we can discuss that in due time as well. Please follow me." With that, Dagbar turned and motioned for them to follow. The dwarves and humans with banners took up position around Dagbar and the knights and guided them towards the gatehouse.

"You said the Emporium, Magister Dagbar. I thought this settlement was known as Dagbar's Freehold," Horth said.

Dagbar gave them an indulgent grin. "Yes, I have heard this name. Some have said we are more... liberal... here, than in other parts of the empire." Magister Dagbar placed his hands together within his broad sleeves and said no more.

As they approached the gatehouse, the large intricately carved set of stone doors swung outwards on well-oiled hinges. Finngyr made out images of dwarves reaching towards what appeared to be living trees, set against a backdrop of swirling vines. Detailed leaves were etched around the outside.

"I did not know there was a contingent of Artificers from the Temple of Art in the Emporium," Kjar said.

"Oh, there has not been a contingent of Artificers in the Emporium for many years, though journeymen priests are here often enough," one of the blue-faced humans volunteered.

Kjar did not look at the human, but said, "I did not address you, human."

The man cleared his throat and suddenly found something on the ground very interesting.

Finngyr took in the armed gate guards. Both dwarf and human, both with half their faces stained blue, working side by side to open the gate.

He glanced back at the human who deigned to speak before being spoken to. "I can see how this place has come to be called Dagbar's Freehold." Bile formed in the back of Finngyr's throat as he took it all in. His gauntleted fist involuntarily tightened on his hammer. Here was a place he would be honored to administer the Rite of Attrition.

All the noise and smells held within the walls escaped through the open doors and crashed over them. Knight Horth put a gauntleted fist to his nose and grimaced.

The banners acted like the keel of a ship, parting the crowds before their entourage. Finngyr found the scene before him a dichotomy. It was obvious the Freehold was overcrowded and had been for some time, something driving the humans behind the safety of the Freehold's walls. The smell of so many living together was overpowering, but still many cheered and called the Magister's name. For every jubilant greeting for Magister Dagbar, Finngyr found a cold stare for himself and his fellow knights. From opened windows, shadowed doorways and rooftops, the humans watching them pass could not hide the fear Finngyr saw behind their eyes, waiting for him like an old friend.

"You arm the humans with steel and allow them to reside within buildings of dwarf make, Magister?" Finngyr said. He noted Horth and Kjar shared a look.

Magister Dagbar responded as if he were commenting on the weather. "There is no law restricting humans from wielding steel weapons within a settlement, Knight Justice. Nor is it written that they may not reside in stone buildings, I'll assume that is what you are referring to, only that they are not allowed to work with stone."

"A thin distinction at best," Finngyr said.

Dagbar motioned to the throngs around them. "There is no law being broken here. On the contrary, we follow it. Do the laws not read we are to watch over humans?"

Finngyr had seen this before. A politician taking the word of Daomur and twisting it to his own ends. Finngyr was tired. He had spent too many days in the saddle and was not going to be drawn into a debate he wouldn't be allowed to win. He knew he was restricted in his actions. The Magister was no more going to change his beliefs than Finngyr was going to change his own. The Magister held the power and was within his rights to interpret the law the way he saw fit in his settlement.

For now.

Those two words gave Finngyr hope and he clung to them in the face of all the blatant abominations of the law before him.

"Since you do not wish to speak of what has caused all the humans to seek shelter behind your walls, perhaps you care to enlighten me on what *that* is?" Finngyr pointed at the wooden structure atop the Bastion.

Dagbar smiled, seeming excited at the change of subject. "Ah, that magnificent creation is my home, Knight Justice."

"It is built of silverwood," Kjar stated in awe.

Finngyr found such a display of wealth sickening. Silverwood was only found within the Deepwood. It was treasured by merchant houses and nobles alike, as a symbol of wealth and prestige. Just to have a few pieces of carved artwork marked one as wealthy. No grandmaster of any trade guild would have less than a few fine pieces of furniture on display or service their guests on a silverwood table – but this?

"Indeed, it is. I find stone so restricting, don't you? I'm especially fond of the view from the larger windows. The smaller windows in the Bastion do not allow one to take in the forest," Dagbar said, warming to the subject.

Kjar quirked an eyebrow at Finngyr and shook his head in disbelief. Finngyr had thought the Magister eccentric, now he thought him mad. Finngyr grunted a response and said no more of it as they continued on through the crowds.

The buildings pushing in on each side of the street fell away behind them as they entered the main square surrounding the Bastion. Finngyr was impressed to see dwarven guards restricting access to the square, even if they too, had blue-stained faces. The guards flowed back into place behind Dagbar's entourage.

"Are your humans not thankful for the shelter you provide, Magister?" Kjar said.

Dagbar seemed confused at first and then realized he referred to the guards. "Oh, no, Knight Justice. The guard is necessary for trade. No matter what happens outside, the Emporium must remain open." Dagbar finished the end of his sentence with his arms spread wide.

Where the street leading to the square was packed with mostly human refugees, the square was filled with trade. Tents of every seeming make and color crisscrossed the square, like a maze of canvas. Hawkers, both dwarven and human, called out over the crowd, their voices a sharp contrast to the underlying din.

The sheer size of the open market was overwhelming and hard to take in all at once. Stalls displaying numerous rugs of vibrant colors were pushed up against others displaying exotic jewels and rare gemstones. The smell of scented oils competed with the smell of spices and cooked meats. The rumbling babel as dwarves haggled prices and the clink of exchanged coins swept over Finngyr, threatening to carry him away. Dagbar's representatives walked through the cacophony like veteran sentinels, undisturbed by the chaos around them.

Finngyr noted Dagbar's representatives consisted of both dwarves and humans alike. They wore long white robes and their faces were stained half white and half blue, making them easy to find in the crowd. Each carried a stone abacus. Finngyr past near a human one overseeing a transaction between two dwarves. The man listened intently as he slid the stones across the abacus with smooth efficiency. Finngyr felt his jaw clenching.

The Emporium would rival the best markets in any of the mountain cities. Though the one difference, not to be seen there, were all the humans. Finngyr could smell their stench seep through all else. Their thin, spindly bodies everywhere, as if they belonged here. He was less bothered when he spotted two orcs and even some Nordlah barbarians trading. Dagbar explained it all away with the simple phrase, "The Emporium is open to all creatures of Allwyn who come to trade."

Each new sight scratched a little more away from Finngyr's sensibilities. He knew why he was here and how important his task. He felt the tick of his clenched jaw like a heartbeat. He tried repeating a prayer to Daomur over and over in his head, tried controlling his breathing, even at one point simply looked down at the back of Dagbar's over-adorned slippers in an attempt to hold it all in. He thought he had made it through the gauntlet of sin when the shadow of the Bastion washed over him and he knew it was almost over.

"By Daomur's beard," Horth said.

Finngyr looked up and stared in disbelief. The Bastion loomed before them. An undergate, at the Bastion's base, its stone doors open wide before them. In front of the undergate a stone statue in the shape of a dwarven priest towered, just shy of clearing the arched entrance. A stone golem, a sacred protector of the forbidden cities, created by the Artificers, stood harnessed to a train of wagons.

"Sacrilege!" Kjar whispered, dumbstruck.

Finngyr snapped. He grabbed Dagbar by the robes, spinning him about and lifting his bulk effortlessly into the air. "What is the meaning of this, coin monger!" He could feel the blood raging through his temples. Finngyr could hear Lord Knight Gyldoon's warning, somewhere in the distant corners of his mind.

The sound of drawn steel echoed around him. All the sounds of the market were gone. He heard the whispered warnings of both the younger knights, saw them from the corner of his eyes, their weapons raised and backs to him.

Finngyr blinked and looked beyond them and down two dozen blades to the blue-stained faces of dwarves. Had even one of the weapons been in the hands of a human, Finngyr wasn't sure he could have controlled himself.

Kjar glanced at him and then back at the guards who had moved to surround them. It was obvious to Finngyr they had been prepared for just such a reaction. Finngyr focused on Kjar's face. It was filled with concern, but also a sort of stoic resolve. Finngyr knew if he decided to break Dagbar in half, Kjar would fight by his side until the end.

The realization that it would in fact be the end, settled on Finngyr then. He could enact justifiable vengeance on this blasphemer now, but pay the ultimate price. Finngyr had no compunction with dying. He would stare Daomur in the eyes when that day came. But the idea of Ghile Stonechosen allowed to go free, and potentially fulfill the prophecies, stayed his hand.

It took all of Finngyr's control to set the Magister down and unlock his trembling fingers from the dwarf's robes.

Magister Dagbar made a deliberate show of straightening his robes and clearing his throat before speaking. If he was shaken from being grabbed, it didn't show on his features, he almost looked... disappointed. "Knight Justice, you have traveled far and are surely tired."

"You go too far—" Finngyr began.

"Let me assure you, I had the full support of the High Council of Daomount in removing the golems from the Fallen City and using them here."

"You are using them as beasts of burden?" Kjar said. He had lowered his hammer and now simply stared at the golem.

"And we have quadrupled the amount of product we deliver throughout the empire as a result," Dagbar said.

"But the city—" Horth began.

"Is protected by the Alvar and their Deepwood," Dagbar finished.

"Alvar?"

"I believe you name them Elves," Dagbar said.

16

The Alvar

HILE lost track of how long he had been walking. As he followed the fae, the bright shafts of light he dodged earlier in the day faded from piercing white, to somber shades of orange and red. Twilight painted itself across what little sky could be seen through the trees, giant sentinels trying to conceal all beneath from the outside world.

Ast and Cuz had awoken from their drug-induced sleep some time ago and now trotted along at his side. Upon waking, they were too accepting of the fae, in Ghile's opinion. Instead of being surprised at being surrounded by the creatures, they seemed excited to the point of wanting to play, and the fae were more than happy to oblige. They only now walked beside him because they were tired from playing chase the pixie and wrestle the hob. Their tongues lolled and they looked half asleep already.

This part of the Deepwood didn't seem much different from when he'd first entered from the village. He had no idea whether he was farther in or if they were traveling along its edge. The massive roots, the size of trees themselves, still dominated the forest floor. He assumed he was moving deeper in, since he could feel the pull of the soulstone getting stronger. He would have thought the wood would become more dangerous as they went deeper, but judging by the hobs swaggering gait and the way the pixies and sprites flitted around them, they had nothing to fear. They chittered amongst themselves, laughing and giggling, as if this was some grand adventure.

Even so, he kept his guard up, his spear in hand and fang blade loose on his belt. He continually probed his surroundings, sensing for life. It had taken some time to get used to all the fae. Even though he could not penetrate past the surface of their minds, he could still sense them, all of them, and their numbers had swelled with new fae joining along the way.

He thought again on why he could mind touch with some creatures and not with others? They felt the same as any other mind, floating out there. He could sense them easily enough, but he couldn't enter. It was almost like pushing on a thin soft membrane and made Ghile think of the surface of water. He just pushed his mind through like a finger, and he was in. Though, try as he might, he couldn't push his way into the fae's minds. It was similar with humans. He wondered if it would be the same with dwarves and that made him shudder. That was a question for another day.

He sensed the minds of some of the Deepwood's larger denizens, great cats, which did nothing more than crouch hidden amongst the limbs and stare at the passing host. He had mind touched with the predators, pushing his way in easily, and found only acceptance of the fae passing nearby. It was as if the fae pacified all they came in contact with. It wasn't the same haze that Ghile had found on Ast and Cuz when they succumbed to the fae's poison, covered in that strange purplish liquid. It was different, more natural, but still felt magical to him.

The fae had never spoken to a human before. And now that their opportunity was before them, their questions seemed endless. Ghile, too, tried to take advantage of his first meeting with them and did his best to squeeze his own questions in between theirs.

"Gutroot, earlier one of you said I wasn't marked. What did that mean?"

Gutroot was just taking in breath to ask his next question and cocked a bushy black eyebrow at Ghile in irritation at being interrupted. "Marked by the Alvar. Once was only humans and dwarves whose faces were covered in blue, like so", Gutroot covered half his face with his hand, "were to be left alone."

The other hobs around them echoed the word 'blue', over and over, to the delight of the other fae.

"By the Alvar?" This question from Ghile sent the hobs into a chorus of "Alvar!"

When Gutroot spoke, his words were almost reverent. "Yep. The Alvar are keepers of the forest. The daughters of Islmur." The nearest pixies swooned at the mention of Islmur.

The Alvar were what Ghile knew as elves. He knew the legends of the elves from Riff. They protected their forest home from all others. They had also taken part in the Great Purge, slaying humans along with the dwarves until the druids awoke Allwyn to save the human race.

"Alvar are real smart," Gutroot continued. "They tell us to keep those who are not marked out of the forest. So that is what we did."

"Did?"

Gutroot nodded. "Yup. Things have changed. Alvar said all must be turned back now." Gutroot made a motion that seemed to be a shrug, or at least would have been, if Gutroot had shoulders. "Strange since it has always been the way to leave the marked ones alone and attack the rest."

"But not kill them," Ghile stated, more than asked.

Gutroot shook his head. "Nope. We capture them and take them to the edge of the forest, to Dagbar's domain. When they awake, they don't remember a thing. Pixie poison packs a punch, puts them right out and makes them forgetful, too." A number of pixies flew past, giggling and shaking their bows at Ghile, their little angular faces full of pride.

"But why allow any to enter?" Ghile said.

"The Alvar will explain," Gutroot said, his voice filled with more than a little exasperation.

Ghile received that answer all too often from Gutroot, but there was nothing for it. Once his line of questioning arrived at that answer, Ghile knew he would receive no further answers. If they told the fae not to kill trespassers, then they couldn't be as bad as the legends said, could they? And if they were as wise as Gutroot said, then maybe they could help him find a way to save Akira and her brother. Maybe even help him remove the soulstones?

Keep dreaming, sheepherder, Ghile heard Riff's voice in his head.

"Are you taking me to their village, Gutroot?"

Gutroot stared through Ghile for a moment. "You humans are none too bright, eh?"

Ghile didn't know how to respond to the blunt statement. Apparently, hobs were not ones to mince words. He wasn't offended, so he could only shake his head and grin.

"Villages? Towns? That stuff is for your lot," Gutroot said. He motioned all around him. "This is home. Home for us and home for the Alvar."

"Then how do you know where to find them?"

Gutroot made swishing movements with his hand. "Not a problem. They don't tend to move about much. There was one down by the river not two moons ago."

Ghile blanched. "Two moons? You mean two full cycles of the moon?"

Gutroot thought for a moment and then nodded.

"What makes you think the Alvar is still there?"

Gutroot gave Ghile another blank stare and shook his head, mumbling. Ghile could just make out the words, "none too bright."

The sound of flowing water filled Ghile's ears, long before he reached the riverbank. The forest abruptly ended where the river, easily fifty spans across, cut through it like shears through wool. The river split the canopy, revealing the deepening sky overhead.

His guides turned to follow it upstream. The fading light seemed to have as little effect on the fae as it did on him. At least, as far as the ability to see. As the darkness thickened, their twittering and singing grew silent. Gutroot and the other hobs watched their surroundings as much as Ghile, But they continued along the river. Sometimes the large roots caused them to go well away from its bank, but he could still hear it flowing nearby.

The ground began to rise, the river sometimes crashing down where it cascaded over a ledge or thundered down a steep bank. The fae's antics brought a grin to Ghile's face during those times, for the sprites would swoop down to scoop up the hobs and carry their grumbling passengers over the harder-to-climb areas and then return them to the forest floor. The hobs would shake fists at their departing helpers and then continue on their way, only to have the whole spectacle repeated at the next patch of difficult ground. The pixies, with their bug-like legs, leaped along and cleared the obstacles with practiced ease.

It was just when Ghile thought they would walk long into the night that the Fae around him became excited. Gutroot took to jumping up and down and pointing. The other hobs began croaking and pointing as well. Ghile could make out the word 'Alvar' in their croaks, but all he could see along the bank of the river were trees and undergrowth. He assumed the Alvar would be experts at blending in with their forest home, so he searched intently, watching between the trees for any movement.

Ghile's breath caught in his throat. Before him, next to the river, a small tree, one of its slender branches touching the water, turned to regard him. He knew immediately it was female, that it was a she. And she was beautiful. Where there should've been a trunk, he could make out a body and two long, thin legs, the white bark freckled with grey, diamond-shaped specks. What he had mistaken for a branch touching the water, was her arm. Her willowy fingers still gently stirred the water's surface. Where there should've been hair were small, light green leaves, a silver sheen playing through-out. It reminded Ghile of the school of minnows he used to chase through the shallow blue waters along the shore of Crystal Lake. The silvery leaves framed a long face and fell past lithe shoulders.

But what captured him more than anything else, were her eyes. They were large, taking up more than twice as much space as a human's and a radiant blue. Even from this distance, he could see little specks of light flowing through them, like a river of stars.

The Alvar rose. She towered over Ghile, easily twice his height. Ghile wondered if all Alvar were so big. With a start, he realized what he had mistaken for bark was smooth, multi-hued skin. She moved slowly, gracefully, and he could only stand and stare. It was when he realized her body was also proportioned like a woman and she wore not a stitch of clothing, that he lowered his gaze. He could feel the blood racing to warm his face.

The fae, spinning and dancing, rushed towards her. Many of them landed upon her shoulders and outstretched arms. That was when Ghile heard the song of the Alvar for the first time.

Ghile couldn't put into words what he heard, other than to say it was like hearing pure emotions. His ears ached. He shuddered as his skin erupted in goosebumps. Beneath the song, through the power of the soulstones, Ghile understood.

"This one's soul sings at the sight of you, little ones." Those sapphire eyes never left Ghile. "Why have you brought this human to me? Please tell this one. Why you have done this?"

Ghile wondered how she could understand anything in the outpouring of answers from the fae. Ghile could only make out a few replies in all the twitters, clicks and croaks. The Alvar seemed to have no trouble and listened patiently, nodding slowly and then, seeming satisfied, began to approach Ghile.

If someone had asked him how a tree might walk, he would've described a lumbering beast, heavy roots dragging across the forest floor. But he knew his description would be forever changed; the Alvar was anything but cumbersome. Her movements were grace itself. She appeared to glide more than walk, floating on tiny feet.

Ast and Cuz trotted forward, tails wagging.

"Ast, Cuz, Stay!" He said the command with some trepidation, his eyes on the Alvar. Would she understand? Would she hurt them for being here, with a human? The Valehounds ignored him.

Ghile mind touched them and they both dropped down on their haunches.

The Alvar stopped as well, then tilted her head slightly. She knelt down and reached out a long, slender hand towards the Valehounds, her fingers twice as long as a human's.

"This one knows sorrow. For now, it knows why the little ones were unable to make you sleep. This one was told of your coming, Stonechosen."

Ghile was so shocked, he lost his mind connection with Ast and Cuz. They sprang forward and ran to the Alvar, who stroked their fur. Questions raced through his mind, each one pushing past the others and demanding to be first. "I'm Ghile... and yes, I'm stone-chosen. But how—"

"This one could feel you reach out to them." She looked to Ast and Cuz, who acted as if they had known her their whole lives and were not being stroked by some strange, living tree they had just met.

She rose and stepped forward to tower over Ghile. "This one is Arenuin of Arenell of Areduin of Arethell of..."

The names continued. Ghile blinked. What should he do? This was the first elf, Alvar, he had met. Did he shake her hand? His need to be well-mannered fought with his need for answers. What did she mean, she felt him reach out to them? She could sense him using the power of the soulstones? Who told her of his coming? He found himself staring at her skin. From a distance, it had looked like bark. He could tell now it was as smooth as his own. He could hear his mother's voice in his head, reminding him of his manners. He stabbed his spear in the ground and presented his open palms, head bowed and eyes averted. Arenuin had apparently reached the end of her lineage.

"I... I'm honored to meet you, Arenuin of... of... the Alvar," Ghile said.

He waited for some response, but none came. It was Ast and Cuz's deep throaty growls that made him raise his head. Arenuin was looking into the forest, her starry eyes unblinking.

"What is it, you two?" Ghile said. He reached out with his mind even as he spoke. The Valehounds enhanced senses assaulted his mind. An acrid scent of musk mixed with the putrid smell of spoiled meat. He could feel their ears, his ears, perk up to catch the snap of twigs and the crunch of debris beneath fast moving feet.

"Gather to me, little ones, it is the fallen!" Arenuin said. "This one would take you now and treestep from here, Ghile Stonechosen, but she will not leave the little ones to these abominations." With that, Arenuin widened her stance and lifted her long slender arms to the sky. "This one asks Ghile Stonechosen to stay close."

Gutroot and the other land-bound fae darted forward to take up guarded positions around Arenuin's feet. The sprites flew in to swarm around her, streaks of color blending together like a rainbow cloud. At any other time, Ghile would have found the scene breathtakingly beautiful. But the fearful faces of the fae and the foreboding silence that descended upon them chilled his heart. Even Ast and Cuz stopped growling and waited.

Ghile found he was holding his breath.

Everything happened at once. Pale white forms exploded through the surrounding foliage. Arenuin began to sing. Ast and Cuz charged forward.

The creatures seemed to come from every direction at once. There were too many to count. Ghile had stones in his hand, but he didn't remember drawing them from his pouch. He could feel his heart beating in his ears but it couldn't drown out the guttural shrieks, barks and howls, all in sharp contrast to Arenuin's song.

A white, hairy shape leaped in the air towards him, all four clawed limbs brought to bear. Stones flew from his hand, driven by the power of the soulstones. The sounds of impact were muted by everything else, but the creature's shudders with each impact, followed by red explosions behind it, told Ghile it was dead even before it crashed at his feet.

He barely had time to take in its white milky eyes and red veined muzzle before two more reared up before him, clawed hands swinging. His force shield sprang into being and he felt their muted blows as they were batted away. These creatures were strong.

Ghile could hear Two Elks voice, "You think too much before you do." This was his test, then. This was what he had been training for and he would not fail.

He saw Ast roll across his vision, tangled up with one of the creatures, this one shaped like a small human. He reached out with his mind and pushed a force shield through and then around Ast. The creature was pushed back, but Ast lay there on the ground, unable to move.

This would not do. He had to protect them and himself, but also allow for movement. He re-envisioned the force shields surrounding him and Ast. He even reached out and mind touched with Cuz. He pictured individual plates, similar to the Cullers metal armor, covering him and the two Valehounds, covering them, but allowing for movement. If he had stopped to think about how many individual shields he had just created, they probably would have vanished, his own doubts defeating him. But he didn't think, he just reacted.

The spear he had stabbed into the ground was in his hand and then pushed through one of the two dead ones, for that was what these things were – the fallen, Arenuin had called them. Whatever they were called, he would not let them hurt Arenuin or the Fae.

He drew his fang blade and heard, "For the Cradle," echo above the din. It sounded like it came from some stranger and not his own throat. He pushed into the second one, swinging and stabbing.

Another fallen slammed into his back and took him to the ground. He could feel it raking with its feet and hands, unable to penetrate his force shield. It even tried to lock its muzzle on his neck, shaking from side to side, trying to squeeze the life out of him. The other charged in and grabbed him by the leg, also trying to bite through the force shield.

He imagined the force shield on his back becoming as thin as a spear and then quickly stabbing forward. He heard the yelp and the pressure holding him down was gone. He replaced the image with the flat plates again and pictured the shield over his leg as a mass of sharp jutting spikes. Another screech and the pressure there was gone, too. He rolled over and pushed out with his force shield as he had done when sparring Two Elks in the Ghost Fens. He landed on his feet.

One of the fallen, a vargan, was on its knees, clutching its chest, blood streaming through its claws. The other, a human male, lay motionless on the ground, several holes oozing blood from its head and hands.

A tree branch crashed down at the same time as the ground erupted beneath the wounded vargan, hurling a boulder up to smash the fallen between wood and stone in a burst of splintered bone and inky gore.

Ghile only had a moment to leap aside as the remainder of the branch crashed over him. He flew into the air with the added help of his force shield, used it again to push off another swinging tree limb, and then extended one hand above him to create a wide shield to catch the air and slow his descent.

For the first time in what seemed like an hour, but was not more than a minute, Ghile took in the battle. Arenuin still stood in the center of it all, surrounded by the fae. All around her was chaos, the forest had answered her call. Trees slammed the ground with their limbs, the ground exploded as stones flew forth and then rolled over the fallen. The river surged up from its bank to slam down with thunderous retorts. Even the wind buffeted the fallen.

Animals had answered the call as well. A black cat, larger than the Valehounds, rolled on the ground with one of the fallen, its rear black claws raking gashes in the pale body as it held the creature's head in its jaws. Across the battlefield, an elk, its bony rack impaling two fallen, drove forward, pumping its back legs, ignoring their gnashing jaws and clawed hands. A myriad of ravens circled above the tumult, diving down to tear at white flesh.

That was when Ghile realized none of the fallen attacked Arenuin or the fae. All milky pale eyes, not fighting or dodging, turned skyward to follow his descent.

They were after him.

He was glad he'd ignored Arenuin's request to stay near her and the fae, though he could see the wisdom of it. The forest, responding to her magic, heaved, trying to drive off the fallen. It was chaos and he was quickly dropping back down into the middle of it.

Ghile thought of fleeing. If the fallen were after him, they should follow. It would keep the others safe. He could sense Ast and Cuz. They were alive and fought on. He could call to them and... what? Where would he go? On to the Fallen City? Would he drag these creatures with him? What about the Alvar? What if they could help him, help Akira? No, no more running.

Ghile reached out with his mind and drew strength from the elk, quickness from the cat. They were large creatures and would not be hurt if he wasn't greedy. He knew not to draw too much.

He released the force shield slowing his descent and fell into the maelstrom. He timed his fall perfectly and pushed off a rising limb with one foot. Turning his body, he added the additional momentum to his fall and landed in front of two fallen who were quickly moving up to intercept him. He continued his forward movement upon landing and spun the fang blade across in front of him. With his enhanced strength, the blade sliced through both creatures as if they weren't there. Limp bodies flew away from Ghile, trailing inky gore.

He ran forward, rolling under thrashing limbs and side stepping bouncing stones. When he passed one of the pale skinned fallen, he lashed out with the fang blade. He kept moving. If they wanted him, they would have to catch him, which meant avoiding the forest's wrath. For every creature he cut down, two more fell beneath wood, stone, or claw. At some point, Ast and Cuz appeared beside him, keeping pace and falling back to savage any creature he laid low. Soon it was over.

The forest once again fell silent. He stood in the middle of devastation. Still white forms lay scattered about the churned earth, some half buried, or floating slowly out into the river. Only the ground beneath Arenuin and the fae remained untouched.

The excitement of battle drained from Ghile and with it, the borrowed powers. He stumbled forward as exhaustion took him. He squinted under a sudden and piercing headache. He had never drawn on that much power from the soulstones. He couldn't even begin to remember how he had held the focus on so many different force shields and still managed to mind touch the Valehounds and other animals.

Arenuin, her face a mask of sorrow, took in the devastation. It was as if every broken limb, every misplaced stone cut her. The elk lay nearby, its fur a mesh of deep gouges and bites. It was not long for this world. Arenuin knelt beside it and began her song anew. This song was different than the one before. The elk stopped its mewling and lay still. The singing washed over Ghile and he could feel his headache fade under the gentle tune. The song drew him to the Alvar and by the time he reached Arenuin, the elk's wounds were gone and it was rolling up onto its legs.

Their curiosity seeming to get the better of them, the fae left the small circle of untouched ground. Gutroot and some other hobs prodded the lifeless form of a fallen, pixies hovered above, watching warily, bows drawn.

Ghile found Ast and Cuz, standing beside him. Cuz nudged against Ghile's waist and he reflexively scratched the Valehound's head. The two appeared unharmed. "How did you do that?" Ghile said.

"This one knows Islmur's tongue. This one is a Spellsinger." She spoke without looking at him, instead watching the elk walk back into the forest, its head held high.

"A Spellsinger?"

"This is not the place, Ghile Stonechosen. It would seem he knows you are here. Come," Arenuin said.

Ghile started to speak, but she was already walking away, stepping gingerly over the ruined ground. Ghile hastened to catch up.

"This one thanks you for bringing the Stonechosen, little ones."

"Wait, you said, *he* knows I'm here. Who knows I'm here?"

Arenuin continued to walk to the edge of the clearing, speaking with various fae as she went. Her stride lengthened as she neared the battlefield's edge and Ghile struggled to keep pace.

"Arenuin, please, wait. Did whoever knows I'm here send these... dead ones, these fallen?"

Arenuin stopped beside one of the largest trees and turned. "Yes. They are abominations from the Fallen City, created by the Sorcerer who rules there."

Ghile tried to take it all in, but his thoughts were a jumble. Akira and her brother, Ashar, were in the Fallen City. Akira had said there were things in the mists, she must have meant the fallen. If these things were what she feared, he had to get to her. But how did this sorcerer know he was here and what did he want with him? Ghile knew these fallen were after him, there was no doubt there, but why?

"Arenuin, I have friends in the Fallen City, I must reach them. Come with me, help me save them from this Sorcerer and then I'll come with you."

"This one cannot. All are forbidden to enter the city. The Fallen City is a cursed place, Ghile Stonechosen. If your friends entered there, then this one grieves for your loss."

How could Ghile explain to Arenuin that Akira was alive and visited him in his dreams? Again Ghile thought of just turning and continuing on his journey. He could feel the pull of the soulstones. If this sorcerer was after him, then wasn't he putting Arenuin and the fae at risk? It was the fear of bringing harm to Riff and the others that made him decide to leave them, Well, that, and because he refused to harm Akira. No one was safe around him. At that moment, he even wished he had left Ast and Cuz with his father. "I don't know what to do," Ghile said.

"Islmur will know."

"What?"

"Islmur will know what to do," Arenuin repeated.

All other thoughts flew away. "Islmur. The goddess?" Ghile said.

"Islmur told of your coming. It is Islmur who forbids entry into the Fallen City. Islmur will know what to do."

"I'm going to meet a god?" Ghile said, more to himself than to Arenuin.

Ghile was vaguely aware of Arenuin taking his hand and saying something about not letting go. Had he not just heard he was going to meet a god, he would have been shocked to see her step into the tree. But, his mind barely registered it. He turned to see Gutroot sitting easily on Cuz's back and waving when he felt his hand begin to tingle. They did not appear to be following. He turned to ask Arenuin why not, when he disappeared into the tree.

17

Without a Trace

 IFF's leg was throbbing. Every step worsened the ache. Two Elks refused to slow their pace and only stared at Riff when he asked for rests. He itched in a dozen places. In hindsight, he should have used the mud the villagers offered, but he just couldn't see rubbing the foul smelling stuff all over his skin, they all looked ridiculous. He could do without the itching, though. ·

He found himself staring at his feet again and quickly looked up into the trees. It was too easy to fall into the habit of looking at the ground just in front of his feet and focusing on his aches and pains. But after the second attack from the great cats that infested this damnable wood, he was not taking any more chances.

The creatures were so bold and difficult to spot before it was too late. They also seemed to favor picking off the last one in the group, which of course, always seemed to be him.Mud-covered Lotte, still grinning like an idiot, helped find the trail and was always up front close to Two Elks. Perfect Daughter Gaidel made it a point to stay right behind them. She didn't even bother to turn and glare when he called for rests. At least they had found a river and he no longer had to concern himself with an attack coming from his left. Of course, there was no telling what was in the river waiting to eat him. Riff moved a bit farther from the river's edge.

It was as if they were setting the pace to punish him. It wasn't his fault Ghile had decided to go it alone. Right now, he couldn't blame the sheepherder. He would give up a warm bed and a hot meal to know what had happened between the oh-so-proud druid and her shieldwarden. They had exchanged some harsh words back in the village. Of course, she had no interest in quenching his curiosity when he asked what the barbarian did to earn her ire.

Riff caught his foot under another root and pulled his sore leg for the umpteenth time. By Daomur's beard, he hated this place and it didn't look like they were going to be leaving it anytime soon. Ghile seemed to be heading into the heart of the Deepwood, following the pull of the soulstone like a Valehound with a scent up its nose and they followed like a band of idiotic hunters with no concern for where the hounds led them.

He leaned forward and grabbed some exposed roots, using them to pull himself up a steep incline. The sun, half way across the sky, broke through an open portion of the canopy to warm Riff's already sweaty neck. *Perfect*, he thought.

If it were up to him, he would have left Ghile in these woods. How could he leave and not take Riff with him? He thought they were friends? Why didn't he just wake him? Riff would have been happy to leave Gaidel and her meat shield with the mud men.

But Ghile had abandoned Riff with the others. Riff kept expecting to catch up with the others and find them standing over the sheepherder's body, laying there on the forest floor, dead eyes staring at nothing.

That won't happen, Riff thought quickly. Ghile couldn't die, could he? He would eventually wake up as good as new. The soulstones would see to that. Good, then Riff could kill him all over again.

He pulled his everflame from his pocket again and focused on the flame. He could feel the lack of power in his magic from being so far away from Ghile. It pained Riff to admit it, but he missed the power Ghile's presence brought him. How many times had he pulled out his everflame and once again experienced the loss?

"Wait, Daughter Gaidel," Riff called.

She was losing him again. They started their journey walking close together, but the more he questioned her about Two Elks, the tighter the set of her jaw, the louder the thump of her staff and the faster her stride.

This adventure was not turning out at all how Riff expected. When Master Almoriz told him he was to accompany Ghile, he had looked forward to it. The wizard had not deigned to leave the Cradle for a number of seasons and they spent most of their time in the outlying villages. It wouldn't have been so bad if Master Almoriz would have visited Lakeside more often, but with his dislike of his old apprentice, that fat oaf Hengon, Riff found the nights spent in a real bed in the town a rare luxury.

Of course, it all made sense now. Master Almoriz knew the soulstone was going to appear and wanted to be there in the Cradle when it did. Riff even believed the wily old sorcerer intended for Riff to be the one who found it. How many nights did he lay awake on some uncomfortable pallet, dreaming of journeying down the Underways from the Cradle to one of the other settlements?

But they hadn't taken the relatively safe Underways from the Cradle, they had left the Cradle through the Ghost Fens, where he was eaten by insects and almost eaten by worse. Only to survive and be walked to death in the bowels of the Deepwood and almost eaten again by its predators. How he hated cats. How he hated his traveling companions and most of all, how he blamed Ghile, since it was all his fault.

Through the trees, he could see the others had finally heard his calls and stopped. Hopefully this time, it would be for a real rest and not that sorry excuse for a break they had last night. Even the forest floor had felt like a freshly stuffed mattress when Two Elks called a halt for them to get some sleep. Riff felt as if he'd just closed his eyes when the barbarian was kicking him awake again, the forest black as it had been when they stopped.

Riff limped up next to the others where they stood in a line at the edge of a clearing. "About time you all listened to reason. My feet are killing—" His words choked off as he took in the clearing.

Pale bodies lay scattered across the churned up earth and the acrid smell of decay hung heavy in the air. Carrion birds eyed them and cawed, warning them not to think of disturbing their macabre meal.

"What by Daomur's hairy backside happened here?" Riff said.

The others stared in silence. Not even Lotte was talking and he definitely wasn't grinning. *At least that was something,* Riff thought absently.

"Are you sure the tracks lead here?" Gaidel said.

"Yes," Two Elks responded.

"I was speaking to Lotte, Shieldwarden," she said, her voice cold and even.

Lotte glanced between the two of them and swallowed. Riff was sure he too had pictured a different type of adventure when he set out this morning; all grins, nods, and aiming to please.

"Sure enuf, to make no nevermind, Daughter Gaidel," Lotte said. He spoke softly, without taking his eyes off the scene before them.

"This looks to be the work of a powerful druid," Gaidel said.

"Powerful Sorcerer."

"What did you say, Riff," Gaidel said.

"This was the work of a sorcerer. Well, at least some of it is. I can feel… something. Someone channeled water and air here recently. That is no small task. Strange, though, no fire," Riff said.

"Why is that strange?" Gaidel said.

"Of all the elements, it is the easiest to control. Stands to reason a sorcerer would channel it first."

Two Elks moved forward cautiously, kneeling down beside the dead as Gaidel stood there, shaking her head. "The ground, the stones. Even the nearby trees – look. The ground around their roots is disturbed. Whoever she was, she was powerful indeed if the trees actually *moved* at her call," Gaidel said.

Gaidel moved forward slowly, Riff close behind. She waved her staff to scatter the ravens and other carrion feeders before her. Lotte remained rooted to the spot.

"Daughter Gaidel, we should git," Lotte called softly.

"In a moment, Lotte."

"Ghile fought in battle," Two Elks said. He motioned to one of the nearby bodies. "This one killed by stones." He made quick thrusting motion towards his chest.

Riff blew out a low whistle. "You don't suppose he…"

"Daughter Gaidel, we shouldn't be here. Gone way too far fer our own good. We should git," Lotte said. He was trying to look in all directions at once.

"In a moment, Lotte. Please—" she began.

"This here is the Elves!" Lotte said in a harsh whisper.

All eyes turned to regard him.

"The Elves did this?" Gaidel questioned.

"How many would it take to do all this?" Riff asked, motioning at the clearing.

"Only take one, Daughter Gaidel. We need to git. The Elves got yur Ghile, fur cert'n," Lotte said. He was backing away as he spoke.

Gaidel apparently forgot she was angry with Two Elks, or just decided Lotte would be unable to focus in his current state.

"Two Elks, can you tell which way they went?"

The barbarian nodded and trotted off towards the far edge of the clearing.

Gaidel made her way to stand on a patch of ground in the center of the clearing, untouched by the destruction. "I wonder what the significance of this area is?"

Riff stepped gingerly towards Gaidel. A pale white face of a human woman, her milky white eyes staring blankly, caught his attention. Half of the dead one's face was stained blue. He wondered if she had come from Lotte's village. The thought that he and Gaidel could have saved her from this came to him. Ghile should have known that. Some of the dead ones were vargan and he wouldn't have tried to cure them of their affliction, even if Gaidel begged him. But the humans could have been spared this fate.

"Lotte, do you recognize any of them?" Riff called over his shoulder.

There was no response.

"Lotte! Did you hear me?" Riff turned back to see Lotte lying face down near the edge of the clearing.

"Lotte? Lotte! Gaidel, something is wrong with Lotte," Riff said as he began half running, half stumbling over the difficult terrain back towards Lotte. His everflame was already in his hand.

Just then Riff heard familiar barking coming from the other side of the clearing. Ghile's Valehounds? Riff spun, thinking to see a tired and ragged Ghile staggering out of the woods. What he saw instead stopped him in his tracks.

The two Valehounds were running across the clearing from the direction Two Elks had gone. A cloud of flying creatures followed, leaving a multihued cloud of rainbow colors in their wake. A small, bearded, brown potato rode on one of the Valehound's back, waving a stick and croaking for all it was worth.

Gaidel called for Two Elks and then raised her staff as the Valehounds and the trailing cloud reached her.

She had time to say, "Ast" and "Cuz", before she dropped her staff to slap at her neck and face. She fell to her knees and then face forward.

The two Valehounds ran right past her and continued towards him.

Riff had no intention of waiting to say hello.

He turned and ran, or at least started to. As he turned back towards Lotte, he saw another cloud surrounding the boy's prone body, more potatoes were jumping up and down on him, croaking.

Riff centered himself and focused on his everflame. He didn't look forward to explaining to Ghile why he had to roast his pets, but he didn't have any choice. Besides, this whole mess rested on Ghile's shoulders. He recalled the ancient words that would summon forth the flames when he felt numerous stings, tiny bites on the back of his neck and exposed arms. Had the bugs from the fens finally caught up with him to finish him off?

This was too much for Riff. He was so tired of all this. Tired in general. Why was he holding his everflame in broad daylight? He sat down to consider it.

Wait, he was in danger, wasn't he?

It didn't make any sense.

The sun was so warm on his skin and the upturned dirt so comfortable. Maybe he would just take a nap.

He felt something warm and wet slide across his face. Oh, it was one of Ghile's Valehounds. What was its name? He would have to ask his good friend, Ghile. Where was Ghile, anyway? Riff wasn't sure, but it would all make sense after he got some sleep. Yes, some sleep would make everything better.

Riff drifted off into a deep sleep with the image of the two Valehounds above him and waving from one of their backs, the ugliest bearded potato he had ever seen.

18

Among the Alvar

"I DON'T understand why we just don't treestep," Ghile said.

He was getting ahead of Arenuin again and made a conscious effort to shorten his stride. Over the last couple of days, Ghile learned that even though the Alvar were much taller than humans, they were nowhere near as fast. Everything they did seemed slow.

Well, that wasn't entirely fair – not everything. He took a steadying breath. He seemed to be doing that a lot lately. He was just irritated by how long this journey was taking.

When they first left the battle against the Fallen, as Arenuin named them, she told him they were going to meet Islmur, the Goddess of Magic. Even the shock of traveling from one place to another through living trees seemed to pale in comparison to the news you were about to meet a goddess.

When they stepped out of a different tree, Ghile expected to find Islmur standing before him, surrounded by light, or floating above him in the sky, or something equally godlike. Instead, what he found was more endless forest. It turned out the Alvar's form of travel, treestepping, had its limits. Arenuin explained the trees they traveled through must be touching and so it sometimes took a few 'jumps' to reach the destination. What she had neglected to add, was she was going to stop after each jump and spend hours singing to the trees.

It was how the Alvar communicated, apparently. The trees 'held' the song somehow. He didn't really understand it, but that was the best Arenuin could explain. She would first spend a frustratingly long time listening to the trees and then sing her message, so when another of the Alvar passed through, the trees would share the message.

So, they treestepped, Arenuin listened, treesung, and then treestepped again. Ghile couldn't tell by sight how far they traveled each time they treestepped, one part of the Deepwood looked much like any other, but he could tell by the pull of the soulstones that Akira was much further away than when they started.

That he was getting further away from the Fallen City, and that they could not bring Ast and Cuz along, hadn't helped his mood much either. Ghile hoped the Valehounds were all right and the fae would keep them safe. The image of his father's disapproving look when he learned Ghile lost the Valehounds made him grimace. That was, if he ever saw his father again.

"Be at ease, Ghile Stonechosen. The destination is close," Arenuin said.

"It's not that! I was just thinking about... never mind."

She ran her long slender fingers along the trunk of a tree as she passed, seemingly oblivious to his irritation, not to mention his rudeness. He had been raised better than to be this disrespectful to anyone, let alone the first Alvar he had ever met. Luckily, Arenuin didn't seem to notice or just chose not to comment.

She touched another tree.

She was always touching the trees, though anything could capture her interest. Feeling the contours of a large stone could hold her attention for minutes on end, if Ghile didn't remind her they needed to keep moving. A strong wind through the canopy or a flock of chirping birds overhead would stop her in her tracks. She would stare unmoving at whatever had enthralled her, looking like nothing more than a young sapling freshly born to the forest.

She did not stop this time and a smile touched her face as she let her hand fall back to her side. "They have heard my call, Ghile Stonechosen."

Movement off to his left caught his attention. Another Alvar came into view a short distance away, stepping out from the trunk of a large oak. Her movements were so fluid as she emerged, it was as if the tree was not even there. Unlike Arenuin, this Alvar's skin was a deep, mottled brown. Her hair was dark green and surrounded her head like a crown.

"An oak tree," Ghile said, his brooding forgotten, "Arenuin, there! Look, another Alvar. She looks like an oak tree."

"Yes, this one sees Karyai… and the others."

No sooner had she spoken than multiple Alvar stepped from the surrounding trees. Ghile almost tripped as he tried to take them all in at once. There were too many to count. Had Arenuin's treesinging called all the Alvar of the Deepwood?

No two were alike, though Ghile could see they all resembled different types of trees. Some had smooth grey skin, others almost black and rough. Their hair either hung down in long braids or bloomed out in all directions. Butterflies danced around many and Ghile saw more than one with a nest perched in their hair, like the feast day ornaments the girls of his village wore.

The one thing they did have in common was they were all obviously female. Numerous downturned, star-filled eyes gazed back at Ghile.

Ghile hadn't realized he'd stopped walking. It was his turn to catch up with Arenuin. She was singing when he reached her side. The forest rang with Alvar song. It was everywhere. It was beautiful.

He realized he had stopped again and his mouth was half open. He shook his head and caught up again, his irritable mood forgotten and replaced with curiosity. "Where are the men?" Ghile said.

"This one does not understand," Arenuin said.

"Why are only the female Alvar answering your call?"

Arenuin didn't answer right away and when she did, her response was full of mirth. "This one understands now. There are no males, like those of your race, among the Alvar."

"Then how..." Ghile trailed off and he felt his cheeks flush.

Arenuin openly laughed now, a melodious chitter, which only made the rest of Ghile's face take on the same color as his cheeks. "Are all humans curious about such things?"

Ghile coughed and shook his head. He decided he wasn't comfortable pursuing this particular line of questioning. Up ahead he could just make out a body of water, its smooth surface dancing with light just visible through the trees. Well, that explained why they couldn't treestep any further. Ghile doubted any of these trees had roots that ran that deep.

They arrived at the edge of a mountain lake. It was then Ghile realized the air reminded him of his home in Upper Vale back in the Cradle. He breathed it in, crisp and familiar. The range of low jagged mountains that bordered the far sides of the lake also reminded Ghile of home. Many of the peaks were tipped with snow. It was then that he saw the island.

At first he thought it was the light reflecting off the waters and he blinked and shook his head, trying to clear it from his vision. It wasn't possible. There in the center of the lake was *his* island. His place in the dreaming. There was even a tree near its center, much larger than all the others.

No, wait, this isn't possible, he told himself. He took it all in again and cautioned his mind to not see what he remembered, but to take in the details of the place in front of him. It wasn't exactly the same. In the dreaming, the mountain range surrounded the lake like a bowl. The Great Oak in the center of the island was gigantic and reached up towards the clouds. But, otherwise, this place was his dreaming recreated on Allwyn. "What is this place," he heard himself asking.

"Welcome to Islmur's Grove, Ghile Stonechosen," Arenuin said. She and the other Alvar stood along the shore of the lake, seeming as awed as he was.

"I have been here before," Ghile said, not sure if he believed his own words.

"That is not possible. The grove is sacred to the Alvar and none other than the Alvar are welcome. The Guardians would never allow it," Arenuin said. "Now, this one asks Ghile Stonechosen to stay close."

With that, Arenuin took up the Dream Song and stepped onto the water. Ghile felt her long limb-like fingers encircle his free hand and guide him forward. He feared falling into the lake and half stumbled, half tripped. The water rose up and caught his feet, steadying him. He couldn't help but laugh as the water gushed under him like moving springs, holding him aloft.

To both sides of him, Alvar stepped off the shore and onto the lake's surface, the water rising up to support them. Surrounded by the lapping waves, they all drifted away from shore.

The mountain winds, freed from the trees, whipped Ghile's brown curls about and filled his ears. He turned back to look towards the fading shore, where more Alvar emerged from the woods and stepped out onto the lake's surface to follow them.

"This is incredible, Arenuin! How do you make the water do this?" Ghile shouted above the dancing water and rushing wind.

"This one asks," she replied, as if he had asked what color was the sky.

Ghile held on tightly to Arenuin's fingers, fearing what would happen if he let go. His legs were soon soaked, but the cold didn't seem to bother him, he found it refreshing against his skin.

As they neared the island, Ghile saw Alvar step from the trees. Even from this distance, Ghile could tell the Alvar on the island were twice as big as Arenuin or any of the others approaching on the water. Even before he could ask, Arenuin spoke.

"The Guardians of the Grove. This one asks Ghile Stonechosen to not speak and do nothing. The Guardians will not be pleased this one has brought you."

Ghile only nodded. As they neared the shore, he could hear the Guardians' song rising above the roiling water. Through the soulstones, he could hear them beseeching the waters to repel the intruders, for the trees and stones to come to the aid of the grove.

They reached the shore and Ghile followed Arenuin onto land. She moved him behind her and waited. Ghile looked about him, waiting to be attacked, but no attack came. The waters of the lake settled as soon as they released their passengers and no trees reached for him, or stones exploded from the earth to crush him.

One of the guardians, a huge Alvar, colored like an elm, stepped forward and swung her arm into Arenuin, knocking her to the ground. "You do not belong here!" she said. The song of the Alvar carried her emotions.

Arenuin made no attempt to defend herself and remained laying there, on the ground.

The guardian stepped forward, towering over Ghile. One swipe had knocked Arenuin to the ground, but what would a blow like that do to him? He was in no hurry to find out. Its face was contorted with rage as it raised both moss-covered arms above its head.

Ghile didn't want to disobey Arenuin, but he was not about to be crushed. He called forth his mind shield and anchored it to the ground around him.

"That is enough!"

The command, though not sung loudly, froze the guardian above him in place. The speaker, obviously also a guardian, based on her size, stepped up next to Ghile's attacker.

"Duanotyn, this one finds your actions shameful."

Duanotyn, lowered her arms and stepped from Ghile. "Keeper, this one only protects the grove. The others are not invited and this human—"

"Does Duanotyn not see that Allwyn does not answer our call?" the Keeper said. "Would Duanotyn further shame us by striking one of our own and then a stonechosen? Look, even now, the power of Haurtu protects him."

Duanotyn looked from the Keeper to Ghile and then lowered her head. "This one asks forgiveness." She reached down and helped Arenuin to her feet.

Ghile let his shield go and glared at Duanotyn. Sorry or not, she had no business hitting Arenuin like that.

"This one understands and asks the Guardians to welcome, Ghile Stonechosen," Arenuin said.

The Keeper inclined her head to Arenuin and then Ghile.

"Though it brings this one no joy, Ghile Stonechosen and those who would call to Islmur are welcome to her grove."

19

The Settlement

 AIDEL was cold. She knew she was on that edge of being awake and asleep. Each time she started to wake the warmth of the sun on her skin and the fresh humid smell of things green and growing lulled her back to sleep.

She was dreaming of the Three Arrows and her father. They used to take walks in the Redwood in the high summer, the sun warming her skin and the smell of green in the air. She had been walking through another forest recently, but couldn't recall exactly where. She was with Two Elks. The thought reminded her of their fight with the vargan in the Drops near the Cradle. Yes, Two Elks was with her. She was angry with him, wasn't she? Yes, she was angry with him. He had overstepped his bounds and said something to Ghile he shouldn't. Ghile spoke the old tongue now and the two talked into the night. Then, the next morning, Ghile was gone. They had all set off after him.

Gaidel heard barking. Yes, Ghile left with Ast and Cuz.

Ghile's Valehounds! Gaidel opened her eyes and bolted upright. She was on the edge of a field, the long leaves of its tall, thin stalks waved lazily in the evening breeze. The sun sat just beyond the stalks. She could still smell its warmth on the plants. Ast and Cuz chased each other, playing through the long rows.

She tried to clear the cobwebs from her mind. Where was Ghile? Had they found him? She pulled her legs under her and sat there for a moment. Where was she? Two Elks, Riff and the boy from the village, what was his name? Lotte, yes, his name was Lotte. The three of them lay nearby, their chests rising and falling in the familiar rhythms of sleep. Gaidel released a breath she didn't realize she was holding. At least everyone was all right.

But where was Ghile? If the hounds were here, then he should be as well. Gaidel called to the two Valehounds, who bounded over to gratefully accept pats and scratches.

"Where is Ghile, you two?" Gaidel said.

She sat there for a short time, taking comfort in petting them and giving herself time to think. How did they get here and how did they end up with Ghile's Valehounds?

She roused the others and explored her surroundings while they came to. They were at the edge of a forest where it met the field, its uniform crop stretching off into the distance like dwarven soldiers. She was too short to see over the tall stalks.

"Two Elks, lift me up," Gaidel said.

Two Elks gathered his weapons and stood, shaking his head to try to clear it. "Where?" he started to say.

His question irritated her. She was still upset with him. "That is what I want to find out. Lift me up."

He put down his weapons and lifted her easily to the full extent of his arms. Below her, Riff rubbed his head and looked around, confused.

"Is Ghile here? Where did his hounds come from?" Riff said, as he tried in vain to push the two Valehounds away from him. They danced around him, trying to get him to chase them.

Gaidel ignored him. The golden-topped plants, whatever they were, stretched off over rolling hills like a blanket. She could just make out the top of some kind of structure peeking over a distant hill, a road running over it, cutting a brown path.

"This way, I see a road," Gaidel said, motioning for Two Elks to let her down.

"Road to where?" Riff said.

"Not sure, I see some kind of structure in the distance, the road must lead to it."

Two Elks had already gathered his tower shield and stone axe. But, Lotte stood near the forest's edge, shaking his head.

"Lotte, what's wrong," Gaidel said.

"This ain't no good, Daughter Gaidel. The elves done got us," Lotte said. He looked left and right, as if he expected the fabled Elves of the Deepwood to come pouring forth.

"What are you babbling about?" Riff said. He sounded irritated, but Gaidel noted he was scanning the woods warily.

"This here crop of corn. We near the Freehold, plum on the other side of the Deepwood and no recollect'n how we got here. The elves done got us." Lotte pointed at the two Valehounds. "And them dogs was with your friend. The elves done got him, too. Got him and kept him by the looks of it. Ain't no good, none of it."

Gaidel took a deep breath and tried to think. As hard as she tried, she could not remember anything beyond setting out with the others from the village. That had been in the morning and it was obviously later in the day. But, she had a hazy memory of being in the woods after dark. Had they fought a black cat?

"Two Elks, what can you remember?" Gaidel said.

Two Elks thought for a short time and shrugged his thick shoulders. "The woods at night, Little Daughter. Nothing more."

"And you?" Gaidal looked to Riff.

"Not much more. I remember setting out from the village. I remember insects and walking at night. Everything else is hazy," he finished with a shrug of his own.

"It's the elves do'n fo sure!" Lotte said. "We need to git. This is Dagbar's domain. Ain't no place for my kind here," Lotte said, backing towards the forest.

Gaidel fixed him with a hard stare and pointed her staff at him. "Don't take another step."

Lotte froze.

This made no sense, but she was not going to lose anyone else to reckless thinking. She sent Two Elks to scout the immediate area and see if they were alone as they seemed. The two hounds bounded after him as he left in a trot.

They waited for Two Elks to return. Time seemed to crawl. Gaidel listened to the insects as they came alive with the evening. She only recognized some of them and though the sound was comforting, since it meant no predators were nearby, it only further reminded her how far she was from home.

Riff sat at the forest's edge, running an idle hand through his everflame, deep in thought. Every so often he would shake his head, as if to clear it and start again.

Lotte no longer smiled and seemed to have slowly shifted from where he had been sitting next to Riff to further within the Deepwood. Would he really be foolish enough to make a run for it?

She went to stand over him. "Lotte. Regardless of where we are or how we got here, you are going nowhere alone, do you understand me?"

He nodded staring up at her, his eyes wide and unblinking.

"You can't blame him for being scared, Gaidel," Riff said without looking up from his everflame.

"That isn't the point, Riff," she said.

They didn't know where they were for sure, or how they had gotten there. They needed to stay together and find some answers. If this settlement was indeed Dagbar's Freehold, then they needed to find Dagbar. If the Elves had found Ghile and captured him, then they were going to need help to get him back.

What if the elves had somehow captured them and brought them here, wiping the entire experience from their minds? That was a lot of ifs. They needed to find answers and they wouldn't find them in the Deepwood.

Riff looked up from his everflame, apparently tired of waiting for her to continue. "Well, what is the point? We can't enter a settlement at night, not and keep our heads attached to our necks."

"Agreed. We need to wait until morning." She kept her voice even. She would not lose her temper with him. Why did everything he say seem to irritate her so much?

"Fine for us," Riff said, pointing at the two of them. "But Lotte here will be killed as soon as they see him or have you forgotten what they do to humans who exist outside the settlements? Two Elks being your warder was the only thing that kept him alive and then just barely."

"Druids and sorcerers can travel between the settlements. As my shieldwarden, Two Elks falls under the same laws. I will think of something for Lotte."

"Oh, I'm sure you will," Riff said, a smirk accompanying his words.

She was just about to let him know what she thought about him when a voice came from somewhere within the corn stalks.

"A Gwa A'Chook dwelling. Empty," Two Elks called.

"Perfect timing," Riff said, hastily scrambling to his feet, his eyes never meeting hers. "Come along, Lotte. You heard her, she'll think of something. Adventure awaits."

20

Know Thyself

 HILE opened his eyes. He was in the dreaming. He was in the clearing surrounding the Great Oak. He found it strange. He assumed he would enter the dreaming at the same place he went to sleep on Allwyn since he was in the same place. He guessed it didn't work that way.

The Great Oak stretched upwards before him, overshadowing the other trees, its upper boughs lost in the dark grey clouds. Thunder played in the distance.

The Great Oak was not the only thing that was different. In Allwyn, many of the trees on the island were silvertrees. Ghile took in the trees around the clearing and didn't see even one.

Even with the differences, it was obviously the same place and Ghile wanted to know why.

"Where are you, Adon?" he called. Only wind answered.

"Muk? What about you?"

Ghile waited, listening intently. There was no answer. He was alone. Of course they weren't there. Why would they be? They probably knew exactly why he was here.

He set off at a run, his face a tight grimace. He didn't know where he was going, but he couldn't just stand there and wait.

The sky glowed as lighting flashed somewhere nearby, the thunderclap followed almost instantaneously. The weather didn't bother him, somehow it seemed fitting, reflected his mood.

He pushed down with his force shield and soared into the air. He touched down on a limb only to push off and soar to the next. He lost himself in the movements, letting his anger play out.

When he found Adon, he was going to get answers. He was in no hurry to return from the dreaming anytime soon. The keeper had made it clear they could not commune with Islmur until more of the Alvar answered Arenuin's call and came to the grove. He didn't know how many they needed for the ritual they would perform. It was obvious the Guardians were not going to tell him anymore than they thought he needed to know, which wasn't much.

Even his questions about the silvertrees seem to upset them. Arenuin was about to explain about the ritual to commune with Islmur and had even gotten so far as to say it had only been done once before in her lifetime, when the Keeper had motioned her to silence. Then he was told to wait. He had not had the opportunity to speak with Arenuin since.

That had been over four days ago. Four days of waiting, watching the island fill with Alvar, and none of them willing to say more than one word to him. He would have thought they would have been curious to speak with a human now that one was here who could understand their sing-song language, but they didn't seem overly impressed. They simply congregated together in small groups and sang to one another. They sang softly on the island; it reminded Ghile of how people acted when they were in trouble and just waiting on the punishment to be meted out.

He landed on a limb and brought himself to an abrupt halt. The mountain lake stretched out before him. He had reached the edge of the island. He pushed off and drifted down to the rock strewn shore, landing in a spray of sliding stones. He reached with his mind and began sending stones, one at a time, skipping out over the black water, its surface a reflection of the roiling clouds. The rocks blurred the image as they skipped along to finally disappear beneath the surface.

He didn't know how long he paced along the beach, buried in his thoughts, sending stones out over the water. But the storm he expected seemed to have passed by, the winds settled and small patches of blue appeared as the clouds thinned.

He sensed rather than heard something behind him and turned to see the shadow creature watching from the forest's edge. It no longer crouched or rubbed its hands, but simply stood there. There was no doubt the shape of it was him. A shadowy representation of him. Even though it had no eyes, or face for that matter, Ghile could feel it watching him. He felt like he was being weighed and measured.

It once again took two steps back and dissolved into black, swirling smoke. The smoke stretched into a large open space between two trees. Within their confines, a swirling black doorway formed.

Finally, some answers, Ghile thought. He tightened his fists at his sides and strode forward. He passed between the trees and was swallowed by the smoke.

$$\wedge$$

He felt a hand on his shoulder.

"Be still, Ghile. The ceremony is about to begin," his mother said.

Ghile swallowed the retort he was about to aim at Gar, who had just been bragging about how the druids would choose him as a Fang after his manhood tests, just like Adon. Beside Gar, pig-eyed Bralf was snickering and talking behind his hand into Gar's ear. Ghile could just hear the sarcastic, "be still, Ghile," when a quick pinch from Aunt Jilla quieted him, much to Ghile's satisfaction. He gave Bralf a quick, satisfied grin then turned back around before Aunt Jilla saw him.

He looked out at the line of young men and women, who were of age, forming up between the two nearest bonfires. The sun had long since lowered behind Lakeside's wooden palisade, muting the colors of the many tents sheltered under its outer wall. The fires in the festival field cast long shadows, causing the faces of the other spectators to dance between shadow and light. Two armored dwarves standing near the dwarven elders held torches of everflame. The light of the bonfires paled in comparison.

He wondered if he might be chosen as a Fang? At ten, he had four more years before he would take his manhood tests. Ghile only hoped he could do as well as Adon had.

The earlier exuberance of the crowd was dying down, quieted by the seriousness of the upcoming Rite of Attrition. His father and Uncle Toren were still grinning with pride from the earlier news and spoke softly with Uncle Dargen, who was still patting Ghile's father on the shoulder and congratulating him.

As was custom, the whole family had stood before the eldest of the druids for Adon's final ceremony of the Manhood Rites – the Choosing. His father and mother right behind Adon, with Ghile to his mother's right. She had sensed Ghile's apprehension and held his hand comfortingly, her other rubbing the side of her small, swollen belly.

They followed along behind Adon as he waited his turn to stand before the druid. The initiates before them each approached and stood before her, waiting. She continued to sing, ignoring them. They moved on and the next group moved forward.

The old druid was lost in the song when they approached with Adon. Several other druids stood behind her, heads bowed, singing along in unison. Mother Brambles reminded him of a shriveled fruit someone forgot and left out in the sun.

It seemed everyone froze when she opened her eyes and pointed her gnarled staff at Adon. Behind her eyes, Ghile saw something flowing, like a river of streaming lights. He started to scream, but luckily his cries were consumed by the cheers of the crowd. Adon was to be a Fang of the Cradle.

It hadn't really surprise Ghile; he had half expected it. Everything great always happened to Adon. He had been the first to emerge from the Redwood that morning and the only one chosen by the druids. Ghile felt a slight pang in his chest and wondered if he had eaten too much of the hard candy he'd traded that other boy his wool hat for. He rubbed his chest and shifted impatiently.

All that was left was the formalities of this Rite the dwarves added on to the ceremonies and then he could go play with all the other boys. All the adults would be celebrating well into the night. Maybe he would find a game of ghost in the graveyard around the tents to join in. The others always wanted him and Adon to play. But Ghile wondered if he would still be invited if Adon wasn't there. He was a man now; he would be celebrating with the adults. Ghile felt another pain in his chest. A horn sounded, announcing the beginning of the Rite of Attrition.

A dwarf in a flowing cloak and heavy armor strode into view. The cloak billowed with each of his steps and his armor shimmered as if it were on fire. Most impressive was the intricate hammer the dwarf carried before him in both hands. The head of the hammer was huge. Ghile forgot about his upset stomach as he watched the Culler step before the first human in line.

Ghile shifted left and right to try and get a better view. He was behind the Culler and couldn't see what was happening. Dwarves were not a tall race, but they were twice as wide as a human and the first one in line was a diminutive girl. The dwarf turned and moved before the next in line. Ghile could see the Culler still held the hammer before him.

This rite was always the most difficult to wait through. Ghile was always confused about it. The initiates from the manhood tests, even the ones who failed, lined up with the young women who had come of age to be handfasted and an armored dwarf would walk before them. Adults and dwarves did a lot of things Ghile didn't really understand, but this ceremony always seemed to scare the older women and irritate the men. Ghile watched his father, who still spoke with Uncle Toren and Uncle Dargen in hushed tones. There was still a slight grin on his father's face, but something about the set of his father's eyes made Ghile uneasy.

Ghile's mother wore concern plainly on her face and he could feel her hand tightening on his shoulder each time the culler moved down the line and closer to Adon.

The culler eventually reached Adon and moved to stand before him. Ghile could see Adon's head above the dwarf's helmet. Adon's eye's widened at the same time Ghile's mother let go of his shoulder and covered a wail.

Adon had been chosen again. Ghile moaned and rolled his eyes – was there no contest his brother wouldn't win? Uncle Toren and his father were holding his mother and she struggled to reach Adon, who was being escorted by another dwarf who looked as surprised as Adon. He was going to get to go into the Bastion.

Ghile stared after his brother as Adon was escorted away towards the main gate into Lakeside, when the pain in his chest became so intense, he clutched at his chest and fell to his knees. He could feel two small solid lumps under his skin. The soulstones.

His mother's cries were gone and the only sound he heard was the flickering of the many bonfires.

Still holding the pressure to his chest, Ghile rose. How had he come to be here? It didn't make any sense. He had been in the dreaming and stepped through the shadow door. He shook his head. Why did he think he was ten?

The festival field was empty. He was alone and himself again. Where was he? He turned to look at the tents along the palisade wall, a flap on one had come undone and snapped lazily in the breeze.

"He was our brother," a young voice said. Ghile had heard that familiar voice before, but it was somehow different.

He turned around to stare into his own ten-year-old face.

"Who are you?" Ghile said. He took a step back, his eyes darting left and right, looking for any other dangers. He reached for his belt pouch and the stones within.

"He was our brother," young Ghile said again.

Ghile didn't see anyone else and focused his attentions on the younger version of himself. He had never heard his own voice from outside his head and the difference was unsettling.

"Who are you? Tell me now," Ghile said. He had pulled the stones from his pouch and held them before him.

"I know who we are," the younger Ghile said. "But do you? He was our brother and he was chosen to be culled, murdered by the dwarves," the younger Ghile said as a grin spread across his face, "and we were happy about it."

Ghile stepped back as if slapped. "What? What are you talking about? He was my brother. I loved Adon!" Ghile remembered the confusion, the guilt, he felt when his father later explained what happened to Adon within the Bastion. He remembered his mother constantly crying and almost losing the baby, the baby that would become Tia, his little sister.

"We were relieved when we found out. We no longer had to live in our older brother's shadow," the younger Ghile said.

"What are you talking about? I loved my brother. I miss him every day. You don't know what his death did to my mother, my father!" Ghile said. His voice trembled with emotion and he tried to blink away the wetness that gathered in the corners of his eyes.

"You keep saying that like it makes things better. We were happy when we found out. Why can't you just admit it?" younger Ghile said. The look of disgust on his face burned as badly as his words.

Ghile shook his head and turned, the stones in his hand forgotten on the ground. He had to get out of here, to escape. He ran towards the gatehouse. Maybe he could stop them from taking Adon into the Bastion. Maybe he could save him.

"Adon!" Ghile cried out, as everything around him turned into swirling grey smoke.

$$\Lambda$$

Ghile sat on the pebbled beach next to the two trees. He turned a small bit of moss over and over in his hand. He wasn't really looking at it, as much as using it for something to distract a portion of his mind from what he had seen and said.

The tears had long since dried, but the emotion was still there, just below the surface, threatening to pour forth. He knew that had been him, his memories of that night. A part of him wished he had used the stones against his younger self. As much for what his younger self said, as the look of contempt on his face.

How could he have been happy that his older brother was taken? Ghile violently shook his head, as if it would throw the black thoughts away, freeing him from them.

Adon didn't deserve to die. The dwarves had no right to take him and kill him. They had no right to take anyone! Ghile felt a fire-like heat wash over his skin.

"Don't change the subject," Ghile said to himself.

"But I have not spoken, Ghile Stonechosen."

Ghile bolted up. "Akira!" The irresistible pull of her soulstone tugged at his chest.

A smile touched her lips and Ghile felt a momentary happiness that passed all too quickly as her look turned to concern.

"You have been crying, what happened?" Akira said, stepping forward and reaching for his face.

Ghile quickly wiped at his face with his sleeve. "Nothing, it's nothing."

She lowered her hand quickly. "I don't know what I hoped to wipe away."

Ghile looked up at the thickness of her voice. She was staring at her hand, made of the same grey swirling smoke as the rest of her. "I'm sorry Akira, I was on my way to help you."

She looked up then and tilted her head slightly to the side. "You're so far away now, Ghile. What happened? Where are you?"

"I'm with the Alvar."

"The Elves? Ghile, you are not safe, the elves have no love for our kind," Akira said.

Ghile raised his hands and tried to calm her. "It's alright, I'm fine. I'm safe, but they've brought me somewhere far from the Fallen City and for that I am sorry."

He went on to tell her about leaving his companions and setting off into the Deepwood, about meeting the fae, Arenuin, and fighting off the fallen.

"I have seen the work of this evil sorcerer first hand, Akira. What he did to those people and those Vargan… it… it was horrible. Is that what you were talking about, when you said there were things in the mists?"

Akira just stared at him, her face unreadable. Finally, she said, "Yes… yes, they are horrible."

"So, I'm sorry, but the sorcerer somehow knew I was coming to help you and sent those things to stop me. I couldn't risk leading them to you and your brother. I need to speak with Islmur. Maybe she can help all of us," Ghile said.

Akira simply nodded and said nothing. *Had he frightened her,* he thought. It made sense. She and her brother were hidden somewhere in the Fallen City and there was some powerful sorcerer hunting for them. She was stonechosen, and Ghile had seen firsthand, how having a stonechosen nearby increased a sorcerer's strength. He said as much to Akira.

"The part that confuses me, though, is how the sorcerer knew I was coming to help you? There's no doubt those fallen were after me," Ghile said.

"I don't know, Ghile. But, I don't think there is time for you to speak to Islmur. How do you know the elves will even let you go, once you do?" Akira said.

He had to speak to Islmur. There were so many things he didn't know. Now that he had gone through the shadow door, there was yet another. "I don't know how to explain it, but I trust them. At least, I trust Arenuin. I don't think the others mean me harm. If they did, they would have done something already," Ghile said.

Akira made to sit down next to him and Ghile moved over to make room. They sat there for a moment and looked out over the waters. Ghile kept glancing at her. He wanted to talk to her about the shadow door and could tell she wanted to talk about something as well and like him, didn't know where to begin.

"This is a beautiful place, Ghile," Akira finally said.

"It is. I remember you said your dreaming was a clearing in a forest, with a stream?"

"Yes, it, too, was a beautiful place."

"But, there was no Great Oak, or mountains?" Ghile said. He wanted to understand what significance his dreaming had. Why was his Islmur's Sacred Grove? He had never been there before.

"Had you ever seen the grove before?" Ghile asked.

Akira tilted her head.

He noticed she always seemed to do this when she thought. He found it endearing. Everything from her small perfect feet, to her strange accent, fascinated him.

"No, I had never seen it before," Akira said.

"What about a shadow creature?" Ghile said. He could tell by the way she jumped and turned to him that she had.

"Yes, there was such a creature hiding in the woods surrounding the glen. My mother told me to be wary of it and not approach it. That it was dangerous," Akira said.

"There is one here, too. I have seen it… and more." Ghile struggled with his thoughts. How much could he tell Akira about his shadow self and what he found beyond the shadow door? The idea of sharing what he had seen made Ghile so embarrassed.

But Adon had also told him to stay away from the shadow creature and that it wasn't safe. It had also attacked Adon. But, now Ghile knew the creature was really him, his shadow. And it hadn't attacked him, but shown him something from his past. But why? And why did Adon not want him to see it?

"Well," Akira said.

Ghile started and blushed when he realized she was staring at him. "I'm sorry, it's just there's a shadow creature here in my dreaming. Adon, my brother – you remember him – you met him when you visited me the first time. He told me the creature was dangerous as well and to stay away from it. Only…"

Akira reached out and held her hand just above his. He knew if she tried to touch him, her hand would give way, but just having it there, near his, gave him comfort.

"Only I did seek the creature and found out it was not really a creature at all. It was *me*. It was *my* shadow. And it didn't try to hurt me. It showed me something, something from my past. That was what I was thinking about when you found me," Ghile said.

"What did it show you?"

Ghile swallowed. Could he tell her? Could he tell anyone? Maybe she could help him understand what it meant, why it wanted him to see that and why it had said those horrible things to him?

In the end, he told her what his shadow self had shown him. Once he began, it came pouring out. She never interrupted him and once he was through, she just sat there next to him in silence, her grey hand hovering above his.

"Oh, Ghile. I am sorry, for what happened to your brother," Akira said.

He nodded. "Thank you." He felt so much better having shared the experience. She had not judged him or called him a monster. "What do you think it means?" Ghile said.

"I don't know, but I wonder what mine would have shown me and why both your brother and my mother didn't want us to see it?" Akira questioned.

"He isn't my brother," Ghile said. It was the first time he'd put words to the thought.

"I know, Ghile. I realized she wasn't my mother, too. But, it doesn't change how wonderful it had been to see her again."

"I know," Ghile said. "Even though I know it's not really Adon, I can't help think some part of him is there, though. Just like with Muk."

"The goblin?"

"Yes, even though it isn't truly him, he remembers what happened in the cave and before. He shared with me his journey over the mountain and how he controlled the worgs from the forbidden city he'd come from.

"I hate goblins," Akira said.

They both chuckled and then laughed out loud. Ghile couldn't remember the last time he had done that. "I will come for you, Akira," Ghile said.

Akira rose. "I must go."

Ghile jumped up. "Wait, don't leave. Why do you have to leave?" How had what he said upset her? He had been sure it would make her happy.

She shook her head, turning to hide her face and faded from view.

Ghile stood there on the shore, playing things over in his head and trying to understand what he'd said wrong.

In the end, he decided he had a lot to learn about women. The best thing he could do was to speak with Islmur as soon as possible, and find out everything he could about the soulstones, the prophecy, and what he could do to help Akira and her brother.

Another thought occurred to him then and it was not one he was familiar with. Ghile had never been one for vengeance, but he would find that sorcerer in the Fallen City and make sure he paid for what he had done.

21

Dinner with Dagbar

INNGYR had grown tired of these private dinners, this settlement, the accents, and most of all, Magister Dagbar.

He drained his tankard of the last vestiges of hardy stout and placed it on the wooden table. Wooden, of all things; the crazy magister and his obsession with wood. The scrape of the pitcher warned him and he leaned back just as a dwarven servant appeared at his side to refill his drink.

Finngyr watched in silence. The servant was an old dwarf, with more than a little grey in his beard. He should have been sitting near a hearth somewhere with younglings on his knee, not serving table. His face was tattooed half blue – ridiculous Allwynians. Dagbar surrounded himself with them, dwarf and human alike. Almost as bad as being waited on by a human. At least the Magister had sense enough to keep his human servants on his side of the table. They looked too old to be servants, as well, for that matter. Everything about this place grated on him.

Finngyr looked about the private dining room. The silverwood walls reflected the light from the fire burning in the hearth and bathed the room in no small amount of light. One of the few rooms at the top of the Bastion, in the Magister's private chambers, it barely held the long banquet table and side serving boards. It looked more like a meeting room than a dining hall. But even with the close confinement, the place felt open to Finngyr. It was all the wood, it felt makeshift and fragile. The placed lacked the permanence of stone.

Finngyr would have preferred eating in the great hall with all the other inhabitants of the Bastion, but Magister Dagbar had insisted he see personally to such important guests from the capital. Keeping them from overhearing all the conversations and so he could question them each evening, was closer to the truth.

For over two weeks they had been the Magister's 'diplomatic guests'. Magister Dagbar was more than willing to give them free reign of the settlement. Though his disappointment was obvious when Finngyr didn't start a riot on the first day. In honesty, it had taken all of Finngyr's restraint not to enact Daomur's judgement on the deserving, and there were many in this place. Instead, the knights had long since scoured the settlement looking for any sign of a stonechosen. Even though they couldn't perform the rites again, nothing stopped them from walking the streets with their hammers in their hands, reciting the words of the rite to themselves. Of course, all this was done under the guise of gathering information about the whereabouts of Knight Justice Griff.

Knight Kjar had been especially useful in setting up a network of well-paid informants who kept him abreast of all the comings and goings. Finngyr had to admit, although begrudgingly, he wouldn't have been able to do it on his own. He had no love of these border settlements with all their human vermin and could barely tolerate the smell in the Cradle. But with the crowding caused by the trouble from the Deepwood, and constant traffic of the trade market, this place positively reeked.

He watched the other two Knights as they engaged Magister Dagbar in conversation. They played their parts well and even seemed to enjoy listening to the Magister's inane ramblings. Finngyr had decided early on that he would limit his own interactions with the Magister, and the younger knights were to go out of their way to win his trust.

After the battle with the orcs, Knight Kjar had told him everything on that rocky outcropping and Finngyr had made sure Knight Horth understood his place and his chances of leaving the settlement alive should he cause Finngyr to fail. It was likely Magister Dagbar knew the part Knight Horth was meant to play and might let something important slip in his impatience to force the young knight's hand and get the excuse he needed to be rid of them. It was no trouble playing the part of the Knight Justice who despised everything about the place and would like nothing more than to purge it clean. It was true.

Finngyr confirmed early on that the Right of Culling had not resulted in any deaths, more's the pity. No one admitted to seeing Knight Justice Griff after the rites, either. Finngyr had searched the Bastion from top to bottom, with no luck. Though he didn't think the Magister would have the audacity to imprison a Knight Justice. Then there was the Knight Justice's griffon. If he was still in the area, his griffon would have been spotted. Finngyr had little doubt he would have heard the complaints about missing livestock, or the odd human.

Though there was no indication where Knight Griff had gone and no traces of any stonechosen, they had gleaned other information during their outings. The settlement was under attack by strange creatures from the Deepwood. White abominations that raided in the night and killed or carried off any they found. Those they took, they somehow infected with their contagion and swelled their ranks. There were as many rumors on where they came from and why, as there were tongues spreading them. As curious as Finngyr was about the creatures, he could not help but see the hand of Daomur in their presence. They had driven every human in the settlement from the outlying hamlets and villages and behind these walls. It made his search that much easier.

Magister Dagbar's treaty with the Elves was of more interest. Rumor placed it on the verge of collapse. The Deepwood was all but closed by the elves, or the Alvar as they named them here. Silly name, really. Who cared what the elves called themselves? They were elves.

It seemed the elves blamed the settlement for the abominations infesting their precious Deepwood. The reason for that, other than humans from the settlement swelling its ranks, Dagbar had not been able to discover. Yet another blessing from Daomur, as far as he was concerned. Anything that would hurt this self-righteous wood lover was welcomed.

"Enjoying your meal, Knight Justice Finngyr? I thought I almost saw a grin. Something sweet, perhaps," Dagbar said.

Finngyr quickly composed his features.

"Dessert, then!" Horth said, rubbing his hands together with enthusiasm.

Dagbar laughed out loud.

Finngyr could only shake his head and even Horth and Kjar looked askance at each other. Such an open display of emotion, had Dagbar forgotten what it meant to be a dwarf?

"No dessert," Finngyr said. He stared at Knight Horth.

"Surely something else, then? Cheese, perhaps?"

Finngyr heard the old dwarf servant already lifting something behind him, before Finngyr could decline. "I said, no."

"You are a most gracious host, Magister Dagbar," Knight Kjar said quickly. "But I believe we are done."

Finngyr slid his chair back from the table, not waiting for the servants to do it for him. He noted the human servants had not moved from the wall and were looking at each other in concern. Magister Dagbar had not moved and even he looked suddenly discomforted.

"Please, remain seated, there are matters I wish to discuss," Magister Dagbar said.

Something odd was going on here. Both Knight Horth and Knight Kjar half stood, waiting for Finngyr to take the lead. He sat back down. "Go on."

"It.... it seems... I think you have been here long enough," Magister Dagbar finally said. He breathed out audibly and seemed to set his mind on his course. That, or he had just settled on this course.

"Most gracious, indeed," Finngyr said. He decided he would play along. "Go on."

"The previous Knight Justice left after the Rites, as was reported to your superiors when they first inquired. You have searched the Emporium and found nothing to the contrary. I see no reason for you to remain."

Both the younger knights could not hide their astonishment. They both watched Finngyr, waiting to see his reaction.

Was Dagbar deliberately trying to anger him? To what end? In all the times they had climbed to the top of the Bastion to dine in this wretched bundle of overpriced sticks, Dagbar had always been diplomatic. He was not wont of emotion, he carried on like a human, but never confrontational.

There had been times where Finngyr felt the Magister tested him with questions concerning their beliefs. Dagbar had even gone so far as to question if their order knew the true meaning of what Daomur meant when he said the dwarves were to shepherd the humans and watch over them. He had even espoused the belief his settlement was following the doctrines closer than the Temple of Justice. Finngyr had not taken the bait and recognized it for what it was, a planned attempt to upset him. But this outburst was sudden. Unplanned.

Finngyr pushed his chair back and stood up abruptly, the younger knights quickly following suit. "You are right of course, Magister Dagbar. We will leave in the morning. Excuse us, it is time for our evening prayers."

The Magister's jaw dropped, but he quickly recovered. "Now see here, I'm not finished."

Finngyr was already walking out of the room, leaving Magister Dagbar shouting at his back.

Knight Horth was the last out of the room and shut the door behind him. He hurried to catch up. "What do you know, Knight Justice?"

Even he could tell something was not quite right. Maybe there was hope for him yet.

"Knight Kjar, what news today?" Finngyr said. They usually waited until after evening prayers to hear what Kjar's informants had shared.

Kjar scratched the side of his large nose as he thought. They passed under an archway and began their descent down the stone spiral stairs.

"Most had nothing to share. The guard on the south gate had something of interest, they admitted a druid and her shieldwarden this morning. Shortly thereafter, a sorcerer and his apprentice entered," Kjar said.

A druid and a sorcerer in the same day? Finngyr stopped and considered. As he thought, he realized he had not seen even one sorcerer in the Freehold. There was comment of a druid and her shieldwarden being here, though he had yet to encounter them, but now there was another pair?

"Did he get a name from this sorcerer?"

"Of course, Knight Justice. It is the law. The sorcerer was Almoriz from Whispering Rock and his apprentice, Rolf or Riff," Kjar said.

"Riff," Finngyr said. "The sorcerer old and grey. Yes, I know of these humans."

"No, Knight Justice. The guard said the sorcerer was young and the apprentice even younger," Kjar said with certainty.

"That's it!" Finngyr said. "Hurry, we have wasted enough time already. Knight Horth, go to your rooms and gather your gear. Take it to the south gate and summon the griffons. Be ready to fly. Go now!"

Horth started to say something, but thought better of it and bowed, then hurried down the stairs.

Finngyr turned to Knight Kjar.

"Knight Justice, I apologize, I don't understand—" Kjar said.

"Of course not. You did not know Almoriz of Whispering Rock is old and grey. Whoever that was who arrived, it was not Almoriz and that was not his apprentice," Finngyr said, already moving towards his room.

Finngyr all but ran through the hallways of the Bastion, Kjar hurrying to keep pace. He knew word would reach Magister Dagbar that they had not gone to the shrine room and had been moving at a brisk pace.

"Do you think it is the stonechosen?" Kjar said in a low tone. They had passed more than a few of the Bastion's residents, who hurriedly got out of their way.

Finngyr stopped outside the low stone door of his chambers. "I think the Magister was trying to keep us there at dinner, stalling. I think he knows of these new arrivals and if he was willing to openly confront us, he hasn't found them yet. I want to find them before he does."

∧

"Do you think I bought Robon enough time?" Dagbar said.

Ulbert listened at the door a moment more before he took the seat Knight Justice Finngyr had just vacated. The older dwarf poured himself a fresh tankard of ale from the pitcher he had been serving from. He made sure to grab a fresh tankard. His hatred of the Cullers was too great to ever allow him to drink from the same tankard.

"By the All Mother, I hope so," Ulbert said. "They know something is up, that is for certain. They ran from here like their beards were on fire. You took a great risk telling them to leave, Dagbar. By law, the Knight Justice could have accused you of interfering with his investigation."

Dagbar nodded and then shrugged. "I am not much for thinking on my feet, old friend. I hoped he had. He would have had to arrest me and who knows how long that would have taken."

"The time it would have taken to whack you over the head with that hammer. Arrested, indeed," Ulbert said.

"I only wish we had news of the stonechosen's arrival sooner, so we could have properly prepared some distraction for the cullers." Dagbar squeezed the bridge of his nose and sighed. It had been a risk he had to take. And why not, he had been walking a dangerous path since the cullers' arrival. He needed them to make a mistake, but was not willing to risk anyone else in the process. What was one more roll of the dice?

By all accounts, Finngyr was a hot-headed zealot who should have struck out at Dagbar any number of times since his arrival. He almost had when he saw the golems. But, there were just too many innocents there in the market and Dagbar's people were too loyal. Too many would have died trying to help him. Dagbar couldn't allow that.

That Horth had been a disappointment. Dagbar was assured by his contacts on the Judges Council that the young knight had been well payed to cause an incident. Though both young knights seemed pliable enough, it became obvious over time they had no intention of betraying Finngyr. Dagbar wondered what had happened there.

The law dictated he had to allow them to investigate the disappearance of the previous Knight Justice, but every day they stayed in the Emporium increased the chances they would be here when Ghile arrived. Now it seemed his fears had come to pass.

But, even this was better than them following the previous knight to the Fallen City and finding Ashar and Akira. Ashar and Akira... how had he let things go so horribly wrong?

"You think of Ashar and Akira again, Magister," Dowynn stated, more than asked. He took a seat next to Dagbar. He knew Dagbar too well. He was a good man and Dagbar was lucky to have him as a member of his advising council and more importantly, as a friend.

Dowynn was a sorcerer and had been Ashar's mentor. He was the closest thing to a parent Ashar and Akira had since their arrival at the Emporium all those years before. Dowynn took them into his home.

Dagbar wished the empire could see the benefit of working alongside humans. The idea to move their dinners from the great hall into Dagbar's private chambers and then replace his normal servants with members of his council had all been Dowynn's idea.

Dowynn's justification for this ruse had served multiple purposes. First, to separate them from some of his more zealous followers. Dagbar had to agree, many of the Allwynians felt the time for change was now and he didn't need them dying in some attempt to instigate said change.

Second, for Dagbar to attempt to upset Knight Justice Finngyr by questioning his beliefs privately. Some were more apt to do things in front of servants that they would never admit to doing, feeling justified to dismiss the word of a servant if ever challenged.

If the knights knew these 'servants' where his true Council of Elders, a mix of dwarves and humans, everyone an Allwynian, well, Ashar and his betrayal would be the least of Dagbar's worries. Unfortunately, Finngyr seemed to be on best behavior and had never taken the bait.

In truth, Dagbar expected Dowynn and the others were there to protect him should he succeed in his attempts, more so than bear credible witness.

"You cannot continue to blame yourself for what happened to Akira, Dagbar," Dowynn said, interrupting Dagbar's thoughts.

Dagbar waved his hands to stop the man from once again trying to relieve Dagbar of his guilt. He had heard all his logic before, it still did nothing to lift the burden Dagbar placed on his own shoulders. Akira. She had been such a lovely young girl and the All Mother knew what Ashar had done to her in his attempts to try and save her. There was no waking from the Elixir of the Sleeping Death. At least Ashar knew who to blame for her condition, in that regard. In that, Dagbar and Ashar found common ground.

"I know, my friend, I know," Dagbar said. "We all know what will happen to Akira, but that doesn't mean I have to like it. But enough; all our talk will not change things. To the matter at hand. We can only hope we have bought Robon enough time to find this Ghile Stonechosen and bring him here."

"Are we sure it is him?" Ulbert said.

Dagbar nodded. "Yes. Those that arrived today match the description Master Almoriz sent me." Dagbar still shuddered from the experience. It was such an uncomfortable feeling to have the old sorcerer's voice suddenly there in his ear. Dowynn called it wind whispering and it had something to do with the element of air, but Dagbar just called it creepy, like a voice from beyond the grave.

"And once Robon sneaks him into the Bastion?" Dowynn said.

"Well, I had hoped for some time to size him up for myself," Dagbar said.

"You still intend to go against Mother Brambles in this, Dagbar? Even with two of her druids and their shieldwardens in the Emporium?" Dowynn said.

"I do," Dagbar said. "And if you had spoken with the Goddess Islmur, as I did, you would not keep asking me the same question every other day!"

Ulbert snorted. "Well, Ashar's abominations have seen that none of us get that chance again".

"Calm yourself, Dagbar. Remember, we all risk much. The sorcerers are aligned with the druids and in following you, I betray them," Dowynn said.

"We follow you in this. For better or for worse," Ulbert said.

Dagbar could only nod. How he wished the others had been there in the Deepwood with him. Seen her and heard her words. Everything he had believed, had worked so hard for all those years, had changed in an instant. If only he could have convinced Mother Brambles and the others. If only they would have listened.

Now, when he was so close, everything seemed to be converging to pull it all down. The first culler had not accepted Dagbar's excuses for removing the golems from the Fallen City and gone there to see the effects himself. Dagbar had done it to ease Ashar's many journeys to the forbidden city, of course. The culler did not return.

Mother Bramble's sent Patron Sister Bosand and her shieldwarden, to remind him of his place in things and to make sure he stayed true to her plan. That was bad enough, but then three more cullers arrived.

Ashar seemed bent on punishing Dagbar and everything he had built to protect those under his care, dwarf and human alike. Ashar had somehow infected humans, goblins and vargan with something that turned them into murderous savages and in so doing, had all but severed Dagbar's communications with the Alvar. Even the blue mark, once a guarantee of safe passage in the Deepwood, no longer offered protection.

He had to do his best to protect this new stonechosen from the cullers, protect him from the druids, and hope he could convince the boy that in completing the Soulstone Prophecy, he would be bringing about the end of the human race.

There was a knock at the door.

"Enter," Dagbar said.

Young Billy, one of his real servants, peeked through the door hesitantly, no doubt fearing the cullers were still present. "Magister, Daughter Bosand wishes an audience."

Dagbar motioned for Billy to show her in. Her timing could not have been any worse. A coincidence? How much did she already know? Her presence was going to greatly complicate matters. Dagbar was not yet ready to reveal his hand.

Ulbert waited for the door to close before giving another one of his meaning-filled snorts. "So now what?" Ulbert said.

"So now we wait and pray for the All Mother's own luck," Dagbar said.

Right now, he needed all the luck he could get.

22

Sacrifice

 AIDEL watched Riff make his way to their table. He slid past the many patrons in the common room of the Happy Trader, the clouds of pipe smoke as diverse as those who created it.

She smiled as Riff tried to clear the air before him with a frantically waved hand. She rather enjoyed the smell, it reminded her of the Three Arrows and home.

"By Daomur's hairy backside, that woman had more metal needing mending, than all the Cradle combined," Riff said, following his words with an exaggerated exhale of breath.

He dropped down on the bench next to Lotte, flinging an empty pouch on the table. "I'm completely out of source. And her roving hands, don't even get me started on her hands!" Riff stared at them for a moment. "I'm fine, thanks for asking."

He reached for the pitcher in front of Two Elks, but quickly withdrew his hand at the stare he received from the barbarian, instead settling for the pitcher Gaidel slid towards him. Two Elks had long since laid claim to the strong dwarven stout, or 'dark drink' as he named it.

"Your head will thank me in the morning," Gaidel said, when Riff skeptically eyed the contents. The paler, human-made beer she and Lotte were sharing was more than a little watered down.

"Well," Riff said, taking a drink and frowning. "Our place here at the Happy Trader is secured. No need to thank me, it was my pleasure to slave away in the kitchens and suffer the attentions of our handsy hostess, while all of you relaxed in the common room. The little coin I received from the moneylender at the gate would not have paid for our drink, let alone lodging."

Lotte clapped and went as far as to pat Riff on the back, before quaffing down the last of his cup's contents.

Riff gave an amused smirk and raised an eyebrow at Gaidel.

She could only shrug. Who could blame him? The boy had been through much in the last couple of days.

Lotte reached under the table to scratch Ast and Cuz. He had become fond of the two Valehounds, and they him. There was something about the bond between boys and dogs. She took the opportunity to slide his cup away from him. No need to let him get too carried away.

"They got off cheap," Riff continued. "I'm doing this place a favor. Apparently, the only other sorcerer in this settlement has been holed up in the Bastion and no one has seen his apprentice in months. Though, this is the best human inn, from what I could discover."

The Happy Trader was easily the largest human owned inn in Dagbar's Freehold. Her father would have been impressed. The entire Three Arrows would have easily fit inside the Happy Trader's common room.

Sitting just outside one of the four entrances to the trade market, the inn was impossible to miss, and where the moneylender had directed Riff when he inquired where a sorcerer and his young apprentice should seek lodging. Gaidel was thankful the inn was not on the market square itself, she didn't want to draw any more attention than was necessary and she knew she would have had to explain herself to the four guards stationed where the road spilled into the market.

Gaidel hated to admit it had been Riff's idea to enter the Freehold separately, and pass himself off as Master Almoriz and Lotte as Riff, his young apprentice. Dwarven law allowed druids and sorcerers to travel outside the settlements, but any other humans found outside a settlement were at the mercy of their captor. She hadn't even considered Lotte. Luckily, Riff's small display of magic had been enough for the gate guards to let the two pass. It was a good idea.

She hadn't thought about food or lodging when she and Two Elks first entered the Freehold either, let alone how they would pay for it. Staying in such a large settlement just wasn't something she knew anything about.

At first, she had tried to retake the reins and inquired about other places to stay, but all of her inquiries resulted in her being directed towards the Bastion. Even the proprietor of the Happy Trader, a buxom, middle-aged woman named Mistress Jolyn, had at first refused to house Gaidel and Two Elks, saying the Bastion was the only proper place for a Sister and her Shieldwarden. It was Riff's sorcerous talents that finally swayed Mistress Jolyn to relent. Well, that, and her obvious attraction to him. She was easily twice Riff's age. It was improper. Gaidel had taken an instant dislike to the woman.

She watched Riff over her cup as he ladled food onto his plate. He still annoyed her beyond measure, but she had to admit he was more than proving his worth in the Freehold. A thought came to her and she raised her cup. "To Riff. Thank you."

Riff locked eyes with her and froze, his food-laden fork only halfway to his mouth. He looked left and right as if expecting a trap. Seeing none, he replied with more than a little trepidation. "You're welcome?"

Two Elks lifted his cup while Lotte searched for his. Gaidel hid her smile with her raised cup. She was sincere in her thanks, but it gave her no small amount of satisfaction to see Riff's discomfort. He was somewhat attractive, when he wasn't so sure of himself.

She froze. What was that? *Attractive?* She looked down at her almost-empty cup. Maybe the beer was not as watered down as she thought. Gaidel set the cup down and took a moment to clear her head.

"So, what is the plan?" Riff asked between spoonful's.

"Hmm? Ah, yes. I want to get a feel for the place, before we approach the Bastion," Gaidel said. She casually slapped Lotte's hand without looking when he made a grab for his cup.

"The storm will stay for days," Two Elks said. "Keep many inside."

The weather had turned as they approached the gatehouse to the Freehold and the small drizzle became a solid sheet by the time they reached the inn. Many of the more recent arrivals to the inn were soaked and congregating near the inn's two enormous hearths. On opposite walls, both were large enough for a tall man to stand in upright. Steam rose from wet heads and damp shoulders, to mingle with the pipe smoke. It would seem the winters here were as cold as in the Cradle.

Riff nodded in understanding. "Won't be as easy to blend in. What if we stain our faces? Half the folk here, dwarf and human, seem to be doing it."

Gaidel shook her head before he finished. "We shouldn't. That is how they identify themselves as Allwynians here. The stain is similar to my own markings. You would not find it so easy to take off, once applied. Besides, marking yourself for the All Mother is not something to do idly."

Two Elks nodded gravely. Gaidel knew his people not only took trophies from those they defeated in battle, but displayed battle scars and tribal markings with honor. He would never have agreed to try and disguise himself that way.

Riff raised both hands. "Just an idea."

Gaidel looked about the room and then leaned in and motioned to four young dwarves, who sat at a corner table gambling with two humans. Each of them wore a veil across their face which hid everything below their eyes.

"What about those veils?" Gaidel said.

"Won't work," Riff said. "I've seen that back in Lakeside. It is what young dwarves do, when they want to go out among the lowly humans and live it up a little."

He elaborated when he noted their confused looks. "Dwarves have their own Public Halls – big long buildings, no humans allowed. Boring places, with serving dwarves standing along the walls and the proprietor sitting on a platform at one end, making sure everyone remembers they're a dwarf. All you can hear is grumbling and belching," Riff said.

Lotte's eyes were as round as wagon wheels. "How did you see inside?"

"What? Oh, Master Almoriz was brought into a kitchen of one once, to do some work for the cook. Apparently, the dwarven smith was overcharging or some such. I snuck a peek when no one was looking."

Somewhere across the common room someone shouted out, "To Dagbar!" It was quickly returned in a storm of tapping cups and cheers. Somehow, Lotte had reacquired his cup and filled it, because he raised it with the rest and followed with a drink.

Gaidel focused her stare on him and he shriveled. "Well, them all keeps a'doin it," Lotte said.

"It is because of the food and shelter," Riff said. "Mistress Jolyn was telling me about it. The dead ones have been attacking here, too. It's what drove everyone into the Freehold. People are afraid to return home and tend the crops. Those who didn't flee, are now dead ones themselves. Many of these people are foresters and the timber trade has completely stopped. Instead of forcing them back out, Dagbar has been having food brought in from throughout the empire and paying for it himself. They love him for it." Riff swallowed down another mouthful of his food before he continued. "Here is another interesting thing. She said he is marked by the All Mother. Apparently, his eyes are blue and white, like all these Allwynians faces. I figured they were staining their faces because of him."

"They should not cower behind dwarf wall. They should fight for land and food," Two Elks said.

Both Gaidel and Riff looked at the barbarian and then their eyes met. She could see her feelings echoed in Riff's. They had saved Ollin together. The dead ones had no control of themselves. No one deserved such a fate. She didn't know what was happening in the Deepwood to make them like that, but she wanted to find out and help them if she could.

A voice in her head reminded her she'd been ordered to stay with Ghile and keep him safe. But what if they didn't find him? What if Dagbar couldn't help? Should she stay here and try to help these people? It was a worthy cause. Somehow, she knew Riff would stay too, if she asked.

"Many pardons, you are Daughter Gaidel?"

Two Elks was up and staring down at the man before Gaidel could respond. The man was older, with wet shaggy hair over a half blue stained face. Unlike his unkempt hair, his mustache and goatee were well trimmed and his robes and cloak, though thoroughly soaked, were clean. He continued to look at her and ignore Two Elks. He was unarmed and if he felt at all threatened, he didn't show it.

She noticed Riff's hands as they slid off the table and rested near his pouches. They had only just arrived and couldn't afford any trouble. "Do I know you?" Gaidel asked.

The man placed the fingertips of both hands on his lips and then his heart before spreading his arms out wide. "You do not. I am Robon, attendant to Magister Dagbar. He was informed of your journey by Master Almoriz. When news of your arrival reached him, he sent me to invite the young man you escort to the Bastion." His accent marked him as a local. Robon looked about the table and finally settled his gaze on Lotte. "Is this him?" There was almost a hopeful reverence to his voice.Robon

Gaidel noticed more than a couple of faces turned their way and motioned for both Two Elks and Robon to sit. As they did so, she asked Riff what Robon meant by Magister Dagbar being informed.

"Wind whispering, I would imagine," Riff said. "It uses air as the source. It's not easy to do over great distances either." Riff leaned closer over the table. "But that means Master Almoriz and this Dagbar have met before. You need to have seen and touched the person you are trying to speak to."

She looked from Robon to Riff, temporarily distracted. Why hadn't Riff mentioned this before? "Why haven't you used this to try and contact Ghile?" Gaidel said.

"Hey, don't even," Riff said. "I thought about it, for all of a second. I'd be lucky to reach someone across the street. It uses the air inside of you as the source. I like being able to breathe."

Two Elks cleared his throat, drawing their attention.

"He is not with you?" Robon said.

"No," Riff said.

The man closed his eyes, visibly resigning himself to the news. "I must go and so should you." He started to rise.

The bond between a druid and her shieldwarden had many benefits. Though they couldn't see into each other's mind and know their thoughts, the ability to sense emotion in the other was strong and she had no more registered Robon's words than Two Elks reached out across the table and locked a hand on the man's shoulder. Robon tried to continue to rise, but was easily lowered back onto the bench.

"You are not going anywhere without us," Gaidel said.

If Master Almoriz had informed Magister Dagbar of their impending arrival and the Magister sent Robon to find them, then Ghile was not here. That meant he was somewhere in the Deepwood and the Magister offered the best chance of finding him.Robon shook his head and tried to rise again, to no avail. "It is not possible. Unhand me." Gaidel could tell Robon was trying to avoid drawing attention to himself, which was good. Attention was the last thing they needed.

"Robon, we need answers. We need to meet with the Magister," Gaidel said.

Robon looked around the table and seemed to be taking a mental tally. "I apparently have little choice, though you should heed my advice and leave."

She continued to stare at him, brooking no further discussion.

"You, I can take you. But not the others," Robon said.

"I go with Daughter," Two Elks said.

Gaidel wondered why he could only take her? Weren't they going to the Bastion? Gaidel knew she would not talk Two Elks into staying with the others. She could feel his resolve through the bond. "You will take the two of us."Robon looked at Two Elks and this time deflated visibly. "Yes. Fine, but no more. We must go now."

Two Elks released the man and Robon was up, hooded, and moving off through the crowd, with Two Elks on his heels.

She looked to Riff, but he was already nodding his head and motioning her to go. "Yeah, yeah, I know. Stay here, look after this lot and stay out of trouble."

She wondered if the worry showed on her face. She turned and hastened after the others.

∧

Dagbar leaned back in his chair and squeezed the bridge of his nose. All luck seemed to have deserted him. He had always been a dwarf willing to take risks. Without real risks, one never achieved real rewards. It was one of the base tenets he lived by. He was now taking the biggest risk of his life, but coming to the realization that the stones in his pile were not a winning set.

He was notified as soon as the cullers left the Bastion, taking their gear with them. He wasn't sure they knew about the stonechosen's arrival, but whatever they knew or planned, it was going to be bad enough they were not going to remain in the Emporium after they played their hand.

Daughter Bosand and her shieldwarden seemed to also know something was going on and had picked the worse time possible to ante in.

Dagbar wondered where the druid or her shieldwarden had gotten their information on the stonechosen's arrival. It was obvious they planned to remain in his presence until this Ghile arrived. And what better way to pass the time, than to reiterate their purpose for being there and to remind him of his promises to Mother Brambles.

"Magister Dagbar, are you listening?" Daughter Bosand said.

He had successfully kept the cullers and the druid away from each other, but there had been too many close calls. He wondered how Finngyr would have appreciated one of Daughter Bosand's tongue lashings. The idea of putting them in the same room had its merits.

Dagbar noted the arch of the woman's eyebrows begin creeping up her forehead. He knew he was about to receive one of those lashings himself, if he didn't answer quickly. "Daughter Bosand, I assure you I am well aware of the promises I made to Mother Brambles," Dagbar said.

Daughter Bosand sat in one of the chairs next to Master Dowynn, her shieldwarden, Rachard, standing behind her. Dagbar noticed Rachard had not only entered the room first, but chose a seat for Daughter Bosand that allowed him to keep his back against a wall and his face to the door. Even here, in Dagbar's private dining chambers, the shieldwarden was wary of an attack.

Dagbar would not lower himself to physical violence against Mother Bramble's envoy, but he had no intention of letting her leave with Ghile Stonechosen, either. He just needed to figure out how to play his hand.

Daughter Bosand seemed placated for the moment, but continued to eye him skeptically. It reminded Dagbar of one of his falcons, eyeing a dead mouse and trying to decide if it was worth eating.

"Nevertheless."

The woman let the word hang there for a moment to make sure it had gathered enough weight.

"She felt it would be best if we took charge of the young stonechosen from here," Bosand said.

Took charge and escorted him to his death, Dagbar thought. And the boy would probably go, too. He was already under the eye of one druid. How could Dagbar convince him to trust a dwarf, instead of his own kind?

The stonechosen would have no reason to trust him other than Master Almoriz's original instruction to seek Dagbar out. There was still the chance Master Dowynn, being a human and sorcerer as well, might be able to persuade the boy to listen to them, but would it be enough? Would he be able to speak away from his druid escorts?

"I thought I had proven myself more than enough times to earn your people's trust, Daughter Bosand," Dagbar said.

"We risk more than any," Elder Ulbert added in.

Dagbar nodded his agreement, thankful for the support.

Dagbar never liked the way humans were treated. In the cities, they were relegated to the role of servant and manual labor, slaves more like. Oh, dwarves would never use that word and would have been insulted by the term, preferring to slather a layer of decency on it with expressions like overseers and protecting them from themselves. Maybe that was the case in the beginning? Maybe his race began with altruistic motives, but humans were little more than commodities now.

"I should think what happened at Oceanwood—"

Dagbar raise his hand. "No. Please, do not speak of that, Master Dowynn. Some things are best left in the past," Dagbar said.

The entire Oceanwood settlement had been razed to the ground under the pretense of quelling an uprising. Dagbar knew and respected Oceanwood's late Magister Bellan. He had been Dagbar's mentor and the very one who taught him the ways of the All Mother and finding a balance in all things. But Magister Bellan made too many changes too quickly, and forgot the one thing that would keep the wolves of the empire at bay. Greed.

"All who struggle for change take risks and make sacrifices," Dagbar said.

Master Dowynn nodded. "The point is, we all work towards the fulfillment of the prophecy, Daughter. We sorcerers believed who better than one of our own, to be Haurtu's vessel? And Magister Dagbar supported us in our quest..." Master Dowynn continued on, though Dagbar had stopped listening.

His mind drifted back to the days when all those refugees arrived from Oceanwood, little Ashar and Akira among them. The thought of all those who hadn't survived still haunted Dagbar. It was the Oceanwood massacre that convinced Dagbar he needed to act. He always said, every situation, no matter how dire, could still produce something positive.

Unlike his mentor, Dagbar would need to put himself out of reach of those who would try to stop him. Then the idea to seek help in the most unlikely of places, the elves, came to him.

He had already established the trade agreements that allowed him to harvest limited supplies of wood from the surrounding forest, but there was nothing special about that. Wood was in plentiful supply and not much in demand. Stone, strong and enduring, was the preferred building material of the empire.

The agreement between dwarves and elves to contain the humans and guard any human cities that fell into the ever-expanding borders of the Deep Wood was in place, well before he became the Magister of the Emporium, dating back to the Great Purge. No, there was nothing that would have protected him from falling victim to the same fate as Magister Bellan.

That was, until his prayers to the All Mother had been answered in a way he never would have expected.

All who struggle for change take risks and make sacrifices.

The Alvar's sacrifice had been silverwood. The trees that were sacred to them and protected above all others in the forest. It had been the suggestion of the Goddess Islmur herself that Dagbar be allowed to harvest them.

How some of the Alvar had raged! But, in the end, they placed their faith in her and almost overnight, as the sole source of the newest and rarest commodity in the empire, Dagbar's heresies had transformed into eccentricities.

Dagbar was brought from his reveries by the door opening. All those gathered at the table turned as one. Shieldwarden Rachard had his blade drawn and kite shield off his back and ready before Robon even entered the room, followed by an exasperated Billy.

"I'm sorry, Magister. He refused to wait—" Billy started to say, before his wide eyes locked on the Shieldwarden Rachard and his sword. The boy usually took delight in announcing guests and probably felt cheated of the chance to announce the two who followed Robon into the room, all forgotten when he saw the drawn blade.

The druid who entered behind Robon was probably one of the youngest Dagbar had ever seen. Her shaved forehead held only a smattering of the druid's blue tattoos. Her red hair and pale skin were wet from the storm and glistening. He had no doubt many humans would describe her as beautiful. But her shieldwarden was even more of a surprise. He was a Nordlah plainsman, and a big one at that.

The young druid stopped abruptly. "Patron Sister Bosand! What are you doing here?"

The smile Shieldwarden Rachard wore as he slid his sword back into its scabbard was a sharp contrast to the expression on Daughter Bosand's face.

"More to the point, what are you doing here?" Daughter Bosand said. Though she spoke to the younger druid, her eyes were on Dagbar. "Care to explain this, Dagbar?"

Dagbar felt like he was just caught cheating at a game of stones. He cleared his throat. "To be honest, I have no idea why she is here. Elder Robon?"

Robon took one of the towels Billy was handing out and wiped his face. Now that the sword was gone, the boy looked equally horrified by the water puddling on the floor. Robon looked at the boy and then Dagbar.

"Ah, yes. Thank you, Billy. That will do for the evening. Please close the door behind you," Dagbar said.Robon waited for Billy to pay proper respects and leave, reluctantly closing the door behind him. "May I present Daughter Gaidel and her shieldwarden, Two Elks."

"Where is the stonechosen?" Daughter Bosand said.

"The stonechosen was not with them. Daughter Gaidel demanded to come with me. They left me little choice, I assure you. My apologies, Dagbar," Robon said.

"So much for earning our trust. You were going to meet with the stonechosen alone?" Daughter Bosand said.

She did not wait for an answer before turning her attention back to Daughter Gaidel. "Where is he?" Her authoritative tone brooked no room for debate. She was taking leadership of this situation with Mother Brambles' authority.

Dagbar had to admit, this young druid was handling the situation better than he was. Her initial surprise was already hidden behind a resolute demeanor and squared shoulders.

"The elves have him," Daughter Gaidel said, as if she was a guard making a report.

Dagbar could have laughed at his good fortune. The idea only lasted for a moment, though as the news silenced the room. The Elders were wise enough to mask their emotions, but all of them cast glances at Dagbar. The two druids had locked eyes and Dagbar could see the internal struggle in each of them. Daughter Bosand pushed down first shock, and then anger, while Daughter Gaidel dealt with fear. Behind each, their shieldwarden's were eyeing the other and looked ready to take the struggle to a more physical place.

Daughter Bosand broke the silence. When she spoke, her words were slow and even. "You were given one task. You were to see him safely here."

Daughter Gaidel's forehead and cheeks took on a shade that almost rivaled her hair. Oh, this one had fire, Dagbar could tell. He took an instant liking to her. She also knew when to control that fire, apparently, as her answer was equally controlled.

"As you say, Patron Sister Bosand."

"Then why did you fail?"

The word had the same effect as a slap. Interestingly, it was her shieldwarden, Two Elks, who seemed more hurt. Dagbar could see there was a story here and he would bet it was a good one.

"It… it is complicated," Daughter Gaidel said.

Daughter Bosand only stared. Dagbar noted Shieldwarden Rachard giving the younger druid an encouraging nod and a quick wink.

"During our journey, Ghile was contacted by another stonechosen, a girl named Akira, she—"

"Akira! Dagbar, could it be?" Dowynn said. He was leaning forward in his chair, all propriety forgotten.

"She is still aware, Dagbar. Trapped! What have we done?" Dowynn said. The look on Dowynn's face caused Dagbar's heart to ache. It was times like this that Dagbar thought he understood why his race thought emotions were something to be controlled.

"Dowynn, enough. We did what we must," Dagbar said.

"What do you know of this, Magister Dagbar?" Daughter Bosand said.

"Patron Sister Bosand, there is more. This Akira, she said Magister Dagbar is not to be trusted. Her brother and her were hurt and in the Fallen City. It is why Ghile ran away from us," Gaidel said. She cast accusing eyes at Dagbar.

"In that I must agree," Daughter Bosand said.

"Dagbar?" Dowynn's voice was pleading.

"Elder Robon, Elder Ulbert. Please escort Master Dowynn to his rooms," Dagbar said.

That he had supported the sorcerers' plan to have one of their own become stonechosen was well known to the Druids, but how bad things had gone was not. It was not only his relationship with the Druids that was at stake. That Akira was a stonechosen they had subdued and that Dowynn's apprentice had fled with her to the Fallen City was not something he wanted known. That it had inadvertently caused the attacks on the settlement and the new animosity of the Alvar, thus ending the silverwood trade most definitely wasn't something he wanted known. Just when he thought luck had returned to him.

Daughter Bosand rose from her chair.

"Daughter Bosand, please. Stay. I—"

"No, Magister Dagbar, I think I've seen and heard enough," Daughter Bosand said.

Dagbar couldn't believe she was just leaving. If Ghile Stonechosen was with the Alvar, then there was a chance he would listen to reason. Dagbar needed to speak to him, try to explain. "Wait. You need my help. If he is with the elves, I am your best chance of reaching him."

"That is not what things in their present situation would have me believe, I'm afraid. I have not spent my time here sitting idly in my room, I can assure you. Your relationship with the elves is strained at best. You know of their pact with your kind concerning the stonechosen. The boy is lost."

"But—"

"But, nothing," Daughter Bosand said. "It is obvious this Ghile Stonechosen is beyond our reach and there is another stonechosen somewhere in the Fallen City, which you were apparently not only aware of, but involved in. Mother Brambles needs to be made aware of this new information. Come, Sister Gaidel, we are leaving."

Daughter Bosand and Shieldwarden Rachard made their way around the table. The elders were still trying to comfort and lead Master Dowynn out, but he seemed on the verge of hysterics and their muttered attempts to calm him were growing louder.

Daughter Gaidel looked taken aback. "What? What about Ghile?" She had not moved and Daughter Bosand stopped in front of her.

"On Mother Brambles' orders, we were to escort him to the Nord-lah Plains where he would be dealt with by the true Stonechosen, Growling Bear," Daughter Bosand said.

"Dealt with?" Gaidel said. "Who is Growling Bear?" She looked between Daughter Bosand and Two Elks.

"I know Growling Bear," Two Elks said, "Strong warrior. Much hate for dwarves."

Dagbar watched the emotions play across Daughter Gaidel's face. It was obvious she was worried about Ghile's fate. If she thought Dagbar was not to be trusted, it was likely Ghile did as well. He would need to convince her of his cause and enlist her aid in convincing Ghile.

"Daughter Bosand, listen to reason – you cannot put your faith into this Growling Bear. He will kill Ghile and take the humans to war. Is war with the dwarves what Mother Brambles wants? There is another way," Dagbar said.

"It is not my decision to make, nor yours. This conversation is over," Daughter Bosand said.

Daughter Gaidel put her hand to her ear as if in pain. Her face took on a focused expression.

"By the All Mother! Riff! How?" Daughter Gaidel said.

"What is it?" Daughter Bosand said.

"Riff, Master Almoriz's apprentice, he is speaking to me."

"Wind whispering," Dagbar said.

"Riff! Riff?" Gaidel's face paled.

Two Elks was already turning towards the door.

"He cannot hear you. What do you know?" Dagbar said.

Daughter Gaidel turned to follow Two Elks, even as she answered.

"Cullers!"

⅄

Riff loved to entertain a crowd. The hearth fire felt warm on his back, but nowhere near as nice as the applause he received with each enchantment he performed.

He could understand why entertainers, like the one sitting on the stool across the way glaring at him, did this for a living. The woman had long since stopped playing her lute and singing. Riff hadn't intended on depriving the woman of her livelihood. It had all started out innocently enough.

It hadn't taken long for Lotte and him to grow bored. He could only take so much of the boy's hard to understand conversation and not even the dark dwarven stout Two Elks had left unguarded could help with that. He had only thought to help pass the time. Surely Gaidel could not begrudge him that?

At first, he had simply made the beer in his mug flow upwards into one he held upside down above it. But once Lotte had gotten used to that, he questioned how far apart Riff could place the cups. It was when Riff stood on the table and stretched the second cup above his head that things became interesting.

Apparently, standing on the table was how entertainers announced they were about to perform at this settlement. His upwards flowing beer trick had been answered with the sounds of a few coins landing on the table. It had progressed from there.

The manipulation of water quickly led to using his everflame to perform tricks with the fire from the hearth. None of them lasted long and so they didn't put too much strain on him. Besides using up whatever source the sorcerer was using, each casting drew a little strength from the caster. Riff thought it felt similar to the exertion to walking up a steep hill. When he kept to small enchantments, it was like taking slow steady steps. Trying something large or something that lasted a long time was like trying to sprint to the top.

Riff focused and spoke the words that allowed him to control the flames. He spoke them at just above a whisper, as Master Almoriz taught him, and the everflame danced and shrank ever so slightly.

Riff never understood why, but he had been taught to protect the words from others, even though being a sorcerer was not something that could be learned. Either you were born with the spark, or you weren't.

Riff wondered if the spark existed in any of those whose faces were lit up by the small ribbons of fire that sprang forth from the hearth to circle around him, before plunging back into the flames.

It wasn't until the crowd parted right in front of him that Riff saw the two dwarfs appear. The flames from his latest spell reflected off the knight's glistening armor and made the screaming face etched in the dwarf's helmet look alive, as if it were proclaiming its owner's arrival. Riff remembered seeing the same helmet on the night of the Summer's Festival at Lakeside. This was the same culler. The one that razed Last Hamlet.

Damn.

Riff recognized the dwarf standing next to the knight and pointing at Riff with equal parts fear and relief on his face. It was the moneylender from earlier.

Twice damned.

The applause slowly died. As others in the crowd noticed the culler, silence fell in its wake, leaving only cautious murmurs. The opaque glass of the windows illuminated briefly, followed by a deep rumble of thunder.

The culler raised his hammer and pointed it at Riff. "You are Almoriz of Whispering Rock." It was more a statement than a question.

Thrice damned.

It always amused Riff how in times of danger, he always noted the oddest things. Right now, he was amazed by how steady the culler could hold such a huge-headed hammer by the handle and point it like that. Riff doubted he could even lift it.

"I am," Riff said, forcing a smile onto his face and showing his palms and bowing low. Master Almoriz would have been proud of him, for remembering to show respect. Though it was easy to respect someone who could snuff you out like a candle. The thought reminded Riff he still held his everflame. He quickly placed it into one of his many pouches. "How may I serve you, Knight Justice?"

The culler lowered the head of his hammer and let it rest on the stone floor, then placed both of his large hands on the tip of the hilt. There was something in the self-satisfied look on his face that more than discomforted Riff. "Where is your young apprentice, Sorcerer?"

Riff fought the urge to look in Lotte's direction and hoped the boy had enough sense to get out of there. More than a few people were making their way towards the front exit.

"Young Riff? Why would you seek him, Knight Justice? Has he done something wrong?"

Riff cursed himself for putting his everflame away. He made a show of looking at the many faces, making sure his eyes didn't linger on Lotte. Luckily, Lotte was not at the table where he had been.

Riff disguised the relief that washed over him as a light hearted chuckle. "You know how kids are," Riff said.

The sounds of Ghile's hounds barking near the door leading to the kitchens killed the chuckle in Riff's throat.

The culler never took his eyes from Riff.

"What do we have here?" Came a deep voice from the back.

Another culler, even larger than the one currently watching Riff like a cat watched a mouse, stepped forward, holding Lotte by the neck with one hand. Lotte's feet barely scraped the floor as he struggled to break free.

The two Valehounds harried the culler, snapping at his armor. He ignored them as he brought Lotte forward.

"Look who I found trying to flee through the kitchens, Knight Justice Finngyr," the taller culler said.

Knight Justice Finngyr continued to stare at Riff for one more moment, before looking at his fellow knight's prize. He did not seem so satisfied at what he saw.

"That is not him, Knight Horth."

Riff knew then who this Finngyr thought Lotte was. Which also meant he knew Riff was not Master Almoriz. Which meant they were in trouble. Riff had to think and think quickly, or they were going to die. He looked about the room, more than a few of the patrons stared at the culler with open hostility. Almost all of them had the half blue faces of Allwynians.

"Why are you hurting that boy?" Riff said. "What crime has he committed?"

Riff was relieved to hear more than a few cries of, "Yeah!" and "Let him go!" from the crowd. The two Valehounds continued to bark and snap at the culler holding Lotte.

Tears streamed down Lotte's face as he struggled to break free.

"Enough," Finngyr said. "I am Knight Justice Finngyr of the Temple of Justice. Do not question me! I walk in Daomur's grace and all who oppose me die in his name!"

Riff was shocked when someone from the crowd shouted, "Someone get the guards!" That was quickly followed by, "They have done nothing, you have no right!" Riff would never have believed humans would have spoken to dwarves in such a way, if he hadn't heard it himself. He was definitely not in the Cradle.

Knight Justice Finngyr lifted his hammer from the ground and grabbed the haft in a wide grip, his face contorted in a mixture of anger and incredulity. Apparently, Riff was not the only one surprised.

"No right? You filthy humans. How dare you question my right?" Finngyr yelled over barking Valehounds and humans who joined in the shouting, spurred on by the courage of the crowd.

One of the veiled dwarves stepped to the edge of the crowd and removed his veil, revealing the half blue face beneath. "The rites are over, Knight Justice, and there are no stonechosen here."

Well, by Daomur's hairy backside, Riff thought, *it was going to work.*

The Knight Justice stared at the other dwarf. The room fell silent, except for the two Valehounds.

"Knight Horth, silence those mutts," Finngyr said.

Riff saw what was coming and tried to stop it. "Ast! Cuz! Down! No!"

Horth's face held no expression as he kicked out with one steel boot at Cuz, followed by a downward jab with the haft of his hammer at Ast. Riff turned away, but still heard the heavy blows fall, the sudden silence. He thought of Ghile, then.

Knight Justice Finngyr stepped over to stand before Horth. When he spoke, he spoke to the whole room and not just Lotte. He placed his gauntleted fist under Lotte's chin.

"Where is Ghile Stonechosen?"

Riff could not see Lotte's face, Finngyr had turned his back to Riff. It was as if he was daring Riff to attack him. Riff could feel the anger coming off the crowd as an almost tangible thing he could grab and hurl at the culler's back.

Riff heard the words through Lotte's choking sobs.

"Da...da Elves, they dun took 'em."

Riff knew then they were going to die.

He quickly recited the words and drew in as much air as his lungs could hold. He brought the image of Gaidel's face into his mind. It somehow calmed him. He saw the almond shape of her eyes and the long slender bridge of her nose. When he spoke, no sound escaped him, but he could feel the air disappearing from his lungs. Darkness closed in around him, but he pushed on.

Cullers. We are lost. Flee!

Riff dropped to one knee.

Finngyr turned then to look at Riff. The flames from the hearth cast a sinister light over the culler's face.

"All those who aid a stonechosen suffer its fate," Finngyr said.

Riff fell on his side. He saw Lotte's body fall to the floor next to one of the Valehounds. Lotte's eyes stared at nothing and his head lay at an odd angle.

Riff spoke the last words he thought he would ever speak. If this was his time, he was going to make the culler's pay. He didn't have time to find his everflame, but he could feel the intense heat of the hearth fire on his back.

He was close.

He slid his leg back until he felt a slight tickling sensation. It soon burst into pain. The pain sharpened his vision for a moment and he could see the steel of the culler's boots before him. He completed the spell and felt the fire rush over him.

Shouts, as if down some tunnel, and long shadows passed before his fading vision. The last image Riff held as darkness took him was of Gaidel's face.

Part III

23

Change of Heart

SHAR stifled his laugh as he crept up to the closet door. It was Oderro's favorite hiding place. Ashar pulled the stone door opened and burst out laughing when he saw the young dwarf squatting on the ground and covering his face, only his unruly red hair exposed.

"Found you!" Ashar shouted.

"Dangit," Oderro said. He grumbled as he got up. "Am I first?"

Ashar shook his head. He knew Oderro would be here, but chose to find a couple of the other children hiding in the Bastion before seeking Oderro. He liked him and didn't want him to be 'it' every time.

"You were cute as a child," Akira said.

He was dreaming. Oderro's relieved grin faded into mist along with the Bastion. When the mists reformed an adult Ashar stood on the cliff before the familiar small wattle and daub hut in Ocean-wood.

"You surprised me," Ashar said.

He cursed inwardly at his lack of control. He normally prepared himself mentally each night before falling asleep, but he had worked late and vaguely remembered sitting down at one of the work benches. He must have fallen asleep. His own dreams could betray his plans.

"Why did you do that, I miss Oderro and the Bastion," Akira said.

She was so beautiful and innocent. He couldn't bear to look at her and instead walked over to the driftwood fence and ran his hands along its sand-worn surface. He thought about her shriveled form lying beneath the stones in the laboratory and shivered. He felt his surroundings start to blur, the wood beneath his hands grow soft.

He concentrated and his surroundings solidified.

"What is it, Akira?" He could feel her eyes on him, searching. He knew his tone was harsh and he'd hurt her. He sighed and closed his eyes. "I'm sorry. You just startled me," Ashar said.

She drifted up next to him and stood there for a moment, as if she was taking in the view. Ashar glanced at her and could tell she had something she wanted to say and didn't know where to begin. "Ghile Stonechosen is with the elves."

"What!" His mist thralls should have him by now? Had they failed? Had the elves intervened and thwarted his plans? He had never been able to maintain contact with the thralls or see through their eyes once they left the dream mists.

"He said he was attacked by humans and vargan, who had been turned into monsters," Akira said.

Ashar could hear the accusation in her voice. He felt his nails digging into the wood of the fence and his jaw clenching. So, they *had* failed him.

"What have you done, Ahsar?"

"We need his soulstones, Akira." He had to convince her to bring the stonechosen to him.

"What have you done?" Her voice was stronger now, determined.

"Do not ask questions you don't want to hear the answers to, Akira."

"Ashar, those people. How could you do that to them?"

The accusation in her voice, the disgust. How dare she judge him? He turned to look down at her. "I did what needed to be done! For the both of us."

The two stood unmoving, there on the cliff, ignoring the gusts off the ocean, heavy with the tang of salt.

"I didn't want to believe Ghile, but what he said is true. Ashar, you must stop. I never wanted to hurt anyone!" Akira said.

Ashar laughed. "You know what we must do to awaken you, Akira."

"Ashar, those people and those vargan have nothing to do with what happened to me, or what you told me we needed to do to awaken me."

"Akira, you must understand. All I do is for you," Ashar said. He knew it was a lie, even as it passed his lips and he hated Dagbar and the others for forcing him to lie to his own sister like this.

"I never asked you to, Ashar. I want you to stop."

The pleading in her voice tore at his soul and boiled his blood at the same time. But, he had come too far to stop now. "It is too late for that, sister. They will not get away with what they have done. I do what needs to be done. I need the boy and you are going to lure him to me."

"No, Ashar. I won't."

Everything he had been through. All the false promises. The outright lies. Now his own sister was going to deny him? It would not stand. "What did you say?"

She stepped back from him then. He could see the fear in her eyes. "This all has gone too far," she said. She hesitated, then the words rushed out. "You have gone too far. I... I said, I won't."

After everything he'd been through, she had the audacity to look at him as if *he* was the monster? He hadn't asked for any of this. Had he not tried to protect her? Protect her from the truth? If she didn't realize all this was necessary and the only way he could convince her to help herself was to scare her, then so be it. "Oh, yes you will, dear sister. Because if you don't you will remain in the dream mists forever."

"I don't care; I won't let you hurt him!" Grey tears streamed down her face and turned to puffs of mist as they fell away from her. She stood there, her tiny grey fists clenched over her eyes, sobbing.

Ashar understood then. It all made sense now. "You love him," he said. He couldn't even begin to hide the contempt in his voice.

She didn't respond to the accusation, but kept her face buried in her fists. When she finally removed them, she refused to look up at him. Akira whispered, "The decision is mine. Let me go, Ashar. Leave me."

"You don't know what you're saying," he said. "Damn that accursed boy for confusing you."

"All he did was tell me the truth."

Emotions warred inside Ashar. There was a small part of him that was tired, so very tired, and for a brief moment, he entertained the idea of walking away from everything. But then the anger and resentment poured in and buried everything else. They all had to pay and he had to do whatever it took, to make sure that happened.

But, he needed the power of those additional soulstones.

"Then you leave me no choice," Ashar said. "I had hoped to use the other soulstones to complete my revenge, but the ones I have will have to do."

"Revenge? What are you talking about? What are you going to do?"

Ashar had already lied to protect her, it would be refreshing to tell the truth and still get what he wanted. If she loved this Ghile and he was with the elves, then she would warn him and bring the boy to him anyway. "I suppose it makes little difference now that my course has been decided for me," Ashar said. He made an offhand gesture and turned to look back out over the sea. "I have already set the elves against Dagbar. All I have done is placed squarely on his shoulders. I have discovered the secrets of the dream mists. Did you know the mists are toxic to vegetation? Only certain slimes and molds seem to be immune, though I couldn't tell you why.

"In any case, I am going to use the power granted by my two soulstones to expand the dream mists beyond the boundary of the Fallen City. More than that, I have discovered how to spread the toxic mists beyond the boundaries of the city and into the trees themselves," Ashar said. "I'm going to destroy the Deepwood, dear sister. Then the elves are going to destroy Dagbar and anything the lying dwarf ever held dear!"

24

Strength of Heart

 HE rain still fell hard against the paving stones of the market square. The many stalls they passed were dark shapes, casting their long shadows before them like grasping fingers, trying to block their way.

Gaidel wiped her face to clear her vision. The rain mixed freely with her tears. She could see the fire and smoke coming from the rooftop of the Happy Trader, on the edge of the market square. The reflection of the flames in the puddles before her danced mockingly, until she splashed through them.

She could hear the others behind her and sensed more than heard Two Elks at her side, keeping pace. Daughter Bosand's demands for her to stop had ceased once they left the Bastion and saw the flames through the storm. She followed somewhere behind as well.

She turned the final corner and reached the edge of the market stalls. It should have been a clear path to the Happy Trader then, but she ran into the back of the gathered crowd. She pushed past people, not slowing. She fell once and felt Two Elk's strong hand bring her to her feet. She pulled free and pushed on through.

Black smoke poured from the Happy Trader's many windows. Flames tried to find purchase on its wet exterior. The inside of the building glowed with a fiendish light.

She heard the sounds of shouted orders mixed with screams and yelling. She added her voice to the cacophony, screaming Riff's name. It was then she saw the line of blackened bodies, splayed out on the ground.

Two Elks grabbed her and refused to let go, no matter how much she struggled. She struck him then. He had to let go, she had to find them.

"Little Daughter, stop. We do not know where they are. Stop!" Two Elks said as he held her close.

Gaidel's shouts turned into convulsive heaves as she simultaneously cried and tried to find breath to fill her lungs. She held onto him, drawing from his strength.

Magister Dagbar was there then, shouting orders. Luckily, the storm was keeping the fire contained and it hadn't spread to the surrounding buildings. Gaidel could see a number of humans and dwarves who had formed a line and were passing buckets of water between them.

She saw Master Dowynn then. He held an everflame in his hand and he walked towards the Happy Trader and right up to the door where the front of the line was hurling buckets of water. Master Dowynn stepped right into the doorway and into the flames, which immediately subsided.

Hurrahs rose behind him as he stepped tentatively into the building, waving his free hand before him. The smoke forced him back. He took a deep breath and waved a hand, and the smoke, too, dissipated. He stepped further into the building, followed by others.

Gaidel patted Two Elks on the chest. "I'm alright, Two Elks. Let me go."

Two Elks released her and Gaidel made a show of straightening her skirt and cloak, even though both were sodden and hung heavy from the persistent rain. She had to get control of herself and help. She fought down the images of Lotte and Riff and focused on the task at hand. "Magister Dagbar, if you could please find out what happened? Our friends were here. One was a sorcerer. Air and fire will not heed my call, I will help those I can," Gaidel said. "Patron Sister Bosand, please help me. Two Elks, help put out that fire." Not waiting to see if anyone followed her orders, Gaidel stepped through the crowd and knelt next to the nearest person lying on the ground. He was an older man, his face and hands badly burned. "I am Daughter Gaidel, of the Redwood druids. I'm going to heal you."

The man simply stared for a moment and then gave a weak nod, never taking his pained eyes from hers.

Closing her eyes, Gaidel breathed in deeply and cleared her mind of thought. She began to sing. Reality faded from view as she entered the song, flowing along with it. She could feel the rain rhythmically slapping the sodden paving stones, the breathy air lilting around the piercing timbre of the flames, both rushing past her song, ignoring her. She found the man's song then, felt the discordant beat of his burns. She focused on them, sang along and then guided them back into the man's natural rhythm.

Gaidel could not see the man's burns lighten and turn a fresh rosy pink of new skin, see the relief come over his face as the pain subsided. She was still lost in the song and going deeper.

The idea came to her while she healed the man and the song flowed past her. It was risky, but she would take the chance. If she sang against the flow of time. She could travel back and find out what happened to Riff and Lotte.

So she began. It felt like fighting upstream against a raging torrent. A current that pulled at her inner being. It would be so easy to give in and flow away with it, like so many other druids had done, become lost in the song. Gaidel focused. She did not have far to go. She sang along, following the flames as they danced back in time, new chords being born where the fires touched instead of being consumed.

She followed the fires back along the ceiling, the smoke flowing past her, returning to where the flames touched wood. She could see the blood and chaos below her. She saw the two cullers as they flowed backwards into the inn through the front doors, dwarven guards leaped up awkwardly from the floor to land in their wake. Back the two flowed, dwarves and humans leaping up from the floor to land before them as the cullers moved backwards towards the hearth.

Gaidel spotted Lotte then, his lifeless form lying next to Ast and Cuz. Gaidel knew all three were gone, because their songs were no longer there.

She almost lost control then, slipped as she struggled into the past, against the flow of time. The song pulled at her, demanded she flow along with it. It was then she saw two men dragging Riff's burnt form towards the hearth.

She found Riff's weak song – thank the All Mother it was there – if barely. She gave in to the pull to time but followed Riff's song instead. She followed the two men dragging him away from the hearth, slapping at the flames that still burned him.

Gaidel pulled herself from the Dream Song, fell to the ground and vomited violently.

"Daughter, are you alright?" It was the man she had just healed. He helped her to her feet. "Thank you, Revered Daughter, thank you."

Gaidel steadied herself and got her feet under her. She half walked, half stumbled past a number of the wounded. The man followed along, offering her support.

"Here now, you need to sit down, me thinks." The man tried to help her sit, but she shook him off and stumbled forward.

She landed next to an unmoving form, black and burnt. Gaidel knew she shouldn't have left them alone. She should have listened to her own inner voice and demanded they be allowed to come with them. If she had, the others—

"Not you, too," Gaidel said. She tried to clear her mind, but saw Riff there in her thoughts, smirking at her. He held one of those ridiculous mushrooms between his fingers. She choked out a laugh between the sobs. "Not you, too," she said again and cleared her mind. She joined the song.

Gaidel didn't remember how long she sang, or when she finally let go, unable to fight the pull of the Dream Song any longer.

Rain patted her face and she blinked open her eyes. It was still dark and the smell of smoke and ash were overpowering. Her head rested on something warm and soft. It shifted beneath her and Riff's face appeared. His skin was smooth and pink and he gave her one of his smirks. "All my sources are ruined," he said.

"Don't leave me again," Gaidel said, before she knew what she was saying. She couldn't say why she had said it, it just came rushing out. She knew she meant those words, but immediately regretted how vulnerable saying them made her feel.

She had obviously caught him off guard. He stared at her, his face a mix of emotions, much like her own, she was sure. He finally answered with a genuine smile and a simple, "I won't."

Patron Sister Bosand came into her vision, along with Rachard and Two Elks. Bosand was kneeling next to her and rested a hand on Gaidel's shoulder. "You risked much to save this young man, Sister. I almost lost you to the song."

Gaidel forced herself to sit up, thankful for the distraction from what was transpiring between her and Riff. Her head swam and ached more than a little. Smoke still issued from the Happy Trader, but the fire was out. Gaidel could see Mistress Jolyn standing near her inn, holding the blackened shingle.

"I helped those I could," Daughter Bosand said. "Can anyone explain what happened here?"

"I can," Riff said. He cleared his throat and struggled for a place to begin. "The cullers were led to us by the moneylender. Lotte tried to escape, but one of them came in through the back. They knew I was not Master Almoriz and I think their leader, Finngyr, thought my apprentice was going to be Ghile," Riff said. He stopped then and closed his eyes, but opened them quickly. Whatever he saw there, he didn't want to dwell on. "Lotte told them the elves had Ghile. They killed Ast and Cuz. Then... then they killed Lotte."

Riff's face darkened. "I knew I was next and wanted to take them with me. After I sent you the warning, I attacked them with fire." Riff motioned towards the gutted remains of the Happy Trader. "I'm afraid that's my fault. I'm not really sure how I survived."

"You were dragged out by two men. The others in the inn, they attacked the cullers. Dwarf and human alike. Even the guards tried to stop them, but they fought through and escaped," Gaidel added.

Riff looked at her, confused, and she added, "I saw it in the Dream Song."

Magister Dagbar stepped up then with a number of the Emporium guard with him. "The cullers made the gate and took to their griffons. They are gone. Do any of you know where they are headed?"

"They know Ghile is with the elves," Gaidel said.

"Then he is lost and our mission failed," Daughter Bosand said.

"Not so," Magister Dagbar said. "We can still help him."

"How do you propose to reach him, when you cannot even enter the Deepwood without being attacked?" Daughter Bosand asked.

Magister Dagbar got down on one knee and looked Gaidel in the eyes. His multi-colored eyes, one blue, the other stark white, locked onto hers. "I have a plan. We can save Ghile. If you'll trust me."

Gaidel heard Patron Sister Bosand's sniff. There was no doubt what she thought about trusting him. Gaidel looked away from Dagbar.

The others stared at her, waiting. It was to be her decision. Even Dagbar had addressed his request at her. Gaidel once again felt the weight of leadership settle on her shoulders. She knew what she wanted to do and would listen to her heart this time. "We go with you, Magister Dagbar. We go now."

Dagbar gave her a toothy smile and helped her to her feet. He clapped his hands and rubbed them together. "You are going to love the irony of my plan, let me tell you."

"Sister Gaidel, I forbid you. You are coming with me," Daughter Bosand demanded.

"No, Patron Sister, I am not," Gaidel responded. She felt bad defying Patron Sister Bosand. A part of her wondered if she realized what she was doing. By defying Patron Sister Bosand, she was also defying Mother Brambles and the entire Order of Redwood Druids. But as wrong as it felt in her head, it felt equally right in her heart. She stared at the older druid and tried not to look defiant, but stern. "Ghile Stonechosen is my friend and I will not abandon him."

"Nor I," Riff said, stepping up next to her. "Even if he is a wool-headed sheepherder."

"Nor I," Two Elks said. He stepped up behind Gaidel and stared down at Daughter Bosand, daring her to disagree.

"Sounds like fun," Shieldwarden Rachard said.

25

Islmur

HILE took his time as he walked. He needed time to
think and it was truly a beautiful day. Unlike the Deepwood, the sunlight filtered unhindered through the
broad trees on the island. The light breeze brushing
his skin still held the warmth of summer.

He didn't need to remind himself that he was in Allwyn. Though
the islands were the same, the silvertrees and Alvar, which didn't
exist in the dreaming, were everywhere. There were so many Alvar
on the island now, the sight of them no longer held him in awe. If
he had to guess, he would say there were more of them than there
were trees on the island.

They gathered in groups and sang in low whispers or walked
alone in silence, their arms outstretched to soak in the sun's rays.
They wore no clothes, which still bothered Ghile, though some dec-
orated themselves with birds' nests or different types of flowering
ivy.

The oddest thing about the Alvar, was Ghile had not seen any of
them eat. He saw a number of them drinking from the lake and some

of the numerous streams that flowed throughout the grove, but they couldn't just live on water, could they? Maybe eating embarrassed them, or it was something they only did in private?

That seemed the most likely explanation. The way some of them stared at him when he called to a fish and then killed it using his mind thrust, you would have thought he'd taken his own head off and shaken it at them. At least the fish had caused a reaction. Most of the time they just ignored him.

That was another thing that was odd. The fish was the first thing he'd eaten in a couple of days. He wasn't really hungry or thirsty even now, though he knew he should be. In fact, he had never felt better. He wasn't losing weight either, just the opposite. Ghile ran his hands along his stomach and felt the hard muscles just underneath the skin. Another gift of the soulstones.

He wondered if Akira noticed his muscles and couldn't help but grin. What kind of thought was that? He looked about, worried the Alvar would be staring at him. He chastised himself for being foolish; they couldn't read minds.

Ghile noticed a large number of them gathered a short distance away. They were circling a conifer tree and singing softly. Ghile turned and began walking in that direction.

It couldn't be the ritual, the Keeper said she would come for him when it was time. Plus, even though there were quite a few gathered together, it was nowhere near all of the Alvar on the island.

His thoughts returned to Akira. He'd thought about her a lot lately. He thought about the time he spent sitting next to her and looking out over the lake. He wanted to see her again, but had been hesitant to return to the dreaming because of what his shadow had shown him.

He had come to terms with his feelings concerning Adon and his culling. Talking about them with Akira had really helped and it didn't make him cringe when he thought about Adon and what happened. He had been much younger then and it was only natural to have those feelings. He was no longer ashamed of them and it wasn't the reason he hesitated in returning. It was the fear of what else his shadow had to show him.

What other things had he done in his life, that his shadow would make him face? The most recent that came to mind was leaving his friends back in the village. *Friends,* Ghile thought. Yes, he saw them as his friends: Riff, Daughter Gaidel, even Two Elks. They were the closest things he had ever had to friends.

Ghile's early height and gangly awkwardness had made him self-conscious and shy around the other children of Last Hamlet. His father being Clan Leader hadn't helped. Once Adon was gone, Ghile was either teased or ignored. If they could see him now.

Ghile shook his head. He might have grown into his own skin with the help of the soulstones, but he was still a child when it came to how to treat a friend. He should have never left them like that. He just didn't want them making him go to Dagbar's Freehold. He wanted to go help Akira. The talk he had with Two Elks about honor and doing the right thing seemed to point him towards helping Akira at the time, so he had left.

He knew now what he should have done was stood his ground and convinced them his decision was the right one and listened to what they all had to say. It would have been a lot harder, but it would have been the right thing to do. That was a lesson he was learning the hard way. The right decisions were most often the harder ones.

"This one greets Ghile Stonechosen," Arenuin said.

Ghile blinked. Arenuin must have seen him coming. She stepped out from the gathered Alvar to greet him. A couple of the nearby Alvar turned to regard him with those magic-infused eyes, but never stopped singing and just as quickly turned back around.

"Greetings, Arenuin," Ghile said. He spread out his hands and bowed his head. "What's happening here?"

Arenuin smiled and motioned him to follow her. "Ghile Stone-chosen is just in time to know answers this one was not allowed to speak, but can show."

Ghile followed as she wove her way past the others. Due to their respective height compared to his own, Ghile quickly found himself keeping his eyes downturned and focused on Arenuin's slender feet. He really wished they would wear some kind of clothing.

As he followed Arenuin, he listened to the song the Alvar sang.

Mother tree release her to us
Islmur guide her to usHear our voice, sister, hear us
Join us
Come forth to us
Allwyn bestows her glories on us
Share them with us
Join us

They sang the words over and over again in a slow, comforting rhythm. Ghile felt his skin tingle. Alvar song was truly the most beautiful sound he had ever heard.

Arenuin stopped at the inner edge of the gathering and knelt down on one knee and spoke to Ghile in a melodic whisper. "A sister joins us."

In the center of the gathering was a tall, dark brown tree, its bark covered in square shaped cracks and thick ridges. Dried needles littered the ground beneath its green, needle-laden boughs.

The trunk nearest the ground was moving. One of the many ridges had opened and a small slender leg hung out of it. Ghile could see the toes flexing.

Ghile suddenly felt self-conscious and wondered if he was supposed to be here. He looked at the circle of Alvar, but if any of them cared, they didn't show it. They all continued to sing and a number of them intertwined arms with those beside them.

One of the Alvar stepped out of the crowd and approached the tree. Ghile noticed her skin color matched that of the tree.

"The mother," Arenuin said, "stepped from the tree this morning. She is blessed to birth a child in Islmur's Grove."

As Ghile watched, the mother Alvar coaxed her child from the birthing tree. It appeared to Ghile that the tree was handing the newborn Alvar to her mother. The newborn stood shakily on her own feet, the mother Alvar supporting her.

No sooner had the baby Alvar left the birthing tree, than the crack closed and its green needles began to rain down. Slowly the tree's deep brown color changed to silver. Ghile could hear a deep crackling sound over the Alvar's singing.

"A silvertree," Ghile said in wonder.

"The Alvar name it, Anualmar," she corrected. "The Alvar honor the Anualmar for their sacrifice."

Through the soulstones, Ghile knew the word translated roughly into ancestor tree.

The other Alvar had slowly moved forward to surround the mother and her new daughter. Many were touching the newly transformed silvertree.

Ghile was in awe at what he had seen, but still felt uncomfortable being there. As if he had stolen something he could never return. How many other mysteries were there in Allwyn that he knew nothing of? At that point in time, Ghile felt quite small and insignificant.

A Guardian Alvar, much larger than the others, strode up to stand before Ghile. He recognized her as the one who greeted him and Arenuin so harshly when he first arrived on the island.

"Ghile Stonechosen, it is time," Duanotyn said. She did not wait for an answer and turned to address the others. "It is time," Duanotyn repeated. This she sang louder.

Slowly at first, and then in increasing numbers, others began to repeat the words.

Arenuin smiled and motioned for Ghile to follow. "It is time."

Ghile swallowed down the excitement. It was time. He was about to meet a Goddess. However small and insignificant seeing an Alvar being born into Allwyn made him feel, it was nothing compared to the feeling that settled into the pit of his stomach as he followed Duanotyn.

He felt certain he knew their destination before any of the Alvar began moving towards it. The Great Oak at the center of the island.

Ghile had to trot to keep up with Duanotyn. Unlike following Arenuin through the Deepwood, Duanotyn did not deviate from her course and strode with purpose towards the Great Oak, all the while singing, "It is time."

The island rang with Alvarsong. Ghile followed past many other Alvar, who walked alone and in groups. The ground reverberated with their movement. The Great Oak towered before him, the sunlight bathing its upper trunk and boughs in golden light. How many times had he sat on those very limbs in the dreaming? It somehow seemed fitting this was where the ritual would take place.

Ahead, he saw the Keeper and other Guardians of the Grove. They formed the inner circle around the Great Oak, the other Alvar fanning out behind them. As Ghile passed, many of the Alvar stopped. Those who did lifted their arms skyward and closed their eyes. Their resemblance to trees was suddenly so profound.

Ghile stopped.

It wasn't a resemblance, he realized – they were becoming trees. Ghile could hear it then, the crackling sound. He could hear the skin of the nearest Alvar thickening. Where their skin was only shaded and discolored like bark, actual bark appeared. Bright green leaves or clumps of pine needles sprouted from hands and arms.

Ghile turned and searched for Arenuin. She was far behind him – he had been so absorbed with everything going on, that he hadn't noticed her stop. The others around her had already begun their transformation, but not Arenuin. Her sapphire eyes met Ghile's as a smile appeared on her lips. She nodded once reassuringly and then closed her eyes. Ghile watched, transfixed, as her face disappeared and she completed her transformation.

Ghile turned slowly and took in the newly formed forest around him. Was he alone?

Sound from ahead around the Great Oak caught his attention, the Guardians were still there and had moved closer to the Oak's enormous trunk.

As Ghile approached, the Guardians stepped back to reveal a woman. A human woman. As she walked towards him, Ghile noted several things at once. She was tall. Easily twice his height, but she was also equally proportioned. She was human, just bigger.

No, he thought. To say she was human would have been to insult her. She was shaped like a human, but she was faultless. Her skin was smooth and glowed with an inner light. Her hair was full and the color of fire. She was radiant.

And clothed, thank the All Mother. A soft green gown hung down to her feet.

She smiled at Ghile then and he panicked. Could she read his mind?

He didn't know what to say, how did you introduce yourself to a God? Luckily, he didn't have to.

"Hello, Ghile."

The simplicity of it left Ghile speechless. Her voice was so melodic. She didn't sing like the Alvar, but even in those two words, Ghile could hear her balanced right there on the cusp of song.

He did the only thing he could think of, he turned his hands towards the sky and bowed deeply.

When he rose, Islmur stood before him, a motherly smile on her face. Ghile couldn't place an age to her. She looked young, barely of handfasting age, but at the same time old enough to be a mother. In her eyes, he saw the wisdom of an elder.

The Guardians remained beside the Great Oak, their eyes following their creator. Ghile felt his cheeks redden. The Alvars' faces held such love and pride in their creator. How would he feel if Haurtu stood before him?

"I sense much of my brother in you," Islmur said.

Ghile averted his eyes. She did see his thoughts. She must sense his shame, as well.

"You wondered why you found this place in your dreaming," Islmur said. "Haurtu lived here with me for a long time. It was special to him."

Ghile realized she had seen his thoughts again and was trying to take his mind from them.

She turned and looked at the Great Oak. "This is the last of the trees from the beginning times."

His curiosity got the better of him. "The beginning times?" Ghile said.

Islmur smiled. "You have found your voice. Good. It is nice to hear you speak. I have missed the sound of words." She looked around the grove and sighed. "I miss a great many things."

"The beginning times, the time when we Primordials walked All-wyn. Things were… bigger then. This is the last tree from that time. It has been my… resting place. I suppose my presence within it has preserved it."

Ghile was still overwhelmed. With every word she spoke, a dozen new questions raced into his thoughts.

Islmur nodded. "I understand, Ghile. Your thoughts are a swirling morass of questions, all fighting to be asked and answered. That is why I asked the Alvar to find you and bring you here. I wish to help you."

"Me?" Ghile said.

Islmur had walked to the nearest Alvar tree, and reached down to caress the leaves that recently sprouted from its upturned arms.

"Yes." She turned to regard him again and Ghile felt the worth of him weighed and measured in that glance. "From the moment you entered the Deepwood. I have hoped you would understand and believe. There is much good in you, Ghile." Islmur said.

She laughed then and all the doubts he felt gathering to rebut her words fled from that joyous sound.

"I am sorry, Ghile. I have overwhelmed you." Islmur sat down then. Even such a simple act as sitting seemed so graceful, so perfect. "Ghile, please, sit down. You will need to overcome this feeling of awe and dwelling on your own inadequacies, or you will never be able to face my brother and he will succeed in his plans to return to Allwyn."

Ghile dropped to the ground, more than a little embarrassed. Of course she wouldn't want Haurtu to return to Allwyn. Islmur and her brother Daomur, the creator of the dwarven race, were the two surviving gods who imprisoned Haurtu and had then began the Great Purge.

Islmur was shaking her head, even before she spoke. "No, Ghile. The histories as you have been taught them are not exactly true. I love my brother, dearly. And he must return to Allwyn. He will return, there is no stopping that. It is only a matter of when and in what form."

Questions jumbled in his mind. This whole conversation, with Islmur's ability to see his thoughts and respond to them before he had put them to words, was confusing.

She started to speak again and then blinked. She couldn't contain a laugh and shook her head.

Ghile felt his cheeks redden. He took a deep breath and calmed himself. All this time he had wanted answers and now was that time. It was all so exciting and more than a little overwhelming.

Islmur waited, patiently, a sympathetic grin on her lips.

Once Ghile felt he had himself under control, he spoke. "Please, tell me."

"I suppose, it would be easiest to start from the beginning, when my kind walked on Mother Allwyn. I am the oldest, you know. I was her first." Islmur sighed. "She was with us for such a short time in the beginning, but she was with us. She had created so much by then..." Islmur caught herself and returned her attention to Ghile. "There is balance in all things, Ghile. A give and take, a push and a pull. When a god creates, they must give up a part of themselves. The more they create, the more they must give."

She motioned with her hands to take in everything around them. "Mother Allwyn created everything that is. She has given much of herself, almost everything. So, she sleeps and dreams."

Ghile nodded his understanding.

"My brothers and sisters and I were her last creations. What remained of her went into us. Do not misunderstand, she still exists. Not as an individual, but there is a part of her in everything. Those parts are all connected and are Allwyn. She exists, but in a different form."

Ghile could remember being taught this when he was young. An image of him sitting in a roundhouse beside the hearth fire in Last Hamlet and listening to the elders explain that everything was created by the All Mother and was thus connected through her. She was the life force that joined all and the dreaming. The place Druids went when they entered their trances and where all magic came from, was that connection, was Allwyn.

"Just so," Islmur said. "In the beginning, the Primordials lived on Allwyn just as you do now. But over time, we too found we possessed the ability to create, to draw from ourselves and create new life. There is an important part in the final act of creation, Ghile. It is important you understand that, as it applies directly to some of those many questions spinning around in your head."

Ghile smiled, a little embarrassed. What must his jumbled thoughts look like to her?

"The act of letting go," Islmur said. "You see, Allwyn sees all we do through her many creations, but she no longer has any control over them. Once you create something, it is no longer in your control. It has free will," Islmur said. "It is the same with the Primordials. We have no control over our creations. They have free will."

Ghile considered that. "So, you mean, if the Alvar did not want you to awaken—"

"Then I could not. They humble me with this gift. Just as they humble me by hearing my council while I'm here. It is important you understand this, Ghile. To create is to let go. It is both the most terrifying and rewarding feeling one will ever experience."

"So, you see what they see?" Ghile asked.

"Yes. You have already experienced a small glimpse of the ability. Through the soulstones," Islmur said.

"When I reach out and mind touch animals."

"Just so," Islmur said.

"But, if the soulstones are of Huartu, then why only animals? Why can't I touch the minds of humans? We were created by him," Ghile said.

Islmur nodded. "In time, you would be able to. Each of the soulstones are but a drop of Haurtu's power. Haurtu has an affinity with animals. Each of the Primordials have an association with different creations of Allwyn. For me, it is the trees. I first knew you when you entered the Redwood on the eve of your manhood tests."

Ghile tried to imagine what that would be like, to see and know everything that happened anywhere in Allwyn through the trees. But at the same time, having no control. That made him think of the soulstones. "So the soulstones are of Haurtu, but are not Haurtu!" Ghile said.

Islmur nodded. "Yes. Once he created them, he no longer has any power over them. Haurtu has no control of you and though the soulstones know of their purpose; to prepare his vessel, they are free thinking creations."

Ghile felt a small weight he hadn't even realized was there, lift from his shoulders. "Can Haurtu see through the soulstones?" Ghile said. He thought of Adon and if it might really be his brother. Ghile could see the compassion in Islmur's eyes and knew she had the answers. "Please, tell me."

"Ghile, Haurtu is imprisoned beyond Allwyn. He is no longer in it, though it is impossible to completely separate him from it. It is through this 'connection' that he was able to introduce the soulstones back into this world." Islmur held up a long thin finger. "But, he is no longer connected to his creations. This includes the life force that remains when their physical bodies, the part of them that is Allwyn, dies. So, what you call Adon in your dreaming, is what the first soulstone took from your memories in creating its form in your dreaming."

"Is it the same with Muk?"

"No," Islmur said, "that is different. I'll try to explain."

Ghile found he was leaning forward and focused on her every word. He knew in his heart it was not Adon, but now he also knew it sort of was. The soulstone was not Haurtu, disguised and manipulating him. It was Adon, as he had known him.

"When a creation of Allwyn dies, the energy, soul, what have you, returns to the dreaming. When something new is born into Allwyn, its energy is drawn from the dreaming."

Ghile nodded for her to continue.

"When a creation of a Primordial dies, its energy is returned to the Primordial," Islmur said. "The energy of Haurtu's creations cannot return to him. They are in limbo. This is why Haurtu must return to Allwyn, to restore balance, make things whole.

"In the case of Muk and the soulstone, his energy entered his soulstone. What dwells in your dreaming is the energy, or soul, of Muk. But you need to understand, it has joined with his soulstone and thus is both. This is why it teaches you," Islmur said.

"And my shadow?" Ghile said. He wasn't sure he wanted to know the answer to this question, but felt he needed to hear it.

"Ah, the shadow. Yes. You recall I said your dreaming, earlier?"

"Yes," Ghile said.

"The island of your dreaming was formed by the soulstone. It created a place of comfort to it. As I said before, Haurtu loved this place as a child, but the place itself is created within you. Have you not noticed your mood affects the weather?"

Ghile blinked. It did? He thought back to the many times he had entered the dreaming. Was she right? Of course she was, but he hadn't really ever considered it.

"The shadow in your dreaming represents the physical part of you. The part of you that is of Allwyn," Islmur said.

Ghile wasn't sure he understood.

Islmur took her two hands and joined them together. When you were born, the energy that is of Haurtu and the physical part that comes from Allwyn join like this. The two become one."

Ghile nodded.

"So the shadow is part of you. The part that hungers, that hates, that part of you that exists below the surface of your thoughts, where your fears and insecurities hide."

Ghile suddenly felt exposed and uncomfortable. He remembered what the shadow had shown him, those feelings he had experienced when Adon was culled.

"It will share more with you, Ghile, and you must listen. It is trying to prepare you."

"Prepare me? For what?" Ghile said. How could showing him something so horrible about himself prepare him for anything?

"For the battle that will come when you free Haurtu," Islmur said. "The battle for your body. That is his goal, Ghile. The soulstones prepare the vessel for Haurtu. You have already sensed the changes both mentally, in the powers you now possess, and physically. Your stamina and strength. Your lack of thirst and hunger. With each soulstone you possess, you become more like a Primordial."

Ghile didn't know what to say. She had not said if, but when. How was he supposed to win a battle against a god? How was it even possible? "No, the part of me that is of Allwyn isn't Haurtu. I thought the histories said Daomur put the perfect lock on Haurtu's prison. Haurtu was the key and he was trapped inside."

Islmur nodded and remained calm, even though Ghile's voice rose with every word. "When I created the Alvar, the part of them that came from Allwyn, I took from the trees. It is because of this that I am able to wake and return to Allwyn." Islmur looked around her. "My children sleep, so that I can wake."

Islmur saw the look of concern come over Ghile's face as he glanced back at the tree that was Arenuin. "Do not fear, Ghile. They will awaken once I return to my slumber. Which will be soon. Even now, I feel its call.

"I am fortunate, Ghile. It was through chance alone that I am able to do this. In the beginning, when we first realized we could create, we did not understand the cost. Of all things Mother created, it was the trees I most cherished and it was from them that I drew my inspiration and created the Alvar.

"Recall I said Haurtu had an affinity for animals. At first, he drew from them for inspiration. From lizards he created goblins. From wolves came the vargan. And there were others. But Haurtu never seemed satisfied with his creations. Also, we began to notice those races created from animals always seemed to lend themselves to darker temperaments," Islmur said.

"And humans?" Ghile said.

Islmur frowned. "Haurtu was never satisfied with his other creations. That was when Haurtu did something none of us ever considered doing. He drew of himself to create humans."

Ghile knew his race was created by the Primordials, but he had never thought of humans as descended from them.

"So you see now, how a human can free Haurtu from his prison. One that has been transformed by soulstones would be able to free him."

Ghile felt the two soulstones beneath his tunic. "How many would be needed?"

"I do not know, Ghile. But, I fear the more you possess, the easier it will be for Haurtu to take control of you."

Ghile ran his hands through his hair and sighed. "Islmur, I do not mean to be disrespectful. You say he must return, then talk as if you know I will be the one to free him, and then hint I can fight him and stop him from taking my body from me. Then you say I need enough soulstones to open the prison that holds him, and you do not know how many that is, but the more I have, the more likely he will be able to defeat me and take my body from me."

Islmur nodded. "Yes, just so, I'm afraid."

"Then why fight? It seems I am doomed, regardless," Ghile said, throwing up his hands. He thought back to the night he had the conversation with Two Elks and felt the same frustration with his situation as he did then.

"Because, you have to fight. It is not just you who is at risk, but your entire race," Islmur said.

"What?" Ghile said.

"I have explained how the act of creation takes from the creator. As the Primordials created, they slowly began to suffer the same fate as Allwyn. As our progeny themselves produced life, it only further drew from us. As the races multiplied and spread throughout Allwyn, we began to sleep longer and longer. But Haurtu pulled from himself both spiritually and physically when he created the human race. The energy your race took was tenfold," Islmur said.

"What did he do when he discovered this?" Ghile asked, though he feared he already knew the answer.

Ghile could see the sadness on Islmur's face.

"Oh, Ghile. He was so proud at first. Your race is so like us. Where the other races seemed content to stay in one place, like the forest or the ocean, you humans wanted to live everywhere. You were curious and intelligent. Haurtu kept nothing from you. He shared all his knowledge with you."

"But," Ghile prompted.

"But, unlike the others, your creator was not content to lie down and give way to his creations. During his waking times, he tried to discover a way to break the process, to stay awake longer. "His first attempt was trying to consume the power of other Primordials," Islmur said.

"He attacked and consumed the others," Ghile said. "We were taught it was because he wanted to become the All Father."

"Yes, I know. My brother was wise, even we have our limits. There was no way for him to destroy the human race alone. None of the other Primordials would have even considered helping him do such a thing, not even Hideon, who so loved war and strife.

"So Haurtu thought and planned. He began telling his progeny his lies of becoming the All Father, of his need to consume the other Primordials and convinced your kind to help him by attacking the other races. The more progeny that was destroyed, the more energy returned to the Primordials. In so doing, he made humankind the enemy of the other races. It was a horrible time, Ghile. The more battles humans fought, the more of them died, the more energy was returned to Haurtu. Do you understand that there are so few humans left on Allwyn now, if he returned, he would be fully awake when no other Primordial would be?"

"You are awake," Ghile said.

"I am, but you do not realize what little power I have, Ghile. I would be but a flea biting at a bull," Islmur said. "Luckily, it was Daomur who finally realized what Haurtu's true intentions were and came up with the plan for us to stop him."

"Was it Daomur's idea to contain us, as well? To keep knowledge from us?" Ghile couldn't keep the resentment out of his voice.

Islmur only showed compassion. "Daomur does not forgive easily. Of all the Primordials, Daomur dislikes Haurtu the most. They were opposites in many ways. Daomur has always been about rules and consequences for breaking them," Islmur said. "Daomur felt if the remaining humans were allowed their freedom, to continue learning and growing, that your race would figure out a way to free Haurtu. Even so, a way was still discovered. So, the Temple of Justice was formed. Enchanted hammers were created, ones that could sense Allwyn's song, sense Haurtu and a future that would be connected to him. The loss of the few for the good of the many, he had said."

Ghile sat there with Islmur in silence. She watched him, but said nothing. He knew she could see his thoughts as easily as he did, but he was beyond caring about Daomur. If Haurtu was allowed to return to Allwyn and take over the vessel that freed him, then he would continue with his plan of destroying humankind, those few that were left. Ghile suddenly felt tired. But he knew what he had to do now.

"How many soulstones are there?"

"There have never been more than nine soulstones discovered on Allwyn at one time," Islmur said.

"What has become of the other soulstones from the times when they appeared in the past?"

"The place between places where Haurtu is imprisoned," Islmur said. "It is not a stationary place. It is difficult to describe, but it passes close to Allwyn for a short time every four hundred and ninety-nine years. The Time of the Stonechosen lasts for one year. Then Haurtu's prison leaves the proximity of Allwyn."

"And the soulstones?" Ghile said.

Islmur stared at Ghile. "The soulstones and the vessels they occupy die."

Ghile had no wish to die, or be responsible for the extinction for his entire race.

How ironic, he thought to himself. Haurtu would be proud of his creation. Ghile was going to fight.

26

Golems

HE stone boot descended with such force, it crushed the foliage beneath it, the ground shaking from the impact. The golem, like its four identical companions, marched through the Deepwood, their thick legs swinging with a measured pace. They traveled in a line, shoulder to shoulder where the forest allowed, but even the giant stone golems, created by master artificers from the Temple of Art, had to give way to the colossal trees of the Deepwood.

Dagbar held on to the stone horn jutting from one of the golem's helmets. The golem's shoulders were wide, flat plates, representing dwarven armor. They offered good footing and made an excellent perch.

The golem lurched violently to the side and Dagbar grabbed onto the horn with both hands. The golem's arm swung out wide, uprooting a tree that blocked its way and sending it soaring. *Well,* Dagbar thought, *made an adequate perch.* At least this would get the Alvars' attention.

He looked back at the wake of destruction marking a clear path through the Deepwood, all the way back to the Emporium. He wished there was another way, but it was the only chance he had and he had already pushed all his chips to the center of the table. He was all in.

If he was going to help Ghile Stonechosen, he needed to get past the fae guarding the borders and into the Deepwood. But most of all, he needed to find the Alvar. He knew finding the Alvar was a near impossible task. One didn't find the Alvar, they found you. So he needed to get their attention. This swathe of destruction would have to do.

The golems were headed home, back to the Fallen City. It wasn't where he wanted to go, far from it, but he didn't have a choice. The clergy from the Temple of Art had been no more impressed with the idea of giving control of their precious golems to a magister than the Knight Justices had. They had reluctantly given him the command gems for each golem, but only shared the commands needed to accomplish the golems' new job as glorified pack animals. But the artificers had been more than willing to give him the command word to send the golems back to the task they were created for – guarding the Fallen City.

So far, things had worked out. He convinced Daughter Gaidel to trust he could get her to Ghile. He had left the Emporium in the hands of his Council of Elders. Ulbert, Dowynn and Robon were more than capable of seeing to the issue with the Happy Trader and calming down those who thought the time to rebel was now. Well, at least, that was what he kept telling himself every few minutes. Right before he reminded himself there was no choice and this was the best chance he had.

The golems had made it past the fae guarding the forest around the Emporium. He had taken no small amount of satisfaction when the golems marched into the Deepwood, sending the fae running. Even those flying fae smart enough to try and attack the golem's riders turned back from a few well aimed bursts of sorcerer's fire. How many of his people had entered the forest to work, only to be found a few days later at the forest's edge with no knowledge of how they got there? Watching them scatter had been uncharacteristically satisfying.

He looked over at the shoulder of the golem to his immediate left where Daughter Gaidel and her shieldwarden rode. Dagbar gave the young druid a broad grin and nodded his head with what he hoped was a confident look of assurance.

The apprehension was plain on her face, mixed in with no small amount of fear, as she clung tightly to the golem's helmet. Nothing like the stoic expression of her shieldwarden, who knelt beside her, his shield raised and ready and his other hand balanced on his stone axe. He reminded Dagbar of a shadow cat who was waiting to pounce.

Dagbar knew the sorcerer, Riff, rode on the shoulder opposite them, but couldn't see past the golem's massive helmet. It wasn't a bad thing, either. The sorcerer had been deeply hurt by the loss of their young companion and his dogs. The hard set of his eyes had not changed since Daughter Gaidel healed him. Dagbar didn't want to think what the sorcerer would do if they reached the Fallen City without finding Ghile. The boy was itching to take his anger out on something. Even the brief tussle with the fae hadn't quenched the fire behind those eyes.

There were still so many loose ends. Daughter Bosand and her shieldwarden had demanded to come along. She had given in to Daughter Gaidel for the time being, but he was certain she planned to take control of the situation as soon as they found Ghile. Daughter Bosand planned to see Mother Brambles' orders carried out and see Ghile turned over to this Nordlah barbarian, Growling Bear. That would not do, of course, and he hoped Daughter Gaidel would see his side when the time came.

Dagbar was also certain the three cullers were headed towards the Fallen City and would see them sooner or later. The closer they got to the Fallen City, the easier for them to be spotted. With their flying mounts and this trail the golems were leaving, he doubted he would even get close before they came to investigate. He had little doubt what the cullers would do to them... Dagbar shook his head. No use thinking on that.

Then there was Ashar and Akira. The journey to the Fallen City would take days and nights. Nights in the Deepwood belonged to Ashar and his creatures. Dagbar knew Ashar would love to get his hands on him. That would be anything but pleasant.

Then if they did find Ghile, what were his intentions? Ghile spoke with Akira somehow and was heading to the Fallen City until he encountered the Alvar.

Finally, there were the Alvar. What had they done with Ghile? Had they taken him to the grove, too? Had they awakened Islmur? Dagbar prayed to Allwyn that is exactly what they did. If Ghile met with her, then he would know the truth of things.

Of course, none of this mattered if the Alvar killed them all. He was pretty sure how they would react to the golems smashing their way through the Deepwood. It was because of their love of nature that Dagbar had spared no small expense, transporting the golems through the Deepwood the first time.

The golem lurched violently and a tree cracked and flew away, trailing splinters and leaves. Dagbar held on and prayed.

"Islmur, I don't know if you can hear me. But, I'm in your Deepwood with Ghile Stonechosen's companions. He is supposed to be with the Alvar and we are coming to help him. He is in imminent danger. Cullers search the Deepwood and the Fallen City for him even now. If you can, please help us!"

Ahead of him, Dagbar saw some of the largest Alvar he had ever seen stepping from the trees.

"That was fast," Dagbar said. He fished for the command gems to call for a halt. It seemed Lady Luck had not deserted him.

$$\Lambda$$

"Well, this is going well," Riff said. He sat on the edge of the shoulder plate of the golem and watched Dagbar dodge yet another swinging arm, or limb, from an elf.

The dwarf had seemed so confident when the dozen or so elves emerged from their hiding places within the trees. He'd called a halt and had his golem lower him to the ground.

That had been his first mistake, Riff thought.

He should have stayed on his golem. These elves were huge, naked, and ticked off. Riff should have been excited to see elves for the first time, not to mention nude ones, but all he could think about was finding Ghile and then finding the cullers. Even discovering that Dagbar could speak the elves' strange singing language couldn't pull Riff's mind from his purpose. They were going to pay for what happened to Lotte and Ghile's Valehounds.

Riff passed his everflame from one hand to the other. He had prepared to fight the elves when they first appeared. He didn't know what they were and he was itching for a fight anyway. From a distance, they looked like walking trees, albeit very curvaceous walking trees, and trees were none too fond of fire.

But Dagbar told them not to attack, no matter what happened. So, here he sat, watching Dagbar and the elves sing at each other and the largest elf stop every so often to try and squash the dwarf. "We are wasting time, Gaidel. This doesn't seem to be going anywhere," Riff said.

Gaidel stood on the other shoulder of the golem, watching. She seemed as baffled as he was. Two Elks stood next to her, shield and axe ready. He seemed to think Dagbar was going to change his mind about not attacking at any time. That brought a feral grin to Riff's face. For once, he had to agree with the barbarian. This was going to end in a fight and he was fine with that.

Gaidel looked from Riff to Dagbar and then Bosand, uncertainty plain on her face.

"Give the Magister time," Daughter Bosand called over the elves' singing.

"We don't have time, Druid. Ghile is out there and these elves know where," Riff said. His response drew admonitory glares from the two shieldwardens. He ignored them, but made sure not to lock eyes with Gaidel. Riff still wasn't sure how he felt about the brief moment they had shared.

Riff almost dropped his everflame as his golem lurched into movement. With the sound of grinding stone, its upraised palm swung into position below Riff.

"It is done," Dagbar called up to them. "The keeper has agreed to take us to Ghile."

"Keeper?" Riff asked as he put away his everflame and jumped down onto the golem's palm.

"Yes, these magnificent creatures are Guardians of Islmur's Grove. Ghile is with the Goddess," Dagbar said.

The dwarf was bordering on giddy. It was like he had already forgotten this 'Keeper' was trying to flatten him just a few moments ago. Gaidel asked Dagbar as much as she and Two Elks jumped down the last few feet from their golem's palm.

"That," Dagbar said, more than a little sheepishly. "Well, the Keeper was just expressing her thoughts on the golems."

Riff watched as more than half the elves went around the golems and began singing to the forest floor. The plants trampled by the golem's passing began to spring back up, unfurling new fronds, or regrowing damaged limbs.

"The golems will have to remain here, I'm afraid," Dagbar said. He reminded Riff of a proud father, just then.

"How are you able to speak their language, Magister?" Daughter Bosand said. She walked up, behaving as if all of this happened twice a day where she was from. At least Rachard had the sense to look skeptical.

"Ah, it was a gift from the Goddess Islmur herself, Daughter Bosand," Dagbar said. He pointed at his face. "It was that very gift that did this to my eyes."

"Fascinating," Daughter Bosand said drily.

"It is nothing compared to what you are about to experience," Dagbar said. He clapped his hands together and produced another one of those unsettling, toothy smiles.

"Treestepping!"

27

Acceptance

HILE appeared in the dreaming. He was on the pebbled shore again. He looked in both directions along the shore and tree line. He was alone. Across the lake, the forests and mountains rose to meet clouds and blue sky, all reflected off the lake's calm water.

This was the same spot he had first appeared, when he first met Adon. He wondered if this particular spot was somehow special to Haurtu. He picked up a smooth stone and felt the weight of it. The thought of skipping it out over the lake came to him and he again questioned if this was his habit, or one of Haurtu's. He tossed the stone down. It was a small thing, but it made him feel better.

"I am Ghile Stonechosen and I am my own person."

He looked up at the clear sky and thought on what Islmur said. This place was a part of him, was him. He considered the position he was in, how all his choices were being taken from him. How unfair it all seemed.

Thunder rolled over the distant mountains. Ghile raised an eyebrow and nodded. That was good to know.

He couldn't hold onto his anger for long and the weather did not change further. His mind was moving too quickly. There was much to consider and things that needed to be done.

He turned and made his way through the forest towards the Great Oak. No sooner had he passed beyond the tree line did he surprise a stag, its head darting up, nostrils flaring as it scented the air.

Ghile mind touched it, almost without thinking. Its senses filled him. He had interrupted it while it dined on a treasured find, hickory nuts, probably hidden there by a squirrel. Ghile opened his mind further. Yes, there it was, on a limb not too far above them. Ghile could feel its agitation. The squirrel was definitely not happy about its stash being raided.

Ghile calmed the stag and squirrel with a thought and released the connection. Was this what it was like then, for the Primordials? To be one with everything? If this place was created from him, was he not like Allwyn, in a way? Why couldn't he sense everything around him, the trees, the land? He knew he was linked with the weather, why not everything else?

No time better than the present to find out, he thought.

Ghile sat down and leaned his back against a tree. He wanted to find Adon and Muk. They had been noticeably scarce his last couple of visits. It would be a good challenge for him. If he could see through his own creations, like Allwyn and Islmur did, maybe he could find where those two had been hiding. He wondered if they knew about his conversation with Islmur? In the past, they had let on they knew about things that occurred in Allwyn, but never gone into detail as to how.

His conversation with Islmur had lasted the rest of the day. She answered all the questions he could think to ask. She never judged him, or grew angry. She seemed content, even with everything that was at risk. Ghile envied her that.

She also told him his companions had entered the Deepwoods in the company of the dwarf, Dagbar. She sent the keeper and some of the other guardians to escort them to the grove. The argument that ensued at that request, surprised Ghile. The guardians took their responsibilities seriously and refused to let any other 'outsiders' on the island. They had settled on the opposite side of the lake.

Islmur also warned them against harming them. Islmur would not explain, but his friends had somehow damaged the Deepwood and Islmur didn't want the Guardians to seek retribution.

The Keeper's curiosity was as piqued as Ghile's at the news, but Islmur got them to promise and sent them on their way.

Ghile was both excited and apprehensive at the thought of seeing the others. He regretted leaving them and didn't know how he would be treated when they were reunited. It would be good to see Ast and Cuz again. He missed their company.

Islmur told Ghile he would need them, Dagbar especially. Dagbar was the one Arenuin had referred to, when she said Islmur had only been awakened one other time. She'd met with Dagbar and told him the truth of the soulstones. Islmur said Ghile and Dagbar were kindred spirits. How he had anything in common with a dwarf, he wasn't sure, but Islmur said it with such certainty, and conviction, he felt inclined to believe her.

With that, she had said goodbye and returned to the Great Oak and her rest. The Alvar had not changed back after she was gone and the remaining guardians ignored him, so Ghile leapt high into the branches of the Great Oak and settled down to wait for his companions to arrive and the Alvar to return.

The calming affect Ghile had on the squirrel had not lasted long and its barking stirred him from his reveries. With a smirk on his lips at the little fellow's persistence, Ghile opened his mind.

Each creature appeared before him as motes of light in the darkness. Little forces of life drifting before him like the sparks kicked up from a fire. As he touched each one with his mind, their senses were added to his own.

He could see himself through the squirrel's eyes from its high vantage point. He had changed, he almost didn't recognize himself. He was much bigger than he thought he was, his shoulders broader. Not only that, his skin and hair were smooth and rich with color. It reminded him of Islmur, just not as intense. He was more than a little uncomfortable with it all and reminded himself not to get a big head over everything. It would be all too easy to get an inflated opinion of himself.

His mind touched the stag's and then moved on to touch a small family of rabbits, deep in their warren. Ghile could feel how warm and comfortable they were, and focused his attention on their sight. He reminded himself he was searching for Adon and Muk. He could see the small sparks that were fish swimming through the lake and turned his attentions away. No, he needed to keep his search on land.

His mind drifted further out; he could see so many different perspectives of the same things, it was almost as if the forest was right before him and he was walking through it in choppy shifts of vision as he hopped from one creature to the next.

Try as he might, he could not sense the trees or other plants, no matter how hard he focused. But his mind touch ability was much stronger and he continued to reach across the island, searching.

It was when he found the ravens that his search truly spread out. They were large enough to establish a firm link without fear of hurting them and allowed him to cover ground much faster. Where he only looked through the eyes of the other creatures, with the ravens, he goaded them into flight.

It was then he found Muk, crouched near the base of a tree. The goblin set off, hopping from one long foot to the other in that bow-legged gait Ghile had come to associate with him. Muk moved quickly to another tree before crouching again and looking about.

Why you little sneak, Ghile thought. *Trying to hide from me are you? Not this time. Show me where my brother is.*

Ghile watched patiently until Muk was a good distance away and then mind touched the next creature closest to the goblin. Ghile soon realized he was headed to the Great Oak. He released the other mind links and focused on the ones closest to the skulking goblin.

Muk reached the edge of the clearing and waited. Ghile was looking through the eyes of a nearby rabbit and sat there, listening to the creature's rapidly beating heart as he watched and waited.

After what seemed like ages, Muk darted across the clearing and climbed up onto a smaller root, before slipping into a hole formed where the root abutted against a larger one.

"Now I have you," Ghile said.

$$\Lambda$$

Ghile could hear their voices coming out of the darkness of the hole. He had used his powers to close the distance from where he'd been seated as he spied on Muk to here, as quickly as possible. Muk had not been in there long.

He mentally prepared himself and leaped into the hole. With his enhanced vision, the darkness hid nothing from him. He slid down a slightly sloped bank before being deposited into an underground room. It was larger than he'd expected and he was easily able to stand. Roots from the Great Oak crisscrossed above him, and protruded from the walls of packed dirt.

The sound of him sliding and the small tumbling debris he pushed before him announced his arrival. Both Muk and Adon were standing in the front of what looked like a wide, curved hump of a root, rising out of the ground. Its upper surface was hollowed out like a bowl and was filled with dark water. They both stared at him, their faces expressionless.

"What is this place?" Ghile said. He dusted off the back of his tunic as he walked up to stand before them. There was more command in his voice than wonder. Though he had to admit he was more than a little excited by the discovery. He felt as if he had just caught some children who'd stolen fresh bread off a windowsill.

"You shouldn't be here, little Brother," Adon said. His face was still expressionless and neither of them had moved.

Ghile walked around them and stared into the smooth surface of the water. He didn't respond right away. This place was created from him, he was the stonechosen.

"There is no place in this dreaming that I do not belong, Adon. I know that now," Ghile said.

Both Muk and Adon followed him with their eyes, but remained motionless. Why didn't they argue with him? Why wasn't Adon trying to reason with him, or Muk throwing one of his epic tantrums, hopping from foot to foot?

"And you know it," Ghile said aloud, as the realization came to him. He looked down into the wide wooden bowl of dark water. "Show me," Ghile said.

Adon hesitated for only a moment before stepping forward and waving a hand over the pool. As his hand passed over the water, daylight emerged from the pool, bathing the room in light. Within the water, just below the surface, Ghile could see crossed arms over a chest that rose and fell steadily – his chest. Under the Ghile in the pool, he could see the limb of the Great Oak and the surrounding forest below. He was looking at Allwyn through his own eyes.

"Well, this explains much," Ghile said, looking up at the others.

Muk crossed his thin arms and glared at him. "Boy too smart for own good."

A thought came to Ghile and he looked at Adon. "You heard what Islmur said, then? About the soulstones?"

Adon nodded. "I did." He looked as if he was about to say more and stopped.

"You thought you were my brother, didn't you?" Ghile said.

"Yes. Well, I thought the memories I had were my own." Adon's eyes stared into the pool, but Ghile could see the inner struggle playing out behind them. The soulstone had taken everything Ghile remembered about his brother and used it to recreate itself as a dream teacher Ghile would trust. Apparently, to the point where not even the creation knew it *was* a creation.

Ghile sighed. He had intended to rage at them for their deception, but now, with them standing before him, he couldn't bring himself to do it.

"Listen, Adon. I don't care what you are or how you came to be. You're the only thing of my brother I have left and if you are made of my memories of him, then you know how much I loved and missed him. You also know he would want to do anything he could to help me. I don't plan to give myself over to Haurtu without a fight. Both of you are a part of me now," Ghile said."

This was it.

"I want your help," Ghile said.

Both Muk and Adon looked at each other then. It was as if they had a conversation in those few moments, came to some kind of agreement. It was Adon who finally spoke. "I want to see Haurtu's return. The desire for it pulls at me. I also want to help you. I care about you, Ghile, and don't want to see you hurt, but you cannot resist Haurtu."

"How do you know that?" Ghile said. "You heard Islmur. She thinks I have a chance."

"Nine," Muk said. "Boy needs all nine soulstones to free Haurtu." The goblin still had his arms crossed over his bony chest. He spoke like he did when he was teaching something.

"With each soulstone, with each one of us that joins you, you will become more like him and less like yourself," Adon said.

"What about my Shadow?" Ghile asked. He could see by their shared expressions he had touched on something. "You knew about the Shadow," Ghile said, "its true purpose. From the beginning, you have been telling me it was dangerous, to stay away from it, but it was never a danger to me, never attacked me. But you, it did attack you. It knows you do not belong here."

Neither Muk nor Adon responded. Muk's face held defiance, Adon's sympathy, and more than a little remorse.

"You say you want to help me, Adon, but you've been lying to me about my shadow."

Adon started to speak when Muk stomped his foot on the ground. "No! Boy know too much already. We prepare vessel for Haurtu."

"Adon, help me!" Ghile said. "*Please.* All I'm asking for is a fighting chance."

Muk raised a scaly brow at Adon and growled.

"I will help you," Adon said.

Muk threw his hands into the air. "Stupid humans! Waste of time. You just make things harder for him. He is vessel! But no matter, you no listen to Muk, stupid humans."

Ghile ignored Muk's tirade. He was grinning and had let go of a breath he didn't realize he was holding. "My shadow?"

Adon nodded. "Islmur spoke true. You must enter your Shadow and experience what it shares. You must come to terms with what it shows you. You must accept yourself." Adon closed his eyes and shook his head. "Even as I speak, something inside of me tells me I shouldn't, Ghile." He smiled weakly. "I'm not the best brother, huh?"

Ghile shook his head. "Right now, I think you're the best brother in all of Allwyn."

Muk groaned audibly. "Right now, Muk think he might throw up."

Both brothers glared at him. The goblin raised his hands protectively.

Behind him, a grey mist appeared, first as a long thin line, then the line expanded and took shape. Muk looked over his shoulder when he noticed he was no longer the focus of their attention. "Great, another human. Now everything will be better," Muk said, rolling his eyes.

Akira had no more than took shape than she ran towards Ghile. "Ghile, you must warn them!" Akira said.

Ghile was taken aback. He had hoped to see Akira, had hoped to share everything Islmur had told him. But from the moment he heard the fear in her voice, all of his own wants vanished. "Warn who?" Ghile said.

"The elves! It's my brother, Ashar. Oh, Ghile! He is the one behind everything. He's been lying to me. Worse, I've been lying to you, trying to lure you to him."

"I don't understand? Slow down," Ghile said.

"There is no time! My brother is the sorcerer who created the fallen ones. He's going to use me and another stonechosen he has, to somehow cause the mists of the Fallen City to kill the trees of the Deepwood. He thinks it will enrage the elves and they will blame it on Dagbar and the settlement," Akira said.

Ghile reached for her then, tried to take her by the arms, to calm her, comfort her, but his hands only passed through her. "I won't let him, Akira. I will stop him."

"No, Ghile, you mustn't! That's what he wants. He wants the power of your soulstones to have his revenge on Dagbar. You must flee."

"I'm not leaving you, Akira," Ghile said.

Adon and Muk stood there watching the exchange, both looking concerned.

"Didn't you hear me? I was luring you to him! You must go! I don't want anyone else hurt because of me, Ghile. Don't you understand? If something happened to you—"

"The soulstones call," Muk said.

"They must be joined," Adon said as if it were the only obvious answer to everything.

"That's enough out of you two," Ghile said.

"No, Ghile. Please understand. It is too late for me," Akira sobbed.

"No," Ghile said. "I'm coming, Akira. I am going to stop Ashar."

"But I've lied—"

"Stop," Ghile said. "I don't care about that."

It was the truth. He didn't care. He knew she was right about the Alvar. They would want retribution if the Deepwood was harmed. He had to tell them about this, explain it so they understood the truth of it. Most of all, he had to save Akira. "I am coming."

28

Reunited

AGBAR opened his eyes and winced. He wasn't used to sleeping rough and his back and neck ached from sleeping propped up against a tree for most of the night. He rose gingerly and began stretching out the worst of his aches. At that moment, he felt every day of his two hundred and twelve years.

It was early and a low mist floated over the waters of the mountain lake. Near its center, Dagbar could see the sun's first rays dance across the forested island of Islmur's Grove. He yearned to get closer, but knew he would never be allowed to step foot on it again. He was lucky the Alvar had allowed him to even come this close.

Dagbar made his way to the water's edge and tried to wash the sleep out of his eyes. The water was cold as ice and shocked him awake. The air was thin and fought to hold onto the night's chill. He covered one nostril and blew forcefully through the other, then repeated the process on the other side.

The Keeper had been none too pleased to see Dagbar in the Deep-wood and even more upset by the damage the golems had caused.

The first time Dagbar moved them from the Fallen City, he had to transport them on wagons to appease the Alvar; a long and arduous process, to say the least.

At first, he was afraid his very presence was going to ruin everything. It was only while the Keeper played out her anger and he dodged her blows that she'd admitted Islmur sent her and wanted all of them, Dagbar included, brought here.

Dagbar opened one of his pouches and took out his tooth cloth, wet a small bit, and dabbed it into the mix of sage and salt crystals in the bottom of the pouch. He began scrubbing at his teeth, spitting out small bits of the old badger that had been last night's dinner.

The Alvar brought the recently deceased creature, shortly after their arrival at the water's edge. It was a weathered and grey haired thing that probably died that very day of old age. Dagbar knew how the Alvar felt about the other race's eating habits and knew they were trying to keep their barbaric guests from killing anything. They probably knew every plant and creature in these parts on a first name basis.

Dagbar rinsed his mouth and worked his jaw. Rocks would have been easier to chew than that leathery old badger. Probably would have tasted as good, to boot. Riff hadn't helped by overcooking it, either.

As Dagbar looked for a place to relieve himself, he saw the barbarian, Two Elks, crouched on his heels off to the side of the camp next to Rachard, their shields and weapons close by. They were talking amongst themselves and keeping watch. Rachard gave Dagbar a curt nod. Two Elks only stared. Dagbar couldn't blame him. There was much enmity between their races and apathy was better than he could have hoped for.

Not too far away, the others still slept. Bosand lay alone, but Gaidel and Riff lay next to each other, backs against a tree. Dagbar had listened to their low muffled talking late into the night. Riff's hand lay atop Daughter Gaidel's.

Good, Dagbar thought. One should find happiness where and when one could.

Dagbar made his way to the water's edge and hiked his tunic and began working the straps of his leggings loose. His first instinct had been to find a nearby tree, but he knew the Alvar wouldn't leave them here without keeping watch. He didn't need an audience, or even worse, choose the wrong tree and really upset an Alvar.

He had barely worked the first strap loose when the sight before him froze his hands in place. Alvar were pouring from Islmur's island in droves. Dagbar had no idea there were so many of them. Their singing drifted clear and beautiful across the water.

Even from this distance, and though he was much smaller than the Alvar, Dagbar could see who could only be Ghile Stonechosen. He soared out over the water in an unbelievable leap, only to come down, touch upon the surface, and soar back into the air.

One by one, the others joined Dagbar near the water's edge. No one spoke. Dagbar was hard pressed to choose which – Ghile, or the mass of Alvar – was the more impressive sight.

Ghile quickly outpaced the Alvar and with one final leap, landed on shore, behind Dagbar and the others.

Dagbar spun around. Other Alvar emerged from the forest, singing. The Alvarsong combined with finally seeing a stonechosen was overwhelming. How long had he worked and planned for this moment? A tear ran down his cheek before Dagbar realized he was crying. It dawned on him he was still holding the front of his tunic up. He let it fall hurriedly and wiped at his cheeks.

Ghile Stonechosen was tall and broad shouldered. He was barechested, the two soulstones obvious just beneath the surface of the skin in the middle of his chest. A necklace adorned with the teeth of some large animal hung from his neck. His thick, brown curly hair hung to his shoulders and almost into his eyes. His skin was smooth and flawless. Dagbar thought him magnificent.

Even though he was young, the intense stare he focused on Dagbar was that of a man with purpose.

Ghile took in the others and Dagbar watched as his eyes softened. Ghile looked about to speak, but only stared. It was Riff who finally broke the silence.

"Where's your shirt?" Riff said.

Ghile smiled and looked down. "It ripped," he said, with more than a little sheepishness in his voice.

"I wonder why?" Riff said, eyeing Ghile from head to toe. "What in the name of Daomur's hairy backside have you been eating, Sheepherder?"

Dagbar cleared his throat and gave Riff a reproachful look.

Riff ignored Dagbar and glanced at Gaidel, who was staring at Ghile with her mouth agape.

"What do you think?" Riff said. He crossed his arms over his chest and quirked an eyebrow at her.

Gaidel looked at Riff and her face reddened to the point of challenging her hair. She cleared her throat. "You have changed since we last saw you, Ghile."

Ghile's cheeks joined hers.

Daughter Bosand cleared her throat and Gaidel quickly nodded.

"Ghile Stonechosen, allow me to introduce Daughter Bos—"

Ghile held up a hand. "Stop. Listen, I have something I need to say first."

"Ghile—" Gaidel began.

"Please," Ghile said.

Gaidel only glanced at Daughter Bosand before nodding.

"What I did back in the village. When I left like that. At the time, I thought I was doing the right thing. I thought I was taking responsibility for myself and keeping those I had come to care about away from danger. I was wrong. I had no right to make that decision for you. I also should have heeded your advice. Had I reached the Fallen City as I originally planned, I would have walked into a trap I don't think I could have escaped on my own." Ghile bowed his head and held his hands up in a show of respect. "For that, I am sorry."

"Ghile, you don't need to apologize," Gaidel said.

"Oh, yes he does," Riff said. "I almost died because of him! Again!"

Riff stepped towards Ghile and pointed a finger at him. "Lotte and your Valehounds *did die*! At the hands of cullers who were looking for you! The very one who tried to cull you in the Cradle. The one who destroyed Last Hamlet. So, yes, Gaidel, I think an apology is only the beginning of what he owes us!"

"Riff—" Gaidel said.

"No, Gaidel, he's right," Ghile said. He moved up to stand before Riff. He looked down at the sorcerer, his hands hanging at his sides. "Ast and Cuz are gone?"

Riff nodded, some of the venom taken out of him by the pain on Ghile's face.

Dagbar had thought the two dogs belonged to the boy who died in the inn. Riff's words and the look on Ghile's face proved otherwise.

Ghile stood there silently for a long time. "I'm sorry to hear about Lotte," he finally said.

Riff nodded. "More important, is what are we going to do about it?"

Daughter Bosand spoke up then. "Ghile Stonechosen, I am Daughter Bosand and I have been sent by Mother Brambles to escort you to her."

Riff huffed and rolled his eyes, but held his tongue.

Now was the time when Dagbar was going to find out if Islmur had shared her knowledge with Ghile.

"Where is Mother Brambles?" Ghile said.

"She awaits you in the Nordlah Plains," Daughter Bosand said.

"Does she?" Ghile looked at Riff and then Gaidel and Two Elks in turn. Finally, his eyes came to rest on Dagbar. "She will have to wait a bit longer," Ghile said.

"Mother Brambles was most clear you were to come at once," Bosand said. Her back was straight and her tone brooked no arguments.

Ghile stared at her for a moment before a smile appeared on his face, but never touched his eyes. "I go to the Fallen City and I would like to see anyone try and stop me."

Riff clapped his hands together and rubbed them eagerly. "Now we're talking!"

Dagbar knew now was the time. He stepped forward and bowed his head.

"I am Magister Dagbar. If you journey to the Fallen City, there is much I must tell you."

Ghile's face tightened as if pained.

"Have I offended you?" Dagbar said.

"No, Magister. It's just... your accent reminds me of Akira."

Dagbar lowered his gaze, suddenly uncomfortable looking Ghile in the eye. "I see."

"Greetings to you Magister. Islmur and Akira have told me all I need to know about you, Ashar, and the prophecy," Ghile said. The momentary lapse in demeanor was gone.

"So, he too has fallen for Islmur's trickery," Daughter Bosand said. "The elves are not our friends, Ghile. The Great Purge should be enough to prove—"

"Enough!" Ghile said. His shouted word was enough to stop Bosand, and even the nearby Alvar stopped singing.

Ghile spoke to one of the nearest Alvar and his voice rang out in clear Alvarsong. Dagbar was already smiling when Ghile motioned towards Daughter Bosand. "The Alvar will take you and your shieldwarden to the edge of the Deepwood, Daughter Bosand," Ghile said.

"My instructions were to find and stay with you," Bosand said.

"It was not a request," Ghile said, as he turned away from her.

Two of the Alvar moved to stand behind the druid and her shieldwarden.

"Daughter Gaidel, it appears the wisdom of the Redwood Druids is no longer needed or wanted here," Bosand said, straightening her robes.

"I am staying, Patron Sister," Gaidel said.

She stepped up to stand beside Ghile and Riff. Riff reached out and took her hand, giving it a reaffirming squeeze.

"You will do no such thing, Daughter," Bosand said.

"You heard her," Ghile said, without looking at the other druid. He walked away, motioning for the others to follow.

Daughter Gaidel only looked at the other older druid for a moment before she followed Ghile, Two Elks right behind her.

Dagbar fell in with the others. He looked back to see Daughter Bosand and Rachard standing there, staring. Rachard seemed... amused. Daughter Bosand held a look that could have melted stone. Ghile Stonechosen had made an enemy this day.

"You have lost your spear?" Two Elks said to Ghile, as Dagbar caught up with them.

Ghile shook his head. "No, I left it. I realized I no longer needed it."

"And the dwarf blade?" Two Elks said.

Ghile ran his hand along the dwarven-made blade sheathed at his side. Dagbar recognized it as one of the fang blades the Magister of the Cradle gifted to the settlement's human protectors. "This reminds me of where I came from and who I fight for," Ghile said.

"Ghile Stonechosen, where are all the Alvar going?" Dagbar asked.

"They go with us, Magister. The sorcerer Ashar plans to use the mists of the Fallen City to attack the Deepwood. We journey there to stop him."

"Is that even possible?" Dagbar questioned. He knew Ashar was gifted and had the power of Akira's soulstone behind him, but could he truly do something of that magnitude? What dark secrets had he uncovered in the Fallen City?

"Akira believes so, and I believe Akira," Ghile stated flatly.

"The Fallen City holds many dangers, least of all the Dream Mists. They befuddle the mind of human and dwarf alike. I have a few vials of an elixir that will protect us, but I do not know for how long. The Alvar fear the mists and are blinded by it. If they enter, then they will be all but helpless."

Ghile nodded as he walked and listened. "They have told me as much. But the threat is to the Deepwood and they will not be deterred."

"Most likely the cullers will be there," Dagbar said.

"I'm counting on it," Riff said.

"Much of the blame for Ashar and the rest lies on my shoulders, Ghile Stonechosen." Dagbar said.

Ghile stopped and placed a hand on Dagbar's shoulder. "There is more than enough blame to go around. Islmur spoke for you, Magister. You know the truth and what is at stake for my race and still you try to help us. She also said I will need your help if I am going to have a chance to defeat Haurtu."

Dagbar felt his eyes moisten. Lady Luck had not left him, she had picked him up and cuddled him against her plump bosom. The boy planned to fight. "I am at your disposal, Ghile Stonechosen," Dagbar said, his voice thick with emotion.

"Am I the only one who feels left out of the conversation here?" Riff said to nobody in particular.

Ghile nodded. "There will be time to explain things later, Riff."

Riff was still holding Gaidel's hand and Ghile looked down at their joined fingers and smiled. "Besides, you are not the only one who has questions."

29

Eye of the Storm

HE winds blew over the mists of the Fallen City, causing them to billow and roll. It reminded Finngyr of the waves on the Innersea. The thought brought Daomount to his mind and he tightened his grip on the handle of his hammer in irritation. *Where was the stonechosen?*

He turned and paced across the uppermost floor of the ruined building. He leaned slightly to the side to make up for the building's uneven tilt. It was one of a scattering of ruins that pierced through the strange mist like desiccated fingers. He stared out from the other side of the ruin and had to shield his eyes from the light of the dying sun.

They should have been back by now to report. He chose this building due to its wide, exposed landing and close proximity to the center of the city. As close as he could find, anyway.

When they'd first flown over the Fallen City, they'd noted the darkening of the mists the further they flew towards its center. The city rested in a deep crater. Few of the ruins were tall enough to reach up from those depths and the few that did, were little more than single jagged spurs, vegetation clinging to every available purchase as if for their lives. Finngyr supposed they did since nothing living seemed to survive within the mists except some noxious-smelling slime. At least in the areas they had tried searching.

Upon their arrival a few days ago, they'd entered the mists looking for signs of the stonechosen. They had found nothing. Not that they had much time.

It affected Knight Kjar first. The dwarf began jumping at shadows and reporting movement out of the corners of his eyes. Then he began stopping every few feet when he heard something that neither Knight Horth or Finngyr could hear. It was when Knight Kjar attacked empty space and Knight Horth started seeing things at the edges of his vision that Finngyr realized something was affecting them. The effects wore off once they were free of the mists.

They'd patrolled above the city since then, only entering when something caught their attention and only for short periods of time.

Finngyr paced back across the uneven surface, kicking at a tile that had come loose under his boot. He watched it clatter down the slope and over the edge to be swallowed by the very mist that thwarted him. The city was just too big to search effectively.

Finngyr knew this was Ghile's destination, just as strongly as he knew that the traitor Dagbar was somehow involved. His suspicions had been confirmed yesterday, when they discovered the golems standing a couple of leagues away during their patrols. The golems' path was as straight as the griffon flies from the settlement towards the Fallen City. He didn't know why they had stopped where they did, but knew enough about the artificers' creations to know someone holding the command gems and who knew the correct words needed to have been there to stop them. His next meeting with Magister Dagbar would be most unpleasant for the freakish-eyed traitor.

Safu vocalized a series of high pitched squawks at him from where she rested a short distance away. His constant pacing must be agitating her. She rested on her rear haunches with her wings folded in close to her sides. She tilted her head quickly and eyed him, before squawking again.

Finngyr made a comforting motion towards her with his hand, but continued pacing.

Where were they?

He'd sent them to patrol opposite sides of the city and to circle clockwise along the forest's edge. He reluctantly admitted the sun had not yet touched the trees, and he had told them to return then, but he was tired of all this waiting.

Finngyr played his encounter with Lord Knight Gyldoon over in his head. There was no room for failure, he had to find the stonechosen. He would not fail this time – he could not. When news of the encounter in the inn reached the High Council, he had little doubt how they would twist what had happened. Even though the humans and the dwarven guard had attacked them! He would like nothing better than to bestow Daomur's justice on the entire settlement. Especially that impudent sorcerer. Finngyr still felt phantom pains on his skin from the burns. Daomur's blessed healing restored the flesh, but did nothing for the memories. At least the creature was consumed in his own tainted magic. Finngyr would have to find some consolation in that.

A distant screech drew his attention. It was followed almost immediately by another, coming in the opposite direction.

Safu answered the call as she stood, extending her white-tipped wings and shaking out the dark feathers along her neck. Finngyr hastily made the hand gesture for her to stay and ran over to gather her reins in his free hand.

"What do you know?" he called to Horth as the knight circled nearby.

"Elves! In his blessed name, hundreds of them. They are attacking the city!" Horth said.

Finngyr was already in Safu's saddle and clipping into the riding harness when Kjar circled in from the other direction.

"Elves attack the city, Knight Justice! Too many to count. As far as I could see," Kjar said.

Safu's front talons clacked across the tiles as she gathered speed and then bounded into the air. He motioned for the others to follow him and then dug his knees into Safu's sides. "Make haste, girl!"

Finngyr directed Safu straight towards the closest edge of the city. Were the elves attacking from all sides? More importantly, what were they attacking? Finngyr had seen nothing but slime and mist down there.

He could hear their singing in the distance. It didn't sound like the battle chants his people sang, but more like a funeral dirge. As they flew closer, a wind buffeted them, followed immediately by another. Finngyr banked Safu tightly as he struggled to maintain control. The sky was a mix of reds and oranges as the sun touched the tree line. It was clear of clouds as far as he could see in every direction, but the winds lashed him harder than a winter's gale over the Innersea.

Finngyr could hear Horth cursing over the winds as the younger knight fought to keep control of his mount. The winds lessened as they were pushed away from the edge of the city. Finngyr realized the winds were pushing back the mists. Below, he could see the remains of buildings and what might have been a defensive wall.

It was the elves! They were somehow controlling the winds and using them to push back the mists. Finngyr directed Safu to climb and as she rose in a slow circle, the winds lessened.

The other knights joined him as he made his way along the edge of the city. He could tell the elves efforts were futile. The mist fought against the winds like something alive. When the winds weakened, it surged forward to reclaim the grey dead ground and slime-covered buildings like a prized treasure.

"There, look! Something attacks from the city," Kjar called.

As the sun dipped lower and the shadows of the Deepwood touched the edges of the mist, small, fast moving creatures emerged. It reminded Finngyr of pale maggots pouring from a bloated corpse. Their numbers were nowhere near those of the elves, but they charged forth without fear.

It appeared the Fallen City was the source of the dead ones infesting the Deepwood and attacking Dagbar's settlement. Had Dagbar sent the golems back to deal with these creatures?

No, they would have resumed their patrols of the city. Even if Dagbar had sent them to fight, someone had to be there to tell them to stop in such an arbitrary spot. It was just too much coincidence they began returning to the city so soon after the stonechosen's allies arrived in the settlement.

"Do we help the elves?" Knight Kjar called.

"No. Our mission is to capture the stonechosen," Finngyr said.

Finngyr turned Safu and they followed the edge of the city, high above the fighting. Why had the elves chosen now to attack the city? The human whelp said they had the stonechosen and now they attacked the city Dagbar felt sure was the stonechosen's destination.

I know you're down there... somewhere.

"We stay together," Finngyr said. "Follow me!"

30

Into the Mists

HILE slid down the remains of the stone wall. It was still mostly intact and offered the quickest way down to the lower level of the ruins. It was also covered with the same pale slime which seemed to grow unhindered on everything in this place. He landed with a grunt and hastily scrambled over wide tiles and up against the base of a jagged column of greenish-black stone.

He pushed himself up against the column and waited for the others. Absently, he began to wipe off the excess slime with one hand, while the other hand unconsciously tightened on the grip of the fangblade, its deer horn handle solid and reassuring in his grasp. The groove along the flat of the blade still held traces of black blood. He had not had time to properly clean the blade since their last fight against the fallen.

The battle to break through the fallens' lines at the edge of the city hadn't been difficult, with the creatures of the Deepwood who answered the Alvars' song along with the trees and winds themselves to help keep the creatures distracted, they were able to fight their way through. But since then, the fallen seemed to know where they were and continued to attack them as they traveled lower and lower within the city. Every level they descended had been hard won. Worst of all, the fallen seemed to feed off the mist. Ghile had to re-engage with more than one fallen who he thought he had dealt a mortal blow. Thankfully, most of the fallen seemed to be fighting the Alvar.

The Alvar had surrounded the sprawling ruins and unleashed their fury upon it. The Keepers had taken the threat of the fallen spreading some kind of poison into the Deepwood as a serious one. All the Alvar who gathered for Islmur's awakening had come. They would keep the mists at bay and no fallen would leave or enter the city while Ghile and his companions dealt with Ashar.

Ghile saw the cullers flying over the city as night fell. Luckily, they were far off and hadn't spotted them. Riff seemed ready to fight the cullers then and there. Ghile knew he would have to face them eventually, he just hoped he could find and deal with Ashar first.

He listened, but heard nothing over the sound of his own breathing. He took a chance and peeked around the pillar, but night and the ever-present mist turned everything into nondescript grey shapes, even to his enhanced vision. He could make out a line of broken columns leading away from the one he sheltered against. He was in some sort of plaza.

The mist lay heavy over the ruins, the moisture of it clung to his clothes and covered his skin with an oily film. It reminded Ghile of how his hands felt, after helping his mother render mutton fat into tallow for candles. The remnants of the fat covered his hands and refused to wash off. The mist made him feel unclean.

That sensation, combined with the nasty taste of the concoction Dagbar had given him had his stomach queasy. The foul tasting stuff was the only thing protecting him and the others from the mind-altering effects of the mist. Ghile forced the saliva that was building in his mouth down with a grimace.

If his regular senses were of no use, Ghile had others. He sent his mind searching out around him. He could feel the minds of the others on the level above him, even Dagbar's.

As he expected, he couldn't push his way into the dwarf's mind any more than he could enter a human's. It seemed only the minds of animals were open to him.

Ghile reached out farther and came upon an unfamiliar mind, one he could penetrate. Then he sensed another, and another. He gently probed the minds, being careful not to enter too fast or go too deep. These creatures were large, whatever they were. Ghile grimaced as the images of leaping from his hidden burrow and landing upon a tiny goblin filled his mind. He saw himself biting down on the creature and feeling his poison enter the succulent creature and render it still so he could feed. Wherever these creatures were, it was dimly lit and Ghile saw the same image from eight different perspectives. They were spiders! Big spiders.

The nearest giant spider had felt his footsteps and was waiting for its next meal to come closer. Ghile had a better idea, though. He reached into their minds.

The sound of someone sliding down the wall caught his attention.

Dagbar stumbled up behind him and half squatted, half collapsed.

"Are you sure this is the way?" Ghile said.

"Yes, quite sure," Dagbar said between breaths. The constant fights and pace he was setting was affecting the others. Ghile had to remember he was no longer a normal human.

"Ashar's laboratory… is near the… center of the ruins. I think… we are in the temple district… judging by these columns… we are close," Dagbar said, between deep breaths.

Ghile nodded. He really didn't need Dagbar to tell him the way, he could feel the pull of Akira's soulstone. He could also feel another sensation, another soulstone. He hadn't been able to tell the two sensations apart before, but now that he was close, it was obvious. Akira was not the only stonechosen down there.

The longing to have the other soulstones pushed its way up from the darkness of his mind. Like cups of water placed before a man dying of thirst, they taunted him to reach out and take them. Ghile squeezed his eyes shut and forced the feeling back down. He would not harm Akira; he was going to save her.

"Does he have to die?" Dagbar said.

Ghile turned to glare down at the dwarf. How could he ask that question? Ashar had imprisoned and lied to his own sister. Had unleashed the fallen upon the Deepwood and the dwarf's own settlement. Ghile could see the pain and confusion on Dagbar's face.

Ghile bit back his harsh retort and just shook his head in disbelief.

"It's just... I set him on this path. Maybe if I spoke to him? I have to believe he can be saved."

"Why?" Ghile said.

"I don't know how to explain, Ghile. It's just I cannot help but see him and Akira as the children they were when they came to the settlement. I know what he has done is wrong. I even accept what will happen to Akira when you find her, but—"

"I am not going to hurt, Akira. There has to be another way," Ghile said. His voice rose with each word.

Riff dropped in behind Dagbar, the hand not holding the everflame clutching his side as he fought for breath. He drew it away from his side to wave it at them dismissively. "Go on, don't mind me."

Dagbar spared a glance for Riff and shook his head. "There are some truths in this life that are hard to face, Ghile, but face them we must. You are stonechosen. You have spoken to Islmur. You now know the truth of what that means. If you do not possess all the soulstones and confront Haurtu, then you will die. Akira will die. And all this," Dagbar said as he motioned around him, "all that we have sacrificed for helping you, will have been for nothing."

"Ghile, what is he talking about?" Riff said.

Ghile and Dagbar stared at each other. Everything Dagbar said was true, but Ghile just didn't want to accept it. He had entertained the fantasy of somehow freeing Akira of her soulstone. The truth of what would happen was there, deep in the shadows of his mind. There were things he had no control of, but there were things he did.

"Ghile?" Riff said.

Ghile shook his head. "Ashar dies."

Riff continued to look between the two, as if he could puzzle the mystery out with sheer effort of will.

Gaidel and Two Elks were behind Riff now. Ghile could see the exhaustion on their faces. Two Elks tilted his head to listen and then quickly raised a hand with three fingers up. Ghile recognized the gestures and stood up. "It's alright, Two Elks. I've found help."

Three large shapes materialized from the dark mist. Their large, hairy legs surprisingly quiet as they plodded into view. Eight pupilless eyes, set into three rows, stared out from grey haired heads.

"By Daomur's backside!" Riff said, as he brought his everflame before him.

"There is no call for that sort of language," Dagbar said, without ever taking his eyes from the spiders.

"Seriously? Now? You're going to choose *now* to address my language?"

Gaidel stepped around Two elks, who had moved up in front of her and touched Ghile on the shoulder. "Are you sure about this, Ghile?"

Trying to look at all the eyes made Ghile dizzy, so he instead focused on the two largest eyes in the middle row. He could feel the instinct to not only attack him and his companions, but the spiders wanted to attack each other as well. Ghile used his will and forced those instincts down.

They had fought through the first line of fallen who had charged out of the mists when night fell. Since then, they encountered roving bands. None wished to fight more than was necessary. The fallen included humans in their ranks and Gaidel and Riff lamented that, given time, they could be saved.

For Ghile, each fight sapped at their strength and they still had Ashar and the cullers to deal with. The spiders were an answer to this problem, but he had little doubt how comfortable Gaidel and Riff were with his chosen solution.

"Yes," was all Ghile said.

Ghile felt the pull of the other soulstones and directed the spiders in that direction. As the creatures turned and moved off into the mists, Ghile followed. He didn't need to turn to know the concerned looks Gaidel and Riff were sharing.

31

Burdens of Fate

SHAR tried to rub away the stiffness that settled into his maimed leg as he watched the scene unfold. The view of the city's edge undulated on the cloud of mist floating before him.

The mist thrall, whose eyes the spell looked through, crouched at the edge of the mists, as it waited for the buffeting winds to stop and the mists to once again surge forward. Its panting caused the scene to rise and fall.

In the middle of the ruins, until just recently hidden by the mists, elves stood in a long row. Ashar found their slow, methodical approach maddening. He would never had believed it possible. They were actually pushing the mists back.

Their size allowed them to easily step over the uneven stones. Stones that had earlier answered the elves' call and erupted from the ground with devastating effect.

Why was this happening now, when I am so close?

Ashar could not hear sound through the spell, but he could see the elves' mouths and knew they were singing.

The winds answered and pushed the mists back. The elves all took a step forward, their limb-like arms upraised.

Ashar could feel the thrall he was casting his spell through stiffen, as one of the elves broke rank and moved forward. The thrall desperately wanted to spring forth from the mists and sink tooth and claw into the elf.

Ashar focused and sent out the mental command for all the thralls on the edge of the city to remain in the mists. He lost control of the thralls when they moved beyond the mists, not to mention they no longer benefited from the mists' regenerative powers. He had already lost too many thralls on their initial attempt to drive the elves back.

The elf stopped just short of the mists, to reach down and touch the body of a fallen stag. The stag spasmed and then rocked up onto its feet. Healed of its wounds, it bounded back to join the other animals that had answered the elves' call.

Ashar did not miss the fact that both sides were healing their wounded, this fight would not be over quickly and he was losing ground. He had to keep pressure on the elves. The further the mists were from the forest, the more difficult it would be for his bloaters to reach it and spread their toxins.

He had never seen so many elves, hadn't known so many even existed. They surrounded the entire city and every fallen he could spare was at the city's edge.

With the spell, the mist flowed forward and with it, his thralls. Ashar focused on the thralls and reinforced the mental command for them to stay within the mists.

Even with the thralls' enhanced vision, it was difficult to see how many animals were behind the elves' line. But no sooner had the mists started to move, than the animals charged forth. Ashar could see great horned stags and sleek black cats, mere shadows if not for their eyes shining through the darkness. A great mass of fur filled the thralls' vision and Ashar just made out the brown paw of a massive bear before it swiped down and the viewing from his spell faded.

They just needed to hold a little longer.

Ashar leaned against one of the many tables that filled the laboratory. He looked at all his equipment and experiments. The various elixirs frothed and boiled in their beakers. He had not wanted to use the large circular chamber to make his stand, but he needed to stay close to his soulstones.

He repeated the words of the mind vision spell and focused its powers to the thralls gathered just outside this tower, his last line of defense. He knew the stonechosen and his companions had entered the city. When Ashar had seen Dagbar among them, he had to fight down the urge to throw every thrall he had at them.

Now was no time to lose his head. He wanted revenge, but Ashar also wanted to survive. So he had sent small packs of thralls against them, to weaken them, but not slow their approach. He had hoped to kill off some of the stonechosen's companions, but had been unsuccessful, more's the pity.

He needed the stonechosen close. As soon as he felt the additional power of the other two soulstones, he would have the strength he needed to send the bloaters forth.

The image of the plaza appeared on the undulating cloud of mist. The thrall the spell had chosen crouched atop a pile of stones that lay against the outside of the tower. Ashar focused and guided the thrall's head with a slight wave of his hand.

Ashar could see dozens of thralls, crouched among the stones, their white forms bobbing with each panting breath, long black tongues lolling. All of his remaining thralls were there. The stonechosen would get no further. Close enough to lend the power of his soulstones for Ashar to complete his plans, but not close enough to be a threat. There were more than enough thralls outside to handle the stonechosen and his pitiful allies.

Dagbar had come to him. The dwarf would die at the hands of his thralls. It occurred to him then, he no longer needed to send the bloated forth. But the unprovoked attack by the elves had angered him and they would learn a valuable lesson and give the Fallen City a wide berth from this night forth.

A deep, gurgling growl interrupted his musings. Ashar dismissed the image on the mist cloud with a wave of his hand.

Collecting his staff, he limped the short distance to the two tombs in the center of the lab and their new guardian. He ran his finger along the creature's slime-covered helmet down one of the many coils that sprouted from it and followed its gurgling contents down to disappear into the creature's wide gorget.

"Do not worry, Knight Justice Griff," Ashar said. "You are my surprise. My 'just in case'."

Ashar smiled as he heard the leather under the dwarf's iron gauntlets tighten on the handle of its rune-covered hammer. The runes had glowed with an intense blue light, ever since the dwarf entered the library.

Ashar knew it had to do with its proximity to the soulstones. He would have to perform some experiments and see if he could not use that to his benefit later.

A muffled explosion from somewhere outside the tower set vials and beakers clinking.

"I see it has begun," Ashar said.

Λ

Finngyr pulled Safu's reins to the right, simultaneously pushing his left knee into the saddle, causing her to bank left. He held that position and stared down into the mists far below. He had climbed to this elevation to try and take in as much of the city as he could. The surface of the mist glowed with reflected moonlight. The night sky was clear and the bloated moon appeared to hang just out of Finngyr's reach.

There!

Below him, near where one of the ruined spires broke the mist's surface, another yellow ball of light appeared. Finngyr knew he had seen something. The knight continued to hold his position and Safu continued down in a tight spiral. He loosened his grip before she plunged into the silver-tipped surface.

Finngyr could hear the sounds of battle rising up from below. "Fly, Safu, we have found him!" The other knights were still monitoring the battle along the city's edge. Finngyr slapped the reins to hurry Safu on. He had to gather the other knights and then capture the stonechosen.

Λ

"By Daomur's hairy backside! Did you see that? I didn't even have to change the incantation," Riff shouted over the battle.

"Is that language truly necessary?" Dagbar called.

Ghile had seen it. The gout of flame Riff normally sprayed forth from his hands had been thrown like a small ball of flame instead. When it impacted with one of the fallen, it exploded into a huge ball of flame, engulfing the fallen and quite a few around it as well.

Riff just laughed at Dagbar's discomfort and hurled another fireball.

Ghile felt the wind and heat of the blast wash over him. The power of the other two soulstones were feeding Riff's magic. Ghile could feel their pull coming from the huge tower behind the fallens' lines. Akira was in there, and so was Ashar.

Ghile had sent the three giant spiders directly into the middle of the fallen and the creatures had swarmed over them without fear. All three spiders were still up, thanks to Ghile's force shield armor, with dozens of fallen scattered beneath them. But for every one that fell, there were three more to take its place.

Riff, Gaidel, and Dagbar stood just behind Two Elks, his kite shield, and the deadly swipes of his stone axe, protecting them as they worked their magics. The barbarian had already racked up an impressive tally, the proof of which lay scattered about him in broken heaps.

Another pack came rushing out of the mists and charged straight towards Two Elks and the others.

Riff held his everflame before him and then slashed over it with his other hand, sending a huge fan of flame trailing out and over the charging fallen.

Two Elks dove in right behind the dying flames, to bring his axe across in a vertical slash. Two fallen, still on fire, flew back in a spray of black blood and bone. Two Elks continued the spin and brought his shield across like a second blade, laying another fallen low.

It was then that Ghile realized Dagbar held no weapons. Ghile had separated from his companions and the spiders, in case the fallen singled him out from the others as they had done when he first encountered them with Arenuin. So far, that hadn't happened. His fang blade already dripped with the blood of numerous fallen, and he held it with the blade down to keep the blood from fouling his grip. He didn't need the weapon slipping out of his hands.

But now, seeing two additional fallen appear from behind one of the columns and bear down on the unarmed Dagbar and Gaidel, he wished he had stayed closer.

Ghile knelt down and touched one of the large stone tiles at his feet. He knew both Dagbar and Gaidel were defenseless and realized he would only have time to stop one of the vargan from reaching its quarry. He made his decision and sent the stone hurtling forwards with a thought.

The large stone tile cut one of the charging vargan through the middle. The upper half spun off to the side in a spinning tangle of hands and entrails. The severed arms and legs rolled forward to settle near Gaidel's feet. Ghile watched as the other fallen leaped on Dagbar, fanged maw snapping. No sooner had it touched Dagbar, than it was hurtling head over heels towards Two Elks.

Ghile blinked. Dagbar had made a graceful twist and spun under the fallen's attack, using the creature's own momentum to redirect it. It landed on its back and Two Elks wasted no time in dispatching it with two sharp blows of his axe.

The battle was far from over, however. More fallen poured around both sides of the tower. As many charged towards Ghile and his companions as engaged the giant spiders. Ghile knelt back down and used his force shield to hurtle tile after tile at the fallen who ran towards him. He gave the fang blade a practice swing, to prepare for those who got through.

The ground before Two Elks exploded in a mass of churning dirt and stone. Then the tumult surged towards the approaching fallen. It brought to mind the way a woolen blanket would roll out with a flick of the arms. Fallen flew in every direction.

"We have a problem," Riff called out over the din. The sorcerer was throwing gouts of flame at the many fallen that lay on the ground around him. "They are healing!" Riff followed his words with another gout of flame on one of the now writhing fallen.

Two Elks merely nodded and brought his axe down on one near him. The creature's head rolled away. "Heal that," Two Elks said.

Dagbar reach down to grab a fallen by the head and chin and spun the head almost fully around with a sharp twist. "We must remove the head of the snake if we are to survive this," he said. "We must find Ashar."

Ghile nodded. "I'll see if I can find some reinforcements first." He reached out with his mind. The part of him that was maintaining the force armor on the spiders tugged for his attention. He would not be able to search far, but maybe there were other spiders nearby. He felt the presence of six minds above him, approaching fast. Three were animal. Three were dwarves.

The cullers! The battle must have attracted them. Ghile had hoped for more time. *Well, there was nothing for it.*

He realized the other minds must belong to their griffon mounts. He tried to force his way into them. He hated to use the power Muk had taught him and shred a creature's mind, but they would not be able to fight three cullers, let alone three cullers mounted on griffons. Something resisted him. It reminded Ghile of his own force shield, smooth and solid. Something was shielding the griffon's minds. He had to get a closer look. "The cullers attack from above!" Ghile said. He charged into the few fallen who reached him and dropped each of them in turn with a thrust of the fang blade.

"I'm not liking these odds," Dagbar said. The dwarf swatted away the attacks from a human fallen. Instead of blocking the next swipe, he let it through. Leaning his head back, the hand past harmlessly before Dagbar's face. He then reached out and grabbed the wrist, and twisted his body into the fallen as he guided the hand around him. With a sudden change in direction, Dagbar extended his other arm and pinned the fallen's arm in an odd position. The fallen had no choice but to fly back in the new direction and crash hard to the ground. Still holding the creature's hand in a locked position, Dagbar stepped down hard on the creature's neck. The dwarf's face looked pained and he pushed and twisted his foot one more time.

"Does battle upset your stomach, Dwarf?" Riff asked, throwing another fireball into a tight group of fallen.

Dagbar released the dead fallen's arm and wiped his hands together. "No, I do not like fighting, young Master Riff." The flash of Riff's fireball lit Dagbar's somber expression. He pointed to the fallen he had just slain. "But I like this fight even less. I knew that man. He was a once a farmer and a father."

Riff looked down at the corpse, his expression losing some of its contempt. He nodded in understanding.

Dagbar patted Riff on the shoulder and moved closer to Gaidel and Two Elks.

Ghile was considering his options when he noticed the numerous bodies of the fallen were being pulled into the upheaved earth. He looked at Gaidel, who was still singing and swaying in a slow rhythmic pattern. Even lost in the song, she must have heard Riff's warning about the fallen healing themselves. He closed the remaining distance between them and called to her. "Gaidel, I need a way into the tower." He hoped she heard him. Ghile leaped high into the air, the sound of rushing wind filling his ears.

The others disappeared from his sight, lost in the mists.

∧

Gaidel held on as the All Mother's Song thundered around her. She could feel the slap of the fallen's feet as they ran across her flesh, feel the dream mists as they hovered over the city like a wolf defending its kill. The mists saturated the song here, attacking everything else. No other plant life save the slime and other eaters of decay could be heard in the song.

Gaidel could hear the songs of her companions, all except Ghile. She could feel the elixir that Magister Dagbar had given them coursing through their veins, holding off the mists for a time. But it was a living thing, if not quite sentient, and she knew it would affect them once the elixir wore off. But unlike other living things, it refused to answer her call.

In the song, Gaidel could feel what the ground felt, taste what the wind touched. Through those sensations, she felt the vibrations of Ghile's voice when he called for a way into the tower.

Gaidel lilted along the song, listening to the deep thrumming of the stone. The stones in this place had long since been taken from the earth and shaped into the needs of man. But even they still held a song. She changed her timbre and began to coax them to shift, to move. It was time for them to join the soil and clay once more.

Slowly at first, she felt one stone join her song, then another. She was the stone. She felt the tremors as she tumbled free and ended the song of more than a few fallen as they were crushed beneath her. She was the stone and had returned to the ground. Soon she would be covered in soil and she could rest.

A creature's discordant song died beneath her. She mourned the loss of those songs; she knew, given time, she and Riff could have restored that song to balance.

Riff, why was that name familiar? She loved a sorcerer named Riff. She was Daughter Gaidel, of the Redwood Druids.

Gaidel fought her way up from the depths of the All Mother's Song. It was time to return to herself.

$$\wedge$$

It was difficult to see, but Ghile could discern the wall of the tower as he flew up towards it. Using his force shield, he slowed his approach.

Reaching out with his mind, he touched one of the giant spiders and pulled a portion of the creature's life force into him. Ghile hands and feet affixed to the surface of the tower. He hung there, in the mists, the battle raging far below him. The tower wall shook, undulating beneath him. He could hear stones crashing down somewhere below. Gaidel had heard his call.

Now to slow down the cullers. He could sense them coming closer in a tight spiraling pattern. They would be close enough soon.

Images of Ast and Cuz herding sheep played through his mind. He saw the pride in his father's face when the two Valehounds obeyed Ghile's commands for the first time. He imagined the look on that same face when he learned of their deaths. One of these cullers was the one responsible for the destruction of Last Hamlet. It was the images of Elana's, and little Tia's face he saw as he sprung from the wall, using his force shield to hurtle forwards. Ghile sensed the minds of the lowest mount and flyer as he closed on them. He knew just where to strike as they swooped down through the mists.

The fang blade cut a deep furrow across the side of the griffon's feathered head. The culler forgot to loosen the reins when he yanked his free hand back to protect his face. The sliced bridle tearing free was the only thing that stopped Ghile's strike from severing the rider's head. The fang blade sliced into the dwarf's upraised arm instead.

As it was, the blow sliced deeply and Ghile's momentum propelled him onwards. He extended force below him to slow his fall and hit the ground in a forward roll. Ghile spun around into a defensive stance. He stared at the mists. When nothing appeared, he reached out with his mind, searching. The dwarves were not follow-ing him. The other two continued in the same downwards spiral.

Of course, they could not see through the mists any better than he could. They would not risk flying into something. More impor-tantly, he could sense the mind of the griffon he had struck and it was no longer shielded.

The bridle!

He reached towards the griffon's mind. Without the magical pro-tection of the bridle, it opened before him. He stayed there, just near the surface. He needed to see around him in case he was attacked.

The griffon was in terrible pain. The fang blade had bitten deep. For some reason, it was fixated on attacking its rider. It twisted and turned desperately trying to dislodge the dwarf. Ghile could see through the griffon's one good eye as it turned and repeatedly snapped its beak down on the dwarf's armored thigh. Pain lanced through the griffon's head as the dwarf's gauntleted fist slammed into it.

Ghile noted a hasty image appear in the griffon's mind. It knew it was falling towards the ground, but the hatred it held for its rider even overruled its own sense of self-preservation. Ghile could see memories of physical abuse and humiliation flash before him, feed-ing the griffon's rage. Ghile saw the ground fast approaching and hastily withdrew from the griffon's mind.

He couldn't see where they crashed down, but the sound of the impact made him wince. He felt for the griffons, trapped and con-trolled by a powerful enchantment. Like his race, they were firmly under the control of their dwarven masters. This one had only just been given its freedom and had turned on its oppressor, sacrificing a chance of escape for a chance of revenge.

A white shape loomed above him. He cut it down with two quick slices and a thrust he delivered even as he turned to get his bearings.

He needed to get into the tower and confront Ashar, but he didn't want to leave his companions to deal with the fallen and the two remaining cullers.

He felt the minds of the nearby spiders. He could only sense two of them now, the other must have died. He could redirect them at the cullers. Would the fallen continue to attack the spiders, or break away to seek him, or worse, his companions?

He berated himself. There was nothing for it, he had to reach Ashar. He also had to accept the fact that the others would have to take care of themselves. They were here because they chose to be. He released the force shield armor he had over the spiders. He would need all his strength for what was to come. Ghile leaped towards the tower. He released his energy shield and dropped amongst a landslide of rubble. A pale light originating from a breach in the side of the tower revealed thick walls and stairs in the distance. Ghile didn't hesitate as he ran into the tower.

$$\bigwedge$$

Finngyr watched as Knight Horth and his griffon tumbled downwards, disappearing into the mist. He had warned the stubborn knight not to abuse his mount. The griffon had attacked him, as soon as his bridle was severed. *Served the beardling right.* Finngyr had been irritated when Horth dove into the mists, taking the honor of being first from him.

How had the stonechosen known about the enchanted bridles?

"Hold your course," Finngyr shouted over his shoulder. The last thing he needed was Kjar flying off, trying to help Horth and slamming into a wall. Knight Horth could heal himself, though he would most likely have to kill his griffon first.

Finngyr's hammer, a most holy relic of Daomur, vibrated in his hand. Holy light poured from its rectangular head. Well, there was no doubt they had found the stonechosen. Daomur was truly with him now. *May he guide my hand.* He would not fail Daomur, and he would not fail the Lord Knight Justice.

With a final beat of her wings, Safu set down in what appeared to be a large plaza. Finngyr could just make out lines of dark columns through the mists, but he had little time for anything else. A white abomination climbed up Safu's side. Finngyr released the reins and grabbed the creature by the throat, hoisting it out to arm's reach.

Eyes black as pitch stood out in sharp contrast to the creature's alabaster skin. The thing's black tongue whipped about like a griffon's tail, before finding his gauntlet and almost completely wrapping around it. He could tell the disgusting thing had once been a human female. Finngyr crushed its neck until his gauntlet stopped his hand from closing further. He tossed the twitching body aside.

Nearby, a battle raged between these creatures and two giant spiders. White bodies littered the plaza and the remains of at least one dead spider. Finngyr used his knees to turn Safu in a quick circle, so he could assess the battlefield. He held his hammer before him, concentrating on its light and the intensity of its vibrations. *Guide me.*

A dull glow a short distance up the side of the tower caught his eye, just as a humanoid figure made an impossible leap from below and disappeared into the exposed tunnel.

Knight Kjar landed next to Finngyr and immediately turned his griffon in the direction Horth had fallen.

"No. Follow me," Finngyr said.

"But, Knight Justice—"

"That is an order. We are here to capture the stonechosen," Finngyr said. He urged Safu into the air, passing over the heads of numerous abominations who raised their pale faces to track him.

Safu closed on the tower, and Finngyr didn't look back to see if Knight Kjar followed. At long last, his quarry was in sight.

Another shape darted into the opening as Safu touched down just outside the hole. Stones and debris cascaded down the slope as the griffon fought for purchase. He could tell Safu wouldn't fit through the opening and had already released the riding harness, sliding down her side before she even had her footing.

Finngyr searched the mists behind him. Kjar was nowhere to be seen but there were more than a few pale shapes making their way over the rocks towards him. There was no time to waste. "Thank you, Safu. Remain here and guard this opening. Let none pass."

With glowing hammer before him, Finngyr charged into the tunnel.

$$\Lambda$$

Horth tried to call for help again, but it choked off in a gurgle of hot blood that sent him into another fit of coughing. He tried to lean back, but the sharp uneven stones he lay on sent spasms of pain shooting through him. He did not want to die like this, pinned under the body of his own griffon at the bottom of this human cesspit. He reached once again for his hammer. Horth stretched out with his good hand and tried touching the handle. His fingers almost reached it. It was so close.

If he could reach the hammer, he could call upon the power of Daomur to heal him. But the cut from the stonechosen rendered his left arm useless. He glanced at it and the odd angle it hung at the forearm. His vambrace was the only thing keeping it attached. Nausea washed over him and bile surged up to sear his throat. He turned his head to vomit. The uncontrollable retching shot another spasm of pain through his ribs and the leg the wretched griffon had mauled. The vomit was bright red. He didn't want to die here, where were Kjar and Finngyr? They'd been right behind him. How far had his griffon's thrashing taken him off course?

If he could just stretch out a bit farther...

A leather boot kicked the handle away, just as his fingers brushed it. Horth's vision was starting to go black around the edges, but he could see the young, dark haired human who stared down at him.

"Remember me?" Riff said.

Horth tried to tell the human what he would do to him if he didn't give him his hammer, but all that came out of his mouth was blood.

Riff stood there watching him for a moment, before raising his everflame.

Horth, Son of Harnuk, screamed as the fire washed over him.

32

Best Intentions

"HERE are the others?" Gaidel asked.
Two Elks could tell the little daughter had not fully
shaken off the effects of the song. Her voice was firm,
but the bond between druid and shieldwarden shared
more than just the other's direction. He could feel her exhaustion
passing through the bond, even if she refused to show it.

She held her staff before her as he had taught her, rear hand a
span from the end of the staff and the other hand two spans above
that one. Even in her weakened state, she was ready to fight. With
that grip she could attack or defend, giving an enemy a false sense
of her reach. She gave him much honor.

Two Elks pointed into the mists. "Riff go that way. Do not know
where Dagbar." Dagbar had been there right behind him. He had not
seen the dwarf since the large section of the tower had collapsed.

"Why did you let them go?" Gaidel said.

Two Elks just stared at her with a blank expression. She knew he
would never leave her side when she was lost in the song. Two Elks

often let the little daughter's questions go unanswered. It was his people's way to allow a person to think for themselves.

Instead she just looked irritated and changed the subject. "Have you seen Ghile?"

The rush of wings and the clicking of talons on stone were all the warning Two Elks needed. He moved into Gaidel and pulled her low as he brought his kite shield before them.

The Little Daughter started to protest until she saw the griffon and its rider land a short distance away.

Two Elks recognized the helmet of the culler, shaped in the image of a screaming dwarf's face. This was the culler from the Cradle, the one who killed Lotte, and Ghile's hounds. There would be much honor in claiming this one's ears.

"It's Ghile," Gaidel said as she pointed towards the tower.

Two Elks thought he saw something near the opening in the tower, but the arrival of the second mounted culler drew his attention. The first culler was holding his glowing hammer up and towards the tower.

"They have seen him," Two Elks said.

"We must help Ghile," Gaidel urged.

Two mounted cullers. Two Elks had often wondered if he would have an honorable death since becoming a Shieldwarden and leaving his home. It seemed the Battle God smiled upon him this night. "No enter song, Little Daughter. You are no strength. Use staff," Two Elks said. He rose into a running crouch. Normally he would have called out the Battle God's true name and charged in, but he knew the Little Daughter could not fight a culler on her own. He had to try to even the odds quickly.

The two dwarves exchanged words, before one took to the air towards the tower.

Two Elks heard Little Daughter curse behind him, but he took it in stride and adjusted his course towards the other mounted dwarf. The past was in the past. Ghile would have to deal with that one. He had fought the cullers in the plains and knew the griffons they rode were deadly both in the air and on the ground. He had seen more than one of his people torn apart by those talons and sharp beaks.

As if the creature heard Two Elks thoughts, it swiveled its head around and screeched just as Two Elks leaped into the air and brought the full weight of his stone axe down on its skull. The griffon fell in a heap, taking its rider down with it. Two Elks wasted no time and jumped up onto the still-thrashing creature. If he was lucky, the dwarf would be pinned beneath it.

The dwarf was there, but had somehow already disengaged from the saddle and was spinning away from the griffon's death throes.

Two glints of steel flashed from the spinning dwarf, right before Two Elks felt the first knife thud into his shoulder. He barely got his kite shield in front of the second knife, which bit into it with a wooden thud.

"So, I'll get to see what you northern barbarians are made of then?" the lean, dark haired dwarf said. "You will pay for my mount with your life, human." It had taken a defensive stance and squinted up at Two Elks, waiting for his charge.

Two Elks had never known a culler to throw knives. He pulled the knife from his shoulder and examined it, before dropping it to the ground. He hopped down from the now-motionless griffon and banged his axe against his shield. "You skinny for dwarf," Two Elks said. He kept his shield before him, in case the dwarf had any more knives hidden away.

The dwarf only shook his head and shifted from one defensive stance to another.

Two Elks charged in, raising his axe above his head in what appeared to be an all-out frontal attack. At the last second, Two Elks shifted his weight and pulled up on the attack, moving to the side. He was too experienced to charge into an unknown opponent. Had he continued forward, he would have felt the bite of another dagger, followed by a parting blow from the dwarf's hammer as the culler spun away from the attack. As it was, the dagger spun off into the mists.

This one was fast for a dwarf and did not depend on his strength in battle. Two Elks nodded his appreciation.

Dwarven hammer met wooden shield and Two Elks accepted the blows as he pressed forward, angling the shield so only a small portion of the attack was absorbed. Two Elks knew his people's refusal to embrace the tools of the dwarves left him at a disadvantage. His wooden kite shield was no match against a steel hammer, no more than his stone axe could break through the dwarf's armor. Likewise, his stone axe, though huge, would eventually crack against the dwarf's plate armor. Sheer strength would not win this fight. Two Elks rushed in with another downward swing, but only put half his strength behind the blow, instead pushing off to the side and using his shield to bash the side-stepping dwarf.

The slippery dwarf accepted the blow and rolled up close to the shield, spinning down and to the side, catching Two Elks in the thigh with a quick jab of the hammer's handle.

Two Elks stumbled when his leg buckled and tried to bring his shield around to fend off the follow up attack he knew would be coming. A sharp crack and cursing greeted him instead.

He spun around to see the dwarf falling back to put some distance between them, his hand over his face, blood pouring out from beneath it.

Gaidel moved up next to Two Elks, her staff before her. "The big thing was too tempting a target," she said.

The dwarf spat onto the ground and rolled his shoulders, adjusting the hammer in his grip. "A barbarian and a druid, then. Fine by me," the dwarf said through bloodstained teeth.

A wall of flame erupted from the ground between them and rose well above their heads. "And a sorcerer, it would seem," Riff said, stepping up next to Gaidel and Two Elks.

As the wall of flame died, they could just see the outline of the culler as he retreated into the mists. Maybe Two Elks would make an effective warband out of this group yet.

"Runs fast, for a dwarf," Riff said, as if he was commenting on the weather.

"Where were you?" Gaidel said, spinning on him.

"The other culler. Where is the other one? And Dagbar, for that matter?"

"We lost Dagbar, but the other culler followed Ghile into the tower," Gaidel explained.

"Lost him? Wait," Riff said, looking around. "Where are the fallen?"

Two Elks realized the sorcerer was right. This was the first time since entering the mists that the fallen had not attacked them for so long a time.

"Must go tower," Two Elks said, already searching through the mists. He saw a flash of light and headed in that direction. It appeared and disappeared many times, before the three of them were close enough to see why.

A lone griffon fought a losing battle against a tide of fallen that fought desperately to get past it and into the tower.

"Is there another way in?" Gaidel said.

Riff lifted his everflame. "I could clear that one."

"No," Two Elks said. "Griffon keep fallen out. Help Ghile."

"We need to find another way in. Hurry," Gaidel said.

They made their way around the side of the tower. The rubble was thick around the base and covered in the pervasive slime. Some areas were piled well above their heads. From within the tower, Two Elks could hear muffled explosions. He worried what they would find if they did discover a way in.

"Alright, I give up. What is that?" Riff said. The sorcerer had stopped and was pointing at something that had just shambled out of a section of the rubble a short distance ahead of them. It looked like a fallen, but unlike the sleek, fast moving creatures they had encountered up until now, this one moved upright with a slow, awkward gait. It was incredibly fat, its skin stretched to bursting over its bulging form.

They stood there watching as another emerged behind it. "Look, there are others," Gaidel said, pointing off into the mists. The bloated fallen didn't move to attack them and seemed to be moving away from the tower.

The sorcerer shrugged after a moment and hurled one of his fireballs at the silhouette of one of the bulbous creatures, little more than an outline in the mists. They all followed the flaming sphere as it arced towards the distant creature. On impact, the fireball's explosion was nothing compared to the explosion that followed. Black fluid and mist flew in every direction. No sooner had the first fallen exploded than the one nearest it vibrated and also burst apart in another equally large spray of dark fluids, then another, each one closer to them than the last.

"Oh, crap," Riff said.

"Down!" Two Elks shouted as he moved to shelter the others behind his shield. As pieces of the closest fallen rained down around them, a horrid stench followed. After a moment of silence, they all slowly rose.

"Do you hear that?" Riff said, from behind the hand that covered his mouth and nose.

Two Elks turned his shield over at the strange sizzling sound. He hurriedly freed his hand from the straps and threw it to the ground. Where the black ichor had landed on his shield, it appeared to be eating its way through. The blackened gouges that riddled the shield slowly creeped outward as the substance that had exploded from the bloated fallen consumed the wood.

All three stared at the shield as it blackened and began to break apart. Two Elks examined his axe handle and then, satisfied it was untouched, turned to stare at Riff with a look that promised pain.

"Sorry?" Riff said. He took a half step behind Gaidel.

"It does not eat the stone, just the wood," Gaidel said, as she looked around them. "Do not attack anymore of those things." She looked at Riff pointedly as she said it.

Riff held up his hands. "Okay, okay."

"At least we might have found a way in," Gaidel said.

⋀

Flames licked Ghile's heels as he leaped away from the explosion. He heard stone crack and fall behind him.

"You are too late, Ghile Stonechosen! Too late!"

The man in the center of the tower, who Ghile could only assume was Ashar, hurled another ball of flame from the end of his everflame-engulfed staff.

Ghile had no sooner landed on a portion of the stone stairs climbing the outer wall than he had to leap away again to avoid another fiery blast. He soared across the huge circular room and landed on the stairs on that side. The portion of stairs he had just left gave way and fell to the floor in a shower of stone and debris. Ashar had barely given him time to react since he entered the room. He needed a moment to take in his surroundings and clear his head.

The intense pull of the soulstones clouded his thoughts. With no distance or walls between him and the two stones, the raw desire assaulted him. He knew both stones were down there, next to Ashar. The desire to have them was so strong, he just needed a moment to think and get them out of his head.

Ghile leaped higher up into the tower and landed on a stony ledge. He backed away from the edge and brought his force shield up before him, anchoring it under the edge beneath him and then up above his head and into the wall. He curved the shield out like a bubble so he could peer over.

Glaring up at him, Ashar stood in the center of the room amidst a chaotic scattering of tables and benches. Every surface was covered with things Ghile had never seen. But it was what was next to Ashar that temporarily made him forget about the soulstones.

An armored dwarf stood beside the sorcerer, a culler's two handed hammer in his hands, guarding Ashar.

Why would a culler be guarding Ashar?

The little of the dwarf's skin Ghile could see was pale like the fallen. Its head was completely covered in some odd, circular helmet that didn't match the rest of its rust-stained armor. Ghile didn't think the dwarf could even see out of the thing.

"My sister is here, Stonechosen!" Ashar screamed, gesturing near his feet. "Your beloved! Think you can save her? Do you?"

Ghile could feel the hatred in the man's voice.

"Only I can save her! You cannot have her, do you hear me?"

Ashar launched another fireball towards him. His fireballs were much bigger than Riff's, they were easily the size of Ghile's head.

Ghile instinctively drew back as the fireball exploded just beneath him. The shelf he rested on shook and debris bounced off his force shield. The wall around him shuddered and he watched dust drizzle down around him snow. Ghile wasn't sure how many spells like that this ruined tower could take. He chanced another look over the edge and his heart broke.

On the other side of Ashar were three low, stone mounds with the top stones removed to reveal the cavity within them. One of the mounds held the pale, desiccated remains of a vargan. The other, a human woman. She too, was little more than pale skin stretched over bones.

Ghile could hear Almoriz's voice. "Do not think this makes you immortal, Ghile Stonechosen. If you do not eat or drink, you will waste away like any of us, but you will not die. I would hate to experience such a fate."

He knew it was Akira. He thought of her when she appeared in the dreaming, how beautiful she was there. Ghile almost released his shield and fell forward then. The shock of seeing her down there, pale and shriveled like that, was almost more than he could take.

The feelings of desire for the soulstones crashed into feelings of helplessness to save Akira from her fate. Beneath all the other warring emotions, an ache he had never put to words churned them all together and pushed up to be recognized.

He loved her.

Dagbar appeared on the stairs near the tunnel entrance. "Ashar, stop this," he said.

Ghile watched as Ashar stood there, transfixed at the sight of the dwarf.

Dagbar shook his head, the pain evident on his face as he looked down on the sorcerer.

"Stop this?" Ashar threw the words at Dagbar like a dagger. "You started this, dwarf! You and your lies!" Ashar gestured at Akira's mummified body. "This is your fault!" Ashar said. "Everything! Everything that has happened is your fault!" He launched a fireball towards Dagbar, who dove headlong off the stairs before it reached him. The stone stairs buckled and collapsed from the power of the explosion. "And everything that is going to happen will be your fault, as well," Ashar said. "You are too late, dwarf! In bringing the stonechosen here, you have given me the power I need to send forth my greatest creations! The bloaters will destroy the elves who dare attack me, and then the Deepwood! Those that survive will destroy your precious settlement and all those stupid enough to believe your lies!"

With that, Ashar shot a gout of flame at the area of the laboratory where Dagbar had landed. Black smoke billowed from the explosions of various potions and elixirs that burst and spewed their bubbling contents into the air. "It is unfortunate that you will not be alive to see it!"

The tower shook violently and more debris rained down around them.

Now was Ghile's chance. He searched the ledge for anything he could use, but on finding nothing, drew the fang blade. Ghile dropped his force shield and with a mental push, the fang blade launched down towards Ashar. He watched the weapon race straight towards the sorcerer. At the last second, the culler's hammer lashed out and deflected the fang blade, sending it spinning away.

Ashar jumped at the movement and returned his attention to Ghile, a triumphant smile on his face. "Nothing can save you, stonechosen. Soon you will be here next to the others."

Did Ashar think the stonechosen would remain there forever, fueling his magic? Didn't he know they would die when Haurtu's prison was no longer near Allwyn?

A roar filled the tower as a second culler leaped from Gaidel's tunnel. Ghile recognized the Knight Justice who had tried to kill him back in the Cradle by his helmet, shaped like the face of a screaming dwarf. He was the one who had destroyed Last Hamlet and killed Ast and Cuz.

In that moment, Ghile couldn't see how he was going to survive this, but if he could take that dwarf with him, it would be worth it.

$$\wedge$$

Finngyr crashed down amidst burning tables and exploding glass. He hit the floor running, his hammer leaving a blue tail of light trailing behind him. He had heard the explosion and seen Dagbar right before the end of the tunnel was filled with flame and debris. He knew he needed to move and keep moving. Most of all, he needed to find the stonechosen.

He searched the room for the whelp, but saw no signs of him or whatever remained of Dagbar. The human lover got what he deserved, as far as Finngyr was concerned.

Through the fire and smoke Finngyr saw a lone human in the center of the large room. He was obviously a sorcerer, judging by the flaming staff he held and likely, the cause of all the explosions. To think these abominations walked free; harmless indeed. The idiot was going to bring the whole tower down on their heads. He would need to be dealt with first. "In Daomur's name, all here die!" Finngyr roared as he charted a path through the debris and headed towards the sorcerer.

The sorcerer's face went ashen and he swung his staff down and pointed it towards Finngyr. A ball of flame appeared and raced in his direction.

Finngyr had already called upon mighty Daomur to bestow his blessings upon his humble servant and enhance his strength. Finngyr could feel the holy power surging through him. This sorcerer's fire was not going to sway him from his righteous path. Finngyr raised his hammer before him and beseeched Daomur for protection. Where flame met hammer, the blue radiance arced out in a protective barrier. Finngyr could feel the heat of the flames around the edges of the magical shield, see the nearby tables hurled back from the force of the explosion, but he never slowed.

"Stop him! Kill him, Griff!" the sorcerer yelled as he hobbled back away from Finngyr's charge.

He recognized the name, but didn't have time to puzzle out why the human would call for help from a Knight Justice, before a dwarf lunged out of the smoke and barreled right into Finngyr. He just had time to brace himself to receive the charge. The two came together like a thunderclap. He felt his very bones vibrate. If not for Daomur's blessings and enhanced strength, he didn't think he would have had the strength to hold his ground. "In his holy name, what are you doing?" Finngyr shouted at the other dwarf.

They stood there, hammer handle against hammer handle, their corded muscles straining, neither able to overpower the other.

Finngyr would have locked eyes with the other dwarf, but his blackened helmet had no opening. It looked more like an iron kettle than a helmet. The hammer the dwarf held was similar to Finngyr's, and the armor was that of a knight of his order, but rusted and unkempt. The dwarf's skin was pale and ashen, black bulging veins crisscrossed it like vines on stone. "Knight Justice Griff?" Could this truly be the Knight Lord the Knight Justice Gyldoon spoke of?

An echoing gurgle was the only response Finngyr received, before Griff broke off the test of strength and went on the offensive, raining blows down on Finngyr.

The stance and attacks were ones Finngyr recognized, and he knew this was indeed a knight from his order, but what had they done to him? The idea that this had been done to a dwarf was horrendous enough, but to one of Finngyr's order? That a hammer of his order, a holy relic, was being used to protect a human? Finngyr fell into a defensive routine and gave ground under the attacks. He didn't have time to size up his opponent and find a weakness. He was going to wait for the attacks to slow, but they didn't. Griff just kept coming, one attack routine rolling into another.

He didn't have time to waste, so he let a blow through his defenses. The strength behind it was unquestionable and Finngyr gritted his teeth through the pain, but he had his opening and used the momentum of the blow to spin to the side and deliver an attack of his own.

His attack landed soundly with the satisfying crunch of bone. The blow sent Griff stumbling to the side. It should have sent him to the ground.

Finngyr watched in disbelief as Griff's bones snapped back into place and the area where the skin had torn filled with an inky black liquid and then knitted back together. Finngyr knew it wasn't blood pumping through Griff's veins. Was Daomur healing him? It was impossible! Finngyr only had a moment to consider before Griff attacked again.

Ghile watched the two dwarves set upon each other with a flurry of attacks, blocks, and counterstrikes. Neither seemed to acknowledge when they were struck and each blow looked enough to crush stone. Now was his time to deal with Ashar. Ghile leaped from the ledge.

Ashar looked up as Ghile fell. Ghile waited for the next fireball to come hurtling towards him, but the sorcerer only tracked his progress and hobbled towards the stone mounds.

When Ghile landed before Ashar, he thought of the fang blade he had lost. He could feel the force shield stretching out from his hand and form into a point, even as it thinned along one side into a sharp edge.

Ashar took a deep breath and said something Ghile couldn't understand. Then the sorcerer laughed as he shimmered and limped in two opposite directions at once, even as he remained still.

Ghile had never seen Riff do that! Where there had been one of him before, there were now three sorcerers laughing at him.

All three spoke in unison. "Well, here we are."

Ghile lunged toward the middle one, only to have his force blade pass harmlessly through Ashar as if he wasn't even there.

"Now!" The three Ashars' shouted. "Do it now!"

A mummified vargan rushed out of the middle Ashar. Ghile just had time to make out the white feral faces of two goblin fallen carrying the body, as he lashed out with his force blade. The blade sliced cleanly through the goblin on the right, but upon hitting the shriveled vargan stopped in a flash of intense light and white hot cutting pain. Unyielding heat seared into his palm. "No!" Ghile shouted.

The force blade vanished and along with it, the body of the vargan stonechosen as if it never existed.

"No!" Ghile shouted again. He reflexively drew his hand to his chest, but he knew it was too late. The pain and simultaneous exaltation mounted as he fell back.

The new soulstone began the excruciating journey under his skin towards his chest.

Ghile's vision blackened around the edges and his mouth went dry. His mind was screaming to give in to the pain and drift off into peaceful oblivion. Ghile knew this was the soulstone trying to draw him into the dreaming, to train him. He knew if he gave in, he would never wake up. Ghile fell to one knee as the room spun around him. "No."

He could hear Ashar's triumphant laughter over the explosions and sounds of fighting. He vaguely remembered the two cullers. The stone slid along his shoulder with a sickening popping sound.

"Now you will join her forever!" Ashar said.

Ghile thought about how easy it would be to give in and lay down beside Akira.

Akira.

"Akira," Ghile said aloud. His vision cleared a little. He focused on that name. He stood up.

He saw a flash of movement coming towards him and lashed out more out of instinct than anything else. He didn't even remember calling forth the force blade again. The other goblin fallen took two more steps before it realized its head was missing and fell.

"No, it's not possible!" Ashar said. The room shook and a table slid against him, sending him stumbling to the side.

The pain reached Ghile's chest. He heard the sound of sizzling meat and he wiped the burning sweat from his eyes. He had to fight, to stay awake. There had only been one voice this time. Ghile focused on it and took a step in that direction.

"It is not possible!" Ashar screamed at Ghile, as if the sheer force of his words would be enough to make it real.

Ghile saw flames appear around him, though he felt no heat. Had he summoned the force shield? He couldn't remember. Ghile took another step forward. Ahead of him, he saw Ashar take a step back and fall backwards over one of the low stone mounds. Ghile shook his head to clear it and took another step forward. His chest was on fire.

∧

Finngyr fell back onto a table that collapsed under his weight, sending glass vials and tubes raining down on him. He climbed to his feet and felt searing pain, as something dragged across his side under his armor. That blow has broken a few ribs. Finngyr tightened his grip on his hammer. He called upon Daomur and felt healing energy flowing into him, resetting his ribs and closing his wounds. He spat out blood and readied himself.

Griff walked towards him, looking as he had when the fight began. Whatever the accursed humans had done to him, he did not seem to tire and his wounds healed as quickly as Finngyr could inflict them.

Finngyr knew he was going to lose this fight. He looked towards the tunnel, hoping to see Kjar or Horth standing there. *Where were they?*

He was so close. He had seen the stonechosen when he jumped down from where he'd been hiding. Why he was fighting the sorcerer, Finngyr had no idea and didn't really care. He needed to get past Griff, capture the whelp, and get out of this tower before it collapsed.

He saw the boy standing there alone in the distance, the sorcerer nowhere to be seen. Had the boy won? Would he flee? Finngyr couldn't stand the idea of losing his quarry again. He knew he had to do something and do it now. An idea came to him and he latched onto it.

Finngyr charged into Griff, his hammer held before him in both hands. As he had hoped, Griff brought his hammer up in a defensive move and their handles clapped together. It was a foolish move. One taught to all initiates of the order. If it worked, it would disarm your opponent.

He drew his elbows in, bringing Griff so close Finngyr could see his breath on the black helmet. He switched his stance, simultaneously releasing his lower grip on his hammer and reaching over Griff's handle to grab it again. Finngyr twisted and pulled up with all his might. He felt the resistance to his move disappear at the same time he saw Griff's arms fly out wide. It had worked. He had disarmed him. He had barely maintained his own grip on his hammer, but he stepped forward to stop Griff from recovering his.

Instead of lunging for his weapon, Griff was staggering back and grabbing at his helmet. Two of the metal tubes that ran from his neck into the helmet had been torn free by Finngyr's move and were spilling their black contents out over Griff's chest. For the first time, it looked like Griff was hurt.

The helmet!

Finngyr dropped his hammer and leaped onto Griff's back, grabbing the helmet in both hands. He locked his legs around Griff with a death grip and pulled. Griff spun, trying to dislodge him, but Finngyr held on. Blow after blow slammed into Finngyr's head, but he refused to let go. He hauled on the helmet, his corded muscles straining, his veins bulging. He lost vision in one eye and felt the cartilage in his nose shatter under Griff's attacks, but Finngyr just focused on pulling.

With a sickening pop the helmet tore free.

Finngyr lost his grip and fell backwards, the helmet rolling to the side. Black murky liquid gushed down over Griff. Finngyr looked up to see a blackened, flesh-covered skull. Both of Griff's eyes were missing and the lids sewn together. Griff's lower jawbone opened and closed, as if he were gasping for air. Griff took two more steps and then fell to the ground.

Finngyr got up and staggered over to his hammer, reaching down for it. "You are mine, Stonechos—"

An explosion of flame sent Finngyr flying from view.

/\

Ghile blinked as Ashar, rising from the stone mound, turned his flaming staff to point it at him. Ghile knew he only had seconds. He rushed forward, slamming into Ashar and the two tumbled back into one of the hollowed out mounds.

Ghile wrestled for the flaming staff and then felt the all-too-familiar white hot pain stab into his back. "No!"

Ashar pulled free of him and scrambled back against the side of the mound. "What have you done?" He reached down to grab a desiccated hand and pull it close to his face.

Ghile watched as the hand vanished and the body it was attached to, the one they had fallen on, disappeared. The pain was overwhelming. The first stone had just reached his chest as the second stone, Akira's stone, seared into his back. He collapsed there, staring straight up, lost in the pain. He watched as large blocks spiraled down from above, to crash into the tables around him. Ghile could feel the stones moving. He took in everything with a sort of detached fascination.

Ashar came into view above him, tears streaking his face. I could have saved her. The answers were here; it was all here!" He produced a small vial from his robes. "You have ruined everything!" Ashar spat. "But you have not won!" He fumbled with the cork stopper. "This is the elixir of Sleeping Death. Now you can share her fate!"

Ashar held up the vial so Ghile could see it. The sorcerer took in the burning lab, the tower collapsing around them.

"Seems we join her in death together," Ashar said, as he gripped Ghile's lower jaw and pried his mouth open. He tipped the vial up and Ghile watched its contents pour forth, unable to stop it.

The tip of the fang blade erupted from Ashar's chest.

The greenish liquid splashed along Ghile's cheek, just missing his opened mouth.

Ashar's eyes locked with his, then slowly lost focus as the sorcerer tumbled from view.

Dagbar appeared and began hastily wiping the liquid off Ghile's face. "I've got you, boy. I've got you."

Ghile watched as Dagbar lifted him from the ground. He could feel himself being lifted, yet at the same time, he could see Dagbar stumbling away from the mound and Ashar's body.

Even as Ghile tried to comprehend how this was possible, he watched as the spirit of Ashar slipped out of the sorcerer's body with his last breath and joined the mist.

Images of Ashar working in his laboratory flashed before Ghile. Ghile somehow knew the place was called a laboratory. He saw Ashar poring over tomes written in the True Language, saw him exploring the ruins with Akira by his side.

What was happening?

Other images replaced those, images of a great human city, more humans than Ghile had ever seen before. Humans working within the city, struggling, laughing, and crying flashed before him.

Ghile felt his body fall and saw Dagbar stumble as the tower floor tipped awkwardly. Dagbar was trying to get him out of the tower.

More images raced before Ghile's eyes.

He was on the walls of the ancient city, looking out at the armies of dwarves, Alvar and even orcs massed there. He saw the other humans on the wall as they chanted together to cast the spell that would protect the city. Ghile could see the memories of the wizards' race before him and knew they felt their race had brought this fate upon themselves. For they had waged war against the other races in the name of their hungering god.

Ghile watched as the spell that was meant to shield them in a protective mist, a spell that came to them in their dreams, a gift from their god in their time of most urgent need, turned on them and consumed them.

Ghile heard Gaidel's voice, felt Two Elks lift him. The thought of the barbarian carrying him once again made him smile.

He could see them running along the tunnel. He could also feel others in the mists, felt it hungering for them. He realized then the mists would take their souls when they died here in the ruin city. Just as it had taken Ashar's. Had it already taken his? Was that why he was here and not within the dreaming?

It was the thought of the dreaming and Akira visiting him there that helped Ghile understand that the mists and the dreaming were somehow related. Her soulstone was now a part of him. She was now a part of him.

Ghile relaxed and felt his consciousness drift along the mist. More images appeared, small flashes from lives of humans taken by the mists. He locked on one, more vivid than the others. It was more recent, of a human settlement he had never seen, but he knew it was Dagbar's Freehold. This memory was different, it was alive. Ghile found he could follow it to its source, something like following a stream back to the spring that produced it. He could feel the mists weaved through it, holding it greedily.

He saw the fallen it belonged to, as it attacked a griffon and dark-haired dwarf. He could see the streams of memories that wove into all the fallen there in the battle.

He followed the memories to the bloated, who staggered through the mists towards the Alvar and the Deepwood. He could feel the perverted mists that roiled inside them, waiting to be released.

He saw all this and knew he could stop it. This was all Haurtu's doing. A spell cast long ago.

Through the four soulstones that were now firmly entrenched in his chest, Ghile reached out and unwove the spell. He couldn't really explain how he did it, any more than he could explain how he understood what all the things were he had seen in those visions.

He just knew.

He felt the spirits as they were released. Those of the dead felt as if they slipped into the soulstones and were then just not there. Those that were from the fallen snapped back into their hosts. Ghile could no longer feel the connection to them, but he saw them collapse, one by one.

It pained him that he could not save those who had been turned into the bloated. Ashar had done too much to them for their bodies to survive. Ghile forced each to explode, well within the confines of the mists and watched as their spirits disappeared into the soulstones to join the others.

The last image he saw, before the mists dissipated and sunlight reached down to touch the lowest reaches of the Fallen City for the first time in a thousand years, was that of a lone griffon taking flight. Its dwarven rider held the limp body of another armored dwarf across the saddle. The screaming dwarf helmet hanging there, reflected the dawn's golden light.

Epilogue

HILE drifted through the dream mists. He felt a pull deep within him, like a rope tied just behind his navel, tugging him onwards.

He did not need to concentrate on his destination. Quite the opposite, the attraction was so strong, he had to fight the pull whenever he entered the dream mists to practice what Akira was teaching him. It seemed odd to be here without her. This was his first time traveling the place between dreams without her, but he felt the need to do this alone.

The small dots of light, he now knew to be dreams, past him in a blur. They no longer held the same fascination for him as they did in the beginning.

When he first entered the dream mists, he was constantly distracted by others' dreams and what they contained.

Though his training with the new soulstones was only beginning, and he still had much to learn, he couldn't put this confrontation off any longer.

His destination appeared before him. It looked identical to the thousands of little lights around it, but Ghile could feel the attraction pulling him towards this one. He floated through the dream wall without slowing.

Ghile stepped into an open, grassy plain. The cloudless sky stretched off in every direction, to touch the distant horizon that surrounded him like a blue lid closed over a green bowl.

Ghile arrived on the outside of what looked to be a deserted training camp. He sought the familiar closeness between the hide-covered huts with their domed roofs, red banners snapping in the unrestrained wind from their central poles. He could hear what sounded like combat coming from deeper in the camp. He made his way towards the noise.

Near the black empty entrance of each tent rested a rack of un-used weapons. Ghile recognized spears, staffs, and great battle axes, like the ones Two Elks favored. Like Two Elk's weapon, each of these was also fitted with stone blades. He wondered if this was what a barbarian camp looked like and if this was the Nordlah plains? The place made him feel open and exposed. The lack of even one tree or bush bothered him.

Ghile passed between the last huts and stepped into the center of the camp. There he found the source of the noise. The largest man he had ever seen, was fighting against four other humans and holding them off with ease.

Obviously a Nordlah barbarian, the man made Two Elks look like a child. Like Ghile, the soulstones had made him larger than normal. His skin also had that inner glow Ghile's had taken on.

"You must be Growling Bear," Ghile said.

The other four other warriors stopped their attacks when Ghile spoke. The man turned slowly to eye the new arrival. He was an ugly man, completely bald, his face and scalp covered in long, deep scars. His wide bare chest held four soulstones. Ghile was used to the constant pull of the other soulstones, but seeing them for the first time still stole his breath. He remembered what Islmur said, there were nine soulstones in total.

Then there was still one out there somewhere.

"And you must be the gwa a'chook whelp the old druid spoke of," Growling Bear said. Growling Bear wasted no time in striding up to Ghile, the other four falling in behind him.

Three men and a woman, three of them were also Nordlah barbarians, but one man was not dressed in a way Ghile had ever seen. The tall thin man had skin as black as night, with wide intelligent eyes. He was garbed in loose white robes that covered everything but his hands and feet, where they were wrapped tightly starting at elbow and knee. His head was likewise wrapped in white and he carried a strange curved metal sword.

The one thing all of them had in common was a look of total disdain for Ghile.

Growling Bear took his axe from his shoulder and swung it through Ghile's neck in one easy swipe. When the grey mist Ghile was made of simply parted and then reformed, Growling Bear smirked and nodded as if it confirmed his suspicions. "Interesting trick. It might be useful to travel into others dreams once I have killed you."

Ghile noted that Growling Bear used his free hand to make wide motions as he talked. "I am Ghile Stonechosen. I have come to speak truth with you." Ghile said the words just as Two Elks had taught him. He even made the same hand gestures Two Elks had used.

The female barbarian scoffed. "Bah, this gwa—"

"Silence!" Growling Bear said.

The woman closed her mouth.

He eyed Ghile for a long time before nodding. Growling Bear laid his axe at his feet and then crossed his arms over his chest. "I will hear your words."

"It is true my people live under the rule of dwarves. My people have forgotten the True Language and speak the tongue of the dwarves," Ghile said. "But, I have spoken with the Goddess Islmur and she has much wisdom. She remembers the time when the Battle God walked on Allwyn, so, I believe her words are true." Ghile knew his next sentence would decide his path in all this. "The Battle God does not wish us to fight the other races so that he can become the All Father and be equal to the All Mother. He wishes us to fight in hope that we will be destroyed and he can take back what he gave up to create us. If you give yourself to him, you will not only be sacrificing yourself, but all of us."

Growling Bear stared down at Ghile, his expression unreadable. He turned and looked at the fourfour humans behind him. There was no question in Ghile's mind what they thought of his words. Each of them had been a stonechosen and had been defeated and consumed by Growling Bear. Like Adon, Muk, and even Akira, the part of them that had existed on Allwyn was still there, but it was now combined with a soulstone and as such had the soulstone's desire that their host be a suitable vessel for Haurtu's return.

"I hear your words, Ghile Stonechosen," Growling Bear said, "Now hear mine."

Growling Bear stepped over his axe and walked to the center of the clearing. He raised his hands like he was addressing an army. When he spoke, his voice carried across the clearing with a deep resonating boom. "I am Growling Bear of the Blood Moon tribe. I now speak truth to *you*, Ghile Stonechosen. My people have not forgotten and hold true to the old ways. I do not believe the words of Islmur. She who schemed with Daomur to trick and imprison the Battle God."

Growling Bear walked over to a large animal hide, concealing something beneath. He pulled it aside to reveal a cage made of bone. Inside cowered a living shadow. "You are not the first to test me, Ghile Stonechosen. But I am Growling Bear and I have not forgotten the old ways. I will prepare for the Battle God's return. I will bathe in the blood of his enemies and lay their cities low. I will call all humans who would remember the old ways to my banner. Then I will release the Battle God from his prison and join him in eternity!"

The others cheered as Growling Bear finished, his hands raised above his head. With a confident smirk on his face, he strode back to stand before Ghile and picked up his axe.

"I will not fight you," Ghile said.

"You will," Growling Bear said. "Because even now my armies march on the dwarven settlements throughout the north." Growling Bear raised a brow. "You are from the Cradle of the Gods, are you not?"

Ghile felt a chill run down his spine.

"Follow the pull of my soulstones. Come to me before I reach your precious Cradle. If you do, I will free your people and allow them to join my army. If not..." Growling Bear's cheek rose in what could have been an attempt at a smile, but his scars turned it into a toothy sneer. "I will kill them all."

⋀

Ghile stepped out of the dream mists and appeared in the clearing under the boughs of the Great Oak. The others were there waiting for him with looks that ranged from hopefulness, to trepidation, to outright fear. He took a deep steadying breath and walked towards them.

There was nothing for it now.

Akira met him halfway and took his hand. She said nothing, but simply smiled up at him and gave his hand a reaffirming squeeze.

By the All Mother, I love her.

Adon stood there with Muk, the goblin, to one side and Ba'groot, the vargan, to the other. They all watched and waited for him to speak. Near the roots of the Great Oak, his shadow appeared and crouched down to watch.

Ghile looked at them all. He looked up at the Great Oak and the surrounding clearing. His path was chosen and for the sake of everything he loved, he would walk it until he reached its end.

"There is much to be done," Ghile said.

Name Pronunciation & Race Guide

Word	Phonetic	Sounds like
Humans		
Adon	\\'ā-'dən\\	'A-done'
Almoriz	\\'al-mə-'riz\\	'Al-muh-riz'
Elana	\\'ē-'lä-nə\\	'e-La-na'
Ecrec	\\'ek-rik\\	'Ek-wreck'
Gaidel	\\'gī-del\\	'Guy-dell'
Ghile	\\'gē-lā\\	'Ghe-lay'
Two Elks	\\'tü-elks\\	'Two-Elks'
Dwarves		
Dagbar	\\'dag-'bär\\	'Dag-bar'
Finngyr	\\'fin-gir\\	'Fin-gear'
Gyldoon	\\'gil-dün\\	'Gill-dune'
Kjar	\\'K-yär\\	'Ka-yar'
Obudar	\\'ō-bu-där\\	'Oh-boo-dar'
Elves		
Arenuin	\\'är-e-nü-ən\\	'R-eh-new-in'
Goblins		
Muk	\\'mək\\	'Muck'
Primordials		
Haurtu	\\'Här-'tü\\	'Har-Two'
Daomur	\\'dā-ō-'mər\\	'Day-O-fur'
Islmur	\\'iz-l-'mər\\	'Izzle-Mur'

About the Author

Thomas grew up in a small town in Illinois where he spent most of his time enjoying scouting and playing role playing games. After graduation he joined the military, obtained a degree in Computer Science and saw the world. Since leaving the military, his job in IT continues to keep him abroad. As of the completion of this book, he hangs his hat in a small town in England, with his lovely wife and children, where he can be found spending most of his time enjoying scouting and playing role playing games. Some things never change.

Made in the USA
Middletown, DE
20 August 2017